Erika Johansen grew up in C⋯
Swarthmore College in Pennsylvani⋯
Fine Arts degree from the celebrated Iow⋯
and eventually became a lawyer, but she ne⋯
writing. Her acclaimed debut, *The Queen of the ⋯*
is the first book in a trilogy and became an international
bestseller. *The Invasion of the Tearling* continues the
thrilling story of Kelsea Glynn and the Tearling kingdom
which concludes with the eagerly-awaited *The Fate of the
Tearling*.

Erika lives in England.

Acclaim for Erika Johansen's *Tearling* novels:

'Builds to a no-holds-barred, pulsating climax . . . Johansen
juggles fantasy, sci-fi and weighty issues of good and evil
with brilliant ease, and leaves us eagerly awaiting
the next instalment'
DAILY MAIL

'An intoxicating brew of dystopian fiction, high fantasy, science
fiction, and a bit of horror . . . in *The Invasion of the Tearling*,
Johansen takes those elements and turns them up to eleven,
making for a thrilling and thought-provoking read that takes
this trilogy to even greater heights'
BUZZFEED

'A dazzling and gripping follow-up . . . Expertly combining
modern and medieval themes, Johansen ratchets up suspense
as she weaves a magical story that crosses time . . . one of the
most original and well-written series in recent memory'
USA TODAY

'Meet the next Katniss Everdeen. If you missed last year's *The
Queen of the Tearling*, run, don't walk, to get it'
ENTERTAINMENT WEEKLY

'Get caught up with Kelsea, a heroine so badass, Emma
Watson's already signed up to play her'
COSMOPOLITAN

'I didn't sleep for about a week because I couldn't put the
bloody thing down. It would be fair to say I became obsessed'
EMMA WATSON

'Enjoyable, fast-paced . . . haunting, tear-jerking moments
that leave you desperate to read the next instalment . . .
a top summer read'
SUN

'Did you love *The Hunger Games*? Partial to an episode of *Game
of Thrones*? Then you're going to want to dive straight in to this
new fantasy . . . brilliantly imagined and captivatingly written'
HEAT

By Erika Johansen

THE QUEEN OF THE TEARLING
THE INVASION OF THE TEARLING

coming soon

THE FATE OF THE TEARLING

THE
INVASION
OF THE
TEARLING

ERIKA JOHANSEN

BANTAM BOOKS

LONDON • TORONTO • SYDNEY • AUCKLAND • JOHANNESBURG

TRANSWORLD PUBLISHERS
61–63 Uxbridge Road, London W5 5SA
www.transworldbooks.co.uk

Transworld is part of the Penguin Random House group of companies
whose addresses can be found at global.penguinrandomhouse.com

Penguin
Random House
UK

First published in the United States in 2015 by Harper
an imprint of HarperCollins

First published in Great Britain in 2015 by Bantam Press
an imprint of Transworld Publishers
Bantam edition published 2016

Map by Nick Springer Cartographies, LLC

Erika Johansen has asserted her right under the Copyright,
Designs and Patents Act 1988 to be identified as the author of this work.

A CIP catalogue record for this book
is available from the British Library.

ISBN
9780857502483

Typeset in 10/13.5pt Ashbury by Falcon Oast Graphic Art Ltd.
Printed and bound by Clays Ltd, Bungay, Suffolk.

Penguin Random House is committed to a sustainable
future for our business, our readers and our planet. This book is
made from Forest Stewardship Council® certified paper.

MIX
Paper from
responsible sources
FSC® C018179

1 3 5 7 9 10 8 6 4 2

Every child should have someone like Barty.

This book is for my father, Curt Johansen.

Fairwitch Sea

FAIRWITCH MOUNTAINS

North Tear

THE COTTAGE

Bolton

Arc
Nord

Cite
Marche

Lake Karczmar

MORT
FLATS

Arc
Pearl

MORTMESNE

REDDICK
FOREST

Lewiston R.

Lewiston

NORTHERN ALMONT
PLAIN

THE TEARLING

BORDER

MT. ELLYRE

ARGIVE PASS

Pike Road

Demesne

The Cold Road

Crithe River

New Dover

Haven

Mort Road

HILLS

MT.
WILLINGHAM

CLAYTON
MTNS.

New
London

Caddell River

SOUTHERN ALMONT
PLAIN

Crossing's End

DRY LANDS

Petaluma

God's
Ocean

CADARE

50 MILES

BOOK I

CHAPTER 1

HALL

The Second Mort Invasion had all the makings of a slaughter. On one side was the vastly superior Mort army, armed with the best weapons available in the New World and commanded by a man who would balk at nothing. On the other was the Tear army, one-fourth the size and bearing weapons of cheaply forged iron that would break under the impact of good steel. The odds were not so much lopsided as catastrophic. There seemed no way for the Tearling to escape disaster.

—*The Tearling as a Military Nation*, CALLOW THE MARTYR

Dawn came quickly on the Mort border. One minute there was nothing but a hazy line of blue against the horizon, and the next, bright streaks stretched upward from eastern Mortmesne, drenching the sky. The luminous reflection spread across Lake Karczmar until the surface was nothing but a glowing sheet of fire, an effect only broken when a light breeze lapped at the shores and the smooth surface divided into waves.

The Mort border was a tricky business in this region. No

one knew precisely where the dividing line was drawn. The Mort asserted that the lake was in Mort territory, but the Tear staked its own claim to the water, since a noted Tear explorer named Martin Karczmar had discovered the lake in the first place. Karczmar had been laid in his grave nearly three centuries since, but the Tearling had never quite relinquished its shaky claim to the lake. The water itself was of little value, filled with predatory fish that were no good to eat, but the lake was an important spot, the only concrete geographical landmark on the border for miles to the north or south. Both kingdoms had always been anxious to establish a definitive claim. At one point, long ago, there had been some talk of negotiating a specific treaty, but nothing had ever come of it. The eastern and southern edges of the lake were salt flats, the territory alternating between silt and marshland. These flats stretched eastward for miles before they ran into a forest of Mort pine. But on the western edge of Lake Karczmar, the salt flats continued for only a few hundred feet before they climbed abruptly into the Border Hills, steep slopes covered with a thick layer of pine trees. The trees wrapped up and over the Hills, descending on the other side into the Tearling proper and flattening out into the northern Almont Plain.

Although the steep eastern slopes of the Border Hills were uninhabited forest, the hilltops and western slopes were dotted with small Tear villages. These villages did some foraging in the Almont, but they mostly bred livestock–sheep and goats–and dealt in wool and milk and mutton, trading primarily with each other. Occasionally they would pool their resources and send a heavily guarded shipment to New London, where goods–particularly wool–fetched a greater price, and the payment was not in barter but in coin. The villages stretched across the hillside: Woodend, Idyllwild, Devin's Slope, Griffen . . . easy pickings, their inhabitants armed with wooden weapons and burdened with animals they were unwilling to leave behind.

Colonel Hall wondered how it was possible to love a stretch of land so much and yet thank great God for the fate that had taken you away. Hall had grown up the son of a sheep farmer in the village of Idyllwild, and the smell of those villages—wet wool caked with a generous helping of manure—was such a fixed part of his memory that he could smell it even now, though the nearest village was on the western side of the Border Hills, several miles away and well out of sight.

Fortune had taken Hall away from Idyllwild, not good fortune, but the backhanded sort that gave with one hand while it stabbed with the other. Their village was too far north to have suffered badly in the first Mort invasion; a party of raiders had come one night and taken some of the sheep from an unguarded paddock, but that was all. When the Mort Treaty was signed, Idyllwild and its neighbor villages had thrown a festival. Hall and his twin brother, Simon, had gotten roaring drunk and woken up in a pigpen in Devin's Slope. Father said their village had gotten off easy, and Hall thought so too, until eight months later, when Simon's name was pulled in the second public lottery.

Hall and Simon were fifteen, already men by border lights, but their parents forgot that fact over the next three weeks. Mum made Simon's favorite foods; Pa relieved both boys from work. Near the end of the month they made the journey to New London, just as so many families had made since, with Pa weeping in the front of the wagon, Mum grim and silent, and Hall and Simon working hard to produce a forced gaiety on the way.

His parents hadn't wanted Hall to see the shipment. They'd left him in a pub on the Great Boulevard, with three pounds and instructions to stay there until they returned. But Hall wasn't a child, and he left the pub and followed them to the Keep Lawn. Pa had collapsed shortly before the shipment departed, leaving Mum to try to revive him, so in the end it was only Hall who saw the shipment leave, only Hall who saw Simon disappear into the city and out of their lives forever.

Their family stayed in New London that night, in one of the filthiest inns the Gut had to offer. The horrendous smell finally drove Hall outside, and he wandered the Gut, looking for a horse to steal, determined to follow the cages down the Mort Road, break Simon out or die trying. He found a horse tied outside one of the pubs and was working on the complicated knot when a hand fell on his shoulder.

"What do you think you're doing, country rat?"

The man was big, taller than Hall's father, and covered in armor and weapons. Hall thought he would likely die within moments, and part of him was glad. "I need a horse."

The man looked at him shrewdly. "Someone in the shipment?"

"None of your business."

"It certainly is my business. It's my horse."

Hall drew his knife. It was a sheep-shearing knife, but he hoped the stranger wouldn't know. "I don't have time to argue with you. I need your horse."

"Put that away, boy, and stop being a fool. The shipment is guarded by eight Caden. I'm sure you've heard of the Caden, even out in whatever shithole town you come from. They could break your puny little knife with their teeth."

The stranger made to grab the horse's bridle, but Hall held the knife up higher, blocking his path. "I am sorry to be a thief, but that's the way it is. I have to go."

The stranger gazed at him for a long moment, assessing. "You've got stones, boy, I'll give you that. What are you, farmer?"

"Shepherd."

The stranger considered him for another moment and then said, "All right, boy. Here's how it plays out. I will *lend* you my horse. His name, appropriately enough, is Favor. You ride him down the Mort Road and take a look at that shipment. If you're smart, you'll realize that it's a no-win proposition, and then you have two choices. You can die senselessly, achieving nothing. Or you can turn around and ride to the army barracks in the Wells, so we can talk about your future."

"What future?"

"As a soldier, boy. Unless you want to spend the rest of your life stinking of sheep shit."

Hall eyed him uncertainly, wondering if his words were a trick. "What if I just ride off with your horse?"

"You won't. You've a sense of obligation in you, or you'd never be off on this fool's errand in the first place. Besides, I have an entire army's worth of horses if I need to come after you."

The stranger turned and headed back into the pub, leaving Hall standing there at the hitching post.

"Who are you?" Hall called after him.

"Major Bermond, of the Right Front. Ride fast, boy. And if any harm comes to my horse, I'll take it out of your miserable sheep-loving hide."

After a hard night's ride, Hall caught up to the shipment

and found that Bermond was right: it was a fortress. Soldiers surrounded each cage, their formations dotted by the red cloaks of the Caden. Hall didn't have a sword, but he wasn't fool enough to believe that a sword would make any difference. He couldn't even get close enough to distinguish Simon; when he tried to approach the cages, one of the Caden launched an arrow that missed him by no more than a foot. It was just as the Major had said.

Still, he considered charging the shipment and ending everything, the terrible future he had already sensed on the trip to New London, a future in which his parents looked at him and only saw Simon missing. Hall's face would not be a comfort to them, only a terrible reminder. He tightened his grip on the reins, preparing to charge, and then something happened that he would never be able to explain: through the mass of tightly packed prisoners in the sixth cage, he suddenly glimpsed Simon. The cages were too far away for Hall to have seen anything, but seen it he had, all the same: his brother's face. His own face. If he rode to his death, there would be nothing left of Simon, nothing to even mark his passage. And then Hall saw that this was not about Simon at all, but about his own guilt, his own sorrow. Selfishness and self-destruction, riding hand in hand, as they so often did.

Hall turned the horse, rode back to New London, and joined the Tear army. Major Bermond was his sponsor, and although Bermond would never admit it, Hall thought that the Major must have spoken a word in someone's ear, because even during Hall's years in the unranked infantry, he had never been pulled for shipment duty. He sent a portion of his earnings home each month, and on his rare journeys to Idyllwild, his parents surprised him by being gruff but proud of their soldier son. He rose quickly through the ranks, becoming the General's Executive Officer by the young age of thirty-one. It wasn't rewarding work; a soldier's life under the Regency consisted of breaking up brawls and hunting down petty criminals. There was no glory in it. But this . . .

"Sir."

Hall looked up and saw Lieutenant-Colonel Blaser, his second-in-command. Blaser's face was darkened with soot.

"What is it?"

"Major Caffrey's signal, sir. Ready on your command."

"A few more minutes."

The two of them sat in a bird's nest deep on the eastern slope of the Border Hills. Hall's battalion had been out here for several weeks now, working steadily, as they watched the dark mass move across the Mort Flats. The sheer size of the Mort army hindered its progress, but it had come, all the same, and now the encampment sprawled along the southern edge of Lake Karczmar, a black city that stretched halfway to the horizon.

Through his spyglass, Hall could see only four sentries, posted at wide lengths on the western edge of the Mort camp. They were dressed to blend in with the dark, silty surface of the salt flats, but Hall knew the banks of this lake well, and outliers were easy to spot in the growing light. Two of them weren't even patrolling; they'd dozed off at their posts. The Mort were resting easy, just as they should. The Mace's reports said that the Mort army numbered over twenty thousand, and their swords and armor were good iron, tipped with steel. And by any measure, the Tear army was weak. Bermond was partly to blame. Hall loved the old man like a father, but Bermond had become too accustomed to peacetime. He toured the Tearling like a farmer inspecting his acres, not a soldier preparing for battle. The Tear army wasn't ready for war, but now it was upon them, all the same.

Hall's attention returned, as it had so often in the past week, to the cannons, which sat in a heavily fortified area right in the center of the Mort camp. Until Hall had seen them with his own eyes, he hadn't believed the Queen, though he didn't doubt that she'd had some sort of vision. But now, as the light brightened in the east, it gleamed off the iron monsters, accentuating their smooth, cylindrical shapes, and Hall felt the familiar twist of anger in his gut. He was as comfortable with a sword as any man alive, but a sword was a limited weapon. The Mort were trying to bend the rules of warfare as Hall had known it all of his life.

"Fine," he murmured, tucking away his spyglass, unaware that he spoke aloud. "So will we."

He descended the ladder from the bird's nest, Blaser right behind him, each dropping the last ten feet to the ground before they began to climb the hill. In the past twelve hours Hall had quietly deployed more than seven hundred men, archers and infantry, over the eastern slopes. But after weeks of hard physical work, his men found it difficult to remain still and simply lie in wait, particularly in the dark. One sign of increased activity on the hillside would have the Mort wide awake and on their guard, and so Hall had spent most of the night going from post to post, making sure his soldiers didn't simply jump out of their skins.

The slope grew steeper, until Hall and Blaser were forced to scrabble for handholds among the rocks, their feet slipping in pine needles. Both of them wore thick leather gloves and climbed carefully, for it was dangerous terrain here. The rocks were riddled with tunnels and small caves, and rattlesnakes liked to use the caves for their dens. Border rattlers were tough brutes, the result of millennia spent grappling for survival in an unforgiving place. Thick, leathery skins rendered them nearly impervious to fire and their fangs delivered a carefully controlled dose of venom. One wrong handhold on this slope and it was your life. When Hall and Simon were ten years old, Simon had once captured a rattler with a cage trap and tried to make it into a pet, but the game had lasted less than a week. No matter how well Simon fed the snake, it could not be tamed, and would attack any movement. Finally Hall and Simon had let the snake go, opening the cage and then running for their lives back up the eastern slope. No one knew how long border rattlers lived; Simon's snake might even be here somewhere, slithering among its brethren just behind the rocks.

Simon.

Hall shut his eyes, opened them again. The smart man trained his imagination not to venture too far down the Mort Road, but in these past few weeks, with all of western Mortmesne spread out before him, Hall had found himself thinking of his twin brother more often than usual: where Simon might be, who owned him now, how he had been used. Probably labor; Simon was considered one of the best shearers on the western slope. It would be wasteful to use such a man for anything besides heavy labor; Hall told himself this again and again, but probability held no sway. His mind dwelled constantly on the small percentage, the chance that Simon might have been sold for something else.

"Bastard."

Blaser's quiet curse brought Hall back to himself, and he snuck a look back over his shoulder to make sure his lieutenant hadn't been bitten. But Blaser had only slipped slightly before regaining his hold. Hall continued to climb, shaking his head to clear it of unwanted thoughts. The shipment was a wound, one that did not heal with the passage of time.

Hall gained the top of the rise and broke into the clearing to find his men waiting, their gazes expectant. Over the last month they had worked quickly, with none of the complaining that usually marked a military construction project, and had finished so early that Hall was able to test the entire operation multiple times before the Mort army had even reached the flats. The hawk handler, Jasper, was also waiting, his twelve hooded charges tethered to a long perch at the crest of the hill. The hawks had cost a pretty penny, but the Queen had listened carefully and then approved the cost without blinking.

Hall walked over to one of the catapults and placed a hand on its arm, feeling a fierce stab of pride as he touched the smooth wood. Hall was a lover of mechanisms, of gadgets. He constantly sought ways to do things faster and better. In his early career, he had invented a stronger yet more flexible longbow that was now favored by the Tear archers. On loan to a civilian construction project, he had tested and proved a pump-based irrigation system that now carried water from the Caddell to a vast, parched portion of the southern Almont. But these were his crowning achievement: five catapults, each sixty feet long, with thick arms made of Tear oak and lighter cups of pine. Each catapult could fling at least two hundred pounds, with a range of nearly four hundred yards into the wind. The arms were secured to the bases with rope, and on either side of each arm stood a soldier with an axe.

Peeking into the cup of the first catapult, Hall saw fifteen large, bulky canvas bundles, each wrapped in a thin layer of sky-blue fabric. Hall had originally planned to fling boulders, like the siege catapults of old, and flatten a significant portion of the Mort encampment. But these bundles, which had been Blaser's idea, were much better, well worth several weeks of unpleasant work. The topmost bundle shifted slightly in the wind, its canvas sides rippling, and Hall backed away, raising a clenched hand into the stillness of the morning. His axemen grabbed their weapons and heaved them high over their shoulders.

Blaser had begun humming. He always hummed to himself in tight situations: an annoying tic. Hall, listening with half an ear, identified the tune: "The Queen of the Tearling," the notes badly off-key but recognizable all the same. The song had taken hold with his men; Hall had heard it more than once in the past few weeks as they sanded lumber or sharpened blades.

My gift to you, Queen Kelsea, he thought, and dropped his hand toward the ground.

Axes hissed through the air, and then the stillness of the morning wrenched wide open, the hillside echoing with an enormous creaking and cracking as the arms of the catapults realized they were free. One by one they levered upward, gaining speed as they lunged into the sky, and Hall felt his heart lift in a pure joy that never evaporated, a joy he'd felt even as a small child testing his first rabbit trap.

My design! It works!

The arms of the catapults reached their limits and halted, with a boom that echoed across the hillside. That would wake the Mort, but it was already too late.

Hall socketed his spyglass and followed the progress of the light-blue bundles as they hurtled toward the Mort camp. They reached their zenith and began to drop, seventy-five of them in all, the sky-blue parachutes unraveling as they caught the wind, their canvas burdens swinging innocuously in the breeze.

The Mort were moving about now. Hall spied knots of activity: soldiers emerging from tents with weapons, sentries withdrawing into the camp in preparation for an attack.

"Jasper!" he called. "Two minutes!"

Jasper nodded and began to pull the hoods from his hawks, feeding each bird a small piece of meat. Major Caffrey, with his uncanny gift for recognizing a dependable mercenary, had found Jasper in a Mort border village three weeks ago. Hall didn't like Mort hawks any more now than he had as a child, when the birds used to swoop across the hillside looking for easy prey, but he still had to admire Jasper's skill with his charges. The hawks watched their handler attentively, heads cocked, like dogs waiting for their master to throw a stick.

A warning shout went up from the Mort camp. They had spotted the parachutes, which dropped faster now as wind resistance decreased. Hall watched through his spyglass, counting under his breath, as the first bundle disappeared behind one of the tents. Twelve seconds had elapsed when the first scream echoed across the flats.

More of the parachutes descended on the camp. One landed on an ordnance wagon, and Hall watched, fascinated despite himself, as the ropes relaxed. The bundle shivered for a moment, then sprang open as five furious rattlesnakes realized they were free. Their mottled skins curled and streaked over the pikes and arrows, dropping from the wagon and disappearing from sight.

Screams echoed against the hillside, and in less than a minute, the camp devolved into utter chaos. Soldiers ran

24

into each other; half-dressed men stabbed wildly at their own feet with swords. Some tried to climb to higher ground, the tops of wagons and tents, even each other's backs. But most of them fled for the boundaries of the camp, desperate to get clear. Officers shouted orders, to no avail; panic had taken hold, and now the Mort army began to pour from the camp on all sides, fleeing west toward the Border Hills or away to the east and south, across the flats. Some even sprinted mindlessly north and splashed into the shallows of Lake Karczmar. They had no armor or weapons; many were stark naked. Several had cheeks still covered with shaving cream.

"Jasper!" Hall called. "Time!"

One by one, Jasper coaxed his hawks onto the thick leather glove that covered his arm from thumb to shoulder and sent them into the air. Hall's men watched the birds uneasily as they gained altitude, but the hawks were well trained; they ignored the Tear soldiers entirely, soaring down the hillside toward the Mort camp. They dove directly into the exodus of men who streamed from the southern and eastern ends of the campsite, talons opening as they dropped, and Hall watched the first of them seize the neck of a fleeing man who wore only a half-buttoned pair of trousers. The hawk ripped out his jugular, spraying the morning sunlight with a fine mist of blood.

On the west side of the camp, wave after wave of Mort soldiers sprinted mindlessly toward the trees at the foot of the hillside. But fifty Tear archers were scattered among the treetops, and now the Mort went down in droves, their bodies riddled with arrows, sinking into the mud of the flats. New screams came from the lake; the men who'd sought shelter there had discovered their error and now they thrashed back toward the shore, bellowing in pain. Hall smiled with a touch of nostalgia. Going into the lake was a rite of passage among the children of Idyllwild, and Hall still had the scars on his legs to prove it.

By now the bulk of the Mort army had deserted the camp. Hall cast a regretful eye toward the ten cannons, which sat entirely unattended. But there was no way to get to them now; everywhere he looked, rattlesnakes slithered among the tents, seeking a good place to nest. He wondered where General Genot was, whether he had fled along with his men, whether he could be one of the hundreds of corpses lying piled at the bottom of the slope. Hall had developed a healthy respect for Genot, but he knew the man's limitations, many of the same limitations that Bermond suffered himself. Genot wanted his warfare quiet and rational. He didn't make allowances for extraordinary bravado or crushing incompetence. Yet Hall knew that any army was riddled with such anomalies.

"Jasper!" he called. "Your birds have done good work. Bring them back."

Jasper gave a loud, piercing whistle and waited, tightening the straps that bound the leather glove to his forearm. Within seconds, the hawks began to soar back in, circling over the hilltop. Jasper whistled intermittently, a different note each time, and one by one each bird dropped to settle on his forearm, where it was rewarded with several pieces of rabbit before being hooded and placed back on the perch.

"Pull the archers," Hall told Blaser. "And find Emmett. Have him send messengers to the General and the Queen."

"What message, sir?"

"Tell them I've bought us time. At least two weeks until the Mort can regroup."

26

Blaser departed, and Hall turned back to stare across the surface of Lake Karczmar, a blinding sheet of red fire in the rising sun. This sight, which used to fill him with longing as a child, now seemed like a terrible warning. The Mort were scattered, true, but not for long, and if Hall's men lost the hillside, there was nothing to prevent the Mort from shredding Bermond's carefully assembled defensive lines. Just over the hill sprawled the Almont Plain: thousands of square miles of flat land with little room for maneuver, its farms and villages isolated and defenseless. The Mort had four times the numbers, twice the quality of arms, and if they made it down into the Almont, there was only one endgame: slaughter.

Ewen had been the Keep's Jailor for several years, ever since his Da retired out of the job, and in all that time, he had never had a prisoner that he considered truly dangerous. Most of them had been men who disagreed with the Regent, and these men generally entered the dungeons too starved and beaten to do more than totter into their cells and collapse. Several of them had died in Ewen's care, although Da had told him that he was not to blame. Ewen had disliked coming in and finding their bodies cold on their cots, but the Regent hadn't seemed to care either way. One night the Regent had even marched down the dungeon steps dragging one of his own women, a red-haired lady so beautiful that she seemed like something out of one of Da's fairy stories. But she had a rope tied around her neck. The Regent led her into a cage himself, calling her bad names the entire way, and snarled at Ewen, "No food or water! She doesn't come out until I say!"

Ewen didn't like having a woman prisoner. She did not

talk or even weep, only gazed stonily at the wall of her cell. Ignoring the Regent's orders, Ewen had given her food and water, keeping a careful eye on the clock. He could tell that the rope around her neck was hurting her, and finally, unable to bear it any longer, he went in and loosened the noose. He wished he was a healer, able to fix the circle of raw red flesh on her throat, but Da had taught him only the most basic first aid, for cuts and such. Da had always been patient with Ewen's slowness, even when it caused trouble. But it didn't take a smart brain to keep a woman alive for the night, and Da would have been disappointed in Ewen had he failed. When the Regent came to collect the woman the next day, Ewen had felt great relief. The Regent had said he was sorry, but the woman had swept out of the dungeon without giving him so much as a glance.

Ever since the new Queen took the throne, there hadn't been much for Ewen to do. The Queen had freed all of the Regent's prisoners, which confused Ewen, but Da had explained that the Regent liked to put men in the dungeon for saying things he didn't like, and the Queen only put men in the dungeon for doing bad things. Da said this was sensible, and after thinking it over for a while, Ewen decided that Da was right.

Twenty-seven days ago (Ewen had noted it in the book), three Queen's Guards had burst into the dungeon leading a bound prisoner, a grey-haired man who looked exhausted but—Ewen noted gratefully—uninjured. The three guards didn't ask Ewen's permission before hauling the prisoner through the open door of Cell Three, but Ewen didn't mind. He'd never been so close to Queen's Guards before, but he'd heard all about them from Da: they protected the Queen from danger. To Ewen, this sounded like the most wonderful and important job in the world. He was grateful to be Head Jailor, but if he'd just been born smarter, he would have wanted most of all to be one of these tall, hard men in their grey cloaks.

"Treat him well," ordered the leader, a man with a head of bright red hair. "Queen's orders."

Though the guard's hair fascinated him, Ewen tried not to stare, for he didn't like it when people stared at him. He locked the cell, noting that the prisoner had already lain down on the cot and closed his eyes.

"What's his name and crime, sir? I have to write it in the book."

"Javel. His crime is treason." The red-haired leader stared through the cage bars for a moment, then shook his head. Ewen watched as the men tromped off toward the stairwell, their voices drifting down the hallway behind them.

"I'd have cut his throat."

"Is he safe with the dummy, you think?"

"That's between the Queen and the Mace."

"He must know his job. No one's ever escaped."

"Still, she can't have an idiot as a jailor forever."

Ewen flinched at the word. Bullies used to call him that, before he got so big, and he had learned to allow the word to roll right off him, but it hurt more from a Queen's Guard. And now he had something new and terrible to think about: the possibility of being replaced. When Da had retired, Da had gone to speak directly to the Regent, to make sure that Ewen could stay on. But Ewen didn't think Da had ever spoken to the Queen.

The new prisoner, Javel, was one of the easiest charges Ewen had ever had. He barely spoke, only a few words to tell Ewen when he had finished his meals or run out of water or needed the bucket emptied. For long hours Ewen even forgot that Javel was there, but then Ewen could think of little but being dismissed from his post. What would he do if that happened? He couldn't even bring himself to tell Da what the Queen's Guard had called him. He didn't want Da to know.

Five days after Javel came to the dungeon, three more Queen's Guards stomped down the stairs. One of them was Lazarus of the Mace, a recognizable figure even to Ewen, who rarely left his cells. Ewen had heard plenty of stories about the Mace from Da, who claimed that the Mace was fairy-born, that no cell would hold him. ("A jailor's nightmare, Ew!" Da would cackle over his tea.) If the other Queen's Guards had been impressive, the Mace was ten times so, and Ewen studied him as closely as he dared. The Captain of Guard in his dungeon! He couldn't wait to tell Da.

The other two guards carried a prisoner between them like a sack of grain, and after Ewen unlocked Cell One, they threw the man on the cot. The Mace stood looking at the prisoner for what seemed to Ewen a very long time. Finally he straightened, cleared something deep in his throat, and spat, a great glob of yellow slime that landed square on the prisoner's cheek.

Ewen thought this unkind; whatever the man's crime, surely he had suffered enough. He was a miserable, shriveled creature, starved and dehydrated. Mud had caked into the thick welts over his legs and torso. More welts, deep red rivets, crossed his wrists. Great hanks of hair had been pulled from his head, leaving patches of scabbed flesh. Ewen couldn't imagine what had happened to him.

The Mace turned to Ewen and snapped his fingers. "Jailor!"

Ewen stepped forward, trying to stand as tall as he could.

Da had chosen Ewen as his apprentice, even over Ewen's smarter brothers, for exactly this reason: Ewen was big and strong. But he still only came up to the Mace's nose. He wondered if the Mace knew he was slow.

"You watch this one closely, Jailor. No visitors. No little field trips outside the cell for exercise. Nothing."

"Yes, sir," Ewen replied, wide-eyed, and watched the group of guards exit the dungeon. No one called him any names this time, but it was only after they'd departed that Ewen realized he had forgotten to ask for the man's name and crime for the book. Stupid! The Mace would surely notice such things.

The next day, Da had come to visit. Ewen was tending the new prisoner as best he could, though the man's wounds were well beyond the power of anything but time or magic. But Da had taken one look at the man on his cot and spat, just like the Mace.

"Don't bother trying to cure this bastard, Ew."

"Who is he?"

"A carpenter." Da's bald head gleamed, even in the dim torchlight, and Ewen saw with some uneasiness that the skin of Da's forehead was getting thin, like linen. Even Da would die eventually, Ewen knew that, deep in a dark place in his mind. "A builder."

"What did he build, Da?"

"Cages," Da replied shortly. "Be very careful, Ew."

Ewen looked around, confused. The dungeon was full of cages. But Da didn't seem to want to talk about it, and so Ewen stored the facts in his mind alongside the rest of the mysteries he didn't understand. Once in a while, usually when Ewen wasn't even trying, he would solve a mystery, and that was a great and extraordinary feeling, the way he imagined birds would feel as they swooped across the sky. But no matter how he stared at the man in the cell, no answers were forthcoming.

After that, Ewen thought he was prepared for anyone to enter his dungeon, but he was wrong. Two days before, two men in the black uniform of the Tear army had burst in, dragging a woman between them. But this was no fancy woman like the Regent's redhead; she spat and kicked, shouting curses at the two men who dragged on her arms. Ewen had never seen anything like her. She seemed all white, from head to toe, as if her flesh had lost all of its color. Her hair was similarly faded, like hay that had sat too long in the sunlight. Even her dress was white, though Ewen thought it might once have been light blue. She looked like a ghost. The soldiers tried to force her through the open door of Cell Two, but she grabbed at the bars and hung on.

"Don't make this any harder than it needs to be," the taller soldier panted.

"Fuck you, you limp prawn!"

The soldier kept patient pressure on her hands, trying to peel back her locked fingers, while the other soldier worked on hauling her into the cage. Ewen hung back, not sure whether to get involved. The woman's eyes fell on him, and he went cold inside. Her irises were circled pink, but deep in the center was a blue so light that it glittered like ice. Ewen saw something terrible there, animal and sick. The woman opened her mouth, and Ewen knew what was coming, even before she spoke.

"I know all about you, boy. You're the halfwit."

"Give us some help, for Christ's sake!" one of the soldiers snarled.

Ewen jumped forward. He didn't want to touch any part

of the ghost-woman, so he took hold of her dress and began to tug her backward. With both soldiers free to work on her fingers, they finally succeeded in prying her loose from the bars and then flung her into the cage, where she ran into the cot and fell to the ground. Ewen was barely able to get the door closed before the woman hurled herself against the bars, spewing more curses at the three of them.

"Christ, what a job!" one of the soldiers muttered. He wiped his brow, where a mole grew like a small mushroom. "Locked in, though, she shouldn't give you too much trouble. She's blind as a mouse."

"Only watch out when the owl comes hunting," the other remarked, and they chuckled together.

"What's her name and crime?"

"Brenna. Her crime . . ." The soldier with the mole looked at his friend. "Hard to say. Treason, probably."

Ewen wrote the crime in the book, and the soldiers left the dungeon, cheerful now, their work done. The soldiers had said that the ghost-woman was blind, but Ewen quickly discovered that wasn't so. When he moved, she turned her head and her blue-pink eyes followed him across the dungeon. When he looked up, he found her gaze pinned on him, a horrible smile stretching her mouth. Ewen usually brought his prisoners their food in their cells, for he was too big to be physically overpowered by an unarmed man. But now he was glad of the little door on the front of the cell that allowed him to slide the woman's food trays through. He wanted the comfort of bars between them. Cell Two was the best cell for dangerous prisoners, since it faced directly into Ewen's small living quarters; he was a light sleeper. But now, when it came time for bed, he found that he could not sleep with that awful gaze upon him, and he finally moved his cot into the corner so that the doorway blocked the view. Still, he could sense the woman, sleepless and malevolent, even in the dark, and for the past few days his sleep had been uneasy, frequently broken.

Tonight, after Ewen had finished his dinner and inspected the empty cells for rats or rot (there was neither; he cleaned his cellblock thoroughly every other day), he settled down with his pictures. He tried constantly to paint the things he saw, but he always failed. It seemed like an easy business, with the right paper and some good paints and brushes—Da had given him these for his last birthday—but the images always escaped somewhere between his thoughts and the paper. Ewen couldn't see why it had to be that way, but it was. He was trying to paint Javel, the prisoner in Cell Three, when the door at the top of the steps crashed open.

For a few moments, Ewen had a bad fright, worried about a jailbreak. Da had warned him about jailbreaks, the worst shame that could befall a jailor. Two soldiers were stationed outside the door at the top of the steps, but Ewen was all alone down in the dungeon. He didn't know what he would do if someone had forced his way in. He grabbed the knife that lay on his desk.

But the crash of the door was followed by many voices and footsteps, such unexpected sounds that Ewen could only sit at his desk and wait to see what would come down the hallway. After a few moments a woman entered the dungeon, a tall woman with short-cropped brown hair and a silver crown on her head. Two great blue jewels hung on fine, glittering silver chains around her neck, and she was surrounded by five Queen's Guards. Ewen considered these things for a few seconds, then bolted to his feet: the Queen!

She went first to stare through the bars of Cell Three. "How have you been, Javel?"

The man on the cot looked up at her with empty eyes. "Fine, Majesty."

"Nothing else to say?"

"No."

The Queen put her hands on her hips and huffed, a sound of disappointment that Ewen recognized from Da, then moved over to Cell One to gaze at the wounded man who lay there.

"What a miserable-looking creature."

The Mace laughed. "He's endured rough handling, Lady. Rougher, maybe, than even I could have devised. The villagers took him in Devin's Slope when he tried to barter carpentry for food. They bound him to a wagon for the trip to New London, and when he finally collapsed, they dragged him the rest of the way."

"You paid these villagers?"

"All two hundred, Majesty. It's a lucky break; we need the loyalty of those border villages, and the money will probably keep Devin's Slope for a year. They don't see a lot of coin out there."

The Queen nodded. She didn't look like the queens in Da's stories, who were always delicate, pretty women like the Regent's redhead. This woman looked . . . tough. Maybe it was her short hair, short like a man's, or maybe just the way she stood, with her feet spread and one hand tapping impatiently on her hip. A favorite phrase of Da's popped into Ewen's head: she looked like no one to fiddle with.

"You! Bannaker!" The Queen snapped her fingers at the man on the cot.

The prisoner groaned, putting his hands to his head. The

welts on his arms had begun to scab over and heal, but he still seemed very weak, and despite Da's words, Ewen felt a moment's pity.

"Give it up, Lady," the Mace remarked. "You won't get anything out of him for a while. Men's minds can break from a journey like that. It's usually the point."

The Queen cast around the dungeon and her deep green eyes found Ewen, who snapped to attention. "Are you my Jailor?"

"Yes, Majesty. Ewen."

"Open this cell."

Ewen stepped forward, digging for the keys at his belt, glad that Da had labeled them all so it was easy to find the key with the big 2. He didn't want to keep this woman waiting. Once a month he oiled the locks, just as Da had advised, and he was grateful to feel the key turn smoothly, with no squealing or hitches. He stepped back as the Queen entered the cell with several guards. She turned to one of them, a huge man with ugly, jagged teeth. "Stand him up."

The big guard hauled the prisoner off the cot and grabbed him by the neck, dangling him just above the ground.

The Queen slapped the prisoner's face. "Are you Liam Bannaker?"

"I am," the prisoner gurgled in a low, thick voice. His nose had begun to trickle blood, and the sight made Ewen wince. Why were they being so unkind?

"Where is Arlen Thorne?"

"I don't know."

The Queen said a bad word, one that Da had once spanked Ewen for repeating, and the Mace cut in. "Who helped you build your cages?"

"No one."

The Mace turned to the Queen, and Ewen watched, fascinated, as they locked eyes for a long moment. They were talking to each other . . . talking without even opening their mouths!

"No," the Queen finally murmured. "We're not going to start that now."

"Lady—"

"I didn't say never, Lazarus. But not for such small chance of reward as this."

She came out of the cell, signaling her guards to follow. The big guard dumped the prisoner back on his cot, where he breathed in great wheezes like an accordion. Ewen, feeling the Mace's eyes on him, assessing, locked the cell immediately behind them.

"And you," the Queen remarked, moving over to gaze at the woman in Cell Two. "You're the real prize, aren't you?"

The ghost-woman giggled, a sound like metal on glass. Ewen wanted to clap his hands over his ears. The woman grinned at the Queen, showing rotten lower teeth. "When my master comes, he'll punish you for keeping us apart."

"Why is he your master?" the Queen asked. "What has he ever done for you?"

"He saved me."

"You're a fool. He abandoned you to save his own skin. You're nothing but chattel to a slave trader."

The woman flew at the bars, her arms flailing like the wings of a bird gone wild inside its cage. Even the Mace took a step back. But the Queen moved forward until she was only a few inches from the bars, so close that Ewen wanted to shout a warning.

"Look at me, Brenna."

The ghost-woman looked up, her face wrenching, as though she wanted to look away but could not.

"You're right," the Queen murmured. "Your master will come. And when he does, I will take him."

"My magic will protect him from harm."

"I have my own magic, dear heart. Can't you feel it?"

Brenna's face twisted in sudden pain.

"I will hang your master's corpse from the walls of my Keep. Do you see?"

"You can't do that!" the ghost-woman howled. "You can't!"

"Sport for vultures," the Queen continued smoothly. "You can't protect him. You're nothing but bait."

The ghost-woman screamed in fury, a high and unbearable sound like the screech of a hunting bird. Ewen covered his ears and saw several Queen's Guards do the same.

"Be quiet," the Queen ordered, and the woman's screams cut off as suddenly as they had begun. She stared at the Queen, her pink eyes wide and frightened as she huddled on her cot.

The Queen turned back to Ewen. "You will treat all three of these prisoners humanely."

Ewen bit his lip. "I don't know that word, Majesty."

"Humanely," the Queen replied impatiently. "Enough food and water and clothing, no harassment. Make sure they can sleep."

"Well, Majesty, it's hard to make sure someone can sleep."

The Queen looked very hard at him, her brow furrowing, and Ewen realized he'd said something wrong. It had been easier when Da was the Jailor and Ewen only an apprentice. Da could always step in when Ewen didn't understand. He was about to apologize—for it was always better to do that before someone got angry—when the Queen's forehead suddenly smoothed.

"You're down here alone, Ewen?"

"Yes, Majesty, since my Da retired. His arthritis got too bad."

"Your dungeon looks very clean."

"Thank you, Majesty," he replied, smiling, for she was the first person besides Da who had ever noticed. "I clean it every other day."

"Do you miss your Da?"

Ewen blinked, wondering if she was winding him up. The Regent had liked to do that, and his guards had liked to even more. Ewen had learned to spot the telltale sign in their faces: a sly meanness that might crouch hidden but never went away. The Queen's face was hard, but not mean, and so Ewen answered truthfully. "Yes. There's lots of things I don't understand, and Da always explained them."

"But you like your job."

Ewen looked down at the ground, thinking of the other guard, the one who had called him an idiot. "Yes."

The Queen beckoned him to stand in front of Cell Two. "This woman may not seem dangerous, but she is. She's also very valuable. Can you watch her every day and not let her trick you?"

Ewen stared at the ghost-woman. Certainly bigger and tougher prisoners had been housed in the dungeon. Several of them had tried to trick Ewen, everything from pretending to be sick, to offering Ewen money, to begging the loan of his sword. The ghost-woman stared at the Queen, her eyes gleaming with hatred, and Ewen knew that the Queen was right: this woman would be a tough prisoner, smart and quick.

But I can be smart too.

"I'm sure you can," the Queen replied, and Ewen jumped,

for he hadn't said anything. He turned and saw something that made his jaw drop in astonishment: the blue jewels that dangled around the Queen's neck were sparkling, glittering brightly in the torchlight.

"Once a week," the Queen continued, "you'll come upstairs and give me a report on all three of your prisoners. If you need to, take notes."

Ewen nodded, pleased that she assumed he could read and write. Most people thought he couldn't, but Da had taught him, so that he could keep the book.

"Do you know what suffering is, Ewen?"

"Yes, Majesty."

"Behind your three prisoners there is another man, a tall starving-thin man with bright blue eyes. This man is an agent of suffering, and I want him alive. Should you ever see him, you send word to Lazarus immediately. Do you understand?"

Ewen nodded again, his mind already full of the picture she had put there. He could see the man now: a looming scarecrow figure with eyes like great blue lamps. He longed to try to paint him.

The Queen reached out, and after a moment Ewen realized that she wanted to shake his hand. Her guards tensed, several of them placing hands on their swords, so Ewen offered his hand, very carefully, and allowed her to shake it. The Queen didn't wear any rings, and Ewen wondered at this. He wondered what Da would say when Ewen told him that he'd met the Queen, that she wasn't at all how Ewen had thought she would be. He stood by his cells, keeping an eye on all of the prisoners, but also peeking at the Queen as the five guards surrounded her and seemed to carry her in a wave, down the hallway and up the stairs, out of his dungeon.

Kelsea Glynn had a temper.

She was not proud of this fact. Kelsea hated herself when she was angry, for even with her heart thumping and a thick veil of fury obscuring her vision, she could still see, clearly, the straight path from unchecked anger to self-destruction. Anger clouded judgment, precipitated bad decisions. Anger was the indulgence of a child, not a queen. Carlin had impressed these facts upon her, many times, and Kelsea had listened. But even Carlin's words had no weight when fury washed over Kelsea; it was a tide that cleared all obstacles. And Kelsea knew that although her anger was destructive, it was also pure, the closest she would ever get to the girl she really was deep down, beneath all of the controls that had been instilled in her since birth. She had been born angry, and she often wondered what it would be like to release her rage, to drop all pretense and let her true self out.

Kelsea was working very hard to contain her anger now, but every word from the man across the table made the dark wave behind the dam swell a bit further. Mace and Pen were beside her, Arliss and Father Tyler in seats farther down the table. But Kelsea saw nothing but General Bermond, seated down at the other end. On the table before him lay an iron helmet topped with a ridiculous blue plume. Bermond was dressed in full armor, for he had just ridden in from the front.

"We don't want to stretch the army too thin, Majesty. It's a poor use of resources, this plan."

"Must everything be a fight with you, General?"

He shook his head, clinging doggedly to his point. "You can defend your kingdom, or you can defend your people, Majesty. You don't have the manpower to do both at once."

"People are more important than land."

"An admirable statement, Majesty, but poor military strategy."

"You know what these people suffered in the last invasion."

"Better than you do, Majesty, for you weren't even born yet. The Caddell ran red. It was wholesale murder."

"And mass rape."

"Rape's a weapon of war. The women got over it."

"Oh Christ," Mace breathed, and put a restraining hand on Kelsea's arm. She started guiltily, for Mace had caught her. General Bermond might be old and lame, but she had still been thinking of dragging him from his chair and giving him several good, hard kicks. She took a deep breath and spoke carefully. "Men were raped along with the women, General."

Bermond frowned, annoyed. "That is apocryphal, Majesty."

Kelsea met Father Tyler's eye, saw him give a slight shake of the head. No one wanted to talk about this facet of the last invasion, not even twenty years later, but the Arvath had received many consistent reports from local parish priests, the only observers to really chronicle the invasion. Rape was a weapon of war, and the Mort did not discriminate by gender.

Kelsea suddenly wished that Colonel Hall could have attended this council. He didn't always agree with her, but he was at least willing to look at all sides of a thing, unlike the General, whose mind had hardened long ago. But the Mort army had reached the border several days ago, and Hall could not be spared.

"We're wandering from the subject, Majesty," Arliss remarked.

42

"Agreed." Kelsea turned back to Bermond. "We have to protect these people."

"By all means, Majesty, build a refugee camp and take in every stray. But don't sidetrack my soldiers from more important business. Those who want your protection can find a way to the city by themselves."

"That's a dangerous journey to make alone, particularly with small children. The first wave of refugees is barely out of the hills, and we've already had reports of harassment and violence along the way. If that's the only option we offer, many of them will choose to stay in their villages, even when the Mort draw near."

"Then that's their choice, Majesty."

The dam in Kelsea's mind shuddered, its foundations weakening. "Do you honestly not know the right thing to do, General, or do you just pretend not to know because it's easier that way?"

Bermond's cheeks reddened. "There's more than one right here."

"I don't think there is. Here we have men, women, and children who have never done anything but farm. Their weapons are wood, if they have weapons at all. Invasion will be a bloodbath."

"Precisely, and the best way to protect them is to make sure that the Mort never invade this kingdom."

"Do you really believe that the Tear army can hold the border?"

"Of course I do, Majesty. To believe otherwise is treasonous."

Kelsea clamped her teeth down on the inside of her cheek, unable to believe the cognitive dissonance implied in such a statement. Hall's reports came from the border, regular as clockwork and grim as doom, but Kelsea didn't need Hall to tell her the true state of affairs. The Tear army would never hold against what was coming. In the past week, a vision had begun to grow on Kelsea: the western Almont, covered over with a sea of black tents and soldiers. The girl who had been raised by Carlin Glynn would never have trusted in visions, but Kelsea's world had broadened well beyond the width of Carlin's library. The Mort would come, and the Tear army wouldn't be able to stop them. All they could hope to do was slow them down.

Arliss spoke up again. "The Tear infantry are out of training, Majesty. We already have reports of tin weapons breaking under impact due to improper storage. And there is a serious morale problem."

Bermond turned to him, furious. "You have spies in my army?"

"I have no need of spies," Arliss replied coolly. "These problems are common knowledge."

Bermond swallowed his anger with poor grace. "Then all the more reason, Majesty, for us to spend the limited time we have in training and supply."

"No, General." Kelsea came to a decision suddenly, as she so often did: because it seemed the only thing that would allow her to sleep at night. "We're going to use resources where they'll do the most good: in evacuation."

"I refuse, Majesty."

"Indeed?" Kelsea's anger crested, breaking like a wave. It was a wonderful feeling, but as always, damnable reason intruded. She could not lose Bermond; too many of the old guard in her army had a misplaced faith in his leadership. She forced a pleasant smile. "Then I will remove you from command."

"You can't do that!"

"Of course I can. You have a colonel who's ready to lead. He's more than capable, and certainly more of a realist than you."

"My army will not follow Hall. Not yet."

"But they will follow me."

"Nonsense." But Bermond's eyes edged away from hers. He had heard the rumors too, then. Less than a month had elapsed since Kelsea and her Guard had returned from the Argive Pass, but prevailing wisdom now held that Kelsea had unleashed a titanic flood on Arlen Thorne's traitors and washed them all away. It was a favorite tale, demanded constantly from storytellers in New London's pubs and markets, and it had done wonders for security. No one even tried to sneak into the Keep anymore, Mace had informed Kelsea, in a tone of near-regret. The incident in the Argive had drastically altered the political landscape, and Bermond knew it. Kelsea leaned forward, scenting blood.

"Do you really believe that your army will defy *me*, Bermond? For your sake?"

"Of course they will. My men are loyal."

"It would be a pity to test that loyalty and come up short. Wouldn't it be easier to simply help with my evacuation?"

Bermond's glare was furious, but Kelsea was pleased to see that it was also weakening, and for the first time since the meeting had begun, she felt her anger beginning to recede a bit.

"The camp's one thing, Majesty, but what will you do when the Mort come? This city is crowded as it is. There certainly isn't room for half a million extra people."

Kelsea wished she had a ready answer, but this problem had no easy solution. New London was already overpopulated, creating issues with plumbing and sanitation. Historically, when disease had broken out in the more crowded sections of the city, it was almost impossible to control. Double the population, and these problems would multiply exponentially. Kelsea planned to open the Keep to families, but even with its great size, the Keep would only absorb perhaps a quarter of the influx. Where would she put the rest?

"New London is not your concern, General. Lazarus and Arliss are in charge of preparing for siege. You worry about the rest of the kingdom."

"I do worry, Majesty. You've opened Pandora's box."

Kelsea did not allow her expression to change, but the satisfaction on Bermond's face told her that he knew he had struck his mark. Kelsea had opened the door to chaos, and while she told herself there had been no alternative, her nights were tormented by the certainty that there *had* been another option, some path that could have stopped the shipment while avoiding the bloodshed to follow, and if Kelsea had only been a bit more clever, she could have found it. She drew a slow breath. "Regardless of blame, General, done is done. Your job is to help me minimize the damage."

"Like trying to dam up God's Ocean, eh, Majesty?"

"Just like that, General." She grinned at him, a grin so ferocious that Bermond recoiled against his chair. "The first wave of refugees will reach the Almont proper tomorrow. Give them some guards, and then begin moving the rest. I want those villages cleared out."

"And what happens if my army is as weak as you seem to think, Majesty? The Mort will make straight for New London, just as they did in your mother's time. Mort soldiers get a salary, but it's a pittance; they build their wealth on plunder, and the good plunder is right here. If I can't keep them from

46

crossing the border, do you really think you can keep them from sacking the city?"

Something was wrong with Kelsea's eyes. A thick cloud seemed to obscure her vision, light at the corners and heavy in the center. Was it her sapphires? No, they had been quiet for weeks, and now they hung dark and still against her chest. Kelsea blinked rapidly, trying to clear her head; it wouldn't do to show weakness in front of Bermond now.

"I'm hoping for help," she told him. "I have opened negotiations with the Cadarese."

"And what good will that do?"

"Perhaps the King will lend us some of his troops."

"Fool's hope, Lady. The Cadarese are isolationists, always have been."

"Yes, but I'm exploring all options."

"Lady?" Pen asked quietly. "Are you all right?"

"I'm fine," Kelsea muttered, but now spots were dancing across her field of vision. She was going to be ill, she realized, and she could not do that in front of Bermond. She stood up, grabbing at the table for balance.

"Lady?"

"I'm fine," she repeated, shaking her head, trying to clear it.

"What's wrong with her?" Bermond asked, but his voice was already growing faint. The world suddenly smelled like rain. Kelsea clenched the table and felt the slickness of polished wood slipping beneath her fingers.

"Grab her, man!" Mace barked. "She'll fall!"

She felt Pen's arm around her waist, but his touch was unwelcome, and she shook him off. Her vision blurred entirely and she glimpsed unfamiliar surroundings: a small compartment and a grey, threatening sky. Panicked, she closed her eyes tightly and then opened them again, looking for her audience chamber, her guards, anything that was known. But she saw none of them. Mace, Pen, Bermond . . . they were all gone.

CHAPTER 2

LILY

"It is merely crossing," said Mr. Micawber, trifling with his eye-glass, "merely crossing. The distance is quite imaginary."
—*David Copperfield*, CHARLES DICKENS *(pre-Crossing Angl.)*

Her eyes opened on a deep grey world, storm clouds promising certain rain. In the distance, through the windshield, she could see a bleak sky dominated by a line of dark grey silhouettes.

Manhattan.

The car hit a bump crossing the bridge, and Lily looked out the window, annoyed. Greg was in charge of their household finances, but Lily had overheard him telling Jim Henderson that he paid a good chunk of money to the utilities every month to use the bridge. In return, they were supposed to maintain the paving. But they never did as good a job as they should have, and lately Lily had noticed bumps and potholes that took longer and longer to repair. Still, the trip beat taking the public bridge; their Lexus was begging to be carjacked on a public roadway. Security regularly patrolled this bridge and its connecting roads, and officers would appear in moments if Jonathan pressed the panic button. A few potholes were a small price to pay for safety.

The bridge ended, and Lily looked eagerly out the window as the high walls tapered down to a low barrier. She came into the city less and less often, and it seemed like things were worse every time, but she still liked to visit. Her own house in New Canaan was beautiful, a stately colonial with white columns, just like those of all of her friends. But even an entire town could get old when everything was the same. Lily dressed more carefully for her rare trips outside the wall than she did for her own dinner parties; dangerous or not, this excursion always seemed like an event.

Looking over the edge of the roadside barrier, she glimpsed the slums, hung with garbage bags to create shelter from the coming rain. Shapeless, shiftless people huddled against walls and beneath overhangs. The first time Greg had brought Lily to New York, just after they married, most of the buildings had already been empty, the windows covered with For Lease signs. By now squatters had torn down even the signs, and so many buildings had been abandoned that Security hardly bothered with the downtown at all. The blank windows made these buildings look empty, but they weren't; Lily shrank from imagining what went on inside. Drugs, crime, prostitution . . . and she'd even read online that people caught sleeping unawares were often killed for their organs. There were no rules outside the wall. Nothing was safe.

Greg said that the people outside the barriers were lazy, but Lily had never thought of them that way. They were simply unlucky; their parents hadn't been wealthy, like hers and Greg's. Greg hadn't been so rigid when he was at Princeton; sometimes, on weekends, he would even work with the homeless. That was how they'd met, both of them volunteering in Trenton at the last homeless shelter left in New Jersey, though more and more, these days, Lily wondered whether Greg had done it for his résumé; he had gone on to a government internship the next summer. Lily went to Swarthmore, studying English because it was the only thing she liked. The books were all purged by then, free of sex and profanity and anything else the Frewell administration had found un-American, but Lily could still enjoy them, could still dig deep beneath the sterilized surface to find a good story. She loved being in school, and the thought of the future made her feel panicky and out of control. Greg was the ambitious one, the one who'd worked summers in Washington, who traveled to New York on countless weekends to network with his parents' friends. Lily had liked that, liked that Greg seemed to have such a handle on where his life was going. When he landed a good job, assisting the liaison for a defense contractor, and asked Lily to marry him after graduation, it had seemed like nothing short of a godsend. She wouldn't have to work; her entire job would be keeping the house and making nice with other people like herself. And of course, taking care of the children, when the children came. None of it seemed like real work. Lily would have plenty of time to shop, to read, to think. The car hit another bump, jarring her against the seat, and Lily felt something almost like a smile stretch across her lips. She had hit the jackpot, all right.

Rain pelted down on the car all at once, hitting the window in spatters that obscured Lily's view. The sky had been darkening all day, and many of the people outside the barrier were wearing some sort of synthetic bags over their clothing in preparation. Lily wondered if they had to find new bags for each rainstorm, or whether they reused the same bags over and over again.

"Detour up ahead, Mrs. M.," Jonathan said over his shoulder.

"Why?"

"Explosion." He pointed out the windshield, and Lily saw an oily sheen of flame through the rain, perhaps a mile ahead. She'd read about this as well; sometimes criminals would climb up and plant explosives on the private highways, trying to block them off, to force people to take public routes. Just one of many constant dangers in traveling outside the wall, but so long as Jonathan wasn't concerned, Lily wasn't either. Greg had hired Jonathan for Lily three years ago, in the week before their wedding. Jonathan was a good bodyguard, but an even better driver; during his service in the Oil Wars, he'd been in charge of security for supply caravans, and he seemed to know the entire eastern seaboard's roadways like the back of his hand. He guided the car through the high streets, which now ran so flush against the buildings that Lily could only glimpse a thin line of darkness over the edge. She pictured the people beneath her, imagining them as rats that scuttled through the gloom. Embeth, a high school friend of Lily's, had come to New York after graduation to be a nanny, but a few years ago Lily could have sworn she had seen Embeth on a corner in lower Manhattan, dressed in rags, skin grimy and hair looking as though she hadn't washed it in years. Just a brief glimpse through a car window and then gone.

As they passed over the crumbling remains of Rockefeller Center, Lily saw that someone had lasered blue words onto the pavement where the old fountain used to be, the graffiti so large that it was visible from the roadway above.

THE BETTER WORLD

That was the slogan of the Blue Horizon, the separatist group, but no one seemed to know exactly what it meant. Most of the Blue Horizon's activities seemed to involve blowing things up or hacking into various government systems to cause trouble. Last year, when the separatists had presented Congress with a request to secede, Lily had been all for it, but Greg told her no; there was too much money at stake, too many customers and debtors to lose. Lily, who thought only of the reduction in violent crime, considered it a good trade, but she left it alone. That had been a stressful time for Greg at work; he was constantly on edge, drinking too much. He had never really relaxed until the petition failed.

Jonathan took a smooth left into the basement of the Plymouth Center and stopped at the Security barrier. Two men with guns in their hands approached the car, and Jonathan presented his pass.

"Mrs. Mayhew, appointment to see Dr. Davis on the fiftieth floor."

The guard peered into the back of the car. "Open her window."

Jonathan rolled down Lily's window and she leaned forward, presenting her left shoulder. The guard had a cheap portable scanner; he had to wave it over Lily's shoulder several times before her tag registered with a small, cricketlike beep.

"Thank you, Mrs. Mayhew," the guard said, and gave her a

smile with no warmth. He went up to scan Jonathan, and Lily settled back into the leather seat as the car proceeded smoothly into the garage.

The body scanner beside the elevator buzzed loudly as Lily went through; she'd forgotten to take off her watch. It was a big, chunky thing, nearly solid silver with a diamond face, and her friends always eyed it covetously when she wore it to the club. To Lily, a watch was a watch, but like so many things Greg had bought her, she wore it because she was expected to. As soon as she made it through the gate, she stuffed the watch into her purse.

The elevator beeped as it read the implant in her shoulder. The tag would show her location, if Greg should check, but what of that? To the outward eye, Dr. Davis was a perfectly respectable doctor, and many wealthy women consulted him for their fertility troubles. Still, Lily felt a guilty blush spreading over her cheeks. She always got caught when she lied, and she had never been able to keep a secret. Only this one, the biggest secret of all, and the longer she kept it, the more frightened she became. If Greg found out . . .

But she didn't let her thoughts go too far down that road. If she did, she would turn around and run out of the building, and she couldn't afford to do that. She took a deep breath, then a few more, until her pulse slowed and her nerve came back. When the elevator doors opened, she turned left and went down a long hallway carpeted with deep, rich green. She passed many doors advertising various specialty doctors: dermatologists, orthodontists, cosmetic surgeons. Dr. Davis's was the last door on the right, a thick walnut slab that looked exactly as it should, with a brass nameplate that advertised "Anthony Davis, M.D., Fertility Specialist." Lily place her thumb against the pad and waited a few seconds, looking up at the pinhole camera fixed to the side of the door, until the tiny red light turned green and the lock clicked.

The waiting room was crammed with women. Nearly all of them were like Lily, white and well dressed, holding high-quality handbags. But a few were clearly from the streets, betrayed by their hair and clothing, and Lily wondered how they had gotten past Security. One of them, a Hispanic woman, perhaps five or six months pregnant, had squashed herself into a chair just beside the door. She was gasping for breath, clutching the arms of the chair, her face pale and frightened. When Lily looked down, she saw that the lap of the woman's jeans was soaked with blood.

Two nurses came hurrying out of the back office with a wheelchair and helped the woman slide into it. She clasped her swollen belly with both hands, as though trying to hold something in. Lily saw tears trickling from the corners of her eyes, and then the nurses pushed her through the door, to the examining rooms beyond.

"Can I help you?"

Lily turned to the receptionist, a young brunette with an impersonal smile.

"Lily Mayhew. I have an appointment."

"Wait, please, until we call you."

There were no seats left but the newly vacated chair, its light green cushion soaked with blood. Lily couldn't bring herself to sit there, so she leaned against the wall, stealing covert glances at the people around her. A woman and a teenage girl, clearly mother and daughter, sat in two nearby chairs. The girl was anxious, her mother was not, and Lily read their dynamic easily. She had felt the same way the first time Mom had brought her to this office, understanding that it was a rite of passage, but also that it had to be kept secret, that what went on here was a crime. Lily hated this appointment, hated this office, the necessity of it, but at the same time she was utterly grateful for this place, that there were people who didn't fear Greg, all the Gregs of this world.

But it was a mistake to think of Greg now; Lily felt as though he were looking over her shoulder, and the idea made her forehead break out in sweat. Each year she came here made it more likely that she would get caught, if not by Security then by Greg himself. Greg wanted children in the same way he had wanted a new BMW, the same way he wanted Lily to wear her diamond-studded watch. Greg wanted children so he could show them off to the world. All of their friends had at least two children already, some even three or four, and the wives gave Lily pitying looks at the club, at parties. These looks didn't hurt at all, but Lily had to pretend that they did. A few times she had even drummed up some tears, small tantrums for Greg's benefit, solid evidence of sorrow over her failure as a wife. Once upon a time Lily had wanted children, but that seemed very distant now, an entire lifetime that had happened to someone else. Greg was the one who had suggested that Lily go to a fertility clinic, not knowing she'd been coming to Dr. Davis for years, not knowing that he had just made things that much easier for her to hide in plain sight.

After an eternity, Dr. Anna leaned out the glass door and called Lily's name. She led Lily into an office and drew the curtain, leaving her with the inevitable paper gown. Dr. Anna was Dr. Davis's wife, a woman well into her fifties. She was one of the few women doctors Lily had ever met. Lily had mostly been too young to understand the Frewell Laws;

President Frewell's term in office had begun when Lily was eight and ended when she was sixteen. But his laws had left their legacy, and medical schools rarely admitted women anymore. Lily, who could no more have let a strange man look between her legs than she could have gone outside naked, was grateful that there was a Dr. Anna at all, but Dr. Anna had the constantly irritated face of the old-time schoolmarm, and she always seemed annoyed at Lily for being there, for taking her away from something more important. She asked Lily the routine questions, making notes on her clipboard, while Lily worked at tucking the paper gown more tightly around her, trying to cover as much skin as possible.

"Do you need more pills?"

"Please."

"A whole year's worth?"

"Yes."

"How will you pay?"

Lily dug inside her purse and produced two thousand dollars in cash. Greg had given it to her for shopping last weekend, and Lily had poked the money through a hole in the lining of her purse, then lied and said she'd bought herself a pair of shoes. The hole in her purse had come in handy several times in the past year, when Greg had taken to making unscheduled inspections of her things. She had no idea what he was looking for; when he found nothing, he would give Lily an odd, cheated look, the look of the store clerk who had failed to catch someone shoplifting. The inspections were unsettling, but that look worried Lily even more.

Dr. Anna took the cash and slipped it into her pocket, and then they went on to the messy, unpleasant business of the

Erika Johansen

exam itself, which Lily endured by gritting her teeth, staring at the cheap plaster tiles on the ceiling, and thinking of the nursery. She and Greg had no children, but Lily had furnished the nursery just after their marriage, back when things were different. The nursery was the only place in their house that belonged entirely to Lily, where she could really be alone. Greg needed people around him, needed someone to respond to him. Nowhere in the house was safe; he might come barging into any room at any time without knocking, seeking attention. But he never came into the nursery.

When Dr. Anna had sent out all of the various tools and swabs, she told Lily, "The receptionist will tell you your test results, and she'll have your pills together. Just give her your name."

"Thank you."

Dr. Anna went for the door, but paused just before opening it and turned around, her schoolteacher's face set in its default expression of pinched disapproval. "You know, it won't ever get better on its own."

"What won't?"

"Him." Dr. Anna's eyes dropped to the ring on Lily's finger. "Your husband."

Lily clutched the hem of the paper gown more tightly between her fingers. "I don't know what you mean."

"I think you do. I see over five hundred women a month in here. The bruises don't lie."

"I don't—"

"Plus," Dr. Anna continued, cutting Lily off, "you're clearly a wealthy woman. There's no reason you can't get contraception closer to home. With black-market prices what they are these days, you could even get a dealer to

58

deliver pills to your house. Unless, of course, you're afraid your husband will find out."

Lily shook her head, not wanting to hear any of this. Sometimes she thought that everything was almost fine, so long as it wasn't brought out into the open.

"Your husband doesn't own you."

Lily looked up, suddenly furious, because Dr. Anna didn't know what the hell she was talking about. That was all marriage meant: ownership. Lily had sold herself for someone to take care of her, to pay the bills and tell her what to do. Certainly there had been some buyer's remorse along the way, but that was the proverbial pig in a poke, as Lily's mother would have said. Mom and Dad hadn't wanted her to marry Greg, but Lily had been so sure of what was best. Thinking of her parents, Lily felt a sudden, hopeless longing for her old room back at their house in Pennsylvania, for the twin bed and oak desk. The furniture had been plain, nowhere near as nice as the things Lily owned now. But her room had been her own. Even her parents didn't come in without knocking first.

Lily's eyes had watered; she wiped a quick hand across them, smearing her makeup. "You don't know anything about it."

Dr. Anna gave a mirthless chuckle. "This dynamic never changes, Mrs. Mayhew. Believe me, I know."

"He's only done it a few times," Lily mumbled, knowing even as she spoke that it was a mistake to answer. Had she ever resented Dr. Anna's clinical, impersonal manner? She longed to have it back now. "He's been under a lot of pressure at work this year."

"Your husband's a powerful man?"

"Yes," Lily replied automatically. It was always the first

thing that popped into her head about Greg: that he was a powerful man. He worked for the Department of Defense, acting as a civilian liaison between the military men and the weapons contractors. His division oversaw supply for all of the military bases on the East Coast. He was six foot two and had played football in college. He had met the president. There was nowhere that Lily could escape to.

"Even so, there are places you can go, you know. Places you can hide."

Lily shook her head, but there was no way to explain to Dr. Anna. Women did run sometimes, even in New Canaan; last year, Cath Alcott had just taken off one night, packed her three kids into the family Mercedes and disappeared. Security had found the car, abandoned in Massachusetts, but so far as Lily knew, they never found Cath. John Alcott, a big, quiet man who had always made Lily feel slightly uneasy, had hired a private firm to find his wife, but it hadn't helped. They couldn't even trace her tag. Cath had done the impossible: she had taken her children and gotten away clean.

But Lily would never be able to disappear, even without children in tow. Where would she live? How would she eat? All of the money was in Greg's name; the big banks wouldn't open individual accounts for married women anymore. Even if Lily had known people who could create a new identity for her—she didn't—she had no skills. She had graduated college with English credentials. No one would hire her, not even to clean houses. Lily closed her eyes and saw the homeless of Manhattan in their shapeless garbage bags, living in clusters beneath the roadways, fighting for scraps. Even if she made it so far, she wouldn't last a day in that world.

"Well, think it over," Dr. Anna told her, face severe again. "It's never too late."

Reaching into her pocket, she produced a card and, with a questioning glance at Lily, tucked it into Lily's purse where it sat on the chair. Then she slipped out, closing the door behind her.

Lily slithered down off the paper-covered exam table, carefully shedding her paper gown so that it didn't rip; her parents' waste-not-want-not upbringing still ruled her sometimes, even in such silly matters as a paper gown that couldn't be reused. Looking down at herself, she saw purple finger-shaped bruises on her upper arms from where Greg had grabbed her on Tuesday. The rest of the cuts and bruises from the bad night almost a month ago had finally healed, but these new marks meant that she couldn't wear anything sleeveless for a while, and Greg liked her in sleeveless tops.

She began to put on the rest of her clothes, trying not to look down at the rest of her body. Greg *had* been under a lot of stress; that, at least, hadn't been a lie, and he had been sorry afterward. But "a few times" was stretching it. There had been six times so far, and Lily could remember each of them in detail. She could lie to Dr. Anna, but there was no use varnishing the truth inside her own head. Greg was getting worse.

When Lily exited the elevator, she found several members of Security clustered around a well-dressed man at the scanner. The man looked respectable enough to Lily's eye, with just a touch of grey in his hair and a very smart navy suit. But the guards hustled him behind the desk, through a blank white door with "Security" painted on it in black letters. All sound ceased when they closed the door behind them.

Under the watchful eyes of the two remaining guards,

Lily moved toward the waiting Lexus. Terrible memory had awoken: Maddy's blonde pigtails, disappearing through the doors. Sometimes there were whole months when Lily managed not to think of Maddy, and then she would see something: a woman being escorted from her car, Security knocking on someone's door, even the faintest glimpse in the distance of one of the sprawling detention centers that lay along I-80. Maddy was gone, but even the tiniest thing could bring her back. Lily jerked the car door open angrily, forcing the image away. This little expedition was hard enough; she didn't need Maddy along for the ride.

"Back home, Mrs. M.?" Jonathan asked.

"Yes, please," Lily replied, feeling the same odd, amalgamated emotions the word always evoked in her: half comfort and half revulsion. "Home."

After Jonathan dropped her off, Lily went right to the nursery. Greg wasn't home yet and the house was empty, silent but for the humming of circuits inside its walls. Jonathan was supposed to stay with Lily at all times, even when she was at home, but she heard the engine gun outside and knew that he had left again. He often ran his own errands on the clock, sometimes at odd hours, but Lily had never mentioned this to Greg. She never felt unsafe by herself, not here in New Canaan. The walls around the city were twenty feet high and topped with electrified fencing. There was never any crime . . . or at least, Lily amended to herself, any violent crime. The city was full of law-abiding thieves.

The nursery was a spacious, airy room on the ground floor. Lily had chosen this room because it was beside the kitchen, but even more so because the nursery opened onto a small brick patio that overlooked the backyard. Lily had liked the idea of being able to bring a baby outside to feed it in the shade of the elms. Three years ago, but it seemed like a hundred, and now Greg's baby was something to avoid having at all costs.

When no children came, the room had become Lily's by default. Greg wasn't the sort of man who would ever enter the nursery anyway; his father, whom Lily had loathed, had raised Greg with very definite ideas of what was masculine and what wasn't, and a room full of stuffed animals didn't make the cut. The fact that Lily remained childless only made the nursery less inviting to him, and despite the toys strewn all over the place, the room had more or less taken on the air of a Victorian lady's parlor: a quiet, sedate space where men never entered. Sometimes when Lily had friends over, they would have coffee in here, but it was always the women, never the men.

Of course, the house's surveillance system was set up so that Greg could watch her in the nursery, even while he was at work. But Lily had taken care of that wrinkle early on by recording several days' worth of innocuous footage—Lily knitting, napping, even staring longingly into the crib, as well as plenty of footage of the empty room—and looping it within the feed. Greg was not particularly computer-literate; in his parents' house, everything had always been done for him by the nanny, the tutor, the bodyguards. Now, at work, he had a secretary who handled his entire life. But Lily knew something about computers, at least enough to alter the surveillance system. Maddy had been something of a hacker; in the last two years before she disappeared—*was taken*, Lily's mind amended; this was a fact she was never allowed to forget inside her own head—Maddy had more or less lived in her room with the door closed, spending long hours on the computer. But sometimes, during weeks when Lily and Maddy were getting along, Maddy would show her interesting things, and this was one of them: how to cut into surveillance footage. If Security ever decided to monitor their surveillance system, Lily would need a new trick, but fortunately Greg's job as a military liaison meant that he and Lily were respectable citizens, and so their house feeds were supposedly closed. Lily had a sneaking suspicion—confirmed the longer she got away with it—that Greg didn't like to look at the nursery, not even on a monitor. If he did check up on her in this room, it was probably limited to a brief glance, certainly not long enough to connect anything he saw with earlier footage. So far, it had worked fine. Her time in the nursery belonged to her and no one else. Even in the past year, as Greg grew increasingly invasive of her few remaining privacies, this place was still safe.

Lily closed the door behind her and took the pills over to the secret place beneath the corner tile. Even if Greg ever did decide to come in here, Lily didn't think he would be able to spot the loose tile, which lay perfectly flush with the wall. Over the years Lily had hidden plenty of contraband here: cash, painkillers, old paperback books. But nothing was as important as the pills, which Lily arranged in neat, careful stacks of three boxes each beneath the tile. She stared down at them, wondering for the hundredth time why she was so different from all of her friends, why she didn't want to be a mother. Being childless was a failure; she heard this message constantly, from her friends, from the minister, from the government bulletins online (the tone of these had grown increasingly panicked in the past ten years, as the ratio of poor to rich had quadrupled). There were even tax incentives now, deductions for people above a certain income level who had multiple children. To the outward eye, Lily had failed at her most important task, but she could only dissemble the shame that her friends would have felt. Inside, she thanked God for the pills. She wasn't ready to have children, and certainly not with Greg, not when he got worse all the time. The night last week . . . Lily had tried not to think of it since, but now the bubble in her mind popped, and all at once, for the first time, Lily found herself seriously considering a new life.

Considering escape.

Even Lily knew that the world was full of dark places to hide. She thought again of Cath Alcott, who had bundled her children into a car and simply vanished. Had Cath had a plan? Had she joined the separatists? Or had she reestablished herself somewhere as an ordinary citizen, with a new name and a new face? There were forgers and surgeons out there who would do such work.

But I have no money.

This was the real stumbling block. Money bought options, the ability to disappear. Lily could ask her mother for help, but Mom didn't really have any money either; when Dad died, his company claimed he had breached his employment contract, and so there was no pension. Mom barely had enough to pay the property taxes on the house. But even if Mom had been rich, she didn't want to hear about Lily's problems with Greg. As far as Mom was concerned, Lily had made her own bed. She had plenty of friends in New Canaan, but no real friends. There was no one she could trust, no one who would help her with something like this, and she suddenly found herself hating Dr. Anna, hating her utterly for trying to upset the status quo. Lily didn't need to peek over the horizon at another, better world that was far beyond her reach. This, right here, was the best possible outcome: to get her pills every year and not have to bring a child into this house.

"Lil!"

She started guiltily. Greg was home. The front door panel on the wall was blinking brightly, but she hadn't noticed.

"Lil! Where are you?"

She shoved the tile back into position and stood up, hastily smoothing her skirt down over her hips. On her way out, she tapped the panel on the wall and was rewarded with the quiet, somehow comforting whirring of the house beginning to make dinner as she went down the stairs.

Greg had gone straight to the bar. This was another thing Lily had noticed lately: Greg used to drink only when something good had happened at work, but now it seemed to be every night, and his intake was increasing. They didn't all turn into bad nights for Lily, but she couldn't help noticing the correlation, the way Greg immediately went for the booze every night now, the way he drank as though he were trying to escape from something.

"How was your appointment?"

"Good. Dr. Davis said it's looking better."

"What's looking better?" He came toward her, tumbler in one hand, and wrapped an arm around her waist.

"He thinks my body will respond well to something called Demiprene. It stimulates my ovaries."

"To release eggs?"

"Yes." The lies flowed glibly, well rehearsed, from Lily's mouth. She had done her research two years ago, knowing that the time would come when Greg would demand real information about what the hell was wrong with her reproductive system. But his questions grew more pointed all the time, and Lily had begun to have the uneasy feeling that he was doing his own research now.

"I got good news today," Greg remarked, and she relaxed a bit; there would be no real interrogation tonight.

"Really?"

"Ted said—well, hinted—that there's a Senior Liaison spot opening up next year. Sam Ellis is retiring. Ted says I'm in line for it."

"That's good."

Greg nodded, but his hands were already pouring another glass of scotch. Lily saw that something was troubling him, badly. "What's wrong?"

"Ted said I was in line for the job, but he made a crack when I was leaving. I think he meant it as a joke, but—"

"What was it?" Lily asked, but that was merely routine, the routine of comforting her husband at the end of the day. She already knew.

Greg's cheeks had stained a dull brick red. "He said that if it wasn't for my little problem, I would have been an SL last year."

"He was joking."

"The first couple of times, maybe. Now I don't think so."

Lily took his hand, trying to project more sympathy than she felt. Greg was under enormous pressure, certainly, but it was a pressure with which Lily couldn't identify. She had never been ambitious. She didn't care whether Greg made senior anything, so long as they had a roof over their heads and a decent life. Other wives at the club took great pride in their husbands' advancements, as though they were all still in high school, where dating the starting quarterback meant you were somehow superior to every other girl in your class. But not Lily. Greg had a good job, and his superiors liked him. He was in no danger of being fired. Who gave a fuck if he became the youngest Senior Liaison in the history of the Pentagon?

Greg does, she reminded herself. But that fact no longer carried the weight it once had. It would have been much easier to cheer for Greg if he had shown some reciprocal concern for her. Early in their marriage things had been better; Greg had treated her like a separate person once. But the tone had shifted, and now all of Lily's actions were evaluated in terms of the main chance, as though she were merely a booster engine on Greg's rocket. These little stories from the office were always the same, and while Greg was certainly looking for reassurance, he was also looking to goad. The message was clear: Lily's shriveled uterus was impeding his career path. The possibility that Greg's testicles might be an issue had never even come up. Lily felt anger climbing up the back of her throat, but then Greg leaned forward, elbows on the bar, burying his head in his hands. He wasn't crying, not Greg; his hateful father had smacked that out of him long before Lily had ever come on the scene. But this was as close as he ever got.

"Greg." She bit her lip, trying to gather courage. She had broached this topic twice in the first year of their marriage and Greg had shut her down each time, but now it seemed like a moment when he might actually be able to listen. Lily reached out and took his hand. "Greg, you know, maybe it's okay."

He raised his head, looking at her as though he'd never seen her before. "What?"

"Lots of people don't have children. Maybe it's not the end of the world."

"What are you talking about? You've always wanted kids."

No I haven't! She bit back the words, but they continued as a kind of scream deep in her mind. *You assumed I did! We never discussed it! You never even asked!*

Lily swallowed, trying to get her anger under control. This was her husband, and once they had been able to talk honestly, sometimes even for hours on end. She reached out and touched Greg's hair, took a deep breath, and continued. "Greg, if we never had kids, I would be okay with it."

He wrapped his arms around her with an incredulous chuckle. "You're just saying that."

"No, I'm not." She pulled back and looked him in the eye. "Greg, we'd be fine."

He reared back, his eyes filling with hurt. "You think I'm infertile, don't you?"

"No, of course not—"

He grabbed her shoulders, clenched fingers digging into the soft skin just above her collarbone. Lily could almost feel the bruises starting. "I'm not."

"I know," Lily whispered, looking away. Already she could sense herself shrinking inward, her personality diving behind any cover it could find. What point was there in pressing onward, when it only made Greg worse?

He shook her, and Lily felt her teeth rattle. "What?"

"I know you're not infertile. You're right. It's important."

He watched her narrowly for a moment longer, then smiled, good humor easing back into his face. "Absolutely, Lil. And I've had an idea about what we can do."

"What's that?"

He shook his head, smiling, the barely hidden grin of a boy who knows he's been naughty. "I have to look into it first, make sure it's viable."

Lily had no idea what he was considering, but she didn't

like that grin. It reminded her of a time in college when Greg's frat had been under investigation for assaulting a pledge. Despite Princeton's best efforts, the news had trickled all over the nearby campuses. When Lily asked Greg about it, he claimed that he'd had nothing to do with it, but the same little gleam had been in his eyes then. The younger Lily just hadn't been smart enough to read the forecast.

"Dr. Davis says the odds are still very good—"

"Dr. Davis is taking too long."

Lily stood still, almost frozen, as he wrapped his arms around her again. "Think how wonderful it would be if we had a baby, Lil. You'd be such a good mother."

Lily nodded, though her throat felt as if there was a tennis ball in there. She thought of being pregnant, having Greg's baby inside her, and a ripple of revulsion traveled just beneath her skin, making her shiver, making Greg clutch her tighter.

"Lil? Say you love me."

"I love you," Lily replied, and he kissed her neck, his hand moving to her breast. Lily had to force herself to hold still and not recoil. She didn't understand how words that sounded so automatic to her own ears could be so pleasing to Greg. Maybe all he really needed was the structure of things. Maybe quality was a different consideration, too graded for him.

I liked this man once, Lily thought. And she had, when they were both young and in college and Lily didn't know her ass from her elbow, when Greg would buy her nice things and Lily would mistake that for love. Greg said he loved her, but Greg's definition of that word had morphed into something dark and invasive. Lily's friend Sarah said love was different in every marriage, but Sarah had been sporting her own black eye that day, and she didn't believe her own platitudes any more than Lily did.

He doesn't know, her mind whispered. *He still doesn't know about the pills.*

But that was no longer a comfort. Lily had known that she couldn't get away with the pills forever, but for a long time they had seemed to provide an almost magical protection, the same talismanic quality that she found in her nursery. Even the bad nights had been easier to get through, knowing that some part of her was ultimately safe, that Greg would not have his way everywhere. But she knew that grin, knew it very well. Greg had gotten away with nearly everything in his life, usually with his father's enthusiastic approval, and now he was once again up to no good. Whatever he was planning, it seemed certain that the status quo wouldn't hold. Greg was groping around under her dress now, and Lily fought not to move, not to push him away. She thought of saying no—she had been thinking of it for months now—but that *no* would open up an entire conversation that she wasn't ready to have yet . . . what would she say, when he asked why? She closed her eyes and pictured her nursery, that quiet space where there was no intrusion, no violation, no—

Kelsea blinked and found herself in the blessedly familiar space of her library. She was standing in front of her bookshelves with Pen beside her, less than a foot away. For a moment the world wavered, but then she saw all of the books, Carlin's books, and felt reality solidify around her, the Queen's Wing settling back in with a solid thud in her mind.

"Lady? Are you all right?"

She rubbed her eyes with the heel of her hand. A hissing sound came from the fireplace in the corner, making her jump, but it was only the fire, dying out in the early hours of the morning.

"I was dreaming," Kelsea whispered. "I was someone else."

But *dreaming* was the wrong word. Kelsea could still feel the man's hands digging into her shoulders, laying the groundwork for bruises. She could remember each thought that had passed through the woman's head.

"How did we get here?" she asked Pen.

"You've been wandering the wing for the better part of three hours, Lady."

Three hours! Kelsea swayed slightly, her hand tightening on the edge of the bookshelf. "Why didn't you wake me up?"

"Your eyes were open, Lady, but you couldn't see or hear us. Andalie said not to touch you, said it's bad luck to lay hands on a sleepwalker. But I've been with you, to make sure you didn't hurt yourself."

Kelsea began to protest that she hadn't been sleepwalking, but then closed her mouth. Something nagged at her memory, something that would shed light. The woman in the Almont! Kelsea had never even learned her name, but six weeks ago she had watched, through the woman's eyes, as Thorne took her two children. That had not been a dream either; it had been too clear, too sharp. But what Kelsea had just experienced was even sharper. She knew this woman, knew the terrain inside her head as well as that inside her own. Her name was Lily Mayhew, she lived in pre-Crossing America, she was married to a wretch. Lily was no figment of Kelsea's imagination. Even now, Kelsea was able to picture a whole host of sights she had never seen, wonders lost centuries before in the Crossing: cars, skyscrapers, guns, computers, freeways. And she could now see chronology, the timing of political developments that had always eluded pre-Crossing historians like Carlin, who had no written record to work with. Carlin had known that one of the biggest factors precipitating the Crossing was socioeconomic disparity, but thanks to Lily, Kelsea now saw that the problem had been much uglier. America had descended into true plutocracy. The gap between rich and poor had indeed been steadily widening since the late twentieth century, and by the time Lily was born—2058, Kelsea's mind produced the year with no trouble at all—more than half of America was unemployed. Corporations had begun to hoard the dwindling supplies of food for sale on the black market. With most of the population either homeless or in unrecoverable debt, desperation and apathy had combined to allow the election of a man named Arthur Frewell . . . and that was a name that Kelsea *had* heard before, many times, from Carlin, who spoke of President Frewell and his Emergency Powers Act in the same tones she used for Hiroshima or the Holocaust.

"Lady, are you all right?"

"I'm fine, Pen. Let me think." Memory had suddenly assaulted Kelsea: sitting in the library, five or six years ago, while Carlin's voice echoed waspishly against the walls.

"The Emergency Powers Act! A lesson in creative naming! Honest legislation would have simply called itself martial law and been done with it. Remember this, too, Kelsea: the day you declare martial law is the day you've lost the game of government. You may as well simply take off your crown and sneak away into the night."

According to Carlin, the Emergency Powers Act had been created to deal with a growing—and very real—threat of domestic terrorism. As the economic divide widened, separatist movements proliferated across America. The better world . . . Kelsea had seen that in her vision, blue letters more than thirty feet tall. But what did it mean? She wanted so badly to know. To *see*. She looked down at her two necklaces, expecting to see the stones shining brightly, as they had when she awoke from that terrible vision in the Almont. But they were dark. The last time she remembered seeing them illuminated had been that night in the Argive Pass when she had brought the flood. For the first time, Kelsea wondered if it was possible that the jewels had somehow burned out. They had worked a great and extraordinary miracle in the Argive, but it seemed to have drained everything from them. Perhaps they were no more than ordinary jewels now. The idea brought relief, followed quickly by fear. The Mort were massing on the border, and any weapon would help, even one as inconsistent and unpredictable as her two jewels. They could not burn out.

"You should go to bed, Lady," Pen told her.

Kelsea nodded slowly, still turning the extraordinary vision over in her mind. Out of habit, she ran a hand over the row of books, taking comfort in their solidity. Sleepwalking or not, she was not surprised that this was where she'd ended up. Whenever she had a problem to consider, she invariably found herself in the library, for it was easier to think when she was surrounded by books. The clean, alphabetized rows provided something to stare at and consider while her mind wandered away. Carlin, too, had used her library as both solace and refuge, and Kelsea thought Carlin would be pleased that she found the same comfort here. Pinpricks of tears stung her eyes, but she turned away from the bookshelf and led Pen out of the library.

Andalie was waiting for Kelsea in her chamber, though the clock showed that it was well after three in the morning. Her youngest daughter, Glee, was asleep in her arms.

"Andalie, it's late. You should have gone to bed."

"I was awake anyway, Lady. My Glee has been sleep-walking again."

"Ah." Kelsea slipped off her shoes. "A cunning sleep-walker, I hear. Mace says he found her wandering in the Guard quarters last week."

"The Mace says many things, Lady."

Kelsea raised her eyebrows. The tone had been judgmental, but she could not interpret the remark. "Well, I don't need help tonight. You should go to bed."

Andalie nodded and left, carrying her small daughter with her. Once she was gone, Pen bowed and said, "Good night, Lady."

"You don't have to bow to me, Pen."

Humor sparked in Pen's eyes, but he said nothing, only bowed again before retreating into his anteroom and drawing the curtain.

Kelsea took off her dress and tossed it into the clothes hamper. She was glad that Andalie had gone so easily. Sometimes Andalie seemed to feel that it was her duty to help Kelsea get undressed. But Kelsea didn't think she would ever be comfortable being naked in front of others. Andalie had hung a full-length mirror on the wall beside Kelsea's dresser, but if she was trying to quietly cure Kelsea of her physical shyness, she had picked the wrong tack. Even this simple device created myriad challenges: Kelsea wanted to look in the mirror, but she didn't want to, and she always ended up looking, and then hated herself. Her reflection did not please her, especially since moving into the Queen's

Wing, where it seemed she was surrounded by beautiful women. But even stronger was distaste for her mother, Queen Elyssa, who had reportedly spent half of her life preening in front of the glass. So Kelsea had made a compromise: whenever she passed the mirror, she would glance at herself quickly, just long enough to determine that her hair was all right and that she hadn't wiped ink on her face during the day. Anything more than a peek would be vanity.

Now, catching sight of herself in the mirror, Kelsea froze. She had dropped weight.

This seemed impossible, for Kelsea was even less active now than when she had first come to the Keep. There was too much to do every day, and most of it involved sitting, either on her throne or at her desk in the library. She hadn't exercised in weeks, and all of her plans to eat less, which seemed so attainable in the morning, were inevitably wrecked by nightfall. But she could not deny what she was seeing now. Her thick legs had slimmed down, and her hipbones were more pronounced. Her stomach, which had always been a special source of embarrassment due to the dimpling that showed just above her abdomen, had retreated to only a slight, rounded protrusion. Kelsea tiptoed closer to the mirror, peering at her arms. They, too, seemed thinner. The thick meat had disappeared from her biceps, and now they tapered neatly down to her forearms. But when had all of this happened? Less than a week ago, certainly, for she had peeked into the mirror before her last meeting with Hall and seen none of these changes. Staring at her face, Kelsea got a nasty shock, for it seemed that something was different there, too . . . but a moment later she realized that it had been only a trick of the firelight.

What's wrong with me?

Should she ask Mace to get the doctor? She shrank from the idea. Mace didn't think anyone needed a doctor unless he was bleeding to death, and the Mort doctor favored by Coryn was wildly expensive. Was Kelsea really going to demand him now, simply because she had lost some weight? She wasn't wounded or bleeding. She felt fine. She could afford to watch and wait, and if anything else happened, then she would tell Mace or Pen. She had been under a great deal of stress lately, after all.

The fire snapped behind her, and Kelsea whirled around. For a moment she was certain that someone was standing in front of the fireplace, watching her. But there was nothing, only shadows. Despite the fire's warmth, her chamber suddenly seemed cold; after a final, uneasy look in the mirror, Kelsea put on her nightgown and climbed into bed. She blew out her candle, then dug her feet deep into the warm pile of blankets, pulling the covers all the way up to cover her cold nose. She tried to relax, but behind her closed eyes, unbidden, came the same image that had tormented her for weeks now: the Mort army, a poisonous black tide that poured down over the Border Hills into the Almont, leaving devastation behind. The Mort had not entered the Tear, not yet, but they would. Mace and Arliss had been stocking for siege and building reinforcements around the city, but unlike Bermond, Kelsea didn't deceive herself; when the Mort really came for the city and put all of their efforts into breaching the walls, no amount of last-minute fortification would keep them out. Her mind turned again to Lily Mayhew, who lived in a town surrounded by walls. There must be some lesson in Lily's life, something helpful . . . but nothing came.

Kelsea rolled onto her back, staring into the darkness.

Her mother had faced the same no-win scenario, and ended up selling out the Tearling. Kelsea hated her for it, yes, but what could she do differently? She clutched her sapphires, willing them to give her answers, but they were silent, imparting only a feeling of doomed certainty: Kelsea had judged her mother harshly, and this was the inevitable punishment, to be dealt the same hand.

I have no solutions, Kelsea thought, curling up into a ball. *And if I can think of nothing, then I'm no better than she was.*

The miners were a rough lot. They had obviously bathed before coming to the Keep, but nevertheless dirt seemed to have grimed its way into their skins, giving them a swarthy appearance. They were independent miners, and this in itself was something of a rarity; most of the miners in the Tearling belonged to guilds, for combination was the only way they could compete against the Mort. One of the miners was a woman, tall and blonde, though she was as grimy as the rest, and wore a beaten green hat that looked as though it had been through a hurricane. Kelsea, who hadn't known that mining crews accepted women, watched her with interest, but the woman returned her gaze with hostility.

"Majesty, we're just out of the Fairwitch," announced Bennett, the foreman. "We've been mining in the foothills for nearly a month."

Kelsea nodded, wishing that she hadn't worn such a thick wool dress. Summer had come, warm and somnolent, but someone had lit a fire anyway. She hated holding audience these days, for it seemed designed to take her attention away from more pressing problems: the Mort and the refugees. The first wave of border villagers would already be making their way across the Almont, but they were only a fraction of what was coming. Five hundred thousand extra people, at least . . . where would New London put them all?

"We were originally a crew of fifteen, Majesty," Bennett continued, and Kelsea tried to keep her attention on him, stifling a yawn.

"Where are the rest?"

"Gone, Lady, in the night. We kept a pretty close camp, even at first, but . . . well, you know, a man has to take a piss sometimes. Men would leave the camp in the night, and sometimes they just didn't come back."

"And why have you come to tell me this?"

Bennett began to reply, but the female miner, who had the air of a second-in-command, grabbed his arm, muttering frantically into his ear. The exchange quickly became a protracted argument, punctuated by grunts and hissing. Kelsea was content to watch. Father Tyler stood closer to the miners than the rest of them; he could probably hear what was being said. She had begun to allow the priest to attend her audiences on occasion, and he had already provided several valuable insights. He enjoyed the audiences, said it was like watching history in action. He also knew how to keep his mouth shut, so much so that he had reportedly incurred the wrath of the new Holy Father, who didn't feel that Father Tyler was providing him with enough information. Kelsea didn't understand what held Father Tyler's tongue, but attendance here seemed like a fair reward.

"Majesty." Bennett finally broke free, though his companion glared at him as he spoke. "We found something in the Fairwitch."

"Yes?"

Bennett nudged the woman, who gave him a disgusted

look but pulled a small black pouch from the pocket of her cloak. Kelsea's guard tightened automatically, doubling up in a line in front of Pen. Something winked blue as Bennett held it up in the torchlight.

"What is that?"

"Sapphire, Majesty, unless I miss my guess. We found a good-size vein."

Now Kelsea understood the argument. "I assure you, your find is your own. We may try to buy it from you at a fair price, but on my word, there will be no seizure."

The words had the desired effect; all of the miners seemed to relax at once. Even Bennett's second-in-command calmed down, her brow smoothing as she doffed her green hat.

"May we inspect your find?"

Bennett looked back to his miners, who gave grudging nods. He moved forward a few feet and held the jewel out to Kibb, who took it and brought it to Kelsea.

She held up one of her own sapphires to inspect them side by side. Bennett's jewel was rough, chipped directly from the vein, and had seen no polishing, but it was also enormous, almost the size of Kelsea's palm, and there was no mistaking the quality of the stone. She waited a moment, struck by a ridiculous hope that the new sapphires would react to her jewels, wake them up somehow. But nothing happened.

"Lazarus?"

"Looks the same stone to me. But what of it?"

"You say you found a lot of this stuff, Bennett?"

"Yes, Majesty. We had to dig deep for the vein in the foot-hills, but I would guess it's shallower up in the Fairwitch proper. We just didn't dare go up there after . . . after Tober."

"What happened to Tober?"

"Gone, Majesty."

"He deserted?"

"To where?" an old miner in the back asked scornfully. "We had all the supplies."

"Well, what do you think happened then?"

"I don't rightly know. But we heard noises out there in the night sometimes, like some big animal."

"Only some of us heard it, Lady," Bennett cut in, glaring at the old miner. "Out in the woods and away up in the higher Fairwitch. It was a big thing, but it moved too stealthy to be an ordinary animal. It took Tober, we're sure of it."

"Why?"

"We found his clothing, Lady, and his boots, a few days later, at the bottom of a ravine. They was all torn up and stained with blood."

Arliss snorted quietly, a sound of disbelief.

"Three other men disappeared also, Lady, before we learned to tighten up our camp at night and work only in groups. We never found a trace of them."

Kelsea turned the sapphire over in her hand. Arliss couldn't know it, but this wasn't the first such story she'd heard lately. Now that there was no shipment, the Census people stationed in every village were anxious to prove that they were still relevant, and information of all sorts poured in to Mace from every corner of the kingdom, including the tiny villages at the base of the Fairwitch. There had been three complaints of missing children in the foothills, as well as several men and women disappeared on the fells. No one had seen anything. Whatever the predator was, it came in the night and then simply vanished with its prey.

"Kibb, return this, please." Kelsea handed him the stone and leaned back against the throne, thinking. "Lazarus, there have always been disappearances in the Fairwitch, yes?"

"Plenty of them, Lady. It's a dangerous place, particularly for children. Scores of young ones disappeared before Tear families simply stopped settling in the mountains. The Mort more or less avoid their portion of the Fairwitch as well."

"Majesty?" Father Tyler spoke up tentatively, raising his hand in the air, and Kelsea bit back a grin.

"Yes?"

"The old Holy Father believed the Fairwitch to be cursed."

Mace rolled his eyes, but Father Tyler plowed on. "I don't believe in curses, but I will tell you: in the late first century, the Arvath sent missionaries up into the Fairwitch, looking for those who'd drifted up there after the Crossing and settled in the mountains. None of the missionaries ever returned. This isn't merely rumor; the report is part of the Arvath records."

"Hasn't anyone ever found any bodies?" Kelsea asked.

"Not to my knowledge. This is the first I've heard of any remains at all, blood or clothing."

This made Kelsea even more uneasy. If people had disappeared, where were the bones? She turned back to the miners. "Bennett, do you plan to return to the Fairwitch?"

"We haven't decided yet, Majesty. The sapphire is good quality, but the risk . . ."

Arliss tapped Kelsea's shoulder and leaned forward to murmur in her ear. "The Cadarese value sapphire highly, Majesty. This stuff would be a good investment."

Kelsea nodded, turning to the miners. "Your choice is your own. But should you go back, I'll buy your haul at . . ."

She looked to Arliss.

"Fifty pounds per kilo."

"Sixty pounds per kilo. I'll also pay extra for any information on what stalks up there."

"How much extra?"

"It depends on the quality of the information, doesn't it?"

"Give us a moment, Majesty."

Bennett led his crew to the far side of the room, where they gathered into a huddle. The old miner, on the outskirts, prepared to spit on the floor and was forestalled only when Wellmer grabbed his shoulder and gave him a forbidding shake of the head.

"Sixty pounds per kilo?" Arliss moaned in an undertone. "You'll make no money that way."

"I know you, Arliss. Your markup is ruthless."

"The right price is whatever the market will bear, Queenie. The ruler of a poor kingdom should remember that."

"Just do your job and make sure the taxes come in on time, old man."

"Old man! You've never had a better tax collector. Ten thousand pounds this month alone."

"Majesty!" Bennett stood at the foot of the dais. "It's a fair deal. We'll leave next Friday."

"Good," Kelsea replied. "Arliss, give them each five pounds' bonus in advance."

"Five pounds each, Queenie!"

"Goodwill, Arliss."

"Much appreciated, Majesty," said Bennett. The rest of the miners grunted agreement, crowding around Arliss with hungry expressions. Arliss pulled out his little book and bag of coins, grumbling the entire time, but Kelsea considered the money well spent. The Tearling didn't have enough metal in the ground to support more than a handful of mining crews. If miners disappeared from the Tear, the kingdom would be forced to get the bulk of its metal from Mortmesne . . . which meant there would be no metal at all.

A loud yawn came from Kelsea's left: Pen. He was very tired; his eyes had a dark, hollow look about them, and he seemed to have lost weight.

"Pen, are you ill?"

"No, Lady."

For a moment, Kelsea was reminded of Mhurn, whose chronic exhaustion had hidden an addiction to morphia. She blinked and saw deep scarlet blood, dripping over her knife hand, then shook her head to clear it. Pen would never be so stupid. "Well, have you been sleeping enough?"

"Certainly." Pen smiled, a private type of smile that had nothing to do with the conversation, and in that moment Kelsea became sure of something she'd only suspected: Pen had a woman somewhere. Two weekends a month, Mace took Pen's place in the antechamber; Queen's Guards didn't usually get time off, but a close guard was a special matter, since he had no downtime. Mace was good company, but Kelsea could always sense Pen's absence. She'd been wondering lately what he did in his spare time, and now, somehow, she knew.

A woman, Kelsea thought, a trifle bleakly. She could ask Mace about it—surely he would know—but then she cut that impulse off at the knees. It wasn't her business, no matter how curious she was. She didn't know why she felt so unhappy, for it wasn't Pen she thought of at night. But he was always there, and she had grown to depend on him. She didn't like the idea of him spending time with anyone else.

She'd been staring at Pen so long and so alertly that he

straightened up in his chair now, looking alarmed. "What?"

"Nothing," Kelsea muttered, ashamed of herself. "Get more sleep if you can."

"Yes, Lady."

Once the miners had received their coin, they bowed and followed Bennett away. The money had enlivened them, for they chattered like children as they headed for the doors. Kelsea leaned back in her chair and found a steaming mug of tea sitting on the table beside her.

"You're a wonder, Andalie."

"Not really, Lady. I've yet to see the moment when you don't want tea."

"Sir." Kibb appeared in front of the throne, an envelope in his hand. "Colonel Hall's latest report from the border."

Mace took the envelope and offered it to Kelsea, who had just picked up her tea. "I don't have hands. Just read it to me, Lazarus."

Mace nodded stiffly, then began to open the envelope. Kelsea noticed small red spots blooming in his cheeks, and wondered if she should have said please. Mace stared at the message for a very long time.

"What is it?"

"Majesty!" Father Tyler jumped forward, so unexpectedly that several of Kelsea's Guard moved forward to intercept him, and he backed off, hands in the air. "I'm sorry, I'd forgotten. I have a message from the Holy Father."

"Can it wait?"

"No, Lady. The Holy Father wishes to have dinner with Your Majesty."

"Ah." Kelsea narrowed her eyes. "I thought he might have some complaints."

"I wouldn't know, Lady," Father Tyler replied, but his eyes

darted away from hers. "I'm only the messenger. But I wondered if the Mace and I might sort it out now, before I need to leave."

Kelsea was not anxious to meet the new Holy Father, whose priests had already begun to give entire sermons on her shortcomings: her lack of faith; her socialist taxation policies; her early failure to get married and begin breeding an heir. "What if I don't want to dine with him?"

"Lady." Mace shook his head. "The Holy Father's a bad enemy to have. And you may need the Arvath if it comes to siege."

"For what?"

"Housing, Lady. It's the second largest building in New London."

He was right, Kelsea realized, though the idea of requesting assistance from God's Church made her skin break out in gooseflesh. She put down her tea. "Fine. Give me that letter, Lazarus, and work it out with the good Father. Let's have His Holiness in here as soon as possible."

Mace gave her the paper and then turned to Father Tyler, who visibly quailed, backing away. Kelsea scanned the letter and then looked up, pleased. "We've scored a tactical victory on the Mort flats. The Mort camp is disbanded. Colonel Hall estimates their recovery time at two weeks."

"Good news, Majesty," Elston remarked.

"Not all good news," Kelsea replied, reading further. "The Mort supply route remains intact. The cannons are undamaged."

"Still, you're playing for time," Pen reminded her. "Delay is important."

Playing for time. Kelsea looked around the room and saw, or fancied she saw, the same question in every face. When the time ran out, what then? There was no anxiety here; her Guard clearly expected her to produce another miracle, as she had in the Argive. Kelsea wished she could hide from them, from the calm trust in their eyes.

Mace finished up with Father Tyler and returned to his place beside the throne. The priest raised his hand in farewell to Kelsea, and she waved back as he headed off toward the doors.

"What's next?" she asked Mace.

"A group of nobles is waiting outside to see you."

Kelsea closed her eyes. "I hate nobles, Lazarus."

"That's why I thought it best to deal with them quickly, Lady."

When the nobles entered, Kelsea was struck first by their clothing, ostentatious as ever. Now, in summer, there were no hats or gloves, but they all displayed a new fashion that Kelsea had seen before: what appeared to be gold and silver, melted down and allowed to run in rivulets across the fabric so that shirts and dresses seemed to be dripping with precious metal. To Kelsea's eye, the effect was merely sloppy, but clearly they thought otherwise. Carlin would have had much to say about this bunch; despite the fact that she had been a noble herself, she loathed conspicuous consumption. Kelsea was not surprised to see the tall, wasplike figure of Lady Andrews near the front of the group, cloaked in red silk. She looked, if possible, even more fleshless than before, but that might only have been the look in the woman's eyes, a loathing for Kelsea that seemed to dwarf everything else in her face.

"Majesty." The man in front, a tiny creature with an enormous beer belly, bowed before her.

"Lord Williams," Mace murmured.

"Greetings, Lord Williams. What can I do for you?"

"We come with a common grievance, Majesty." Lord Williams swept an arm toward the group behind him. "All of us hold property in the Almont."

"Yes?"

"The evacuation is already incredibly destructive. Soldiers and refugees march across our lands, flattening the crops. Some of the refugees even loot in our fields. The soldiers do nothing."

Kelsea bit down on her tongue, realizing that she should have foreseen this issue. These people, after all, had nothing to do but sit and count every last penny of profit.

"Do you have complaints of violence, Lord Williams? Armed thievery, harassment of your farmers?"

Lord Williams's eyes widened. "No, Lady, of course not. But we lose money on the damaged and stolen crops, as well as lost work time."

"I see." Kelsea smiled, though it hurt her face. "What would you suggest?"

"Majesty, it's not really my place—"

"Speak plainly."

"Well, I . . ."

Another noble stepped forward, a taller man with a tightly clipped mustache. After a moment's thought, Kelsea placed him: Lord Evans, who owned vast fields of corn north of the Dry Lands. "I have reports, Lady, that while your soldiers protect the refugees on their journey, they make no attempt to supervise them. You could order better enforcement."

"I will do that. Anything else?"

"My farmers can't work with an army of vagrants marching across their fields. Why not conduct the evacuation at night? That way, it won't interrupt production."

Something flared behind Kelsea's ribs. "Lord Evans, I suppose you have a residence in New London?"

"Why, yes, Majesty. My family owns two."

"So long before the Mort come, you will simply move your household and all your valuables into town."

"For certain, Majesty."

"How convenient for you. But these people are being transplanted from their homes with no such ease. Some of them have never left their villages before. Most will be on foot, and many are carrying infants and young children. Are you honestly suggesting that I force them to cross unfamiliar territory *in the dark*?"

"Of course—of course not, Your Majesty," Evans replied, his mustache twitching in alarm. "I only meant—"

"I am suggesting it," Lady Andrews announced, stepping forward. "Property rights have always been inviolate in the Tearling."

"Be careful, Lady Andrews. No one is violating your property rights."

"They cross our lands."

"So did the shipment, once a month. It must have done a good bit of damage to your roadways. But you did not complain then."

"I profited!"

"Precisely. So let's talk about what's really at stake here. Not right to property, but right to profit."

"Profit is where we find it, Majesty."

"Is that a threat?"

"No one is threatening Your Majesty!" Lord Williams cried. He looked around to the group behind him, and several of them nodded frantically. "Lady Andrews does not speak for all of us, Majesty. We simply wish to minimize the damage to our lands."

Lady Andrews rounded on him. "If you had any balls at all, Williams, I would not have needed to attend this farce!"

"Keep it civil!" Mace barked. But the admonishment sounded automatic, and Kelsea suspected that Mace was enjoying himself.

"At some point, Majesty," Lady Andrews continued, "the Mort will have to cross my lands. I can make it difficult for them, or I can stand aside."

Kelsea stared at her. "Did you just tell me you mean to commit treason? Here, in front of thirty witnesses?"

"I have no such intention, Majesty. Not unless I am forced to it."

"Forced to it," Kelsea repeated, grimacing. "I know how you conduct yourself in wartime, Lady Andrews. You'll probably greet General Genot himself with a glass of whisky and a free fuck."

"Lady!" Mace pleaded.

"Majesty, I beg you!" Lord Williams interrupted. "Please do not take Lady Andrews's words as representative of–"

"Be quiet, Williams," Kelsea replied. "I understand what Lady Andrews is about here."

Lady Andrews had begun to examine her nails, as though she found Kelsea uninteresting.

"You all have property rights, for certain. But property rights are not inviolate, not in my Tear. These people must be evacuated, and their safety is more important than your profit. Try to stand on your rights in this matter, and watch me bring out the principle of eminent domain."

Several of the nobles gasped, but Lady Andrews merely looked up at Kelsea, bewildered. Lord Williams grabbed

Lady Andrews's arm and began to hiss in her ear. She shook him off.

"I will do my best to curtail the looting," Kelsea continued. "But if any of you"—she looked around the group of nobles—"*any* of you hinder the evacuation in any way, I will not even think twice before I seize your lands for the greater good. Do you understand me?"

"We understand, Majesty!" Lord Williams bleated. "Believe me. Thank you for doing what you can."

He tugged Lady Andrews away from the throne, but she shook him off again, staring up at Kelsea with eyes like daggers. "She's bluffing, Williams. She wouldn't dare. Without the support of the nobles, she has nothing."

Kelsea smiled. "What do I care for your support?"

"If we abandon the monarchy, Kelsea Raleigh—"

"My name is Glynn."

"If we abandon you, then you have no money, no protection, no structure. Even your army is shaky. Without us, what do you have?"

"The people."

"The people!" Lady Andrews mimicked. "They'd as soon kill any highborn as look at us. Without force or arms or gold, you're as vulnerable as the rest."

"My heart flutters."

"You're taking my threat lightly. That's an error."

"No, your threat is real enough," Kelsea admitted, after a moment's thought. "But your overestimation of your own importance is staggering. I knew it the first moment I ever laid eyes on you."

She returned her attention to the rest of them. "I am sorry for the inevitable impact on your profits. You will simply have to content yourself with a bit less gold on your clothing

91

this year, and hope the strain doesn't become too much. Get out."

The nobles turned and moved off toward the doors. Some of their faces betrayed anger, but most of them only looked a bit bewildered, as though the ground had shifted beneath their feet. Kelsea gave a great sigh of impatience, and that seemed to hurry them onward.

"Wondrous diplomacy, Lady," Mace muttered. "You realize you only make my job more difficult."

"I am truly sorry for that, Lazarus."

"You need the support of your nobles."

"I disagree."

"They keep the public in line, Lady. The people blame the nobles and their overseers for their problems. Remove that buffer, and they might start looking higher up the chain."

"And if their eyes come to rest on me, I will deserve that."

Mace shook his head. "You're too absolutist for power politics, Lady. Who cares if your nobles are hypocrites? They serve a function for you, and a useful one."

"Parasites," Kelsea remarked, but the retreating group had reminded her, again, of Lily Mayhew. Lily had lived in a town with walls, high walls built to keep out the poor. And yet both she and her husband still had to be afraid of the world outside. Was Kelsea any better? Mace and Arliss had ordered the construction of an enormous temporary camp just outside of New London's walls to house the refugees, but if the Mort came, these refugees would have to be moved inside the city, probably into the Keep itself, since New London was already stuffed to bursting. Would Kelsea mind having them there? She thought for a moment and realized, with some relief, that she would not.

"Now I'll have to keep an eye on all of these fops," Mace

continued, looking troubled. "I doubt any of them would open direct negotiations with Mortmesne, but they could do so through an intermediary."

"What intermediary?"

"Most nobles are churchgoing folk, Lady. The Andrews woman is a regular guest in the Arvath, and the new Holy Father is no admirer of yours."

"Are you spying on the Church?"

"I keep myself informed, Lady. The new Holy Father has already sent several messages to Demesne."

"For what purpose?"

"I don't know yet."

"That Andrews bitch is no more devout than I am, Lazarus."

"And when has that ever stopped anyone from being a pillar of the Church?"

Kelsea had no answer.

"Aisa?"

Marguerite was teaching them fractions, and Aisa was bored. School was harder to get through on the days when she hadn't had enough sleep the night before. The air of the schoolroom always seemed too warm, and it put Aisa into a semi-doze, awake and asleep at the same time.

"Two-fifths," Aisa answered, feeling smug. Marguerite had been trying to catch her napping. Marguerite, who liked all children, didn't like Aisa at all. Aisa seemed to create instinctive distrust in adults, as though they could sense that she was watching them, looking for errors and inconsistencies. But it was frustratingly hard to find mistakes in Marguerite. She was too pretty, and Aisa gathered from overheard conversations that she had been the Regent's concubine, but even Aisa had to admit that neither of these things was Marguerite's fault.

Something prodded Aisa sharply in the ribs: Matthew, sitting behind her, nudging with his foot where Marguerite couldn't see. After a few more pokes, Aisa turned around, baring her teeth.

Matthew smiled wide, a malicious smile that spoke volumes: he had achieved his objective, broken Aisa out of her head. Her brother was the worst sort of bully: one who couldn't stand the sight of other people sitting quietly and contentedly, one who simply had to ruin things. Maman made allowances for Matthew, said that Da had been hard on him and he wasn't equipped to handle it well. Aisa thought that was nonsense. She had taken the worst from Da, even Wen admitted that, but it hadn't turned her into a little prick who couldn't leave other people alone.

Matthew's foot nudged her again, digging right into the space between her ribs. Something struck inside Aisa, a thick, deep, gonglike reverberation, and before she could think, she whipped around and flung herself on Matthew, punching and kicking. He shook her off and ran, and without thinking Aisa got up and ran after him, out the door and into the hallway. Matthew was a year older and much bigger, but Aisa was quicker, and just as Matthew reached the end of the hallway, she launched herself at him and brought him down. They fell to the stone floor together, Matthew screaming and Aisa snarling. She got a fist up into Matthew's throat, making him cough and gag, then bloodied his nose with a good, hard slap from the heel of her hand. She loved the sight of the blood against Matthew's white, frightened face, but then a man's hands were locked beneath her arms, hauling her backward. Aisa kicked her heels, but she could get no leverage on the smooth stone of the floor. None of this seemed real; even when Aisa looked up and saw Maman, the Queen, the rest of the Guard, the wide eyes of the crowd assembled in the audience chamber, it seemed only another phase of the insomnia, the hours before sleep that caught Aisa like a long, continuous fever dream. Any moment now she would sit up in the dark, mouth dry and heart pounding, and be pleased that nothing truly terrible had happened before she jerked awake.

"Majesty, I apologize!"

Maman, apologizing for her. She had embarrassed Maman. The Queen merely shook her head, but Aisa could sense irritation in the gesture, and this was almost as bad. Marguerite had arrived in the audience chamber now, and she bent over Matthew, shooting Aisa a venomous look as she did so. Whoever had laid hold of Aisa was now dragging her backward, toward the hallway, and Aisa's mind conjured up a rogue memory of Da, who always pulled and tugged.

"Let go!"

"Shut up, brat."

The Mace, Aisa realized, and that brought home the seriousness of what she had just done. She planted her heels on the ground, but that was no help; the Mace simply took one of Aisa's arms and swung her around, clamping her wrist in an iron grip and dragging her down the hallway. Where was Maman? Aisa wondered frantically. Memory was growing stronger and stronger, overtaking fact; the Mace even smelled like Da at the end of the day, sweat and iron, and Aisa couldn't go with him. She dug her heels in again, and when the Mace turned, she brought her foot up and around, launching a kick into his stomach. It caught him squarely, and even in her fright, Aisa felt a brief moment of satisfaction; it was no small thing to sneak a move on the Captain of Guard. The Mace coughed and bent double, but his other arm snapped forward and flung Aisa against the wall. She hit, hard on her shoulder, bounced off, and staggered to the ground, black spots in front of her eyes.

It took her a few seconds to recover, but Aisa came up ready, prepared to kick and scratch. But the Mace was leaning against the opposite wall, one hand on his stomach, watching her with that same speculative gaze.

"You have a great deal of anger in you, girl."

"So?"

"Anger is a liability for a fighter. I've seen it many times. If he doesn't let the anger go, or at least harness and drive it, it brings him down."

"What do I care?"

"See here." The Mace detached himself from the wall, his bulky frame towering over hers, and Aisa tensed, preparing. But he merely pointed to her foot. "A kick in the guts is good. But you didn't plan it well, and so I wasn't disabled. In a real fight, you'd be dead now. What you want to do is point your toe, catch me with the tip rather than the arch or ankle, knock the wind out of me. It's very few men who can keep fighting without breath. Point your toe hard enough, and you could even damage one of my organs. As it is, all I'll have is a good-size bruise."

Aisa considered this for a moment, sneaking a glance at her own feet. She never planned anything; it just happened, actions exploding out of her. "Still, I hurt you."

"And what of that? Any man in this wing can keep fighting through much worse. I watched the Queen finish her crowning with a knife stuck in her back. Pain only disables the weak."

Pain only disables the weak. The words struck a chord inside Aisa, making her think of all those years under Da's roof. Wen and Matthew each had broken bones, and Wen's shoulder had never healed properly, giving him a strange, slightly hunched appearance when he tried to stand up straight. Maman had taken so many beatings that some of her bruises never went away. And Aisa and Morryn . . .

Pain only disables the weak.

"Come along, hellcat." The Mace resumed his course down the corridor, rubbing his stomach. "I want to show you something."

Aisa followed him cautiously, a few feet behind. She had never been so far down the hall; it was mostly the guards and their families down here. Near the end, the Mace opened one of the doors and swung it wide.

"Have a look."

Warily, keeping an eye on him, Aisa peeked around the doorway and blinked in surprise. She had never seen so much metal in one place before. The entire room gleamed in the torchlight.

"The arms room," she breathed, her eyes wide.

"Welcome to my domain." A tall, lanky man with a hooked nose emerged from behind a table on the other side of the room. Aisa recognized him: Venner, the arms master. Even on the rare occasions when he emerged into the audience chamber, he always had a weapon in his hands, sword or knife or bow, fine-tuning them as though they were musical instruments. "Come inside, child."

Aisa only hesitated for a moment. Children were never allowed in the arms room. Wen would be so jealous. Even Matthew would be jealous, though he would try to hide it with scorn. Swords and knives covered the tables; armory sets hung on the walls; there were even some long, twisted metal weapons, taller than a man, which rested against the wall, pointing toward the sky. Several maces, a rack of bows, their wood a deep, polished bronze, and bundles of tied sticks that Aisa eventually recognized as arrows, hundreds and hundreds of them, piled in the corner. So much weaponry! And then Aisa realized what this stockpile was for: siege. Maman had explained siege, but only to Aisa and Wen. Maman thought the Mort army would reach New London by autumn.

The Mace had followed her into the room, and now he paused beside a table that held row after row of knives. "You can't keep starting brawls with the other children. It's a distraction we don't need."

"It only distracts Marguerite."

"Today it distracted everyone. Your little squabbles are both noisy and dangerous."

Aisa flushed. She added up the number of fights she'd been in since they'd come to the Keep, and her cheeks burned brighter. Did they all think she was a brat? The Mace's gaze was hard, almost contemptuous; he was waiting for her to make an excuse. She would surprise him, just as she had caught him off guard with a kick to the stomach.

"Sometimes the anger runs me, and I can't control it. I hit and kick before I know what I'm doing."

The Mace settled back on his heels, his mouth crimping in a small smile. "That's a strong admission. Many men refuse to face the fact of their anger."

"Maybe it helps that I'm not a man."

"In this room it won't matter," Venner interrupted, striding forward. "It's a lesson I learned from the Queen. Here you're a fighter, and I will treat you like one."

98

Aisa looked up, instantly suspicious, and found Venner holding out a knife on one palm, offering her the hilt.

"What do you say, hellcat?" the Mace asked. "Want to learn?"

Aisa looked at the room around her, the weapons piled everywhere, the walls hung with metal. She used to spend days of her childhood fearing that Da's shadow would appear on the ground beside her, and when she looked up to find him standing there, her stomach would fall to pieces. Staring at Venner and the Mace, Aisa saw that their faces were hard, yes, and grim . . . but she saw none of Da's meanness there, none of his taking.

She reached out and grasped the knife.

CHAPTER 3

DUCARTE

In an era rife with butchery, we must still make special mention of Benin Ducarte.

—*The Tearling as a Military Nation*, CALLOW THE MARTYR

"Where is he?"

The Queen heard the peevish edge in her own voice. That was bad, but she couldn't help it.

"He'll be here, Majesty," Lieutenant Vallee replied in a quiet voice. The lieutenant was new to her Security Council, a replacement after the death of Jean Dowell, and he always seemed to be on the edge of things, afraid to speak up. The Queen, who usually valued restraint, found the new lieutenant's tiptoeing manner irritating, and signaled him to be silent. "I wasn't speaking to you. Martin?"

Lieutenant Martin nodded in agreement. "He'll be here shortly, Majesty. The message said that urgent business delayed him."

The Queen frowned. Ten men were seated in a semicircle in front of her throne. All of them looked exhausted, and

100

none more so than Martin. For the past month, he'd been in the north, putting down unrest in Cite Marche. Hundreds of people had planted themselves in front of the Auctioneer's Office and refused to move until the Crown addressed the economic conditions in the city. It was irritating, but nothing to really contend with. They had no leader, these radicals, and rebellion without a leader was like a tidal wave; it went like hell until it met a cliff wall. The rebellion in Callae had failed in a similar fashion when its momentum simply petered out. But the fighting in Cite Marche had been hard, with several soldiers killed. There was no doubt that many of these men could use some rest. After this meeting, she would give some of them a few days off.

But the meeting couldn't begin without Ducarte. Her Chief of Internal Security was no doubt more exhausted than any of them. His men had spent weeks trying to figure out who was organizing the protests in Cite Marche, with no answers yet. But Ducarte would get results eventually; he always did. Physically, he was beginning to show his age, but there wasn't a more skilled interrogator in Mortmesne. The Queen tapped her nails on the arm of her throne, her fingers going automatically to her breastbone. They seemed to go there all the time, of their own accord. It had, in fact, become a tic, and the Queen of Mortmesne had no tics. Such things were for the weak and mindless.

The invasion of the Tearling had begun in disaster. Word had reached the Palais a week earlier: her army had been taken by surprise and scattered throughout the Mort Flats. It would take weeks to reassemble the soldiers and clear the camp. The entire thing was a catastrophe, but there was no one on whom the Queen could unleash her fury; General Genot had simply disappeared. More than a thousand Mort soldiers had died on the Flats, but Genot's body hadn't been among the corpses.

He'd better pray he's dead. If I find him—

Movement to her right drew her attention. A slave was kneeling in front of the fireplace, lining the base with paper.

"What do you think you're doing?"

The slave looked up, her eyes wide, terrified yet resentful. Tear, there could be no doubt of it; although she was dark-haired and quite beautiful, she had the sullen, stupid expression of a Tear peasant. The Queen switched languages. "No fireplace is to be used within this building."

The girl swallowed and replied in Tear, "I'm sorry, Majesty. I didn't know."

Was that possible? The Queen had given a blanket order about fires. She would have to speak to Beryll about it. "What's your name, slave?"

"Emily." She even pronounced it in the Tear fashion, without accent.

"Be the last to know again, Emily, and you'll find yourself for sale on the streets."

The slave nodded, gathered up the paper from the fireplace, and stuffed it back in the bucket, then stood waiting with a bewildered expression that only irritated the Queen further.

"Get out."

The girl left. The Queen sensed her Security Council's eyes on her, questioning. The throne room was cold this morning; no doubt many of them wondered why there was no fire. But the only fires the Queen allowed now were torches and the ovens in the Palais kitchens, some twenty floors below. Not even to Beryll could she admit the truth: she was frightened. In the past two months, disturbing rumors had begun to trickle in from the Fairwitch: miners taken, children disappearing, even an entire family that had simply vanished from a home at the base of the foothills. The dark thing was always hungry; the Queen knew that better than anyone, but something had changed. It had always been satisfied with explorers and fortune hunters, those foolish enough to venture into the Fairwitch proper. Now it was expanding its hunting grounds.

But how?

That was the real question. The Queen didn't know the whole of the dark thing's strange history, but there was no doubt that it was bound to the Fairwitch, enspelled there in some way. It could only travel by fire, and even that effort could exhaust its abilities. So how had it managed to take an entire family in Arc Nord without leaving a trace?

Has it gotten free?

The Queen quailed at the thought. The dark thing had forbidden her to invade the Tearling, and by now it would know that she had disobeyed. But what choice did she have? Left unpunished, the delinquent Tear shipment was an incitement to every revolutionary in the New World. The riots in Cite Marche were only the latest example. The last Cadarese shipment had contained goods of markedly diminished quality: poorly insulated glass, defective horses, second-rate gems whose surfaces revealed multiple flaws. In Callae, silk production had dropped to such a low level that it could only mean deliberate sabotage. These signs were easy to interpret: fear, that powerful engine that drove the Mort economy, was waning. The Queen had to invade the Tearling, if for no other reason than demonstration. An object lesson, as Thorne would say. But she had disobeyed the dark thing, and by now it had surely found her out. Damping the fireplaces was a temporary measure, one that could not work forever.

It doesn't matter, her mind insisted. She would invade the Tearling and do what she should have done years ago: take the sapphires. The reports from the Argive Pass, though still spotty and unconfirmed, made her course very clear. The Tear sapphires still had power, all right, and once the Queen had them, she would tear through the New World like a hurricane. She would light all the fires she wanted, and even the dark thing would cower from her sight.

But still she was worried. Thorne had vanished. It was a special gift of his, disappearing without a trace, but her guard captain, Ghislaine, had evaluated Thorne correctly long ago: "Dangerous, Majesty, always, even if he stands before you wearing nothing." She wished she knew where he was.

None of her military men were brave enough to ask about the fireplace. Vallee's mouth still held a hint of sullen displeasure at being silenced earlier, his pout that of a small boy denied a sweet.

Children, the Queen thought grimly. *My soldiers are all children.*

A throat cleared behind her, such a perfect mixture of signal and respect that it could only be Beryll. "Majesty, Ducarte has arrived. He will be here shortly."

The Queen nodded, but her eyes remained on the darkened fireplace. She thought she'd heard something over there, a soft hiss like the sparking of a flame. Her patience had shortened, and she found herself unwilling to wait for Ducarte even a moment longer. "Let's begin. What of Cite Marche?"

"The rebels are contained, Majesty," Martin replied. "For now, at least."

"Let's not call them rebels," Vise interrupted. "Let's call them adolescents with too much time and money on their hands."

Martin shook his head. "I would advise caution in that assessment. We found many overfed young people, yes, and most of these ran at the first sign of real conflict. But we also found a considerable number of idle poor, apparently directed by a man named Levieux. Several of those we took into custody died hard without even revealing his name."

"What else?"

"Barely anything, Majesty. None of them had much information to give. No one had ever seen Levieux's face, only received orders through intermediaries. He seems to be operating from outside Cite Marche."

"That's all?"

"That's all they had, Majesty, I promise you. They didn't know anything. Thus, my caution: the rabble may have found a leader, someone who knows how to organize. That would be a serious development."

The Queen nodded slowly, a thread of disquiet worming through her belly. Another low hiss came from the direction of the fireplace. She whirled, but there was nothing there.

Stop falling to pieces!

The double doors to the throne room opened with a creak of wood, and there, finally, was Ducarte, still wrapped in his traveling cloak. He dragged a prisoner behind him, chained and hooded.

"My apologies for the delay, Majesty!" he called across the room. "But I bring you a gift!"

"Bring it quickly, then, Benin. We've been waiting for you."

Ducarte hauled the prisoner forward, heedless of the

man's groans as the manacles bit into his bloody wrists. Ducarte's nose and cheeks were still reddened with the morning cold, and his black hair was beginning to thin on top, but when he reached the table and turned his heavy-lidded eyes to the Queen, she found herself comforted, as always, by the dark confidence she found there. Here, at least, was a man she would never need to doubt.

"What have you brought me this time, Benin?"

Ducarte jerked off the prisoner's hood. The man straightened and blinked in the torchlight, and the Queen's spirits lifted as though infused with helium. It was General Genot.

"I found him hiding out in Arc Pearl, Majesty," Ducarte announced, tossing the end of the chain to Lieutenant Vise as he removed his cloak. "In the basement of a knockhouse, and not a wound on him, either."

The Queen gazed at Genot, considering. Two thousand dead in a surprise attack on his watch. It would be good to make an example of him . . . but not a public example. As yet, few in Mortmesne knew of the disaster out on the Flats, and she wanted to keep it that way.

Still, it never hurt to remind her War Council who was in charge here. Sometimes they tried to forget.

"We behead our deserters, Vincent. But a general who fails so spectacularly and then deserts? I believe you're a special case."

"Majesty!" Genot protested. "I carry extensive knowledge of the army, of tactical planning. I did not want my knowledge to fall into Tear hands."

"How noble of you. And which ignorant but well-meaning whore agreed to take you in?"

Genot shook his head, but when the Queen turned to Ducarte, he nodded.

"Good. Have her executed."

"Majesty, there was nothing I could have done!" Genot cried. "The attack, it came so suddenly—"

The Queen ignored the rest. She had slept with Genot once, years ago, when he was only a lieutenant, and a different woman might have taken that into consideration. But the Queen was already sifting through her memories. Genot had been talkative after sex, babbling endlessly while she tried to sleep; it was one of the reasons she had never invited him back for a repeat performance. The Queen wasn't the only one afraid of fire these days; Genot's childhood home had burned down, and he had narrowly escaped being caught inside the flaming building, taking several bad burn wounds in the process. The incident had left its mark on the adult Vincent, who still had a deep-rooted horror of fire, of being burned.

The Queen leaned forward, lacing her fingers together, and stared into Genot's eyes. He wrung his bound hands, trying to look away, but it was too late. Something had woken inside the Queen, a hungry, grasping rage that traveled her bloodstream, igniting individual nerves. She sensed Genot's body, tasted the contours of it: a soft mass of vulnerable cells in her hands.

Dimly, she sensed her Security Council shifting uncomfortably around the semicircle. Martin crossed his legs, looking down at the floor. Vallee had actually turned away to stare into the dark fireplace. Only Ducarte was really watching Genot, his expression the same as on those rare occasions when the Queen allowed him to observe in her laboratory: alert and interested, curious to see what would happen next.

Genot began to scream.

He tore his gaze from hers, but the Queen had him now, and she bore down harder, feeling his skin as a thick, malleable fabric of flesh that darkened and burned in the oven of her mind. His body blackened before her, the skin charring and crisping until the Queen knew that she could turn him inside out and shed his skin as easily as if he'd been a pig on a spit.

The military men were unable to ignore the spectacle; even those who'd tried to look away now stared at Genot, transfixed, as his howls echoed between the walls of the audience chamber. The Queen went to work on his vitals, and Genot fell to the ground, his screams quieting until he could only emit a shallow gargling. His heart was the easiest thing of all: a thick wall of muscle that the Queen tore through as though it were paper, lacing it with fire and then shredding it apart. She felt the moment when he died, the connection between them breaking sharply inside her head.

She turned back to the rest of them, looking for argument. The fire inside her was ravenous now, difficult to control; it cried out for another target. But none of them would meet her eyes. Only a charred, vaguely manlike shape remained on the floor.

A throat cleared behind her. The Queen whirled, delighted, but it was only Beryll, his face expressionless, holding out an envelope. The Queen fought down the thing inside her, but it didn't go easily. She was forced to tamp it down as one would extinguish a fire, stomping and kicking until it was only ashes. As her pulse returned to normal, she felt both relief and regret. She rarely used this particular talent, understanding that repetition would lessen its impact on others, but it was a wonderful feeling, to let go and give free rein to her anger. There were so few opportunities now.

She took the envelope from Beryll, noting that he had already opened it, and read the enclosed note, unease deepening inside her with every word. All of the satisfaction of the previous few minutes had evaporated now, and she was suddenly afraid.

"You're going back to the north, Martin. A fire has destroyed the central barracks in Cite Marche."

"What kind of fire, Majesty?"

"Unknown."

"How many dead?"

"Fifty-six so far. Likely more buried in the rubble. Someone barricaded the doors from the outside."

Her commanders stared at each other in wide-eyed silence.

"You're dismissed, all of you, except Ducarte. Go and take care of this mess, and bring me the heads of those responsible."

Martin spoke up, an audible quaver in his voice. "The army needs a new commander, Majesty."

"Dismissed."

They leapt from their seats. Each took a wide path around the charred corpse of Genot, and the Queen restrained herself from smirking. There would be no more griping complaints or secret meetings from this bunch for a while.

"Shall I remove that, Majesty?" asked Beryll, nodding toward the corpse.

"After we're done."

Beryll ushered the soldiers out, the oak double doors closing behind him. Only the Queen and Ducarte remained.

"Well, Benin, you know what I'm going to ask of you."

"I would have thought you'd want me in Cite Marche,

Majesty. A barracks doesn't burn flat without inside help. There's conspiracy here."

"What do you know of this Levieux?"

"I've heard the name a few times in interrogation. No one seems to know what he looks like or how old he is, which is a bad sign; whoever the bastard is, he's prudent as well as cunning. The terrorist tactics we've seen recently are new, well planned, and designed to inflict maximum damage. These are severe security problems, Majesty."

"Severe," she agreed reluctantly. "And I know you're the best man to solve them, Benin. But I can't put any of them"– she gestured toward the door–"in charge of the army. It's been too long since we went to war, and none of them are experienced enough. We can put that second-in-command of yours in charge of Cite Marche while you're gone; he seems capable to assist Martin. But I need you on the border."

"I'm getting a little old to go off to the front again, Majesty. And I've grown to enjoy my current job."

She sighed. "What do you want, Benin?"

"Ten percent of plunder."

"Done."

"Not done." Ducarte smiled, a vulpine smile that slid like ice along her spine. "Also first pick of the children from Cadare and Callae. There aren't enough since the Tear shipment stopped, and I've been losing out lately to Madame Arneau; she's made some sort of underhanded arrangement with the Auctioneer's Office."

The Queen nodded slowly, staring at the floor, ignoring the taste of bile in her throat. "You'll have them."

"Then we're agreed. Any special instructions?"

"Push the Tear out of the hills and into the Almont. We can't cross the border anywhere else."

"Why not simply flank them? Go farther north, toward the Fairwitch?"

"No," the Queen replied firmly. "I don't want the army within a hundred miles of the Fairwitch. Steer clear."

He shrugged. "You know best, Majesty. Give me a few days to tidy some loose ends here, and send Vallee to let the border know I'm coming. I don't want to have to settle any questions of rank when I arrive." Ducarte swung his cloak over his shoulders. "Incidentally, one thing does keep coming up about the rebel leader, this Levieux."

"Yes?"

"His accent, Majesty. Several prisoners have mentioned it. It's well hidden, but the man's enunciation says he isn't Mort. He's Tear."

"What would a Tear be doing fomenting rebellion in Cite Marche?"

"I could find that out for you, Majesty . . . but no, I'm heading to the western front."

The Queen opened her mouth to reprimand him, and then closed it as he left the room in a swirl of cold air and black cloak. Yet even this exit, abrupt and disrespectful, was comforting. Ducarte would find a way to dislodge the Tear from the Border Hills; he was a ruthless strategist. Ducarte was the commander she needed now, but her unease resurfaced almost immediately after his departure. Why had the dark thing forbidden her to invade? Did it shield the girl? An unpleasant suspicion crossed her mind: perhaps the dark thing *valued* the girl. Perhaps it valued her the same way it had once valued the Queen herself. With the dark thing's help, she had ascended to great dominion, but she had always known that this assistance was not free; in return, she was to find a way to set it free from its confinement in the

Fairwitch. But she had reached the limit of her powers, at least until she got hold of the Tear sapphires. If the dark thing had no more use for her, then she held no leverage at all. Counting off problems in her mind, the Queen realized that she was in trouble. The Mort army had been humiliated out on the Flats. The dark thing was moving beyond its own borders. The rebels in Cite Marche had found themselves a leader, a cunning Tear leader with no face. The Queen's mind gnawed away at these new developments, repeatedly biting down on each of them as one would bite down on a canker, relishing the pain but finding no solutions.

Around the corner, in the hallway that led to the stairwells, the slave girl, Emily, straightened from her crouch in the deep shadows. She had come to Demesne in the previous October's shipment, but she had never faced the auctioneer's block. Two men, both of them very polite, had chosen her from the cage, stripped her, and inspected her thoroughly— for lice or some deformity, Emily supposed—before placing her in a wagon with several other male and female slaves, all of them bound for the Palais. Emily was a tall woman, pretty but well muscled, just the way the Red Queen liked her female slaves. That was why she had been chosen. Emily missed her parents, her brothers and sisters, longed for them every day … but that longing paled in significance beside the fact that none of them would ever be hungry again. After a quick look in each direction, Emily moved lightly down the hallway, her face a pleasantly stupid mask in case she was intercepted, her mind already composing a message to the Mace.

G lynn Queen."
    Kelsea dropped her pen, startled. She was alone in the library today, a rare occurrence. Father Tyler was

supposed to be here, but he had sent his regrets: unexpected illness. Pen was with her, of course, but he didn't really cut into Kelsea's solitude, and anyway, he had nodded off on a nearby sofa while Kelsea worked. If Mace should walk in, he would give Pen hell for napping, but Kelsea was just as happy to have him get some sleep. Now, as the thin, lisping voice spoke again, Pen jerked awake.

"You ride toward death, Glynn Queen."

Kelsea turned and saw Andalie's youngest daughter standing before her. The child was tiny, a pixie really, fine-boned like Andalie, with dark hair that grew in a close cap around her head. Kelsea hesitated; she was never sure how to deal with children. The best she could seem to do was talk to them like tiny adults. But then she saw that the girl's eyes, as grey as her mother's, were distant and unfocused. Her usually ruddy face—all of Andalie's children seemed to have taken their father's complexion—was pale now, a milky luminescence in the candlelight. The girl was no taller than Kelsea's work desk, little more than a toddler, but Kelsea felt a sudden urge to back away.

"I see you, Glynn Queen," Glee lisped. "I see you riding toward death."

Kelsea turned a questioning glance to Pen. Glee was supposed to stay with Andalie or Marguerite at all times, but even Kelsea knew that there was a wraithlike quality about this particular child. Mace said she was a sleepwalker, and several times Glee had been found wandering the Queen's Wing in unexpected places, even rooms that were supposed to be locked. But Mace had said nothing about what Kelsea was seeing now. The girl wasn't sleepwalking, for her eyes were open and staring. She didn't seem to know where she was.

Kelsea got up from her desk. "Glee? Can you hear me?"

"Don't touch her, Lady," Pen warned.

"Why not?"

"She's in a trance, just like you were a week ago. Andalie told us not to touch or disturb you. I don't think we should touch the girl."

"The queen of spades," Glee murmured hollowly, staring straight through Kelsea to the wall beyond. "Crossing. The dead hand grasping and empty."

The dead hand. Kelsea paused at that, for "dead hand" translated roughly into Mortmesne. Several members of the Guard, notably Coryn, had taken to asking Andalie when they needed advice on something uncertain, health or weather or women. Whether Andalie would answer was another matter entirely; she dismissed questions that she considered beneath her, and she adamantly rebuffed all of Arliss's clever attempts to elicit information on coming betting events. Andalie had the sight, all right, but here was something Kelsea had never considered: that her children might have it too. Glee moved forward until she was only a foot away, and Kelsea reached out to block her before they collided.

"Don't touch her, Majesty." Andalie had entered the library just as soundlessly as her daughter. "Leave her alone, please. I will handle it."

Kelsea scrambled backward. Andalie knelt in front of her daughter, speaking softly, and Kelsea, who had always assumed that Andalie loved all of her children fiercely and equally, suddenly saw that she had been wrong. Andalie did have a favorite child; it was clear in her face, her hands, the quiet tone of her voice.

"You're in a dark place, my poppet," Andalie murmured

gently. "And you must come out. You can follow me."

"I can follow you, Maman," Glee repeated in her child's lisp.

"Follow my voice, poppet. See the light, and then you can wake."

Glee stood, staring blankly, for a few more moments. Then she blinked, staring up at her mother with wide eyes.

"Maman?"

"And here you are, poppet. Welcome back."

Glee climbed into Andalie's arms. Andalie sat down on one of the sofas and began to rock the girl, who appeared to already be falling asleep.

"Pen. Leave us alone, and make sure we're not disturbed."

Pen left, shutting the door behind him.

"I apologize, Majesty," Andalie murmured quietly. "My Glee is not like my others. I can have both eyes on her, and a moment later she's gone."

Kelsea paused for a moment. "Does she have your sight, Andalie?"

"Yes. She is too young to control it. I have been trying to train her, but it is difficult to find time alone, so that my other children will not be jealous. Glee still doesn't know how to differentiate between what should be said and what should be kept to herself."

"I'm sure she'll learn."

"She will, but the sooner the better. A child like Glee makes a valuable prize."

"She's safe from me, Andalie."

"I am not thinking of you, Majesty." Andalie continued to rock her daughter, her gaze thoughtful. "Even before my Glee was to go in the shipment, her father had already begun planning a way to use her. His spoken thoughts went no further than dragging her to the dogfights for his own benefit, but I saw the possibility of sale in his mind. He may have told others about Glee."

"I see." As always, Kelsea had to fight a morbid curiosity about Andalie's marriage. "Was it equally hard for you, as a child?"

"Even worse, Lady, for I had no one to guide me through it. My mother sent me away for fostering when I was newly born."

Like me, Kelsea thought, surprised. Andalie and her children were so tightly knit that Kelsea had never imagined Andalie raised in anything but a close family.

"For a long time, my foster parents thought I was merely mad. They treat these things with great suspicion in Mortmesne."

"Despite the Red Queen?"

"Perhaps because of her, Lady. The Mort are a science-minded people. They hate what the Red Queen can do, yes, but she is too powerful for them to hate the woman herself. Ordinary Mort quickly learn to hide such gifts."

"Lazarus tells me—though it's only a rumor in the Palais—that the Red Queen's laboratories have been working on the sight. They wish to find out if it's genetic."

Andalie smiled, her expression brittle. "Trust me, Lady, it is. My mother was one of the most powerful seers of our age. My gifts are only a shadow of hers. And I am terribly afraid, Majesty, that Glee is more my mother than me. It will make the world very dangerous for her."

"In what way?"

Andalie considered her thoughtfully for a moment. "We have trust, Lady, you and I?"

"I trust you with my life, Andalie."

"Then I will tell you a story. I cannot speak to the truth of the entire story, you understand, for some of it is Mort legend, but instructive nonetheless. There is a woman, a plain wife, who lives on the edge of the Foret Evanoui. Her life is uneventful. She has grown bored with her husband, a miner. She does not like keeping house. She has nothing to occupy her mind, until one day a fortune-teller comes to the village. He is handsome, this fortune-teller, and he does parlor tricks: reads palms, offers charms, even carries an ancient crystal ball. But his tricks are very good, and he is no stranger to bored wives in small towns. The woman is enchanted, and enchantment makes her foolish. Nine months later, the fortune-teller is long gone, but a child is born, a child as different from the woman's other children as can be. This child can predict the weather, knows when visitors approach the village. Useful information for a community, certainly, but the child's gifts reach even further. She can see not only the future but the past and present, the truth of things. She knows when people are lying. She is a boon to her tiny mining village, and the village prospers, far out of proportion to others in the surrounding countryside.

"And yet the villagers are extremely foolish. They talk freely about the child. They praise her to the skies. They brag about her in Cite Marche, not thinking of the fact that their country has a new queen now, a queen who believes that she has a right to anything she can grab. And one day, inevitably, soldiers come to the village and take the girl away. She is a commodity, you see, just as valuable as a good assassin or spymaster. More valuable, even, for her gifts only sharpen as she reaches adolescence. She lives a gilded life in Demesne, but still she is a prisoner, destined to sit at the right hand of the Queen until she dies."

The Red Queen's old seer, Kelsea realized. *Dead now.* Carlin had spoken of her several times. What was her name?

"And yet, for all that, the woman is not entirely subservient. She has a secret life, you comprehend, and she is so clever, so gifted, that she is able to hide that life, even from the Queen of Mortmesne, who has the most feared surveillance apparatus since the old Etats-Unis. The seer has a man, she conceives a child. Yet she knows the child will never be safe. Her mistress, the Queen, is interested in heredity. Even if the child shows no gifts at all, it will spend its life in a laboratory, subject to horrors. So the seer smuggles her newborn girl from the Palais. She gives the baby to good people, so she thinks, kind people. They live in the Jardins, one of the poorest sections of Demesne. They have always wanted a child. The baby will be safe there.

"And yet here the mother's sight has failed her. The child does have her mother's gifts, sporadic and inconsistent, yes, but there. She too can predict the future, see the present. Sometimes she can even see other people's thoughts as clearly as if they were her own. Such a child will always hold a dangerous value. When her adoptive parents fall into debt and need quick money to keep from losing all they own, they sell her to a man in the neighborhood, a man who has always coveted the child. Not for the usual reasons, you understand. He is a businessman, and he wants her sight for the market. She is a tool to him, and when she cannot perform, she is beaten."

Kelsea swallowed. "How did you get out?"

"I made my own great mistake, Lady. There was a boy, a Tear slave whose masters lived next door to mine. He was a stupid boy, but persistent. He began coming around when I was ten years old, and he would not take no for an answer. He told me of the Tear, told me that we could escape and live a free life here. I had no interest in the boy, but when I was fifteen, my owner fell on hard times, and he had no leisure to market my particular gifts. He planned to sell me to a knockhouse."

"Is that—"

Andalie nodded. "In your Tear, Majesty, a whorehouse. Faced with that, I turned to the Tear boy. I thought him harmless."

Andalie looked down at her daughter, who was fast asleep now, breathing easy. "Always, my sight seems to fail when it is most crucial that it should function. Borwen raped me the first night out of Demesne, and every night after that. We were on foot, and I could not outrun him. By the time we reached the Tearling, I already knew that I was carrying. I did not speak the language, but even if I had, Borwen had misled me about the nature of opportunity in the Tearling. For all of its terrors, Mortmesne at least allows a competent woman to earn her living without being on her back; many Mort women are miners or artisans. But I saw very quickly that there were no such options in the Tearling. Borwen is strong; he quickly found work. But I could find none, Majesty."

Andalie's voice was rising, and Kelsea realized, horrified, that Andalie seemed to be trying to justify herself, to ward off some inevitable condemnation.

"No fifteen-year-old can make good decisions, Andalie. I can barely make easy decisions for my own life now."

"Perhaps, Majesty, but had I known that my children would also pay for my mistakes, I would gladly have taken the knockhouse. I knew that Borwen was a brute, but I didn't realize precisely what he was until Aisa was five years old. I tried to send both Aisa and Wen away, but we had no friends who would take them to safety. Heaven help me, I even tried our local priest, to see if he would take them for fostering in lieu of tithe. But the priest told Borwen what I had done. Finally I tried to run away, but it is difficult to disappear with children, and it seemed that I was always pregnant. Each time, Borwen found me, and if I refused to come home, he would snatch one of the children. In the end, it seemed better to keep them with me; at least I could help them, shield them somewhat."

"That seems reasonable," Kelsea ventured, not knowing whether it was true. What she was hearing now was so far beyond her own experience that she couldn't begin to imagine what she would have done. Her mind skipped back to the pre-Crossing woman, Lily Mayhew. Lily had wanted to run, but as a lone woman, there was no safety for her to run to. The Crossing was more than three centuries past, but that world suddenly seemed very close, separated by only a thin veil of time.

Great god, Kelsea thought bleakly, *are we really no better?*

"Perhaps it was reasonable, Lady," Andalie mused. "And yet my children suffered, and badly. The boys took beatings, the girls took worse. My husband is not a clever man, but his very stupidity makes him dangerous. He has never asked himself whether he has the right to do the things he has done. He is not intelligent enough to consider such questions. This, I think, is the crux of evil in this world, Majesty: those who feel entitled to whatever they want, whatever they can grab. Such people never ask themselves if they have the right. They consider no cost to anyone but themselves."

"Surely part of that is upbringing," Kelsea objected. "It can be eradicated."

"Perhaps, Lady. But I believe Borwen was born as he is." Andalie looked down at Glee, who was fast asleep now, her mouth rounded into an O. "I know what my girl has received from me. But I fear constantly what the rest may have taken from their father. I am not sure whether Aisa's temperament comes from Borwen's blood or his mistreatment. The boys have their own problems."

Kelsea bit her lip, then ventured, "Lazarus tells me that Aisa has real skill, particularly with a knife. Venner enjoys teaching her, certainly more than he ever did me."

Andalie made a face. "It's not what I would have wished for her, Majesty, the fighting. But I see now that her problems are beyond my ability to repair. I appreciate that you have given her this outlet; perhaps it will ease some of her anger."

"Don't thank me; the idea came from Lazarus."

"Ah." Andalie shut her mouth, an entire conversation there. Andalie and Mace were unlikely allies, thoroughly disapproving of nearly everything about each other. Kelsea considered saying something else, but Andalie's next remark seemed deliberately abrupt, designed to close the previous topic as though she were slamming shut a book.

"My Glee's visions may be unfocused yet, Lady, but I would advise you to take heed of them."

"In what way?"

"The Mort problem torments you, Lady. You are not sleeping. You have lost an alarming amount of weight."

So Andalie sees it too. Kelsea didn't know whether to be relieved or not.

"I have considered the problem as well. I see no solutions; the Mort army is too strong. But Glee and I see the same

121

common elements in your future. A hand holds your two jewels, but the hand is somehow empty at the same time. A beguiling man whose face conceals a monstrosity. A playing card: the queen of spades. A chasm beneath your feet."

"And what does all of that mean?"

"I can't say, Lady."

"Then I'm not sure what good it does me."

"Often no good at all, Majesty. It's a mistake made by many, to place too much faith in visions. But I would urge you to remember these elements, for they may prove useful when you least expect it. That has been my experience."

Kelsea considered these things, one by one. The queen of spades. Once a week, Kelsea played poker with five of her Guard, and she knew the spade queen well: a tall, proud woman with a weapon in each hand. But what of that? Only one of Andalie's omens really seemed to mean anything: the beguiling man. That could easily be the Fetch, but despite all that she knew of him, Kelsea did not believe him to be monstrous. Her instincts had failed her several times since she had taken the throne, but she refused to believe that they could fail so badly as that. The Fetch had his own agenda, certainly, but he made no effort to beguile. Kelsea had done that to herself.

"Be careful, Majesty," Andalie cautioned. "I know your dark-haired rogue. I speak of another. Handsome as sin, this one, but beneath the facade is a horror, and suffering comes with him. Be on your guard."

Not sure how much of this she really believed, Kelsea nodded. She looked down at the sleeping child in Andalie's arms and felt anew the massive weight of responsibility on her shoulders. So many individual lives to look out for each day, and arching above all, the great Mort nightmare on the horizon. It was a heavy responsibility, but it was Kelsea's, and even in her most self-pitying moments, she recognized that she had bargained for it. If she had known everything on that late afternoon when the guards rode up to the cottage, she would still have come, and now it was her burden to bear, all the way to the end.

What end?

Kelsea didn't know, but one of Andalie's images stayed with her, ruining her concentration for the rest of the afternoon: the queen of spades.

S ir!"

Hall looked up, startled. The razor slipped in his hand, scraping jaggedly along his jaw, and he hissed in annoyance.

"What is it, Blaser?"

"Scouts are back, sir. There's a problem."

Hall sighed and wiped the lather from his face, smiling wryly. It seemed that every time he tried to get in a shave lately, there was a problem. Throwing the towel into the corner of his tent, he grabbed his spyglass from the table beside his cot and ducked outside.

"What is it?"

"Five men rode out of the western Verinne around dawn, sir. We thought they were messengers, but we've been tracking them all the same."

"And?"

"Llew's pretty sure now, sir. It's Ducarte."

Hall's stomach sank. The news was not wholly unexpected, but it was bad all the same: Benin the Butcher. Hall would much rather have dealt with Genot, but Genot hadn't been seen in camp since the attack. He was dead, or fled, and there would be no more easy victories. Blaser looked uneasy as well, so Hall forced a smile and clapped him on the shoulder. "How far away?"

"A few hours. At most."

Hall trained his spyglass on the sprawling mess of tents below. He and his men had gotten plenty of entertainment watching the Mort clear the camp; the rattlers were crafty bastards, their sense of self-preservation not at all impacted by the sudden removal from their hillside rookeries, and having fed well, they'd gone to ground, finding the best hiding places in the camp and sleeping during the day. At night, the screams continued, a steady diet. For the first two weeks, Hall had been pleased to see the Mort camp lit up like a Christmas tree at night. They must have used up the lion's share of their ready oil.

But more food and oil always came, an unrelenting stream of supply from the southeast, and snakes or no, the cannons remained heavily guarded in the middle of the campsite. Dozens of plans for dealing with them had been heard and discarded, and Blaser and Major Caffrey often ended up shouting at each other until Hall ordered them to shut up. These were signs he could read: despite the victory they had scored, morale was beginning to fail.

Hall refocused his spyglass on the foot of the hill, where the Mort had piled their dead in an enormous pyre. This pyre had burned for the past week; even now, wisps of smoke still drifted into the air from the charred remains. The smell had been bad, and Hall had been forced to change shifts at double time. But now the camp was entirely cleared of the dead, and Mort soldiers leaned against tents, chatting, their shirts off to absorb the June sunlight. Three separate groups of soldiers were hunched over tables, downing pint after pint of ale while they played cards. Hall even saw one soldier sunbathing atop a supply wagon. Still excursionists on vacation. The Mort had tried several assaults on the foot of the hill, but found themselves repelled by Hall's archers each time. In the absence of Genot or another general, these attacks were poorly planned, disorganized in execution. Hall could see them coming a mile away, but that would not last. He turned his spyglass east and found the party easily: a clutch of dark-clad figures moving slowly and steadily across the flats. He couldn't make out their features, but there was no reason to doubt Llew, who'd been born with a built-in spyglass of his own. Hall had never fought Ducarte himself, but he'd heard plenty from Bermond, whose reminiscences about the Mort general could chill the blood.

"Ducarte will be more inventive," Hall remarked. "And much more trouble."

"If they try to flank us to the north, we can't hold them," Blaser cautioned. "It's too much ground to cover."

"They won't flank."

"How do you know, sir?"

"The Mace has a source in the Palais. The Mort have orders to avoid the Fairwitch, even the foothills. It's this stretch or nothing." Hall set down his spyglass. His palms were sweating, but he hoped that Blaser hadn't noticed. "Put fresh men in the trees and tell them not to let their eyes wander. Any changes in the Mort sentry line come directly to me."

Blaser left, humming to himself, and Hall began to shave again, though his hand wasn't quite as steady this time; he drew the razor down his bare jaw and felt the blade slice through his skin. Hall had no people; his parents had died several years ago, victims of a winter fever that had swept through all of the villages on the hillside. But what faced the

Tear now was infinitely worse, and Ducarte's arrival only darkened the outlook further. In the last invasion, according to Bermond, Ducarte had liked to throw his Tear prisoners into pens with starving bears. There would be no mercy for the taken, not even the wounded, and part of Hall could not help wondering whether the Queen had considered these eventualities before she had violated the treaty and opened the door wide. The Queen had brought this upon them, and for a rogue moment Hall cursed her, sitting safely on her throne back in New London. There was some Bible story Hall remembered vaguely from his childhood, something of a little man who took on a giant and emerged victorious . . . yet the Mort were ten giants. Even after Hall's victory two weeks ago, the Mort army still had more than four times the men, enough to divide and crush the Tear army from multiple angles. The Queen had not thought of her soldiers, only of principle, and principle was cold comfort to men who were going to die. Hall wondered if she truly had magic, as the rumors said, or whether that was simply a fairy tale that the Mace had allowed to spread. The rumors were difficult to reconcile with the woman who sat on the throne, the child-adult with the gaze of an owl. Hall had already made his military assessment—all was lost—but intuition was not logical, and his gut would not allow him to give up.

She could *save us*, he thought stubbornly. *She could.*

— CHAPTER 4 —

MATTERS OF
CONSCIENCE

Flee, we are in the hands of a wolf.
    —*Giovanni de' Medici, upon the ascension of Rodrigo Borgia,*
                                                    POPE ALEXANDER VI

Father Tyler should have been at ease. He was reading, sitting in the comfortable chair at his desk, and reading usually calmed him, reminded him that there was a world beyond this one, a better world that seemed almost tangible. But this was the rare day when reading calmed nothing. Tyler had covered the same two pages several times before he finally put down his book and gave up. The candle on his desk was covered with dried drips of wax, and without thinking, Tyler began to peel them off. His fingers worked independently of his brain, peeling and peeling, as he stared out the window.

The Holy Father had died two weeks ago, on the last day of May. Cardinal Anders had succeeded him, in a conclave so short that a few of the more distant cardinals arrived to find him already in the Holy Father's seat. The Holy Father, recognizing a political mind as sharp as his own, had hand-picked Anders as his successor years ago, and everything had proceeded as it should.

But Tyler was afraid.

The new Holy Father had attended to many things since taking the robes. He immediately fired five cardinals, men with known reformist sympathies, men who'd spoken against Anders during his tenure. Their sees went to nobles' sons for more than a thousand pounds each. The new Holy Father had also hired sixteen new bookkeepers for the Arvath, increasing the total to forty. Some of these new bookkeepers were not even ordained men; several of them looked and sounded as though the Holy Father had plucked them right off the streets of the Gut. Tyler and his brothers had heard nothing, but the conclusion was clear: more money would be coming in.

Then there was Tyler's own position. The old Holy Father had been too preoccupied with fighting death to take Tyler to task, but Tyler knew that he would not escape the new Holy Father's housecleaning attentions for long. Already, last Sunday, Tyler had found Anders's eyes seeking him out in the crowd during the convocation. Anders wanted information on Queen Kelsea, damning information, and Tyler had given him nothing. The Queen had already made several moves that presaged trouble for the Church, beginning with a proscription on the use of underage clerical aides to satisfy tithing debts. Tyler, who had been one of these aides himself, had enjoyed his childhood, but he understood the argument; not all priests were Father Alan. Now parishes would have to hire real aides, aides whose salaries would be paid from money already earmarked for the Arvath treasury.

But worse had followed: the Queen had announced that the Church's property tax exemption would end in the coming year. Starting in January, the Church would have to pay tax on all of its holdings up and down the Tearling, including the big prize: thousands of acres of high-producing farmland in the northern Almont. For the Arvath, this was a financial cataclysm. With the help of her foulmouthed but undeniably clever Treasurer, the Queen had also preempted the Holy Father's protests by decreeing that the Crown's private landholdings would no longer be exempt either. The Queen would pay property tax alongside the Church, and the money would be earmarked for public works and social services.

Without enforcement, these decrees would mean nothing. But from overheard conversation in the Keep, Tyler also knew that the Queen and Arliss had begun to quietly convert a large portion of the Census Bureau over to the business of tax assessment and collection. It was a clever move. Census men were already entrenched in every village of the Tearling, tracking the population, and it would not be a stretch for them to track income as well. Arlen Thorne would have screamed bloody murder, but Thorne was nowhere to be found, and without him, the Census was a far more malleable animal. There would be plenty of Crown employees to make sure that God's Church forked over every last pound due.

This morning, word had gone like quicksilver through the halls of the dormitory level: they were all wanted in the chapel at nine this evening. No one knew what it was about, but the Holy Father required every priest in the Arvath to be there. Such a gathering was unlike Cardinal Anders, who always worked in the shadows, meeting one-on-one so that no one else knew his plans. Tyler sensed something terrible on the horizon. It was eight thirty.

"I know that you know, priest."

Tyler jumped to his feet, knocking over the candle. He turned, and the Mace was there, leaning against the wall beside his bookshelves.

"You know that I can't read."

Tyler stared at him, speechless and frightened. He had known that he was treading on thin ice the other day, jumping into the Queen's conversation, but he had been unable to watch the Mace wriggle there, like a hooked fish. And Tyler's move had worked, for the Queen had forgotten about the note. It was only when Tyler met the Mace's gaze afterward that he saw fire, hell, murder.

"How did you find out?" the Mace asked.

"I guessed."

"Who have you told?"

"No one."

The Mace straightened, and Tyler closed his eyes, trying to pray. The Mace would kill him, and Tyler's last, odd thought was that the man had done him a great honor by coming in person.

"I want you to teach me."

Tyler's eyes popped open. "Teach you what?"

"How to read."

Tyler glanced at the closed door of his room. "How did you get in here?"

"There's always another door."

Before Tyler could consider this idea, the Mace darted forward, catlike and silent. Tyler tensed, pressing backward against his chair, but the Mace only grabbed the other chair from beside the bookshelves, placed it facing Tyler, and sat down, his expression truculent.

"Will you teach me?"

Tyler wondered what would happen if he refused. The Mace had not come here to kill him, perhaps, but that could always change. The Mace had joined Queen Elyssa's Guard at the age of fourteen, and now he was at least forty years old. Illiteracy was a difficult thing for anyone to hide, but it must have been nearly impossible for a Queen's Guard. Still, the Mace had gotten away with it all of these years.

Tyler glanced down and saw something extraordinary: the Mace's hand, resting on the arm of the chair, was trembling, a slight flutter that was almost imperceptible. As unbelievable as the idea seemed, Tyler realized that the Mace was afraid.

Of me?

Of course not, you old fool.

Then of what?

After another moment's thought, he knew. The Mace couldn't bear to ask for help, not from anyone. Tyler stared, marveling, at the terrifying man sitting across from him—*the courage it must have taken him to come here!*—and before he knew it, the words were out.

"I'll teach you."

"Good." The Mace leaned forward, businesslike. "Let's start now."

"I can't," Tyler told him, lifting apologetic hands as the Mace's expression darkened. "All of us are supposed to attend a meeting in the chapel at nine o'clock." He checked his watch. It was a quarter to nine. "In fact, I should go now."

"A meeting about what?"

"I don't know. The Holy Father demands the presence of every priest in the Arvath."

"Have there been many of these meetings?"

"This is the only one."

The Mace's eyes narrowed.

"Come back tomorrow, just after supper. Seven o'clock. We can start then."

The Mace nodded. "Which chapel is this meeting in? The main, or the Holy Father's private?"

"The main," Tyler replied, raising his eyebrows. "You know the Arvath very well."

"Of course I do." A hint of contempt crept into the Mace's voice. "It's my business to know of danger to my mistress."

"What does that mean?"

The Mace went to Tyler's clothes rack and pulled a robe from its hook. "You are not a stupid man, priest. Pope and kings make poor bedfellows."

Tyler thought of the new appointees to the accounting office, men who looked more like criminal enforcers than priests of the Arvath. "I'm only a bookkeeper."

"Not anymore." The Mace put on his weekend robe. Priests' robes were meant to fit loosely, but the material hung tight on the Mace's huge frame. "You're the Keep Priest, Father. You can't avoid picking a side forever."

Tyler stared at him, unable to reply, as the Mace ran his hand over the wall beside Tyler's desk. His hand stilled, then pressed hard, and Tyler's mouth dropped open as a door swung inward, a door whose edges had been cleverly concealed by the uneven mortar of the wall. The Mace stepped into the darkness, then leaned back into Tyler's room, a twinkle of humor in his dark eyes.

"Seven o'clock tomorrow, Father. I will be here."

A moment later, there was nothing facing Tyler but a blank stone wall.

The bell for convocation rang, and he jumped; he was going to be late. He grabbed one of his chapel robes and threw it over his head as he hurried down the hallway. The arthritis in his hip began clamoring, but Tyler ignored it, pushing himself harder. If he entered late, word would surely get back to the Holy Father.

Hurrying through the door of the chapel, Tyler found his brother priests already assembled in long, straight rows on either side of the central aisle. Up on the dais, the Holy Father stood behind the podium, his sharp eyes seeming to burn through Tyler as he stood frozen in the doorway.

"Ty."

He looked down and saw that Wyde, sitting on the end of the last bench, had scooted over to make a space. Tyler gave him a grateful look as he squeezed in, bowing his head respectfully. But his unease persisted. The sight of Anders in the white robes was still a shock to Tyler; to him—and no doubt, many of the older priests—the Holy Father was, and always would be, the old, shrunken man who now lay entombed beneath the Arvath. Tyler didn't grieve the old Holy Father, but he couldn't deny that the man had left his mark on the place; he'd sat in the seat for too long.

Anders held up his hands for silence, and the shuffling stopped. The room was as still as stone.

"Brothers, we are not clean."

Tyler looked up sharply. Anders gazed across the room with a benevolent smile, a smile that suited a Holy Father, but his eyes were deep and dark, filled with a righteous fury that made Tyler's stomach tighten with anxiety.

"Disease begins with contagion. God has demanded that

we root out the contagion and eradicate the disease. My predecessor tolerated it, turning a blind eye. I will not."

Tyler and Wyde stared at each other, bewildered. The old Holy Father had tolerated many vices, certainly, but they seemed like the sort of vices that wouldn't bother Anders at all. Anders kept two private servants, young women who had been turned over to the Arvath by their families in lieu of the tithe. When Anders had moved into the Holy Father's lavish apartments in the pinnacle of the Arvath, the women had followed, even though the new residence came equipped with an army of acolytes ready to serve the Holy Father's every whim. Anders might call his women servants, but everyone knew what they were. The new Holy Father was no stranger to vice, but now, as he turned and gestured to someone behind the dais, light glinted off the tiny golden hammer pinned to his white robes, and Tyler froze in sudden comprehension.

Two of the Holy Father's aides emerged from the hallway behind the dais. Between them was Father Seth.

Tyler bit back a groan. Seth and Tyler had received their ordinations in the same year, but Tyler hadn't seen him in a long time. Ever since Seth had been given his own parish in Burnham, out in the southern Reddick, he rarely visited the Arvath. He was a good man and a good priest, so no one ever spoke of it, but all the same, everyone knew about Seth. Even back when they were all novices, Seth had always liked men. Due to Tyler's position as a bookkeeper, he knew that Father Seth kept a companion out in the Reddick, a man far too old to be a clerical aide, although Seth's records listed him as such. When the clerical aide had appeared, Seth's board expenditures had increased significantly, but Tyler had never called attention to this; priests and cardinals all over the Tear kept questionable companions and paid for them with the same contortionist's accounting. But Seth's aide was the wrong gender, and Anders must have found out.

"I will go through the Church and root out the backsliders!" Anders thundered. Tyler had never heard Anders preach before, and a distant part of his mind noted that the man had a wonderful speaking voice, deep and booming, reaching the farthest corners of the chapel and echoing back. "We will purge and cleanse! And we will start with this creature, a priest who has not only violated God's law, but used Church funds to subsidize his sickness! Supporting his foul lifestyle with his parish's tithe!"

Tyler bit his lip, wishing that he had the courage to speak. It was wrong, what was happening here, and Wyde, beside him, knew it too; he looked at Tyler with helpless, gleaming eyes. Wyde and Seth had been good friends too, all those years ago, when they had all been young together.

"God has been wronged! And for every wrong, God demands vengeance!"

At this, Wyde closed his eyes and bowed his head. Tyler wanted to shout, loud echoes that would bring the vaulted ceiling down over their heads. But he remained silent.

"Seth has forgotten his duty to God! We will remind him!" Anders's voice dropped suddenly; he had ducked behind the table. When he straightened, he was holding a knife.

"Dear God," Wyde muttered. Tyler merely blinked in surprise, wondering if this entire evening was a dream that had suddenly veered into nightmare . . . the Mace's strange visit, the disturbing sight of the guard captain in clerical robes, and now this horrible torchlit scene: Seth's pale face, alarm dawning in his eyes as he spotted the knife in Anders's hand.

"Strip him."

The two aides laid hold of Seth, who began to struggle. But Seth, like Tyler and Wyde, was in his seventies now, and the two younger men overpowered him easily. One pinned Seth's arms behind his back while the other ripped his robe down the front and tore off the remains. Tyler averted his eyes, but not before he'd seen the evidence of time on Seth's body: a narrow, sunken white chest; arms and legs that had lost all of their taut muscle and now hung with loose skin. Tyler saw much the same thing when he looked down at his own body, a body that had grown pale and slack. He recalled a summer, half a lifetime ago, when their ecclesiastical class had journeyed all the way to the coast, to New Dover, for a look at God's Ocean. The water was a miraculous thing, vast and sparkling and endless, and when Wyde had thrown off his robes and dashed for the cliff edge, they had all followed him without thinking, leaping off the rocks and hurtling thirty feet down. The water had been brutally cold, agonizing, but the sun had been shining, a bright golden face above the limitless blue ocean, and in that moment Tyler was certain that God was looking directly at them, that He was infinitely pleased with what they were becoming.

"Our belief has grown slack," Anders announced. His eyes glowed with a terrible fervor, and Tyler recalled a rumor he had once heard: that during his years with the Regent's antisodomy squads, Anders had nearly killed a young homosexual, beating him with a plank of lumber until the boy was unconscious and covered in blood. The Regent's other thugs had to haul Anders off, or he would undoubtedly have murdered the young man right there in the street. Panic slowly dawned as Tyler realized that this was no mere shaming exercise; Seth could be in real danger. Looking heavenward, he caught sight of a hulking, white-robed figure concealed in the shadows of the gallery: the Mace, his grim visage inscrutable beneath the cover of his hood, his eyes pinned on Anders, a hundred feet below.

Good, Tyler thought, almost angrily. *It's right that an outsider should see.*

"Hold him."

Anders moved in swiftly and his hands worked with almost surgical precision, so fast that Seth barely had time to make a sound before the deed was done. But Tyler and Wyde screamed together, their voices joining a chorus of cries that echoed back and forth between the stone walls of the chapel. Tyler looked down, unable to watch, and found Wyde's hand in his, their fingers clasped in the unconscious manner of children.

When Anders straightened, his face was splattered with bright crimson. In his hand was a dripping red mass, which he flung into the corner of the chapel. Seth had gotten his breath back now, and his first scream was a mad cacophony of sound that seemed to bounce off the highest rafters of the chapel.

"Make sure he survives," Anders ordered the aides. "His work isn't done."

The two acolytes took Seth between them and dragged him forward, down the stairs and then up the aisle between the rows of priests. Tyler didn't want to look, but he had to. Red sheeted down Seth's thighs and calves, and a crimson trail followed him up the aisle. Mercifully, Seth appeared to have lost consciousness; his eyes were closed and his head lolled against his shoulder. The acolytes staggered under his deadweight.

"Look and remember, brothers!" Anders thundered from the dais. "God's Church has no room for panderers and sodomites! Your sin will be discovered, and God's vengeance is swift!"

Tyler felt his dinner, barley soup, climbing up his throat, and swallowed convulsively. Many of the faces around him looked similarly ill, white and frightened, but Tyler spotted plenty of exceptions: smug faces, vindicated faces. Father Ryan, eyes bright with excitement, nodding vigorously at Anders's words. And Tyler, who had not experienced true fury since the early, starving days of his childhood in the Almont, suddenly felt rage contract within him. In all of this, where was God? Why did He remain silent?

"Backsliders," Anders intoned solemnly. "Repent your works."

Tyler looked up and found the Holy Father's gaze locked on him.

"Ty?" Wyde asked in an undertone, his voice plaintive. "Ty? What do we do?"

"We wait," Tyler replied firmly, his eyes pinned on the river of scarlet at his feet. "We wait for God to show us the way."

And yet even this statement sounded hollow to Tyler's ears. He looked toward the dome of the chapel, toward heaven, waiting for some sign. But none came, and a moment later he saw that the gallery was empty. The Mace had disappeared.

When Kelsea had finished with Arliss, she dismissed Andalie and returned to her own chamber alone. She was tired of people today. Everyone seemed to have constant demands, even Arliss, who knew better than anyone how strapped the Crown was for men and money. Arliss wanted to provide armed protection for a small portion of farmers to stay out in the Almont until the eleventh hour. Kelsea could see the argument; with the Almont emptied, the entire autumn crop harvest would be lost. But she had no idea where to get the manpower. Bermond would howl if she asked for even a fraction of his soldiers, and though Kelsea disliked the old general, she knew that he was indeed stretched extremely thin. Perhaps a fourth of the Tear army was deployed in and around the Argive Pass, making sure that the Mort didn't open it up as a potential supply line. The rest of Bermond's men were scattered across the eastern Almont, busily moving refugees inward toward New London. Hall's battalion was entrenched on the border. There were simply no more men to spare.

Kelsea left Pen behind in the antechamber without a word, drawing the curtains closed behind her. Andalie had made her a mug of tea, but Kelsea ignored it. Tea would only keep her awake. She brushed her hair and rearranged her desk, feeling restless and exhausted but not at all sleepy. What she really wanted to do was return to her library, to the continuing puzzle of Lily Mayhew. Who was she? Kelsea had gone through more than ten of Carlin's history books now, looking for any reference to either Lily or Greg Mayhew, but there was nothing, not even in the books published closest to the Crossing. Whoever the Mayhews were, they seemed to have faded into obscurity, but still the riddle of Lily seemed infinitely solvable compared to the problem on the eastern border. Kelsea was certain that if she could only find the right book, the answer would present itself and Lily would become clear. But no solutions were forthcoming for the problem of the Mort.

She couldn't go back to the library now. Pen needed his sleep. Kelsea had gone to bed early for the last three nights, but Pen still looked very ragged. She had begun to wonder whether he ever slept, or whether he simply sat there on his pallet, sword across his knees, as the night turned into morning. There was no reason for him to be so vigilant; Mace now had well over thirty Queen's Guards under his command, and the Keep itself was more secure than ever. But still, the image of Pen sitting there, motionless, staring into the darkness, was strangely persuasive. Kelsea didn't know how to make him sleep, when she barely slept herself.

After a moment's thought, she tiptoed toward the mirror. She had deliberately avoided looking for the past week, and although she ascribed this to Carlin's strictures about vanity, the real reason was much simpler: she was terrified.

Except for a few moments of rogue longing, Kelsea had more or less resigned herself to the fact that she would spend her life with a round, friendly farm girl's face, good-natured but unremarkable. She had often wished that she were beautiful, but it simply wasn't in the cards, and she had come to terms with her appearance as best she could.

Now she felt a deep ripple of fear as she studied her face in the mirror, remembering something Carlin had once said: "Corruption begins with a single moment of weakness." Kelsea couldn't remember what they had been talking about, but she seemed to remember Carlin looking at Barty, judgment in her gaze. Now, staring at herself in the mirror, Kelsea knew that Carlin was right. Corruption didn't happen all at once; it was a gradual, insidious process. Kelsea neither felt nor saw anything occurring, but change had crept up on her back.

Her nose was transforming, that was the first thing. It had always sat in the middle of her face like a squashed mushroom, too big for its surroundings. But now, to Kelsea's searching eyes, her nose had lengthened, become tapered, so that it emerged quite naturally and gracefully from the ridge between her eyes. The rounded, slightly piggish upturn had softened at the tip. Her eyes were still a bright cat's green, the shape of almonds. But the pockets of flesh around them had been steadily eroding, and now the eyes themselves seemed larger, dominating Kelsea's face in a way they never had before. Perhaps the most noticeable change was Kelsea's mouth, which had always been full-lipped and flat, too wide for her face. Now it too had shrunk, the top lip thinning slightly so that the bottom looked fuller, a deep healthy pink. Her cheeks had dropped weight as well, so that her face was oval rather than round. Everything seemed to fit better than it had before.

She wasn't beautiful, Kelsea thought, not by any stretch. But she was no longer plain either. She looked like a woman someone might actually remember.

At what cost?

Kelsea shrank from the question. She was no longer afraid that she might be sick, for she had plenty of energy, and the image before her was the very picture of health. But beneath the initial pleasure she felt, looking at this new woman, there was a sense of great falsity. Here was beauty blooming from nowhere, beauty that reflected no change inside.

"I'm still me," Kelsea whispered. That was the important thing, wasn't it? She was still fundamentally herself. And yet ... several times lately, she had caught Mace giving her hard looks, as though trying to analyze her face. The rest of the Guard, well, who knew what they talked about once they retreated to their quarters at night? If things continued in this vein, they might well think her a sorceress, just like the Red Queen. They were still worried about the trance she'd had, that night in the library; whenever Kelsea stumbled these days, there seemed to be several guards at her arm to hold her up. She closed her eyes and saw, again, the pretty pre-Crossing woman with the sad eyes, the deep lines around her mouth. The bruises.

Who are you, Lily?

No one knew. Lily had vanished into the past with the rest of humanity. But Kelsea couldn't be satisfied with that. Her sapphires operated outside of her control, their actions inconsistent and maddening. But they had never shown her anything she didn't need to see.

What makes you think it's the sapphires? They've been dead for weeks.

Kelsea blinked at that. True, the sapphires had done almost nothing since the Argive. But Kelsea was not like Andalie; she had no magic of her own. All of her power, everything extraordinary that she had ever done, was bedrocked on these two pieces of blue stone, both of which could fit comfortably in her pocket. Kelsea risked another look in the mirror, and almost flinched at the calmly attractive woman she saw there.

How can the jewels be dead? They're transforming your face!

"God," Kelsea whispered, shuddering. She whirled away from the mirror, almost as if preparing to flee, and stopped short.

A man stood in front of the fireplace, a tall black silhouette against the flames.

Kelsea opened her mouth to shout for Pen, then held back, drawing a long, shaky breath. The Fetch, of course; it was well known that no doors kept him out. She tiptoed a few steps closer, and then, as the firelight crossed his profile, she

142

started. The man before her was not the Fetch, but all the same, she found herself physically unable to scream, or to make any sound at all.

He was beautiful. There was no other word. He reminded her of the drawings of Eros in Carlin's books of mythology. He was tall and thin, not dissimilar to the Fetch in build, but that was where the similarity ended. This man had a sensualist's face, slightly hollowed cheekbones tapering to a full-lipped mouth. His eyes were deep-set but somehow wide, their color indeterminate; by a trick of the firelight, the eyes seemed to gleam a deep red for a moment, before fading.

Tear heir.

Kelsea shook her head to clear it. He hadn't spoken out loud, she was sure. But still, his voice echoed inside her head, a low hum with a clear Tear accent. Her pulse sped up and her breath shortened, as though both reactions had been set to a metronome. Her palms, dry as a bone moments before, had begun to sweat.

She opened her mouth to speak, and he put a finger to his lips.

We meet in the quiet, Tear heir.

Kelsea blinked. Behind the curtain drawn over the doorway, she could still hear Pen moving around, getting ready for bed. He hadn't heard a thing.

Nothing to say?

She peeked down at her sapphires, but they lay dark and quiescent against the black silk of her dress, silk that now hung loosely on Kelsea's frame. Her mind tilted dizzily, and she felt intoxicated, as though she should slap herself awake. She met the man's eyes and a thought arrowed out of her, as cleanly as breathing.

Who are you?

A friend.

Kelsea thought not. Andalie's warnings recurred to her, but she didn't need Andalie to know that this man didn't come in friendship. His gaze seemed to pin her where she stood, and she had the sense that all of his attention was focused on her, that nothing was so important to him as Kelsea Glynn at this moment. Handsome as sin, Andalie had warned, but she had failed to do him justice. Kelsea had never had any man seem utterly absorbed in her before, and it was a seductive feeling.

What do you want? she asked him.

Only to help you, Tear heir. Do you wish to know of the Mort Queen? Of the movements of her army? Where she is weak? I can tell you all of these things.

Free of charge, I suppose.

Wise child. Everything has a price.

What's the price?

He pointed to her hand, which had crept up, almost unconsciously, to clutch her two sapphires. *You hold jewels of enormous power, Tear heir. You could do me a great service.*

Enormous power? After the Argive, Kelsea supposed that was true, but what good was all the power in the world if she couldn't control it, couldn't summon it on command? Inconsistent power would not mitigate the Mort army's massive advantage in size and weaponry.

What power?

I have seen one jewel alter time and create miracles. But the other has the power of flesh, and you have a strong will, Tear heir. You will be able to flay skin and crush bones.

Kelsea considered this idea for a moment, darkly

fascinated. She closed her eyes and saw it suddenly: the Almont, stretched between horizons, and the Mort army cowering, fleeing before her ... was it possible?

The man in front of her smiled, as though he had read her mind, and gestured toward the fireplace. *Look and see.*

Kelsea found a wide mirage in front of the flames, a broad vista of salt flats and black water that could only be western Mortmesne. Lake Karczmar, it must be, where the Mort army lay massed at the base of the Border Hills. But now the hillside was in chaos, treetops aflame and men in black uniforms fighting wildly. A pall of smoke covered the trees.

Here are your soldiers, Tear heir. They will fall.

The Tear were being pressed back now, overwhelmed by superior numbers and forced back up the hillside. Hall's battalion, Kelsea realized, and they were going to die. Pain sliced through her, and she reached out toward the mirage, wanting to grasp them, to carry them away.

The man snapped his fingers and the mirage winked out, leaving only firelight. She thought of calling for Pen, but the stranger's gaze seemed to hold her frozen.

The Mort Queen has vulnerabilities. They are exploitable. And the service I ask in return is very small.

Thinking of Andalie's warning, Kelsea shook her head. *I want no part of you.*

Ah, but that's not true, Tear heir. I have watched you for some time. You long to be an adult, but those around you often treat you like a child. Is it not so?

Kelsea didn't reply. The man stepped forward, giving her every chance to back away, and placed a hand around her waist. His hand was warm, and Kelsea immediately felt the skin beneath turn hot and feverish. Pressure echoed deep in the pit of her stomach.

I will never treat you as a child, Tear heir. I have never cared whether you were pretty or plain. I have known myriad women, but I will treat you as unique.

Kelsea believed him. It was the voice, its hollow tones so smoothly confident that they seemed to weave certainty out of thin air. She met his eyes and found them understanding, full of some sort of dark knowledge of Kelsea that he had no business having. For a moment she was tempted, so strong was the pull of being an adult with a life of her own, of making terrible mistakes the way everyone else was allowed to. And this man would be a good choice, for he had been the ruination of many women, she had no doubt.

But weaker women than me, a voice spoke up quietly inside her. *I'm not one to be taken in.*

Carefully, she removed his hand from her waist. His skin was oddly dry, but even this was exciting in its own way; she couldn't help wondering what such dry hands would feel like between her legs, whether they would elicit the same sensations as her own. She backed away from him, trying to regain some control of herself, some equilibrium.

What do you want? she demanded. *Be explicit.*

Freedom.

Who imprisons you?

Mine is not a dungeon of walls, Tear heir.

Speak more plainly or get out.

Admiration sparked in the man's eyes. He moved closer, but stopped when Kelsea held up a hand.

I am imprisoned, Tear heir. And you have the power to set me free.

In exchange for what?

I offer you a chance to defeat the Mort Queen and achieve greatness. You will sit on your throne long after all you know has crumbled into dust.

Did you promise her the same thing?

This time it was his turn to blink. A stab in the dark, but a good one. The Red Queen's extraordinary age had never been explained. And it stood to reason that a man—*is he a man?* Kelsea wondered for the first time—who would try this with one queen would certainly try it with another.

I have no wish to emulate the Red Queen.

You will say so, he replied, *until the moment when her legions smash your army into rubble.* The words were so close to what Kelsea had seen in her mind that she shivered, and saw that this gave him pleasure somehow. *You'll beg for the opportunity to be cruel.*

I will not, she replied. *And if you seek cruelty in me, you won't find it.*

Cruelty is in everyone, Tear heir. It takes only the right application of pressure to coax it out.

Leave, now, or I will call my guard.

I have no fear of your guard. I could wring his neck with little effort.

The words froze Kelsea, but she merely repeated, *Leave. I am not interested.*

He smiled. *But you are, Tear heir. And I will be waiting when you call.*

The man's form dissolved suddenly, coalescing into a black mass that seemed to hover in the air. Kelsea stumbled backward, her heart thudding. The mass streamed like shadow into the fireplace, falling on the flames like a curtain, dimming them and then putting them out entirely, leaving the room cold and dark. In the sudden blackness,

Kelsea lost her balance and landed against her bedside table, knocking it over.

"Shit," she muttered, feeling her way around on the floor.

"Lady?" Pen asked from the doorway, and she gasped; for a moment she had forgotten the existence of anyone but her visitor, and that seemed the most dangerous development of all. "Are you all right?"

"I'm fine, Pen. Just stupid."

"What happened to your fire?"

"A draft."

Even in the dark, she could hear Pen's silent skepticism. His soft, catlike tread moved across the chamber toward the fireplace.

"Don't bother." She fumbled on the floor among the items that had fallen off the bedside table. "I'll just light a candle."

"Have you been practicing sorcery, Lady?"

Kelsea paused in the act of striking a match. "Why do you ask?"

"We're not blind. We see what's happening to you. Mace has forbidden us to speak of it."

"Then perhaps you'd better not." Kelsea lit the candle and found Pen a few feet away, concern in his face. "I'm not practicing sorcery."

"You've become quite pretty."

Kelsea scowled. Pleasure welled up in her, that Pen thought her pretty, but the pleasure was quickly subsumed under anger: she had not been pretty enough before! She felt as though she couldn't win. Her heart rate was still elevated and her body felt frazzled. Pen's handsome face was open, filled with the same honest concern as ever, but then Pen had always been good to her, all the way back to the Reddick Forest, when most of the Guard would probably have been just as happy to leave her behind. As Pen helped her up, Kelsea couldn't help noticing other things. Pen was muscular; he had that whipcord body, well developed on top and lithe on the bottom, that Venner extolled as an absolute necessity for a top-notch swordsman. Pen was quick and strong and intelligent. And, perhaps even more important, he was trustworthy, exceptionally so, even in a cadre of guards chosen for their ability to keep their mouths shut. Anything that happened in this room would stay here.

"Pen?"

"Lady?"

"You think I'm pretty."

He blinked in surprise. "I always found you so, Lady. But it's true that your face has changed."

"You always found me pretty?"

Pen shrugged. "It doesn't matter, Lady. Some women are defined by their appearance, but you have never been one of them."

Kelsea didn't know how to take that. Pen had begun to look uncomfortable now, and she wondered if he was being deliberately obtuse. "But do you—"

"You seem tired, Lady. I should let you sleep." Pen turned away and headed for the door.

"Pen."

He turned back, though he seemed unwilling to meet her eyes.

"You could sleep in here. With me."

Pen's eyes snapped to hers, and his face suddenly seemed to drain of all color, as though Kelsea had slapped him. He shoved his hands into his pockets and turned away. "Lady, I'm a Queen's Guard. I can't."

This was an outright lie, one that made blood darken

Kelsea's cheeks. Her mother's entire Guard had tumbled in and out of bed with the Queen. If Arliss was to be believed, even Mace himself had done so.

Pretty, indeed, Kelsea thought. *So pretty that even with no cost attached, he wants no part of me.* Blood roared in her ears, and she felt a terrible realization creeping up on her: the knowledge of how badly she had just humiliated herself. It took only a moment for humiliation to ignite into anger.

"You're full of shit, Pen. You *could*. You just don't want to."

"Lady, I'm off to bed. In the morning—" Pen swallowed again, convulsively, and Kelsea felt a moment of grim satisfaction; at least he was embarrassed as well. "In the morning, we'll forget about all of this. Sleep well."

Kelsea smiled at him, but the smile felt bitter and frozen. She had made the worst possible choice for this little experiment: the one guard she would have to see constantly, day in and day out. Pen went back into his antechamber and prepared to pull the curtain.

"Pen?"

He paused.

"Despite your active social life, I'll need you at your best in the coming weeks. Whoever she is, tell her to let you get more sleep."

Pen's face froze. He jerked the curtain shut, and she heard the distinctive thump of his body falling onto the mattress, then silence. A deep, wounded part of her mind hoped that he would lie awake for hours, but within a few minutes he began to snore.

Kelsea had never felt further from sleep. She stared at the lit candle on her bedside table, willing herself to blow it out, but she couldn't seem to work up the energy. The entire odd evening seemed to beg for analysis, but she didn't even have the energy for that. Her body was still a mess of involuntary reactions. She rolled over and punched the pillow, hating the frenzy inside her. She reached down to touch herself, then realized it would be no good right now. She was too angry, too ashamed. What she really wanted was to hurt someone, to—

Flay skin and crush bones.

The handsome man's words echoed inside her head. He had offered immortality, but that was only a word. Immortality for Kelsea would not solve the problems of the Tearling. He was imprisoned, the man had said, a prison without walls. He wanted Kelsea to set him free.

Kelsea took her sapphires in her palm and stared at them for a thoughtful moment. Perhaps the man didn't know that they barely worked anymore, that Kelsea didn't truly command them. Flay skin and crush bones . . . but whose skin? Whose bones? She hated Pen in this moment, but she knew that he had not done anything wrong. Pen did not deserve her hatred. There was no one to harm but herself.

Kelsea raised her left arm, staring at it. She had already endured terrible pain . . . the knife in her shoulder, the wound from the hawk . . . but what her mind dug up instead was Lily Mayhew. Lily's life was relatively comfortable for her times, but even in that brief moment of memory, Kelsea had sensed something terrible in Lily's future, an oncoming trial by fire. She studied the smooth white skin of her forearm, trying to focus, imagining the layers of flesh beneath. Just a scratch . . . it would barely hurt, but Kelsea sensed her subconscious mind revolting at the idea, all the same.

Flay skin and crush bones.

"Just the skin," Kelsea whispered, staring at her arm,

focusing all of her will on a tiny inch of flesh. She had borne worse; surely she could handle this. "Just a scratch."

A shallow line of red appeared on her forearm. Kelsea bore down, watching the line deepen, her breath hissing through her teeth as the skin parted with a sting, allowing a thin line of blood to well up and hold. At the sight of the blood, Kelsea smiled wide. She felt connected to her body, to each nerve. Pain was not pleasant, certainly, but it was good to feel something more than helplessness. She blotted her arm on the sheet and turned on her side, barely feeling the sting of the wound, not hearing the rumble of Pen snoring in the next room at all. She was too busy staring at the fireplace, thinking of Mortmesne.

L ady?"

Kelsea looked up and found Mace standing in the doorway. Andalie gave her hair a hard tug, and Kelsea winced.

"The Holy Father is here."

Andalie set down the brush. "It will do, Lady. I could've done a better job with more time."

"His Holiness won't appreciate it anyway," Kelsea muttered, her voice petulant. She had been dreading this dinner all week, but her discomfort in this moment had nothing to do with the Holy Father. What she saw in the mirror was beyond belief. Mace had said nothing about it, and neither had Pen, but Andalie, who did her hair every day, could hardly fail to notice. Kelsea's hair had grown at least eight inches in the past week, and it was now below her shoulders. She was no longer worried about being ill, but even illness would have been something definite, something known. Andalie must have seen some of Kelsea's upset, for she put a firm hand on Kelsea's shoulder and murmured, "It will be all right."

"I've had an interesting report from Mortmesne, Lady," Mace continued.

"The army?"

"No, the people. Mort discontent has been spreading ever since you stopped the shipment, and now there's apparently a protest movement afoot. Right now, it's concentrated primarily in Cite Marche and the northern market villages, but cells are already spreading south toward Demesne."

"Led by whom?"

"A man no one has ever seen, named Levieux. Apparently, he's very anxious to conceal his face."

"The Fetch?"

"Possible, Lady. We've heard nothing from the Fetch since he left that little bit of decor on the Keep Lawn. Arliss has received many tax payments from noble estates in the past month, but we've had no complaints of robbery or harassment. Something keeps him busy."

Kelsea took a deep breath that she hoped was unobtrusive. "Well, if it keeps him from stealing my taxes, so much the better."

"Also, the Red Queen has given an odd set of orders. No one, throughout the entire Palais, is allowed to light a fire in any fireplace."

Kelsea's mind went immediately to the handsome man who had appeared in her chamber. Given the loyalty of her Guard—and despite the mistakes of the past, Kelsea did consider that a given—there was certainly no way for a stranger to simply waltz into the Queen's Wing. The man had departed via the fire; it seemed a reasonable assumption that he had come from the fire as well. The handsome man had mentioned the Red Queen, hadn't he? Kelsea struggled to remember his exact words. If the Red Queen was afraid of this creature, he must be dangerous indeed.

You already knew he was dangerous, her mind mocked gently. *Ten minutes of conversation and he nearly had your dress off.*

"Does this mean anything to you, Lady?" Mace asked. Kelsea had not been as careful as she should have been; Mace had always had a gift for reading her face, even in the mirror.

"No. As you say, it's odd."

Mace watched her for another moment. When Kelsea said nothing, he moved on, but she knew that she hadn't deceived him. "Be careful with the Holy Father, Lady. He's nothing but trouble."

"You can't be concerned about violence."

Mace opened his mouth and then closed it. "Not tonight."

He was going to say something else. Kelsea thanked Andalie and headed for the door, Mace and Pen trailing behind her. For the past two days she had done her best to make no eye contact with Pen, and he seemed just as happy to have it so. But this state of affairs could not hold for long. Kelsea wished she could think of a way to punish Pen, to make him feel as much regret as she did. And then she realized that her appearance wasn't the only thing that had changed. She was different now. The handsome man's words about cruelty recurred: *It takes only the right application of pressure to coax it out.*

I'm not cruel, Kelsea insisted. But she didn't know whom she was trying to convince.

"God's Church holds a vast amount of sway in this kingdom, Lady, like it or not," Mace continued as they headed down the hallway. "Watch your temper tonight."

"Telling me to watch my temper is the first and best way to wake it up, Lazarus."

"Well, I've put Father Tyler between you. At least have a care for him."

They entered the audience chamber to find Father Tyler waiting with his usual timid smile. But tonight the smile betrayed anxiety as well, an anxiety that Kelsea read easily. Father Tyler's two worlds were colliding, and Kelsea, who had long suspected that she saw a different man than the one who lived in the Arvath, wondered if he dreaded the evening as much as she did. She needed the resources of the Arvath now, but she didn't like the idea of going to the Holy Father with hat in hand.

I'm not, she reminded herself. *We're here to trade.*

"Hello, Father."

"Good evening, Majesty. May I introduce His Holiness?"

Kelsea turned her attention to the new Holy Father. She had pictured an old man, shrunken and shriveled, but this man was no older than Mace. He didn't radiate Mace's vitality; rather, Kelsea got no impression from him at all. His features were thick and heavy, the eyes dark, opaque pits, and upon seeing her, his face remained immobile. Kelsea had never received such an impression of blank nothingness from anyone. After a few seconds, she realized that God's mouthpiece was not going to bow; rather, he expected her to bow to him.

"Your Holiness."

Seeing that Kelsea would not bow either, the Holy Father smiled, a functional lifting of the corners of his mouth that did nothing to change the lifelessness of his face. "Queen Kelsea."

"Thank you for coming." She gestured toward the

155

enormous dining table, which had been laid out for ten people. "Have a seat."

Two acolytes, one tall and one short, followed at the Holy Father's elbow. The tall one had the pointed face of a weasel, and he seemed vaguely familiar to Kelsea. He was clearly the favored assistant; it was he who drew the chair out, then pushed it back in after the Holy Father had seated himself. Both acolytes stationed themselves behind the Holy Father's chair; they would not be eating, were clearly meant to fade into the landscape, but Kelsea's attention returned to the tall acolyte several times over the course of dinner. She *had* seen him before, but where?

"No guards?" she whispered to Pen as they sat down.

"The Holy Father always travels with a complement of four armed guards, Lady," he whispered back. "But the Captain insisted they remain outside."

Father Tyler was seated on Pen's other side, only one seat from Kelsea. The Holy Father blinked in surprise when he took his place.

"Do you always eat with so many of your Guard, Majesty?"

"Usually."

"Are security concerns so great?"

"Not at all. I prefer to eat with my Guard."

"Perhaps when you begin a family, that will change."

Kelsea narrowed her eyes as Milla began to ladle soup into her bowl. "My Guard are my family."

"But surely, Majesty, one of your first duties is the production of an heir?"

"I have more pressing concerns right now, Your Holiness."

"And I have many worried parishioners, Majesty. They would have both heir and spare as soon as possible. Uncertainty is bad for morale."

"You would have me get pregnant as my mother did, then, under the table?"

"Certainly not, Majesty. We don't preach wanton sexuality, though it's undeniable that your mother was guilty of such. We would have you married and settled."

Pen nudged her with his foot, and Kelsea realized that the entire table was waiting for her to begin eating. She shook her head. "Forgive me. Please start."

Milla's tomato soup was usually quite good, but tonight Kelsea could barely taste it. The remark about her mother had been too crude, too overt. The Holy Father was trying to goad her, but to what end? His two acolytes stood behind him, motionless, but their eyes were constantly moving, clocking the room. The entire evening already felt wrong. Father Tyler was taking careful spoonfuls of soup, but Kelsea saw that he was eating nothing, that each spoonful went right back into the bowl. Father Tyler never ate much; he was an ascetic. But now his eyes were sunken in dark pockets of flesh, as though bruised, and Kelsea wondered, again, what had happened to him.

The Holy Father hadn't even picked up his spoon. He merely stared at his soup bowl, his eyes empty, as the others ate. This was so rude—particularly since Milla hovered anxiously ten feet from the table—that Kelsea was finally forced to ask, "Is there something else we can bring you, Your Holiness?"

"Not at all, Majesty. I simply don't like tomato."

Kelsea shrugged. A man who didn't like tomato was to be more pitied than despised. She ate mechanically for a few minutes, breathing slowly in and out between spoonfuls, but she was unable to ignore the Holy Father, who seemed to be lurking in wait across the table. Since he clearly wished to make her angry, Kelsea tried to smooth her temper, a mental exercise akin to laying a velvet carpet across a field of spikes. She didn't want to ask this old liar for help, at least not outright, not as a supplicant. But she couldn't wait all night for an opening to come up in the conversation.

Movement over Elston's shoulder distracted her. Her Guard had just admitted the magician, a sandy-haired man of medium build. The last time Kelsea had seen him, she had been a frightened girl riding through the city, but she had not forgotten, and at her request, Mace had tracked the magician down. His name was Bradshaw, and until now he had been strictly a street performer; an engagement at the Keep would be quite an opportunity for him. Kelsea's attention was drawn to his fingers, which were long and clever, even in the quotidian acts of removing hat and cloak. Mace didn't rate the magician as a particular threat to Kelsea's person, but as always, he remained wary of all things magical, and had warned Kelsea that security might tighten in odd ways over the course of the evening.

Kelsea's instincts had been right. When she finally finished her soup and set down her spoon, the Holy Father pounced.

"Majesty, at the request of my congregation, I must bring up several unpleasant matters."

"Your congregation? You still give sermons?"

"All of humanity is my congregation."

"Even those who want no part of it?"

"Those who want no part of God's kingdom are the most in need, Majesty."

"What's the first unpleasant matter?"

"The destruction of the Graham castle some months ago."

"I understand it was gutted by an accidental fire."

"Many of my congregation believe that fire to be no accident, Majesty. Indeed, the prevailing belief is that the fire was set by one of your own guards."

"Prevailing belief is very convenient. Have you any proof?"

"I do."

Kelsea drew a sharp breath. Mace, on her right, had frozen, but the Holy Father only continued to stare blandly at Kelsea; he seemed to have no fear of Mace at all. Kelsea considered asking the Holy Father to produce his proof, but discarded the idea. If he really did have something linking Mace to the fire, there was nowhere else to go. She shifted ground.

"An assassination attempt on the Queen is treachery. I believe the common law states that treachery renders the traitor's lands forfeit."

"So it does."

"Lord Graham put a knife to my throat, Your Holiness. Even in the unlikely event that one of my Guard was involved with that fire, his property was mine to burn."

"But not the people inside, Majesty."

"If they were on my property, they were trespassing."

"But your ownership of that property depends entirely on your own accusations of treachery."

"My accusations," Kelsea repeated. "What else would you call Lord Graham's actions?"

"I don't know, Majesty. As you say, there's so little proof. What do we know? Only that you had a young, attractive lord in your chamber in the early evening, and you killed him."

Kelsea's mouth dropped open.

"Perhaps you had your eye on his lands all along."

Pen pushed back from the table, but Kelsea grabbed his arm and whispered, "No."

"Lady—"

"*Do nothing.*" Meeting Pen's gaze was a mistake; in that moment, Kelsea seemed to live her humiliation all over again. This was her oldest friend, the guard who had been kind to her long before any of the others, but all Kelsea could see was the man who had turned her down. How could they ever get back to where they had been before? She turned back to the Holy Father and found him watching her and Pen with an interested gaze.

"So this is the story your priests tell from the pulpit, Your Holiness? Young Lord Graham was a victim of *my* wanton sexuality?"

Elston and Dyer began sniggering.

"Majesty, you misunderstand me. I am only a mouthpiece for my congregation's concerns."

"I thought you were the mouthpiece for God."

The shorter acolyte gasped.

"Such a statement would be blasphemous, Majesty," the Holy Father replied, his tone gently reproving. "No man can speak for God."

"I see."

She didn't see, but at least she had gotten him off the subject of Mace and the fire. Milla took the pause in conversation as an opportunity to bring the main course: roast chicken with potatoes. Kelsea snuck a glance at Pen and found him staring with cold fury at the Holy Father. All of her Guard were angry now, even Mace, whose mouth had tightened. Kelsea tapped her nails on the table, and they returned their attention to the food, though some of them appeared to have difficulty swallowing.

"Have you heard the reports from the Fairwitch, Majesty?" the Holy Father asked.

"I have. Children disappearing and some invisible murderer that stalks in the night."

"How do you plan to address the matter?"

"Difficult to say, until I get some hard evidence of what's going on."

"While you wait, Majesty, the problem grows worse. Cardinal Penney tells me that several families have disappeared in the foothills. The Cardinal himself has seen dark shadows in the night around his castle. It's the devil's work, for certain."

"And how would you suggest that I fight the devil?"

"Prayer, Majesty. Devotion. Have you never considered that this might be God's vengeance on the Tearling?"

"For what?"

"For laxity of faith. For backsliding."

Father Tyler dropped his fork. It hit the ground with a clatter, and he crawled under the table to retrieve it.

"Prayer will not save us from a serial killer, Your Holiness."

"Then what will?"

"Action. Judicious action, taken after all the consequences are weighed."

"Your faith is weak, Majesty."

Kelsea put down her fork. "You will not goad me."

"I had no thought to goad, only to offer spiritual advice. Many of your actions subvert God's will."

Kelsea saw where this was going now, and she leaned her chin on both hands. "Do tell, Your Holiness."

The Holy Father raised his eyebrows. "You wish me to list your transgressions?"

"Why not?"

"Fine, Majesty. I will. Three heretics and two homosexuals were in Crown custody at the start of your reign, and you have freed them all. Worse, you tolerate open homosexuality in your own Guard."

What was this? Kelsea fought down the urge to look at Mace, or at any other member of her Guard. She had never heard a whisper of any such thing.

"Your own failure to marry sets a terrible example for young women everywhere. I have heard speculation that you may have homosexual sympathies yourself."

"Indeed, Your Holiness, the sexual freedom of consenting adults is the greatest threat this kingdom has ever faced," Kelsea replied acidly. "God knows how we've lasted so long."

The Holy Father was not derailed. "And most recently, Majesty, I have been informed that you mean to tax the Arvath, like any secular body, on its landholdings. But surely this must be a mistake."

"Ah, so we finally come to it. No mistake, Your Holiness. God's Church is a landholder like any other. Beginning in February, I will expect monthly payments on all of your property."

"The Church has always been exempt from taxation, Majesty, all the way back to David Raleigh. The exemption encourages good works and selflessness on the part of our brothers."

"You reap profit from your land, Your Holiness, and despite your mandate, you're not a charitable institution. I don't see the vast bulk of your income flowing back to the public."

"We distribute bread to the poor, Majesty!"

"Well done. Saint Simone herself could hardly do more." Kelsea leaned forward, trying to soften the edge in her voice.

"However, since you bring up the point, I have an offer for you."

"What is that?"

"If my estimates are correct, by the end of July, most of the Tearling will be housed at the Caddell Camp outside the walls. When the Mort come, all of the displaced will need to be brought into the city."

"That will make New London terribly crowded, Majesty."

"Indeed, and since you claim to be a charitable institution, I thought you could show some of that Christian spirit by providing food and housing as well."

"Housing?"

"I will be opening the Keep to refugees, but you have the second largest building in New London, Your Holiness. Nine floors, and I'm told that only two of them are actually used for housing."

"How do you know that?" the Holy Father asked angrily, and Kelsea was dismayed to see him shoot a glare at Father Tyler. "The Arvath is sacrosanct."

"Seven empty floors, Your Holiness," she pressed on. "Think how many displaced people you could house and feed."

"There is no extra space in the Arvath, Majesty."

"In return," Kelsea continued, as though he had not spoken, "I would be willing to consider all of the Church's New London property as charitable, and forgive the tax on those landholdings."

"Only New London?" The Holy Father burst out laughing, an unexpected sound from his mirthless face. "New London constitutes only a tiny fraction of our property, Majesty. Now, if you were willing to throw in our holdings in the northern Almont, there might be an arrangement to make."

"Ah, yes . . . your farmlands. Where the poor work for pennies a day and their children start in the fields at the age of five. Charitable property indeed."

"These people would otherwise have no employment at all."

Kelsea stared at him. "And *that* allows you to sleep at night?"

"I sleep well enough, Majesty."

"I'm sure you do."

"Majesty!" Father Tyler stood up abruptly, his face panic-stricken. "I must use the restroom. Excuse me."

Somewhere during the argument, Milla had slid a dessert plate in front of Kelsea: cheesecake dotted with strawberries. Kelsea made quick work of it; it wasn't one of Milla's best efforts, but there really was no bad cheesecake, and even Kelsea's temper was not enough to blunt her appetite. Mace gave her a pleading glance, but Kelsea shook her head. While she chewed, she cast surreptitious glances at her guards, wondering for whom that remark about homosexuality had been meant. Perhaps, like so many things in God's Church, the Holy Father had simply produced it from thin air, but Kelsea didn't think so; it was too odd a claim. And was it any of her business anyway? According to Carlin, the institutionalized homophobia of the pre-Crossing had wasted vast amounts of time and resources. Barty, with characteristic practicality, always said that God had better things to worry about than what happened between the sheets.

No, Kelsea decided, *it's not my business.* She wished she could simply tell the Holy Father to go fuck himself—it would feel wonderful—but where would she house all of those remaining refugees, if not in the Arvath? Bedding, sanitation, medical care . . . without the Church, it would be a disaster. Briefly, Kelsea considered threatening to seize the Arvath itself under eminent domain, just as she had threatened that group of idiot nobles a few weeks ago. But no, that would be a disastrous move. A direct attack on the Arvath would only confirm every dire warning the Holy Father's people recounted in the pulpit, and too many people believed the Church's nonsense. The Holy Father had been trying to make her angry, Kelsea realized now, and he had succeeded. Anger made Kelsea strong, but it weakened her as well; she saw no route to wend her way back into negotiation now, not without losing ground.

"I think His Holiness and I have provided enough entertainment for one evening," she announced, standing up. "Shall we move on to the real performance?"

The Holy Father smiled, though the smile did not meet his eyes. He hadn't touched his cheesecake either, and Kelsea cast her mind back, trying to remember if he'd eaten anything at all. Was he worried about poison? Surely this man would not scruple at making one of his acolytes taste the food.

You're wandering. Focus on the Arvath. The Mort.

Kelsea tried, but she didn't see what could be done to repair the situation now. And wasn't this all academic anyway? The Mort would be here long before the new tax year, and New London would never stand up to a prolonged siege. Debating next year's taxes was like painting a house that lay right in the path of a hurricane. Perhaps she should just relent, but at the mere thought of it, Kelsea's mind conjured the Arvath steeple: pure gold, worth many thousands of pounds. She could not give in.

As the group moved toward the throne, Father Tyler

reappeared beside Kelsea, speaking in a low voice. "Lady, I beg you not to antagonize him further."

"He can take care of himself." But Kelsea paused, seeing anew the priest's pale face, the weight that had dropped from his already thin frame. "What is it you're frightened of, Father?"

Father Tyler shook his head stubbornly. "Nothing, Majesty. My concern is for you."

"Well, if it's any consolation, I do plan to be on my best behavior for the rest of the night."

"And yet that plan so often fails."

Kelsea laughed, clapping him on the back. Tyler's grimace became more pronounced, and she bit her lip; she had forgotten that she wasn't supposed to touch a member of God's Church. "Sorry, Father."

He shrugged, then grinned mischievously, a rare occurrence for Father Tyler. "It's fine, Lady. Unlike His Holiness, I'm not concerned about your wanton sexuality."

Kelsea chuckled, and gestured for him to come with her to the top of the dais, where two armchairs had been set up. The Holy Father was already seated, and he gave Kelsea one of those disturbingly bland smiles as she sat down. His acolytes remained standing at the foot of the dais; Mace gestured for Elston to stay with them. So Mace, too, was worried about the tall acolyte with the weasel's face. Memory tugged at Kelsea for a moment before letting go.

Mace snapped his fingers at the magician, Bradshaw, who came forward and made a shallow bow. He didn't wear the brightly colored clothing Kelsea had seen on so many street performers; rather, he was dressed very simply, in black. A table had been set up nearby to hold his props: an assortment of objects, including two small cabinets placed perhaps two feet apart. Bradshaw opened the cabinets, lifted each to show that there was no false bottom, then took a cup from the dinner table and placed it in one cabinet, shutting the door tightly. When he opened the door of the other cabinet, the cup was there.

Kelsea clapped, pleased, though she had no idea how the trick was done. Not magic, surely, but it had the appearance of magic, and that was good enough. Bradshaw made a quick succession of objects appear in each cabinet: one of Dyer's gloves, a bowl from the table, two daggers, and finally, Mace's mace. This last caught Mace out with a bewildered expression that turned momentarily to anger, then back to bewilderment as Bradshaw took the mace from the cabinet and presented it to him with a smile.

Kelsea clapped loudly; few people could put one over on Mace, and even fewer would have dared to try. Mace inspected his favorite weapon for a moment, as a jeweler would inspect diamonds, and finally appeared to conclude that it was indeed the same mace. In a low voice, Kelsea told Elston to give the magician a fifty percent tip.

The Holy Father was clearly unimpressed; he had watched the entire performance with an increasingly sour expression and had not clapped once.

"Not a fan of illusions, Your Holiness?"

"Not really, Majesty. All magicians are con artists, deceiving the common people into belief in pagan magic."

Kelsea nearly rolled her eyes, but stopped herself. Her window of opportunity was closing here; once the Holy Father walked out the door, he was never coming back. And perhaps he would be more amenable to reason now, when there were fewer people to overhear. Bradshaw was waving his hands in a performative fashion below; Kelsea waited until he produced a mouse from nowhere before asking quietly, "What would tempt you to accept my offer?"

"Perhaps we could reach a compromise, Majesty. Forgive the taxes on both our New London holdings and half of our acreage in the Almont, and the Church will happily feed and house four floors' worth of the displaced."

Kelsea looked up at Mace. "How much tax money is that?"

"Only Arliss would know for certain, Lady. But you're talking at least a thousand square miles of producing farmland. A year's taxes would be a good sum."

"Not just a year," the Holy Father interjected. "In perpetuity."

"In perpetuity?" Kelsea repeated in an incredulous whisper. "I could build my own damned Arvath with the money the Tearling would lose over five years alone."

"You could build it, Majesty, but you don't have the time." The Holy Father grinned, and for the first time his eyes showed a glimmer of light . . . but it wasn't a good sort of light at all. "The Mort will be here by autumn, and you're over a barrel. That's why we're having this conversation."

"Don't make the mistake of thinking that you're anything more than a convenience to me, Your Holiness. I don't need your pile of gold."

"Then don't make the mistake of thinking *I'm* frightened of your tax collector, Majesty. By the time the New Year rolls around, you'll be in no position to tax anyone."

Kelsea had been thinking the same thing not five minutes before, but this fact only made her angrier. She turned fully toward him, no longer even pretending to take interest in the magic show. "And what good is all that gold doing you, Your Holiness? Who is it you're trying to impress with that steeple of yours? God?"

"God is not interested in such trifles."

"My point exactly."

"Devout parishioners donated that gold, Majesty, as a matter of repentance and good works. Your uncle was one of them."

"My uncle had seven concubines and no marriage in sight. How devout could he be?"

"Your uncle confessed those sins to Father Timpany, Majesty, and was absolved."

"A fascinating system. Children of four are subjected to more discipline."

The Holy Father's voice tightened in anger. "You have criminal laws for secular punishment, Majesty. My concern is simply salvation of the soul."

"But the gold helps, right?"

"How dare you—"

"Your Majesty!" Bradshaw gave another elaborate bow at the foot of the dais. "For my final trick, may I ask one of your Guard to volunteer?"

Kelsea produced a wilted smile. "Kibb."

Kibb headed down the steps, to the chuckles of the other guards, but Kelsea barely paid attention. Her hands were clenched tightly on the arms of her chair. It was all she could do not to throttle the man sitting next to her.

All that room, she thought, staring at the Holy Father, her temples throbbing. *All that room and all that gold. You don't use it, you don't need it, but it's not to be shared. If we live through the invasion, my friend, I am going to tax you until you scream for mercy.*

The Holy Father stared back at her with the supreme arrogance of one who had nothing to fear. Kelsea remembered a remark Mace had made, weeks ago: that the Holy Father wasn't above dealing with Demesne under the table. If the Holy Father had already made his deal, then of course he wouldn't be threatened by Kelsea; he need only sit and wait until the Mort army rolled in, sparing the Arvath and laying waste to everything else. And now Kelsea felt the first seeds of despair take root in her heart. She had spent the last month running back and forth, moving frantically from one option to the next, trying to find a solution, and now she looked up and found herself surrounded by cannibals.

"In honor of your holy guests, Majesty!" Bradshaw produced the cup he'd used earlier and filled it with water from a small canteen, then handed it to Kibb. "Have a sip, sir, and please confirm that it's water."

Kibb sipped gently at the cup. "Water indeed."

The magician brought the cup to the front of the dais and held it up for Kelsea's inspection, waiting until she nodded to continue. With a small, polite bow to the Holy Father, Bradshaw covered the mouth of the cup with one hand and snapped the fingers of the other. A small flash of light appeared between his fingers, and then Bradshaw held the cup up to Kelsea again, removing his hand. The water in the goblet was now a deep, dark red.

"For her Majesty's pleasure!" Bradshaw announced. "Where's my able assistant?"

Kibb raised his hand, and the magician danced over to him, holding out the cup. "Taste it, sir. It will do you no harm."

Kibb, smiling with a touch of anxiety, took a small sip from the cup. An astonished look came over his face, and he took a second, larger sip. Turning to Kelsea, he announced in an amazed voice, "Majesty, it's wine."

Kelsea chuckled, then giggled, and finally could not stop

herself from roaring with laughter. She didn't miss the look of fury on the Holy Father's darkening face, but that only made her laugh harder. Below the dais, Bradshaw smiled, his face flushing with triumph.

"Get up, get up!"

The shorter acolyte had fainted dead away, and the taller one was shaking him, hissing commands. But the young man was out cold.

The Holy Father rose from his seat, his face a deep, rich red that pleased Kelsea no end. Father Tyler was murmuring gently in his ear, but the Holy Father shoved him away. He showed no concern for the unconscious boy on the floor.

"I see no humor in an insult offered to guests," the Holy Father snarled. "That was a blasphemous joke, Majesty, in poor taste."

"Don't look at me, Your Holiness. I don't keep court performers. His tricks are his own."

"I want an apology!" he snapped, and Kelsea, who had assumed that this sort of ludicrous outrage was part of a Holy Father's job description, found herself hesitating, because his anger was clearly genuine. But even if Bradshaw had produced Mary the Virgin from a hat, no one could possibly take a magic trick seriously. The smart move was conciliation, but Kelsea was long past that now. She tapped her nails on the arm of the chair and asked sweetly, "An apology from whom?"

"From this impostor, Majesty."

"Impostor? I'm quite sure he didn't mean to represent himself as the actual Christ, Your Holiness."

"I demand an apology."

"Did you just give the Queen an order?" Mace asked, his voice deadly soft.

"I certainly did."

"Refused!" Kelsea snapped. "What kind of fool takes offense at an illusion?"

"Majesty, please!" Father Tyler had moved up to stand beside the Holy Father, his thin face blanched nearly white now. "This is hardly constructive."

"Shut up, Tyler!" the Holy Father hissed. "All magicians are charlatans! They promise quick solutions and undermine faith in the straight and righteous path."

Kelsea narrowed her eyes. "Don't even think about playing the devout card with me, Your Holiness. I've heard all about you. What of those two women you keep in the Arvath? Do they kneel down before the Holy Spirit every night?"

At this, the Holy Father's face turned an apoplectic purple, and Kelsea suddenly wished that he would simply have a heart attack and keel over right in front of her throne, consequences be damned.

"Have a care, Majesty. You have no idea how delicate your position is."

"Threaten me again, you greedy fraud, and I will end you."

"I'm sure he meant nothing of the kind, Majesty!" Father Tyler exclaimed in a high, panicky voice. "It was no threat, only–"

"Tyler, stay out of this!" the Holy Father roared. He turned and lashed out with one arm, catching Father Tyler in the chest. Tyler momentarily pinwheeled for balance, then fell backward, down the stairs of the dais. Kelsea heard the dry, crisp snap of a breaking bone, and all thought ceased, the voice of reason in her head falling mercifully silent. She jumped to her feet, pushed past Pen, and slapped the Holy Father across the face.

172

Mace and Pen moved very quickly, and the rest of the Guard was right behind them. Within a few seconds, more than ten men stood between Kelsea and the Holy Father. The guards obscured her view, but not before she had seen and memorized the white mark of her handprint against the Holy Father's red cheek, wrapped it in her mind like a gift.

"Sacrilege!" the taller acolyte hissed from the bottom of the stairs. "No one can lay hands on the Holy Father!"

"If you value that hypocrite, get him out of my Keep right now."

The acolyte scrambled up the steps to assist the Holy Father. Kelsea turned back to her armchair, determined to ignore them, but then she heard gasping breaths below her, behind the wall of guards.

"Father, are you all right?"

"Fine, Majesty."

But Father Tyler's voice was hoarse with pain.

"Stay there. We'll get you a doctor."

"Tyler will come with us!" the Holy Father snarled. But Mace had already pushed his way down the steps and positioned himself between Father Tyler and the priests.

"The Queen says he stays."

"My own doctors will attend him."

"I think not, Your Holiness. I've seen the work of your doctors."

The Holy Father's eyes widened, full of surprise and something else . . . guilt? Before Kelsea could decipher his reaction, Mace sprang across the room and laid hold of the taller acolyte, grabbing him by the neck. "We'll be keeping this one as well. Brother Matthew, is it?"

"On what charge?" the Holy Father demanded, enraged.

"Treason," Mace announced flatly. "The Thorne conspiracy."

The Holy Father's mouth worked for a moment. "We came here under promise of safe conduct!"

"I promised safe conduct to *you*, Your Holiness," Kelsea snapped, though inwardly she cursed Mace; he never told her anything. Now she placed Brother Matthew easily: one of the men from the Argive, crouched around Thorne's campfire in the middle of the night. "You're free to go. But your toadies came at their own risk."

"I suggest you leave now," Mace told the Holy Father, tightening his grip on the struggling priest's neck. "Before I have a chance to ask your weasel any questions."

The Holy Father's eyes narrowed, and he kicked the shorter acolyte, who was still unconscious on the floor. "You! Wake up! We're leaving!"

Somehow or other, they got the young man to unsteady feet. Mace handed Brother Matthew off to Elston and followed the two Arvath men to the doors. The second acolyte, his face white as milk, cast several appalled glances over his shoulder, but the Holy Father, walking stiffly at his side, never looked back.

Kelsea hurried down the stairs to crouch beside Father Tyler, whose left leg was twisted at a dreadful angle. He was breathing in shallow pants, enormous beads of sweat rolling down his pale cheeks. Kelsea gathered the hem of her dress to wipe his forehead, but when Coryn tried to examine the leg, Father Tyler groaned and begged him to stop.

"Broken in multiple places, Lady. We're going to have to put him out to reset the bone."

"We'll wait for the doctor," Kelsea ordered, casting a

murderous glance toward the Holy Father's retreating back. "God's good work, I suppose."

Father Tyler giggled, a wild, disconnected sound. "I got off light, Majesty. Seth will tell you so."

"Who's Seth?"

But Father Tyler gritted his teeth, and although Kelsea asked her question several more times before the doctor arrived, he refused to answer.

CHAPTER 5

DORIAN

The success of a great human migration depends on many individual pieces falling into place. There must be discontent with an unpleasant, perhaps even intolerable status quo. There must be idealism to drive the movement, a powerful vision of a better life beyond the horizon. There must be great courage in the face of terrible odds. But most of all, every migration needs its leader, the indispensable charismatic figure whom even terrified men and women will follow headlong into the abyss.

The British-American Crossing met this final requirement in spades.

—*The Blue Horizon of the Tear*, GLEE DELAMERE

Lily was sitting in the backyard, struggling to record a message to her mother. The day was too hot; something must have gone wrong with the climate control. That happened more and more often lately. Greg said it was the separatists and their hackers, sabotaging the satellites; the military men he dealt with at the Pentagon had been complaining about it for weeks. Over the past few days, the temperature in New Canaan had climbed into the high nineties, and now heavy wet air blanketed the backyard.

Weather aside, this had been a good week. Greg had gone on a business trip to Boston, some sort of convention with other players in the military. Lily always pictured these meetings as a larger version of the parties they held at their house: drunken men, their voices growing louder and hoarser as more and more liquor poured forth.

Still, she was grateful. When Greg was gone, she could almost pretend that this was her house, that she needed account to no one for her day. There was no need to hide in the nursery; Lily could move freely around the house. But tonight Greg would be coming home, and Lily was trying to snatch the last few hours to record her letter. It was hard to make her lies sound natural, particularly for Mom, who didn't want to hear about anything unpleasant. Lily had just hit record again when a woman toppled over the back wall into the garden.

Lily looked up, startled. The woman rolled down the wall, a hissing sound following her descent as she scraped against the ivy that clung there. She ended up buried in the patch of hydrangea bushes, disappearing from sight with a low, wounded grunt.

Jonathan materialized from the kitchen doorway, his gun drawn. "Stay back, Mrs. M."

Lily ignored him, got up from her Adirondack, and tip-toed over to the stone wall. The intruder had flattened the hydrangea bush. Lily felt Jonathan's restraining hand on her arm, but she peered over the jagged edges of the bush until she found the woman who lay there.

She looks like Maddy!

The woman did look remarkably like Lily's younger sister.

Her hair, now tangled in the bush, hadn't been washed in some time, but it was the same dirty blonde, even the same springy texture. She had Maddy's snub nose, her freckles. She was a few years too young; Lily bit her lip, trying to remember how old her sister would have been now. Two years younger than Lily, so twenty-three. This girl couldn't be more than eighteen.

Now Lily heard sirens, their wails muted by the thick stone wall. Security hardly ever used sirens in New Canaan; on the rare occasion when they came into Lily's neighborhood, it was a quiet, efficient business. But this woman clearly didn't belong in New Canaan. Her face was streaked with some kind of grease, and she wore jeans and a torn sweater that looked about three sizes too large. The edges of the sweater were bloody. Lily peered more closely, then drew back with a hiss. "She's been shot!"

"Go on inside, Mrs. M. I'll call Security."

The woman opened her eyes. They shone, bright green and remarkably clear, too old for adolescence, before they slipped closed again. The woman breathed in shallow pants, her hand clamped against the bloody patch on her stomach. She seemed too young to even contemplate crime, and she looked so much like Maddy, Maddy who had disappeared years before.

"You're injured," Lily told her. "You need a hospital."

"No hospital."

"She's a trespasser!" Jonathan hissed.

The sirens were louder now, perhaps as close as Willow Street. The woman opened her eyes again, and in them Lily saw resignation, a tired sort of acceptance. Maddy had looked that way when they came for her, as if she were already imagining what came next. Lily didn't want to think

178

about that day, about Maddy. Jonathan was right; they should call Security. But Maddy was upon Lily now, and she found herself unable to do it, unable to turn the woman in.

"Help me get her inside."

"What for?" Jonathan asked.

"Just help me."

"What would Mr. M. say?"

Lily looked up at him, her voice sharpening. "It wouldn't be the first secret we've kept, would it?"

"This is different."

"Let's get her up."

"She's not a random wall trespasser, Mrs. M. You hear those sirens? You think they aren't for her?"

"Into the house. We'll put her in the nursery. He'll never know."

"She needs a doctor."

"Then we'll get her one."

"And then what? Doctors have to report gunshot wounds."

Lily hauled the woman up, slipping an arm under her shoulders and wincing when the woman groaned. It seemed very important to hurry up and get the woman inside before she thought too hard about possible consequences, about Greg. "Come on, inside."

Grumbling, Jonathan pitched in. Together, they helped the woman across the garden and into the house, an air-cooled oasis of darkness. By the time they reached the living room, the woman had dropped into unconsciousness and become much heavier than her skinny frame would have suggested. Lily groaned as they hauled her through the foyer, but her mind was already clocking off the things she would have to do. First, the surveillance. Lily had no backup footage of the living room and stairway, but she could do a onetime erase and Greg would chalk it up to a glitch . . . *probably*, her mind amended. The separatist's shoes were covered with mud, and she had left several patches of it on the living room carpet. The house sterilized itself, but not that quickly. Lily would need to clean the mud up by hand before Greg came home.

They muscled the injured woman into the nursery and deposited her on the sofa. Lily could feel Jonathan's glare, even before she looked up.

"What are you doing, Mrs. M.?"

"I don't know," Lily admitted. "I just . . ."

"What?"

A picture of Security popped into Lily's head: the door through which they hustled people who never came out again. When Lily was a child, there hadn't been such doors, and even as she became an adult, she had paid very little attention to the world changing around her; she often thought that it was this very inattention to implications, to the future, that had allowed her to marry Greg in the first place. Maddy had been the political one, the one who cared about the wider world. Lily's immediate concerns were keeping the house running and dealing with Greg, finding ways to tiptoe around his newly volatile anger, to stay one step ahead of it. That was a full plate, certainly, but she couldn't escape a nagging sense of shared responsibility, of many good people, all of them with their eyes on the ground, who had allowed the faceless door of Security to become the status quo. Maddy would not have allowed it, but Maddy had disappeared.

Jonathan was still waiting for an answer, but Lily couldn't explain, not to him. Jonathan had been a Marine, had fought in Saudi Arabia in the final, desperate battle for the last of the world's oil. He was a loyalist. He carried a gun.

"I'm not going to turn her in," Lily finally replied. "Are you going to tell Greg?"

Jonathan looked down at the woman on the sofa, his gaze contemplative. "No ma'am. But you need to get her a doctor. If you don't, she's going to bleed to death right here on your couch."

Lily ran though the list of local doctors she knew. Greg's friends, none of them trustworthy. Their family doctor, Dr. Collins, had offices less than five miles away, in the center of town, but he wasn't an option either. Dr. Collins had never asked Lily whether she wanted to have a baby. On her last visit, he'd told her that she needed to relax more during sex, that relaxing was a good way to conceive.

"My purse. There's a card in there. My doctor in New York."

"Davis? This isn't his area. He's a fixer."

"He's a fertility specialist!"

"Right, Mrs. M."

She stared at him for a moment. "Are you going to tell Greg?"

Jonathan sighed, pulling the Lexus keys from his pocket. "Stay here. Keep pressure on the wound. I'll be back with a doctor."

"What doctor?"

"Don't worry about it."

"Not one of Greg's friends?"

"*Don't worry about it*, Mrs. M. You were right; we both know how to keep a secret."

Jonathan was gone for more than an hour, giving Lily plenty of time to imagine the worst: Jonathan arrested for transporting an unlicensed physician; Jonathan unable to find a doctor at all; but mostly, Jonathan gone straight to Greg's office, straight to Security, to tell them everything. Jonathan had been her bodyguard for nearly three years, Lily told herself, and he knew about Dr. Davis. If he'd wanted to get her in trouble, he could have done so a long time ago.

But still she was afraid.

The woman on the sofa was visibly dehydrating before Lily's eyes. Her lips were chapped nearly white, and when she tried to speak, it was a hoarse croak. Lily went downstairs and filled a bowl with chipped ice. She didn't know anything about taking care of sick people, but she'd had pneumonia when she was little, and for that entire week, all she could stand to eat was ice chips. She wet a cloth with freezing water and dumped it into the bowl as well.

When she returned, the woman on the sofa asked where she was. Lily tried to tell her, but the woman passed out again before she'd finished. Another three hours and Greg would be home. Where was Jonathan? And what was Lily doing anyway? The pills were one thing, one secret to keep, but hiding a person was something else.

"What's your name?" Lily asked the woman when she woke up again.

"No names," she whispered back. Lily felt as though she had heard those words before, perhaps on one of the government's countless pamphlets and flyers. What had the woman been doing here? From time to time, Lily heard sirens cruising the neighborhood, sometimes far away and sometimes very close. She checked the news sites on the wall panel, but there was nothing, no local news about a trespasser or any nearby crime. She went out to the surveillance room and deleted that afternoon's footage. There was always a chance that Greg had seen it in real time, but that was very unlikely today; at the end of his conference, Greg would be busily glad-handing before he got on the plane. On her way back to the nursery, she cleaned up the mud.

The woman was still unconscious. She was too young to be Maddy, yes, and a bit too tall as well, but still, it was almost like having a ghost on the sofa. As the afternoon advanced, the line of sun from the window moved across the woman's shoulder and Lily spotted a scar there, just above the collar-bone. Lily had a scar in the same place, a neat surgical line from having her tag implanted when she was young. But this scar was much more noticeable. It was not the thin, pristine line that a laser would leave. It looked as though it had been done with a scalpel.

Lily stared at the scar for a very long time, a wild idea taking hold in her mind: the woman had somehow removed her tag. That should have been impossible; each tag was armed with a toxin, a deadly chemical that would release on impact if anyone tried to tamper with the device. But the longer Lily considered the scar, the more certain she became: this woman had managed to get rid of her tag. She could move freely wherever she wanted, without Security tracking her every movement. Lily couldn't even imagine what that would be like.

Jonathan finally came back at four, with a small, neat grey-haired man in tow. The little man looked just the way a doctor should look, to Lily's mind; he wore a professional-looking grey suit and old-fashioned wire-frame glasses, and he carried a small black leather bag that clinked as he set it down. He ignored Lily entirely, going straight to the woman on the sofa. After a moment's assessment he turned, speaking as he would to a nurse. "Boiling-hot water and some towels. Cotton towels."

For a moment, Lily was too surprised to move. She wasn't used to being ordered around in her own house.

Except by Greg, her mind whispered, and that got her moving, out of the nursery and down to the kitchen. After she had fetched the water, she went to the linen closet and tried to decide which towels Greg would miss the least. He had a strange, sporadic eye for details around the house; Lily would throw out a set of threadbare sheets and then, a year later, Greg would ask where the sheets had gone. None of their towels were dark enough to hide blood; whichever set she chose would have to be tossed.

Just pick and go, dammit.

Lily grabbed a set of pine-green towels she'd always hated, a wedding gift from Greg's aunt. When she returned, she found that Jonathan and the doctor had moved the sofa into the direct sunlight beneath the windowsill. The doctor had removed the woman's oversize sweater to reveal a discolored man's undershirt beneath, and now he was cutting the undershirt off with some scissors he'd produced from his little bag. Lily bent down to deposit the towels beside him.

"That'll do, miss."

"Lily."

"No names."

That phrase again. Feeling rebuked, Lily turned to Jonathan and found that he'd taken out his gun, a gleaming black thing that never failed to make Lily uneasy, and was fiddling with it, taking out the bullets and putting them in again.

"I need you to hold her down," the doctor said. Lily didn't know who he was talking to, but both of them moved forward, Lily toward the woman's arms and Jonathan, tucking the gun away, toward her feet. Looking down, Lily saw a glint of panic in the woman's eyes, and she placed a hand on her forehead, feeling like the world's biggest fraud as she murmured, "It'll be all right."

The next half hour would stay with Lily in clear, sickening detail for the rest of her life. The doctor had a laser probe, at least, but when he began to poke around with it, the woman's arms strained until Lily's face and neck were slicked with sweat in the effort to hold her down. Every few minutes the doctor would mutter, "Buried deep, little bastard," and these mutterings were Lily's only way to mark the passage of time.

She spent much of the operation staring at Jonathan, trying to puzzle him out. He was a good bodyguard and a gifted driver, but he was also a former Marine and—Lily had always thought—a loyalist. How on earth did he know an off-the-grid doctor? How would either of them be able to keep this from Greg?

The doctor finally found the bullet, then began to work a small set of tongs into the hole. The woman passed out again somewhere in the middle of this process, her arms going mercifully slack against Lily's hands. The temperature in the nursery felt as though it had climbed sharply, though the wall panel only read 74 degrees. Lily was dizzy, as though she'd lost all the blood in her head. Jonathan, no surprise, was steady as ever, his face immobile as he watched the doctor work. He'd probably killed men in Saudi Arabia with the same stone face.

At last the doctor held up the tongs to display a deformed piece of scarlet-dripping plastic. Jonathan held out a towel and the doctor dropped the bullet into it, making the cotton bloom red, then began to seal the wound.

"Was she successful?" the doctor asked.

"I don't know," Jonathan replied.

"One of us should let him know she's here."

"I'll do it. How long will she have to stay?"

"Ideally, she needs a few days' rest. She's lost a lot of blood. There's no way to get her out anyway, not until she can walk; I would think there are roadblocks up by now." The doctor gave Lily a doubtful look. "But can she stay *here*?"

"Yes, she can," Lily replied, trying to sound firm. But the rest of the conversation had mystified her. What kind of doctor patched wounds and asked no questions? The doctor wiped his hands on one of Lily's bath sheets, then threw it on her armchair. "She'll need fairly constant care."

"I'll do it," Lily volunteered. "During the day, I can be in here all the time. At night, maybe every few hours."

"What does a woman like you want with something like this?"

Lily flushed at the judgment she saw in his eyes. Her nursery was bigger than most people's homes. She wished she could tell this neat little man about Maddy, but she didn't know where to begin. "I just do. She'll be safe here."

The doctor considered her for another moment, then opened his bag and dumped a pile of medical paraphernalia onto the sofa: bandages, syringes, pill bottles. "You need to change the bandage at least once a day. If she becomes feverish, give her this. Have you ever given someone an injection?"

"Yes." Lily nodded vigorously, feeling more confident now. The new syringes had guides to pinpoint veins, but even if the doctor's syringes were the older kind, Maddy had been a diabetic. Lily knew how to give a shot.

The doctor held up a green-wrapped syringe. "Antibiotics. Give her an injection every evening at the same time. The vein in her forearm."

He turned back to Jonathan. "She can stay here for a few days, but she could easily develop infection. The sooner he gets her out, the better."

He who? Lily wondered now. The doctor's voice was so reverent that for a moment Lily thought he was talking about God.

"I need to take the doctor back, Mrs. M., then run some errands. I might be gone until late."

Lily nodded slowly. "I'll tell Greg you went to pick up my new dress in the city."

This wasn't precisely a lie. Lily had ordered a new dress from Chanel several weeks ago: fifteen thousand dollars, amethyst silk with hand-sewn sequins. Now, looking down at the unconscious woman on the sofa, she felt sick.

"We need to go. Her husband will be home soon."

The doctor gathered up his instruments, wiped them down with the bloody towel, and stuck them inside his bag. "These towels need to be burned. You can't just throw them away."

"I know that," Lily snapped, glaring at him. Then she looked down in bewilderment. The floor tiles had begun to tremble beneath her feet.

A giant thunderclap echoed outside, an explosion of noise that made Lily cover her ears. Dimly, from the other end of the house, she heard glass shatter. The doctor had covered his ears as well, but Jonathan merely stood staring out the window, a faint smile on his face. For a few seconds the walls and doors continued to rattle, and then they were still. The Security alarm went off downtown, its distinctive bray loud enough to penetrate even the unconscious brain of the woman on the couch; she rolled and murmured in her sleep.

187

The doctor reached out to clasp Jonathan's hand. "The better world."

"The better world," Jonathan repeated.

Lily stared at him with wide eyes, a hundred tiny things coming together in her mind. Jonathan's encyclopedic knowledge of the public roadways. His inexplicable decision to keep Lily's secrets. His mysterious nighttime errands. Now Lily understood why the injured woman had rolled over the wall into this particular garden: because Jonathan was here. Jonathan, a separatist.

"I'll be back later, Mrs. M."

She nodded, watching him go. Deep down, she secretly hoped that the doctor would shake her hand as well, but he didn't, only gave her another distrustful look as he went. Lily was left staring at the woman on the couch, her mind already categorizing the various types of trouble she was in. If she were caught harboring a fugitive, she would be arrested, taken into custody. But even the dangers of arrest paled against what would happen if Greg found out. Greg called the separatists filth. He crowed whenever one of them was caught and watched with a grim but smug pleasure as they were executed on the government site.

I need to be smart now, Lily thought, staring at the woman on the couch. She wondered how it was possible to be terrified and, at the same time, deeply excited. She had gone to a party one weekend in high school, years before she had met Greg . . . she had been drunk, yes, but not so drunk that she didn't know what she was doing, and at the end of the night she had followed a boy into a darkened room and given up her virginity, just like that. Lily had never learned the boy's name, not even in the morning, but he had been shy and kind, and she had never regretted the incident, a moment of wild abandon that had seemed, in that time and place, to define her.

I'm here, she thought now, terrified but buoyant, as though she were floating in midair at a great height. *Really and truly here.*

It had been a long time.

When Greg walked through the door, Lily could already tell that it was going to be a bad night. His head was lowered like a bull's, and there were sweat stains under his arms. Although he'd never said so, Lily was fairly sure he was scared of flying. She could smell him all the way across the living room, a mixture of bitter fear-sweat and the sandalwood cologne he wore every day. The cologne smelled like a dead animal.

If he'd only been wearing it when I met him, Lily thought, biting her cheek against a sudden peal of awful laughter, *maybe I would have told him to get lost.*

She had taken a shower, straightened her hair, and put on her best dress, knowing that Greg would come home angry. The news sites had begun to carry the story almost immediately: three East Coast Security bases, one only six miles from New Canaan, had suffered some sort of cataclysmic chemical explosions in their jet proving grounds. The casualties had been low; the terrorists had clearly been aiming for equipment, not men, and they had succeeded. More than one hundred jets had been destroyed. Two civilian contractors from Lockheed had died as well, but they hadn't been workers, only management.

Only management. That sounded like something Lily's father would have said. Dad had been a chemical engineer, and by the end of his life he'd been management himself, making upward of five million a year. But his sympathies had always been with the workers. When Lily was very young, Dad even tried to organize a union at Dow, but that attempt had died with Frewell's Labor Facilitation Act. When quality control went to complete automation a few years later, there weren't even any workers to unionize anymore. Dad was well off, yes, but Lily knew he was unhappy. He had died two years ago, and even in those last hours, sitting beside his bed in the hospital, Lily could sense him longing, still dreaming of his more equitable world. She couldn't escape the feeling that she was the wrong daughter to be there, that it was Maddy he really wanted.

Greg dumped his coat on the sofa and went straight for the bar. Another bad sign. Lily noted the hunch of Greg's thick shoulders beneath his suit, the way his dark brows had knitted together over his fraternity-handsome face, the clench of his jaw as he dumped gin into a glass. Liquid sloshed over the rim onto the bar, but Greg didn't wipe it away. That would be her job, Lily thought, and was surprised to feel a dim throb of anger trying to break through her anxiety. The anger struggled briefly, then drowned.

Security sirens had been sounding in and out of their neighborhood all afternoon. They hadn't come to Lily's door, but they had gone to see Andrea Torres down the block. On the rare occasions when something happened in New Canaan, Andrea was always the first one questioned, because her husband was half Mexican and had once been arrested on suspicion of helping illegal immigrants cross state lines. But Andrea was a tiny, shy woman who could barely gather the courage to go down and get her own mail at the foot of her lawn. Lily always invited her to parties as a matter of form, since they lived in the same neighborhood, but Andrea never came.

Security was looking for an eighteen-year-old woman, five foot six, with blonde hair and green eyes. She had been hired as a civilian cleaner at Pryor Security Base three months ago, and today, somehow, she had made her way onto the jet fields and planted a bomb. She had taken gun-fire as she fled from the scene, and they believed she was wounded. Her name was Angela West.

No names, Lily had thought, almost reflexively. The woman in the nursery was not an Angela. Lily decided that she must have been mistaken about the scar on the woman's shoulder; no one would have been able to get Security clear-ance on a military base without a tag. The news sites said that the woman had known affiliations with the Blue Horizon, but no one seemed able to explain what domestic terrorists wanted with jets designed for transcontinental flight. The sites postulated that the separatists were mad dogs, simply going after the nearest military installation; everyone knew they were headquartered in New England somewhere, although neither Security nor private bounty hunters had been able to find a trace. The news said that naval bases were a convenient target.

Even to Lily, this explanation didn't ring quite true. Every few months Greg would invite a Security lieutenant named Arnie Welch over to dinner, and the last time, after a few drinks, Arnie had admitted mournfully that the Blue Horizon were efficient, well-organized terrorists; they tar-geted carefully selected goals and usually succeeded. Lily watched the online news because there was nothing else, but she knew the news sites were heavily censored. Security was determined to keep the size of the problem under wraps, but

Arnie could always be persuaded to talk on his third glass, and according to Arnie, the Blue Horizon was a much bigger problem than most civilians knew.

"You haven't asked me about my day."

Lily looked up and found Greg staring at her, a hint of petulance in his protruding lower lip. She got up from the armchair, taking a deep breath, and went and kissed him. He tasted like salami and olives. He'd already been drinking martinis on the plane.

"I'm sorry."

"I had a bad day," he told her, pouring himself a scotch.

Lily nodded with what she hoped looked like sympathy. Every day was a bad day for Greg. "Did the trip go all right?"

"It did, right until terrorists blew up every jet on the East Coast."

"I saw it on the news."

Greg looked down at her, irritated, and Lily realized that he had wanted to tell her about it himself. "I didn't know it was terrorists. I thought they were just accidents. Explosions."

"They weren't. Three saboteurs got Security clearances. One of them was even a woman! I don't know what the hell has happened to this country." Greg took a swig of whisky. "I have to go down to Washington in a couple of hours. The Pentagon will need more jets in a hurry, and they're going to want me to take care of it."

"That's good," Lily replied tentatively.

"No, it isn't!" he snapped. "The fucking separatists have bombed damn near every jet production facility on the East Coast over the past two years. Only two of them are still up and running; the rest are still being repaired. There's no way for us to come up with even a fraction of the jets the Pentagon is going to ask for. Every time we build something, the Blue Horizon blows it up!"

Lily wanted to ask questions about the woman, to see if Greg had more information, but she knew better. She'd seen Greg like this several times in the past year, and they always came with injuries: two black eyes and a night in the emergency room with a broken arm. The last time had been the worst; Greg had wanted to have sex almost as soon as he came in the door, and when Lily pushed him away, he'd slapped her. While he was fucking her, he had bitten her shoulder hard enough to draw blood. Lily shook off the memory, a quick, reflexive mental movement almost akin to a shiver. Greg always said he was sorry afterward, and there was usually a present of some kind attached, earrings or a dress. There was nothing to do but forget these things . . . until they happened again.

"Now I'll have to go down to Washington, stand in front of ten three-star and higher generals, and explain that what they want can't be done."

Lily tried for empathy, but none was forthcoming. In fact, she realized in astonishment, she almost wished Greg would hit her, as he plainly meant to at some point, and leave. She wanted to be back in the nursery. It had been nearly an hour, and the woman would be thirsty.

"What was her name?" Lily asked.

"Huh?" Greg had begun stroking the crack of her ass, something she hated. She willed herself to be still, not to brush his hand away.

"The terrorist, the woman. What was her real name? Did they find out?"

"Dorian Rice. She escaped from the Bronx Women's Correctional a year ago! You believe that?"

Lily did.

"I have just enough time for dinner before I leave."

Lily knew her role now: she was supposed to serve dinner, then ask if he wanted anything, if there was anything she could do for him. She sensed Greg waiting for her to ask; he knew this routine as well as she did. And yet Lily found herself unable to act.

If he decides he wants to screw, I'll go out of my fucking mind.

Greg's hand had stopped stroking her crack, a small favor that suddenly seemed worth whatever might happen next. Lily slipped out of his arms. "I'll go get you some food."

He grabbed her arm before she'd taken two steps toward the kitchen, his hand clamping hard. "What are you thinking about?"

"You." Lily wondered if Dorian Rice would be hungry, if she could eat solid food. She should have asked the doctor.

"No, you're not," Greg replied, his voice petulant. "You're thinking about something else. I don't like it when you do that."

"Do what?"

"I don't like it when you go somewhere else in your head. You're supposed to be here with me."

You fucking candyass. Lily bit down on the words, bit down hard. *Candyass* . . . it was Maddy's favorite insult; she'd applied it to at least half the people in Media by the time she was fourteen.

"Why don't you say you love me? I've had a lousy day."

Lily opened her mouth, even found her lips edging into an oval to shape the words.

I can't say it.

But what if he hits you?

Well, what if he fucking well does?

That was Maddy again. She and her perennially foul mouth seemed to have taken up residence in Lily's head. Greg's hand had coiled in her hair, and he yanked her head backward, not hard enough to be truly painful, but enough for a warning. Lily felt a muscle pop in her neck.

"Everything I do for you, Lil . . . don't you love me?"

She looked up into his eyes (brown, with just a hint of green) and gritted her teeth. It was going to be one of those nights; it had gone too far now for it not to be. But she might reduce the oncoming damage by playing her part.

At what price, Lil? Maddy asked. Lily could almost see her now, smirking, her blonde hair tied up into the Goth-girl pigtails she'd favored since she was about nine. Maddy had never met Greg; she'd disappeared two years before Lily first brought Greg home. And yet, even in the beginning, the good days, Lily had always known deep down what Maddy would have thought.

Greg tugged harder now, pulling Lily's hair, hurting her scalp, and she opened her mouth, not knowing if she meant to say it or not. Even if Dorian couldn't eat solid food, she would need something; maybe Lily could bring her some soup. Chicken broth; that should be safe enough. That was what invalids always ate in books. Lily should give Dorian some books, too, from her hidden stash, so that she wouldn't be bored.

"You do love me, don't you Lil?"

What if she can't read?

"Lil? Say you love me."

"No."

The word was out before she could pull it back, and Greg flung her across the living room, into the teak cabinet that housed the screen. Lily's forehead hit first, splitting open and leaving a smear of blood on the dark wood. The cut didn't hurt so much, but then her midsection also ran into the corner of the cabinet, knocking the wind out of her. It felt like someone had kicked her intestines in. Lily opened her mouth but couldn't speak; her breath was stuck somewhere in her throat, trying to get down into her lungs, allowing only a series of hoarse gasps. Blood trickled into her left eye, and when she looked up, she saw Greg approaching through a haze of scarlet. The rug was scattered with drops of blood.

"What did you say to me?"

Good question. Lily had put a lock on her throat a long time ago, so that everything would need to pass through a filter before coming out. There was a very real lock there now, a physical one; she struggled to draw breath. But the other lock, the one that mattered . . . it had broken wide open. She wiped blood from her eye and braced herself as Greg bent down toward her. His face was red with anger, and the corners of his eyes had squeezed down into deep pockets, but the eyes themselves . . . they were empty.

"Want to apologize?"

Part of her did. If she apologized, and did it well, he would fuck her and then leave her alone for the rest of the night. If she wasn't such a good actress, he might give her a few more sporting injuries and then fuck her anyway.

Going to be a bad night.

He was about to hit her again. His fist hadn't even clenched, but over the past year Lily had developed good radar for such things. She sensed the oncoming blow, perhaps even before the impulse had left Greg's own brain. She grabbed the leg of his grey suit pants with one bloody hand and pulled herself up into a crouch before he could jump backward. Her stomach was still hitching, but as she straightened and stood, everything relaxed inside her and she drew a pure, clean breath of air that seemed to fill her up.

"You got blood on my suit." Greg's tone was astonished, as though Lily had defied gravity. "Now I'll have to change."

"How terrible for you."

He grabbed her by the hair and threw her out of the corner. Lily tripped over the coffee table, barking her shin and landing in a pile of government flyers that flew everywhere, scattering across the living room floor. She tried to shove herself up, but Greg was behind her, pushing her back down as if she weighed nothing, pinning her against the coffee table. He pulled up her dress, and Lily fought harder, suddenly understanding what was going to happen next. She thought of the woman in the nursery, the bullet hole in her stomach, how brave she'd been . . . she held the idea tightly as Greg ripped her panties off and shoved inside her. He'd planted his arm in the small of her back to keep her still, but Lily hitched involuntarily as she felt something tear deep inside her on the left side. A groan was climbing up the back of her throat, but she bit down on the skin of her hand. Greg would like it if she made a hurt sound. There was no logic to this, it was simply something she knew.

Movement from over her shoulder caught her eye. She looked backward, past Greg's arm pinning her neck, and saw an upside-down Jonathan standing in the front hall behind her, frozen, his eyes wide. His car keys were still in his hand.

Shame crashed down on Lily. She did her best to hide the bruises, knowing very well that she wasn't fooling anyone. Jonathan knew the score; he had taken her to the emergency room when Greg broke her arm. But this was much worse, and everything in Lily screamed that it had to be hidden. She couldn't watch it reflected in anyone's eyes but her own.

Jonathan took a step forward, reaching beneath his jacket and pulling out his gun.

Lily shook her head frantically. Jonathan could probably stop Greg, even without the gun; Greg was bigger, but Jonathan was combat-trained. But then what would happen? Greg would fire Jonathan without a thought, hire Lily a new bodyguard. Jonathan might even go to prison. And then what would happen to the woman in the nursery?

Or to me?

Jonathan took another silent step forward, raising the gun, his eyes fixed on Greg.

Lily drew a hitching breath and gasped, "No!"

This only served to egg Greg on; he began to thrust faster. But it had also stopped Jonathan. He paused, gun in hand, on the bottom step into the living room.

Lily gave him a small smile through gritted teeth, a smile meant to tell him that she would get through it, that she was looking beyond the next few minutes. She rolled her eyes to the left, toward the nursery. The separatist.

Jonathan hesitated for a long moment, eyes gleaming and hand clutching the banister. Then he tucked the gun back inside his jacket and disappeared into the shadows of the hallway, as silently as he'd come.

Two hours later, Lily hobbled slowly toward the nursery. She'd meant to check on the woman much sooner, but in the end she broke down and took a hot bath. Even after an hour soaking in the tub, she could barely walk. She would have taken some aspirin and gone to bed, but she didn't like the idea of the injured woman sitting in the dark nursery alone. Lily didn't know whether Jonathan had gone to check on her; he appeared to have disappeared from the property again.

Greg had gone to Washington for his crisis meeting at the Pentagon. Above the stone wall around the garden, Lily could still see the orange bloom of flames, the thick smoke that obscured the moon. They hadn't been able to get the fire under control yet, and Pryor was still burning. Had Dorian Rice built the bomb herself? Where had she learned that kind of thing, young as she was? The Blue Horizon recruited many veterans, both men and women, who had returned from the oil wars to find themselves unemployed. But Dorian looked too young to have done a single tour of duty.

When Lily reached the nursery, she slid the dimmer switch on the wall panel up slowly, not wanting to scare the woman if she was asleep. But Dorian was awake, lying on the couch and staring at the ceiling, looking lucid for the first time. Lily set a bowl of broth and a glass of water on the table in front of her, and Dorian nodded thanks. She had sharp eyes; they tracked Lily's every movement and grimace as she limped across the room.

"Looks like we've both been through it today," Dorian remarked. "Where are we?"

"My nursery." Lily reached the loose tile, but now she faced a logistical problem: squatting was simply not going to happen, not tonight. She was reduced to pawing at the tile with her toes. After an interminable period, during which she could feel the young woman's eyes pinned to her back, she managed to work a toenail beneath the edge of the tile and flip it up and over. She bent one knee and stuck her other foot out, gracefully, like a ballet dancer, flipped two books out of the hole, and pushed them over to Dorian, who picked them up off the floor and flipped through them appreciatively.

"Where's a woman like you get real books?"

Lily bit her lip, not sure how much to tell. What if this woman were taken for interrogation?

Dorian grinned, showing a missing incisor. "You're already in plenty of trouble, honey."

"There are a few other wives in the neighborhood who like to read. One of them has family in California with some kind of collection. They bring her books whenever they come to visit, and we pass them around." Michele could also procure pharmaceutical-grade painkillers for anyone who needed them. Lily wished she had some now.

"Does anyone know I'm here?"

"Jonathan does. He went to let some other people know."

"I won't be here long, then."

"You can stay as long as you like."

"Dangerous for you. I bet Security's all over this town."

"Yes."

"When they don't find me, they'll start searching houses."

Something new to worry about. But Dorian didn't look particularly worried, so Lily shrugged and tried to look non-chalant as she sat down carefully in her favorite armchair. She tightened up everything in preparation for the landing, gritting her teeth, but when her ass met the cushion, it still started all over again. She should have taken the aspirin.

Dorian yawned. "I'm getting sleepy. If you decide to call Security, do me a favor and shoot me in the head first."

"I won't call anyone."

"Good. Because I'm not going back into custody."

Lily swallowed. She thought again of the blank door, that day in Manhattan, the group of uniformed men hustling the man in the suit inside. She had never found a single article or news report about what went on behind that door. "What's it like?"

"What?"

"Custody."

"Oh, it's wonderful. They serve you steak and whisky, and when you go to bed, there's a little mint waiting on your pillow."

"I'm only curious."

"Why do you care?"

"My sister—" But Lily found she couldn't finish that thought. Did she really want to know what had happened to Maddy behind that door? "Nobody talks about it."

Dorian shrugged. "It's bad. For women especially."

"Women have a bad time everywhere."

"Oh, get off it, rich lady. Sure, you walked in here limping and shuffling, but we've all done that walk. You should be thankful he was the only one."

Lily swallowed again. The throb between her legs, the raw-rubbed skin, suddenly felt much worse.

"I need to sleep. You can go."

"I'll stay until you're asleep."

"There's no need for that."

Lily leaned back in the armchair, crossing her arms.

"Fine. Christ." Dorian closed her eyes. "Wake me up if he comes."

Who? Lily almost asked, then answered herself: *No names.* She lit the small scented candle that sat on the table beside the armchair, then whispered to the house to turn off the overhead light. Shadows flickered on the walls, highlighting Lily as a matronly figure, an old woman in her rocking chair.

We've all done that walk.

She watched Dorian fall asleep. Her mind kept on trying to turn to Greg, to go over the evening, but Lily wouldn't allow it. She would think about these things tomorrow, in the light of day . . . not now. But the images, the sensations, kept on coming, until she thought she might bolt from the chair and scream.

What would Maddy do?

But that was easy. Maddy wouldn't have shied away from remembering. Maddy would have gone all the way through it. Maddy had always been tough, and Lily, who had been delighted at the idea of a younger sister, quickly became disenchanted when she realized that Maddy was never going to want to play any of the same games as herself: no dress-up, no beauty parlor, no cooking in the fake kitchen that sat in the corner of the living room. Maddy liked baseball, insisted on wearing pants. By the time she was twelve she was the best pitcher in the neighborhood, so good that the neighborhood boys not only allowed her to play in their impromptu baseball league but always picked her first.

But being a tomboy was only part of it. Maddy was much smaller than Lily, tiny and pixie-like, but she had no tolerance for bullshit. She was unable to keep silent, even when silence would save her trouble or pain. Their elementary school had had two bullies, and by the time Maddy started sixth grade, she had dealt with both of them. In eighth grade, she took several suspensions for arguing with the canned government information being peddled by her history teacher. Maddy was born to be a defender of the weak, of the helpless. Maddy was the first to tell Lily that millions of people were living outside the fences that surrounded Media, people who didn't have enough food, people who owed so much money that they would never be free of their debts. Until then, Lily had had no idea that not everyone lived the way their family did. Dad told her the truth as well, but many years later, when Lily was fifteen. Even though Maddy was the youngest, Dad had clearly told her the truth of things long before.

The woman, Dorian, moaned in her sleep, jerking Lily back to the present. Drops of sweat gleamed on Dorian's forehead in the candlelight. Lily cast around and found the bowl of melted ice she had brought up earlier. She hauled herself from the chair, wincing, dipped a towel in the cold water and wrung it out, and then placed it gently on Dorian's forehead. The towel turned warm almost immediately, and Lily dipped it again, replaced it. She should get Dorian some aspirin. But no, the doctor had left some pills for fever. Lily seemed unable to feel sure of anything. She'd been at her father's sickbed, but she didn't know how to take care of sick people. The nurses and machines had done all of the work. Toward the end, when Dad was pumped full of drugs, he had asked for Maddy, and Lily couldn't bring herself to explain where Maddy was, to make him go through it again. She had told him that Maddy was down the hall, talking to the doctor, but Dad kept on asking, right until the end. They had a special bond, Dad and Maddy, and because that bond seemed to have always been there, Lily had no time to develop resentment. Dad took Maddy to Phillies games in the summer, and he would sit with her in his study at night, the two of them reading endless books together. Even though Maddy was two years younger than Lily, she was the first to learn to read on her own. This was the crucial difference between the two of them, and the crucial similarity between Maddy and Dad: Maddy cared deeply about things.

"If we could be better people," she would say, "if we could

care about each other as much as we do about ourselves, think about it, Lily! Think what the world would be!"

Lily would nod, for this sounded good in theory, but Lily had no such deep drives; anything she cared about was discarded as uninteresting two months later. Maddy's passions were exhausting. They demanded not only interest but commitment and effort. Sometimes Lily had wished that Maddy would just think about boys and clothes and music, as all of Lily's friends did, as Lily did herself.

The candle flame flickered sharply, and Lily looked up at the walls, where the shadows of her familiar nursery furniture had turned grotesque in the thin candlelight. The house was supposed to be airtight, to protect against a chemical attack, but she felt a draft from somewhere, chilling her toes. The cold had not woken Dorian, though; she slept on peacefully, her head lolling sideways on the pillow. For a moment she looked so much like Maddy that Lily could almost believe this woman was her sister . . . but then the shadows shifted again, and the illusion was broken.

That Maddy would be politically active was almost a foregone conclusion. Their childhood was not a good time for anyone to be political, but Lily had only realized this years later, when she learned about the Frewell administration. One of Lily's English teachers, Mr. Hawthorne, had disappeared when she was halfway through eighth grade, and Lily had not questioned the school's announcement that Mr. Hawthorne had moved to California. Only in college did she remember that Mr. Hawthorne had been prone to sweeping pronouncements about the impact of religion on society, that he often assigned books with this theme. Back then, federal editing of individual works of literature was still new, and Mr. Hawthorne had always managed to secure the original versions for their readers. But one day he was simply gone, replaced with a substitute who used the approved editions. Mr. Hawthorne vanished perhaps two months before Maddy did, and Lily, who had barely cared at the time, often wondered now—again, in those moments before sleep, when everything took on an exaggerated importance and even fever dreams seemed reasonable—how he had gotten caught. A student, probably . . . a student as thoughtless as Lily, talking because she loved to talk, meaning no harm.

She was being watched.

Lily knew it suddenly, in every nerve ending. Someone was standing just inside the door to the patio, looking down at her. Greg, back early, here to check on her, to see what his doll was up to. Greg didn't come into the nursery, but that wouldn't be the only line crossed tonight, would it? Lily would look up and see his grinning face, his bully's cheerfulness, and she would have nothing left.

She made herself look up, and relief nearly choked her; it wasn't Greg. The man had entered the room without making a sound, and now he leaned against the closed door, watching her. He was perhaps forty, a tall man with a military bearing that showed clearly despite his relaxed posture. He wore all black. His blond hair was cropped almost brutally short, but it suited the face beneath: a severe, clean-shaven face, all angles and hard curves.

"How is she?"

Lily blinked at his accent, which wasn't American. "She's fine. She's got a fever, but the doctor said that might happen. I'll stay with her until it breaks."

The man inspected her closely, studying her face. "You're Mrs. Mayhew."

Lily nodded slowly, identifying the accent: English. She

hadn't heard an English voice in a long time. It had been more than ten years since Security had closed the border to the UK and expelled all of the Brits; what was he still doing here?

"Have you ever seen me before?" he asked.

"No."

"You sure?"

"Yes." She was sure. She would have remembered this man; he exerted pull, a magnetism that Lily could feel all the way across the room. He lifted a black canvas bag, smaller than the doctor's but still clearly medical; Lily heard the light ring of metal instruments inside when he set it on the table.

"I don't know why you helped her, but thank you. Unexpected help is the best kind."

"Why is it unexpected? Because I'm rich?"

"That, and your husband."

For a moment, Lily could only think of the scene in the living room. Then she realized that he must be talking about Greg's job. Greg didn't work for the government, not exactly, but by now, Security practically was the government; in the eyes of the Blue Horizon, Greg was just as bad as any politician. The man's eyes were beginning to hypnotize her; with an effort, Lily turned back to Dorian. "Why did she blow up the naval base? It seems so pointless."

"Nothing we do is pointless. You only judge because you can't see the whole picture."

"I don't judge."

"Of course you do. Why wouldn't you? This is a lofty perch you sit on."

Lily flushed, and she suddenly found herself wanting to contradict him, to explain about Greg, to tell this man how the perch wasn't so lofty at all. But she couldn't say any of that to a stranger. She couldn't even say it to her friends.

"Boss?" Dorian asked from the couch.

"There you are, love."

Dorian smiled, a sleepy smile that turned her face into that of a child. "Knew you'd come. Did it work?"

"Beautifully. Months before they can fly again. You did a good job."

Dorian's eyes brightened.

"Sleep, Dori. Heal up."

Dorian closed her eyes. Lily didn't know what to make of this exchange. Clear affection between the two of them, yes, but what man sent the woman he loved to plant explosives, to be shot?

"I have to get her out of here," the man murmured, his eyes troubled.

"She can stay as long as she needs to."

"Until you tire of the novelty and turn her in."

"I won't!" Lily snapped back, stung. "I would never do that."

"Forgive me my skepticism."

"The doctor said she shouldn't be moved!" Lily insisted, alarmed, for the man had risen from his armchair, and she saw that he meant to pick Dorian up and carry her out. Lily sprang from her own armchair, then hissed in pain as all of her separate wounds woke up at once.

"Seen some rough handling, haven't we, Mrs. Mayhew? Who's done that to your face?"

"None of your business."

He nodded, his eyes bright, and Lily saw that he already knew . . . maybe not everything, but more than she wanted him to.

"Don't take her away, please."

"Why not?"

Lily cast around for more of the doctor's words. "There might be roadblocks."

"There are three roadblocks around New Canaan, Mrs. Mayhew. They're no impediment to me."

"Please." Lily was appalled to find herself near tears. The entire day seemed to have crashed down on her all at once: the horrible surgery, Greg, Maddy ... and now this man, who wanted to take Dorian away before Lily could atone for anything. "Please let her stay."

"What's your interest here, Mrs. Mayhew? Might as well tell me; I'll know if you're lying. Are you looking to collect a reward?"

"No!"

He bent toward Dorian again. Lily fumbled for words, for any excuse, but she came up with nothing. Only the truth.

"I turned my sister in."

He looked up sharply. "What?"

Lily tried to stop, but the words came tumbling out. "My sister. I turned her in to Security, eight years ago. I didn't mean to, but I did. Dorian looks just like her."

He studied her closely for a moment, his eyes narrowed. "What's your maiden name, Mrs. Mayhew?"

"Freeman."

"Good name for a separatist. What did your sister do?"

"Nothing." Lily closed her eyes, feeling tears threatening to swamp her again. "She had a pamphlet in her room. I didn't know what it was at the time."

"You showed it to someone?"

Lily nodded, and the tears began to slide down her cheeks. "My friends. One of them had a father who worked for

Security, but I never thought about that. I just wanted to know what Maddy was doing."

"How old were you?"

"Seventeen. Maddy was fifteen."

"Did they come for her?"

Lily nodded again, unable to speak. She had no way to explain that morning, the way it never changed in her memory no matter how badly she wished it to: Lily, standing by her locker, surrounded by her own friends, all of them glued to their phones; Maddy, coming out of a classroom thirty feet away; and just around the corner, not yet seen, the four Security officers, closing in. Sometimes Lily had dreams, hopeless nightmares in which she reached for Maddy, grabbed her arm at the last minute and helped her duck into a classroom, behind a door, out the window. But even her dreaming self knew it was futile, that any moment the four men in black uniforms would come around the corner, that two of them would grab each of Maddy's arms and escort her down the hallway, that Lily's last glimpse of her sister would be a flash of blonde pigtails before the doors closed.

At dinner the three of them, Mom and Dad and Lily, had waited for Maddy to turn up. They had waited through the night as well, and into the next morning. Dad got on the phone with every important person he knew, and Mom cried almost nonstop, but Lily was silent, some deep and awful part of her already beginning to put two and two together, to understand what she had done. Dad was only an engineer; his clout was nowhere near strong enough to get a prisoner released, especially not one with suspected separatist ties. They had waited for days, and then weeks, but Maddy had never come home; she had vanished into the vast, dark mechanism of Security. The doctors said that Dad had died of cancer, but Lily knew the truth. Dad had been dying for a long time, dying slowly and horribly of Maddy's disappearance years before. Mom didn't want to talk about it, didn't even want to think about it. She told friends that Maddy had run away, and when Lily tried to talk about it, Mom would simply ignore her, turning the conversation into a different path. Mom's attitude was maddening, but Dad's grief had been terminal.

I killed him too, Lily often thought to herself, in those defenseless moments right before sleep. *I didn't mean to, but I killed my father.*

She looked up at the man in front of her, expecting judgment. But his face was neutral.

"It's been eating you up, I see."

Lily nodded.

"And you're using Dorian as . . . what? Self-punishment?"

"Fuck you!" Lily hissed. "I'm not the one who sent her to blow up a jet field."

"She volunteered," he replied mildly.

"Please. Your group recruits people with nowhere else to go."

"True, most of them have nowhere else. But that's not why they volunteer."

"Then why?"

He leaned forward, his remarkably light eyes gleaming in the candlelight. He steepled his hands, and Lily saw that his fingers were scarred and burned in several places. Whatever she had imagined when she thought of the Blue Horizon, it wasn't this man.

"Tell me, Mrs. Mayhew, have you ever dreamed of a better world?"

"Who hasn't?"

"Anyone who profits by keeping the world as it is. You and your husband, for instance."

"I don't profit by it," Lily muttered, wiping the tears from her cheeks.

"Maybe not," he replied, his eyes going to the cut on her forehead. "Profit is a relative thing. But regardless, there's a better world out there. I see it all the—"

The Englishman broke off abruptly, tilting his head to one side. A moment later, Lily heard it as well: a siren, no more than a couple of streets away.

"Time for me to be going." He began digging in the medical bag on the table. "I thought I'd need this, but the doctor seems to have done well. Did he leave antibiotics?"

Lily nodded. "I'm supposed to give her one shot per day."

"Good. Don't go shopping and forget."

Lily's cheeks colored, but she didn't take the bait. "She can stay?"

"Until I find a safe way to get her out. A few days at most." He pulled a small white packet from the bag and held it out to Lily. "Take this. Pour a bit in the bath for a few days."

"Take it for what?"

He stared down at her, his face unreadable. "You put on a good show, Mrs. Mayhew, but men like your husband rarely limit the damage to the outside."

Lily took the packet, trying not to touch his fingers. "I suppose you think I have options."

"Oh, I know you don't." He closed the flap of his medical bag. "But don't lose all hope of the better world. It's out there, so close we can almost touch it."

"What better world?"

The Englishman paused, deliberating. Lily had thought

211

that his eyes were grey, but now she saw that they were actually bright silver, the color of moonlight on water.

"Picture a world where there are no rich and poor. No luxury, but everyone is fed and clothed and educated and cared for. God controls nothing. Books aren't forbidden. Women aren't the lower class. The color of your skin, the circumstances of your birth, these things don't matter. Kindness and humanity are everything. There are no guns, no surveillance, no drugs, no debt, and greed holds no sway at all."

Lily fought against his voice, but not hard enough, for she glimpsed his better world for a moment, clear and limned in shades of blue and green: a village of small wooden houses, of pure kindness, beside a river, surrounded by trees.

Wake up, Lily!

She dug her fingernails into her palms. "I'm told that pipe dreams go better with lubricant."

His shoulders shook with silent amusement. "That's late night, Mrs. Mayhew. But you did ask the question."

He opened the patio door and stood framed for a moment in the doorway, listening to the night. He was taller than Greg, Lily saw now, but whereas Greg was still bulky from his football years, this man was agile, with the lithe muscles of a runner or a swimmer. When he turned back to her, she noticed a long, jagged scar running down the side of his neck.

"Do you want to help us further?"

"Help you how?"

"We can always use information. Anything you can pass along via Jonathan would be helpful."

"How did Jonathan join up with you?"

"That's his story to tell."

"How did you get over the New Canaan wall?"

"There are ways through every barrier, Mrs. Mayhew."

Lily blinked, stunned by the calm assurance of this statement. "Who are you?"

She knew what she would get: no names. The Englishman stepped through the door, and Lily ignored him, staring resolutely at the sleeping woman on the sofa. He had allowed Dorian to stay, but Lily felt as though she had already lost something. Soon they would both be gone, Dorian and this man, and what would Lily have then? A lifetime with Greg, an eternity of nights like tonight. This brief glimpse of another life would make that future a thousand times worse. When the man spoke, his reply was so unexpected that Lily froze in her chair, and by the time she looked up, he had already vanished into the night.

"My name is William Tear."

BOOK II

CHAPTER 6

EWEN

Even small gestures of kindness have the potential to reap enormous rewards. Only the shortsighted man believes otherwise.
—*The Glynn Queen's Words*, AS COMPILED BY FATHER TYLER

The Cadarese ambassador, Ajmal Kattan, was a charmer: tall, sharp-witted, and handsome, with almond-colored skin and a blinding white smile. Kelsea liked him immediately, despite Mace's warning that this was exactly the sort of ambassador the King of Cadare always sent to women: smooth and plausible and seductive. Kattan's Tear was imperfect, but even his accent was engaging, riddled with pauses before long words and a sharp drop on the penultimate vowel. He had brought Kelsea a beautiful chess set carved from marble, kings and rooks and bishops with intricately detailed faces, and she accepted the gift happily. After their return from the Argive, she had sent several Keep servants to clean out Carlin and Barty's cottage, and among assorted other things, they had brought back Carlin's old chess set. Both Arliss and Mace were good players; Arliss could beat Kelsea two times of three. But Carlin's set was old, whittled—by Barty, no doubt—of plain wood and beginning to show its wear. It had great sentimental value to Kelsea, but the new set would be more durable for play.

Mace had warned Kelsea that the Cadarese placed great value on appearances, and as such, she had not wanted to conduct this meeting in the large central room of the Queen's Wing that usually served for such functions. At her urging, Mace had finally relented and moved the throne back down to the massive audience chamber several floors below. When not filled with people, the chamber felt ridiculously cavernous, so they had also thrown this audience open to the public. Tear nobles had more or less stopped attending Kelsea's audiences once they realized that no gifts would be dispensed from the throne, and Mace and Kelsea had decided on a simple, fair system: the first five hundred people who came to the Keep Gate could attend the audience, so long as they submitted to a search for weapons. Kelsea had found that clothing was a fairly reliable index of wealth; some of the people who stood in front of her were clearly of the entrepreneurial class, probably dealing in lumber if not something less legal. But the majority of the audience was poor, and Kelsea had the regrettable thought that most of them had come here for entertainment. Her first few public audiences had featured quite a bit of talk and some occasional catcalling from the crowd, but Mace had taken care of that, announcing that anyone who captured his attention could look forward to a private conference. Now Kelsea barely heard a peep.

"My master begs that you will honor him with a visit," the ambassador said.

"Perhaps one day," Kelsea replied, seeing Mace frown. "At the moment, I have too much to do."

"Indeed you have the full plate. You have provoked the Ageless Queen. My master admires your bravery."

"Has your master never provoked her?"

"No. His father did, and received a painful reminder. Now we pay twice as much in glass and horses."

"Perhaps that's the difference. We were paying in humans." A moment later Kelsea remembered that the Cadarese also sent slaves to Mortmesne, but the ambassador did not seem to take offense.

"Yes, we've heard this as well. You forbid human traffic within your borders. My master is greatly entertained."

There was an insult wrapped in the last statement, but Kelsea made no attempt to unpack it. She needed help from the Cadarese king, and she could not offend the ambassador by questioning him in front of his aides, but neither did she have time to engage in the lengthy and circuitous prelude to serious discussion that was fashionable in Cadare. This morning, a message had arrived from Hall, with bad news: General Ducarte had taken command of the Mort army. Everyone in the Queen's Wing seemed to know a horror story about Ducarte, and although the border villages had already been evacuated and Bermond was now beginning to clear out the eastern Almont, even a successful evacuation would accomplish nothing if Ducarte got to New London. The city's defenses were weak. The eastern side had a high wall, but that wall was too close to the Caddell River, built on watery ground. The western side of the city had nothing. Her mother had trusted the natural defense of the Clayton Mountains to protect the west against a prolonged siege, but Kelsea was not so sanguine. She wanted a western wall around the city, but Mace estimated that they had less than two months until the Mort reached the city. Even if she conscripted every stonemason in New London, they would never build it in time.

But Cadare had many masons, the best stoneworkers in the New World. Even if the King was unwilling to supplement the Tear army with his own forces, perhaps Kelsea could get him to lend her some of his craftsmen. At the very least, she needed him to stop sending horses to Mortmesne; there was a saying, only lightly exaggerated, that a sick Cadarese mare could outrun a healthy Tear yearling. Better horses weren't much use to the Mort up in the Border Hills, but once they got down into the Almont, superior cavalry would be a crushing advantage. She needed these negotiations to bear fruit.

"Shall we get down to business, Ambassador?"

Kattan's eyebrows rose. "You move quickly, Majesty."

"I'm a busy woman."

Kattan settled in his chair, looking a bit disgruntled. "My master wishes to discuss an alliance."

Kelsea's heart leapt. A murmur ran through the audience chamber, but Mace did not react; he was too busy staring at the ambassador with narrowed, suspicious eyes.

"My master likewise wishes to reduce his tribute to the Mort," Kattan continued. "But neither Cadare nor the Tearling is strong enough to do so alone."

"I agree. What would the terms of this alliance be?"

"Slowly, slowly, Majesty!" Kattan insisted, waving his hands, and that was Kelsea's real clue that she would not like what was coming: the ambassador felt the need to wend his way into it. "My master recognizes your bravery in defying the Mort, and would reward you accordingly."

"Reward me how?"

"By making you first among his wives."

Kelsea froze, dumbfounded, hearing several of her Guard mutter around her. She swallowed hard and managed to reply, though it felt as though her throat were full of moths. "How many wives does your King have?"

"Twenty-three, Majesty."

"Are they all Cadarese?"

"All but two, Majesty. Those two are Mort, gifts from the Ageless Queen."

"What are the ages of these wives?"

The ambassador looked away and cleared his throat. "I am not sure, Majesty."

"I see." Kelsea wanted to kick herself. She should have seen it coming. Mace had told her that the Cadarese were isolationists, that their assistance would come with heavy strings. But she didn't think that even Mace had foreseen such an offer. She scrambled to think of a counterproposal. "What is the value of being the first wife?"

"You sit immediately beside the master at table. You have first pick of all gifts delivered to the palace. Once you have produced a healthy son, you have the right to refuse the master's attentions if you wish."

Coryn had begun tapping his fingers on his sword. Elston appeared to be thinking of creative ways to disembowel the ambassador, and Kibb placed a warning hand on his shoulder. But Mace . . . Kelsea was glad that Kattan could not see Mace's expression, for there was murder there.

"What of an alliance without marriage?"

"My master is not interested in such an alliance."

"Why not?"

"The King of Cadare cannot have an alliance on an equal

footing with a woman. Marriage ensures that Your Majesty is seen to submit her will to my master in all things."

Mace moved in sharply, blocking off Kelsea's right side. She blinked in surprise, for she had sensed no threat from the ambassador or his guards. It took a few moments for her to see it: Mace had actually moved to protect the ambassador. Some of Kelsea's anger ebbed away then; she smiled at Mace, and felt a rush of affection when he smiled back.

Turning back to Kattan, she asked, "Would your master expect to share my throne?"

"It is difficult for one man to govern two kingdoms, Majesty. Rather, my master would appoint a"—Kattan paused for a moment, searching for language—"castellan, yes? A castellan, to oversee your throne on his behalf."

"And I would live in Cadare?"

"Yes, Majesty, with my master's other wives."

Elston had begun to crack his knuckles now, slowly and obtrusively, one at a time. Kattan, clearly sensing the thin ice beneath him, did not elaborate on the further joys of living in the King's harem, but merely waited silently for Kelsea's response.

"This is the only offer you bring?"

"My master has not empowered me to make any other offer, Majesty."

Kelsea smiled gently. If she were the ruler Carlin had been trying to train, she might have taken Kattan's deal, distasteful as it was. But she could not. An entire life seemed to flash before her eyes, the life of a Cadarese concubine outlined clearly, before she pushed the thought out of her head. If it would save the Tearling, she would gladly give up her own life, stick a knife in her heart tomorrow. But this . . . she could not.

"I refuse."

"Yes, Majesty." Kattan looked up, his black eyes twinkling with sudden amusement. "I cannot say that I am surprised."

"Why not?"

"We have heard all about Your Majesty, even in Cadare. You have a will."

"Then why offer?"

"It is my job, Majesty, to carry the master's wishes and offers. Incidentally, this offer will remain open until my master withdraws it." The ambassador leaned a few inches closer, lowering his voice. "But for your sake, I am glad that you do not accept. You are not such a woman, to be content in my master's *harim*."

Kelsea met his smiling eyes and felt her mouth twitch back. She found him attractive, she realized . . . attractive in a way that only the Fetch had been before. It was a wonderful feeling, almost like freedom. "Will you be staying with us long, Lord Ambassador?"

"Sadly, Majesty, I am to report back to my master as soon as negotiations are concluded. We will beg your hospitality for one night only."

"A pity." But Kelsea knew it was probably for the best. She already spent far too much time thinking about the Fetch, and another handsome man would only be a further distraction. Deep in her mind, a small voice rose in protest: would she never deserve any pleasure for herself? But Kelsea smothered it easily. Whenever she needed a cautionary tale, her mother was always there, waiting in the back of her mind.

Mace cleared his throat, reminding Kelsea of her duties as a hostess: Cadarese hospitality had well-defined rules, and they would expect to share at least one meal with her before they left.

"Well, gentlemen, we have—" Kelsea began, but she got no further, for the doors at the other end of the throne room suddenly exploded in commotion.

Kelsea's guards drew in tight. Her memory doubled back to that terrible day of her crowning, and the muscles of her shoulder tensed automatically, bunching up beneath her scar. Something was happening at the doors; a group of Queen's Guards and Tear army had coalesced into a huddle. Several men shouted to be heard.

"What is it?" Mace called across the room.

No one answered him. An argument was clearly going on, army men bickering with the Guard. But finally a group won through, two men hauling a third between them. They approached the throne slowly, haltingly, followed closely by soldiers and guards.

"Good Christ," Mace muttered. Kelsea, whose eyesight was not good, had to wait a few moments, but as the three men came closer, her mouth dropped open.

On the left was her Jailor, Ewen, his open, friendly face now scuffed with bruises, one eye swollen shut. On the right was Javel, the prisoner from the Argive. His wrists were manacled, but he appeared to be unharmed.

Between them, nearly unconscious, bound with thick rope and bleeding from multiple wounds, was Arlen Thorne.

Ewen recognized the man the moment he saw him. He didn't need the silence at the top of the dungeon stairs, where two soldiers were supposed to be on duty at all times. He didn't need the swift intake of breath by the woman in Cell Two or the way her eyes blazed as she stared up through the bars. He didn't even need the glimpse of the knife tucked behind the man's back. A tall, starving-thin man with bright blue eyes, the Queen had said . . . and when Ewen looked up and saw the scarecrow, he simply knew.

Still, he was determined to handle things the right way. The scarecrow had a knife, and Ewen had three prisoners to think about. He was big enough to knock the scarecrow flying, and it was good to know that he would need no weapons to do so. But he also knew that he was big enough to accidentally kill the scarecrow with such a blow. Da had always warned Ewen to remember his own size, and the Queen, Ewen reminded himself, wanted this man alive.

"Good afternoon," the scarecrow greeted Ewen, leaning over the desk.

Javel, the prisoner in Cell Three, sat bolt upright from his cot.

"How can I help you, sir?" Ewen asked. From the corner of his eye he saw that his other two prisoners, Brenna and Bannaker, had moved up to stand at the bars. The torchlight played cruelly over the now-healing welts that covered Bannaker's body, but his face was sly and expectant.

"The Queen has ordered me to transfer all three of your prisoners to the central New London Jail," the scarecrow told Ewen. He had a low, somehow unpleasant voice, and Ewen didn't even question how this man had gotten past the soldiers at the top of the stairs. He guessed they were already dead. "I'm to escort them myself."

"This is the first time I've heard about a transfer," Ewen replied. "Give me a moment to note it in the book."

He pulled out the logbook and began to ink up his pen, trying to think. Da had always told Ewen that he had the ability to be clever; it would just take some time and work. After Ewen finished with the book, the scarecrow would expect him to get up and walk over to the cells with his keys.

If Ewen could only get the scarecrow to walk in front, it would be easy to disarm him . . . but something told Ewen not to be too sure even of that. The scarecrow was skinny, yes, but he looked quick. He wore the black uniform of the Tear army. If he was a soldier, he might have another knife hidden somewhere.

"Your name, sir?" Ewen asked.

"Captain Frost."

Ewen wrote as slowly as possible, his face screwed up as though in concentration. He couldn't simply launch himself at the scarecrow while seated at the table; the table itself would flip over and act as a shield, if it didn't kill the man outright. Ewen also had to make sure the man's knife didn't get into any of the cells. Da had told Ewen that prisoners could use any sharp object to pick a lock.

Javel had moved up to stand at the bars of Cell Three, and Ewen, who had grown accustomed to the man's dull, expressionless face, was shocked at what he saw there now. Javel's expression was that of a hungry dog. His eyes, deep and dark, were glued to the scarecrow's back.

There could be no more delays. Ewen pushed back his chair and got up, pulling the ring of keys from his belt. He came around the right edge of the table, where it would be only natural for the scarecrow to move out of his way, to go in front of him. But the scarecrow merely backed away a single step and pressed up against the wall, sweeping a hand toward the cellblock.

"After you, Master Jailor."

Ewen nodded and moved forward, his heart thumping in his chest. He warned himself to be on guard, but even so he was taken by surprise, had only the barest fraction of a second to sense the hand around his neck, the knife coming for his throat. He reached up and batted the knife away, heard it clatter to the ground in the far corner behind him.

The scarecrow jumped on Ewen's back, wrapped his arms around Ewen's throat and squeezed. Ewen bent double, trying to throw the scarecrow over his shoulders, but the man clung to him like a snake, his arms pressing tighter and tighter around Ewen's neck until the cells in front of Ewen were covered with black spots that bloomed wide when he tried to focus. He sought for air, but there was none. Blood was roaring in his ears, but he could still hear the woman, Brenna, hissing encouragement. Bannaker, too, was holding the bars of his cell, hopping up and down in his excitement. And then there was Javel, silent, his eyes wide and unhappy, his hands outstretched as though to ward something off. The agony in Ewen's chest had become a fire that burned everything now, his arms and legs and head, and he didn't have the strength to pry the man loose.

Stinging pain arrowed up from Ewen's palm. He thought for a moment and then realized that he was still clutching his ring of keys, gripping them hard enough to draw blood. The world had turned to a dark, bruised purple, and Ewen suddenly realized that without air to breathe, he was going to die, that the scarecrow would kill him. Da was dying, Ewen knew, but Da was dying of old age, of sickness. This wasn't the same. Javel's unhappy face swam before him, and without warning Ewen's mind made one of its odd connections: Javel didn't want this to happen. Javel was a prisoner, yes, a traitor. But somehow, he was not the scarecrow's friend.

All of Da's old lectures about jailbreak echoed through Ewen's head, but before he could think about them, he had already flung the keys toward Cell Three. He watched them clang off the bars and land just between them, saw a dirty hand scrabbling for them on the ground.

Then the purple world darkened to black.

Whit hen Ewen woke up, his head and chest were aching. His neck stung as though it had been scraped with a brick. He opened his eyes and saw the dungeon's familiar ceiling above him, grey stones caked with mold. Da always said that whoever had built the Keep had done a good job, but it had become harder and harder over the years to prevent seepage from the moat.

What had woken him up?

The noise, of course. The noise to his right. Snarling sounds, like a dog would make. A thick thud, like a baker's fist sinking into dough. They had lived right next to a bakery when Ewen was growing up, and he loved to stand on his toes and watch the bakers through the windows. He wanted to close his eyes and go back to sleep, just as he would have on a Sunday morning long years ago, before he began to apprentice with Da in the dungeon.

The dungeon!

Ewen's eyes snapped open. Again he saw the familiar pattern of mold on the ceiling.

"STOP!" a woman shrieked, her voice echoing around the stone walls. It hurt Ewen's ears. He looked to his right and saw the ghost-woman, clutching the bars, screaming. On the floor beneath her, Javel was crouched over the scarecrow, pinning him down. Javel was laughing, dark laughter that made Ewen's arms prickle. As he watched, Javel reared back and hit the other man squarely in the face.

"I have only one question for you, Arlen!" Javel's high cackle drowned out the woman's scream. Another blow landed, and Ewen winced. The scarecrow's features were awash with dripping red.

"Can you do the math? Can you, Arlen? Can you, you flesh-peddling bastard?"

Ewen struggled to sit up, though his head pounded so hard that he groaned and blinked tears from his eyes. When he opened his mouth, nothing came out. He cleared his throat and found new agony, roaring pain that barreled down to his chest and back again. But he was able to produce a weak croak. "The Queen."

Javel paid no attention. He hit the scarecrow again, this time in the throat, and the scarecrow began to cough and gag.

Now Ewen spotted his keys, still stuck in the lock of Cell Three, dangerously close to the reach of Bannaker. He crawled over and retrieved them, then approached Javel cautiously from behind.

"Stop," Ewen whispered. He couldn't seem to raise his voice. His throat felt as though someone had set it on fire. "Stop. The Queen."

Javel didn't stop, and Ewen realized then that Javel meant to hit the scarecrow until he was dead. Ewen took a deep, painful breath and grabbed Javel beneath the arms, hauling him backward off the unconscious man. Javel snarled and turned on Ewen, attacking him with his fists, but Ewen accepted this with patience; the Queen would not wish Javel to be hurt either. Ewen certainly didn't want to hurt him; Javel had been a good and well-behaved prisoner, and even when Ewen had thrown him the keys, he had not fled. Ewen kept his arms around Javel in a bear hug, dragging him toward the wall, not letting go even when Javel hit Ewen in his right eye, snapping his head backward and sending sparks across his vision. He threw Javel up against the wall, hard enough for the man's head to rap against the stones. Javel groaned softly and rubbed his scalp, and Ewen took the moment of sudden silence to croak, "The Queen wants this man alive, do you hear? She wants him alive."

Javel looked at him with bleary eyes. "The Queen?"

"The Queen wants him alive. She told me so."

Javel smiled dreamily, and Ewen's stomach tightened with worry. Even after Da's many lectures about minding his size, Ewen had injured one of his brothers while wrestling, rolling Peter into a fence post and breaking his shoulder. He might have thrown Javel against the wall too hard. Javel's voice, too, was odd, hazy, seeming to float somewhere over their heads. "Queen Kelsea. I saw her, you know, on the Keep Lawn. But she was older. She looked like the True Queen. I don't think anyone else saw."

"What's the True Queen?" Ewen asked, unable to help himself. Whenever Da told fairy stories, it was always the queens that Ewen liked best.

"The True Queen. The one who saves us all."

A shrill cackle echoed behind them, and Ewen whirled, certain that the scarecrow had only been shamming, that he had somehow recovered his knife. But it was only the woman, Brenna, clutching the bars of her cage, grinning happily.

"*The True Queen,*" she mimicked in a ghastly, cracked voice. "Fools. She goes to her death before the first snowfall. I've seen it."

Ewen blinked and then cast a quick glance toward the ground. The scarecrow lay motionless, but Ewen was sure he had seen the man move. He turned back to Javel, who was still rubbing his head. "Will you help me tie him up? I have rope."

"I can't kill him, can I?" Javel asked sadly. "Not even now."

"No," Ewen replied in a firm voice, certain of this one thing. "The Queen wants him alive."

Aisa trudged slowly down the hallway, a lit candle in one hand and the red leather-bound book in the other. Two weeks ago she had turned twelve, and Maman had given her permission to get up and read when she was wakeful. Maman didn't have insomnia, but she seemed to understand Aisa's misery at being stuck there, alone in the dark. She must have passed the request along to the Queen or the Mace as well, because now the guards ignored Aisa when they saw her wandering through the Keep in her night-gown, clutching her book.

She always went to the same place to read: the Arms Room. Venner and Fell were too important to work the night shift, so the room was always empty at night, save for the rare guard who came in to sharpen a sword or grab a replacement piece of armor. Aisa liked to take the five straw men that Venner kept there for beginning sparring, arrange them into a big pile in the far corner, and curl up with her book. It was a good reading spot, quiet and private.

She passed Coryn, leaning against the wall. He was in charge of the night guard this week. Aisa liked Coryn; he always answered her questions, and he had shown her the best way to grip a knife for throwing. But she knew better than to talk to him when he was on duty. She gave him a small wave with two of the fingers holding her book, and saw him smile in return. None of the other guards lining the corridor were her friends, so she kept her eyes down until she reached the Arms Room. The cavernous chamber, large and dark, should have frightened her; many dark rooms did.

But Aisa loved the glitter of weapons in the candlelight, the tables and tables of swords and knives and armor, the slight residual smell of old sweat. Even the long, looming shadows cast by her candle didn't frighten Aisa; all of these shadows seemed to have the tall, careful aspect of Venner, and they were a comforting presence in the dark. Aisa knew that she was becoming a better fighter every day; a few days ago she had even gotten through Fell's guard with her knife, while the men lining the walls hooted and cheered. Aisa took it as a point of pride that several of the Guard spent their free time watching her spar. She was getting better, yes, but that wasn't all. She sensed her own potential to be more than better. To be great.

Someday I'll be one of the greatest fighters in the Tear. I'll be the Fetch himself.

Aisa had told no one about this dream, not even Maman. Even if other people didn't laugh, she knew that to speak the dream out loud would curse it, hex it somehow. She gathered the straw men in the far corner of the Arms Room, and when they were arranged just right, she collapsed contentedly and opened her book to its mark. She read for hours, through a great battle and the pleas of a woman who dreamed of holding a sword, and her mind raced ahead of her to the day when she would stride across the world, weapon in hand, finding evil and stabbing it out. These thoughts spun out before her, faster and faster, a grand dream, and finally Aisa slept. The candle continued to burn beside her for perhaps forty minutes until it guttered and died, leaving her in the dark.

She awoke to the sound of the door opening, of voices. Her first instinct, learned from earliest childhood, was to freeze, to make herself invisible. She had escaped from Da, but in waking moments, that never mattered. Some little part of her was always awake, waiting for his thick, ponderous movement in the dark.

Slitting her eyes open, she saw faint torchlight inching its way around the edge of the table. She drew her knees up, curling into the smallest ball possible. It was two men, she realized after a moment: one with a younger, lighter voice, and one with the older, roughened tones of a longtime Queen's Guard. This second voice took her only a few seconds to identify: the Mace. Aisa had heard his angry growl often enough lately to recognize it now, even when he spoke calmly and quietly.

"Had a good break?" the Mace asked. His tone was pleasant, but Aisa heard unpleasantness just beneath it, lurking. The other man must have been able to hear it as well, because his voice, when he answered, was low and defensive.

"I'm sober."

"That's not my concern. I know you'll never make that mistake again."

"Then what's your concern?" the younger man asked, his tone aggressive.

"You and her."

Aisa curled into a tighter ball, listening closely. This would be about Marguerite, for certain. All of the guards, even Coryn, had a certain look on their faces when they watched Marguerite, even if she was just walking across a room. Aisa had been jealous for a bit, but then she remembered that Coryn was old, thirty-eight. Too old for Aisa, even in her fantasy life.

The Mace's voice remained measured and careful, but there was still that tone, lurking underneath. "You can't hide much from me, you know. I've known you too long. You're not impartial. That's fine; perhaps none of us are. But none of us have your job."

"Leave off!" the younger man snarled.

"Don't take your anger out on me," the Mace replied mildly. "I haven't done this to you."

"It's just . . . difficult."

"You've noticed the change in her, then."

"I never cared which face she wore."

"Ah. So this isn't new."

"No."

"That makes it worse, I think. Do you want me to choose another for your job?"

"No."

Aisa's brow wrinkled. Something pulled at her memory; the identity of the younger guard was right there, almost identifiable. She thought about leaning around the corner of the table and taking a peek, but she didn't dare. The Mace saw everything; he would certainly see the tip of her head if it poked out. He was sneaky himself, but he would not take kindly to an eavesdropper. And if she got caught, they might not let her come in here to read at night anymore.

"My skills aren't compromised," the younger guard insisted. "It's a nuisance, not a problem."

The Mace remained silent for a long moment, and when he spoke again, Aisa was surprised to hear that his voice had softened. "You may think you're the first one this has ever happened to, but I assure you that this is an old problem for close guards. I understand it well, believe me. I'm not sure that it doesn't actually make you a better guard. You'd throw yourself in front of the knife without a thought, no?"

"Yes," the younger man replied bleakly, and Aisa finally

identified him: Pen Alcott. She crouched lower, trying to remember the rest of the conversation, to puzzle it out.

"What of that woman you've found?" the Mace asked. "Does she offer no relief at all?"

Pen laughed without humor. "Ten minutes of relief, every time."

"We *can* find another shield, you know," the Mace told him. "Several of them are ready. Elston would jump at the chance."

"No. It would be a greater torment to be out of the room than in."

"You say that now, but think, Pen. Think about when she takes a husband, or even just a man for the night. How will you feel then, being right outside the door?"

"She may not take either."

"She will," the Mace replied firmly. "She has her mother's recklessness, and her mind grows older by the day. It won't be long before she finds that outlet."

Pen was silent for a long moment. "I don't want to be replaced. Partial or no, I'm the best man for the job, and you know it."

"All right." The Mace's voice lost its gentle edge and became iron-hard as he continued. "But mark me: I'll be watching. And if I see one sign of impaired performance, you're done, not just with your post but with this Guard. Do you understand?"

Silence. The pile of straw men began to collapse behind Aisa's back, and she dug her heels into the floor, clutching her book, trying to keep the entire mountain from shifting down in an avalanche.

"I understand," Pen replied stiffly. "I'm sorry to put you in this position."

"Christ, Pen, we've all been there. You won't find a man in her mother's Guard who didn't go through this at one point or another. It's an old problem. A difficult thing."

Aisa was losing ground. She pushed hard with her legs, pressing back against the corner, holding the pile of straw men in place. If they would only leave!

"Better get about it now. She'll wake in a few hours."

"Yes, sir."

Footsteps retreated toward the door.

"Pen?"

"Sir?"

"You're doing a good job. She doesn't mind having you a foot away, I can tell, and that's really a remarkable accomplishment. I'm not sure she wouldn't have killed anyone else by now."

Pen didn't reply. A moment later, Aisa heard the door open and close. She relaxed and felt one of the straw men topple to the ground on her right.

"And you, hellcat?"

Aisa gave a small shriek. The Mace loomed over her, his hands clenched on the table edge. Despite her fright, Aisa couldn't help staring at those hands, which were covered in scars. Venner and Fell had told her that the Mace was a great fighter, one of the greatest in the Tear. To have hands like that, he must have been battling for a lifetime.

That's what I want to be, Aisa realized, staring fixedly at the three white scars across one knuckle. *That dangerous. That feared.*

"I've heard of your nightly wanderings, girl. Venner and Fell tell me you've a great gift for the knife."

Aisa nodded, her face flushing slightly with pleasure.

"Do you come here every night?"

"Almost. I wish I could sleep in here."

The Mace was not distracted. "You've heard something you shouldn't. Something that could be very dangerous to the Queen."

"Why?"

"Don't play foolish with me. I've watched you, you're a quick little thing."

Aisa's paused for a moment. "I am quick. But I won't tell anyone what I heard."

"You're not an easy child." The Mace looked closely at her, and Aisa shrank back. His eyes were terrible things, invasive, as though he were turning her inside out with his gaze. "What do you mean to do with your knife one day? If you're as gifted as Venner and Fell claim?"

"I'll be a Queen's Guard," Aisa replied promptly. She had decided this three days ago, at the very moment she had snuck under Fell's guard and dimpled his jugular with her knife.

"Why?"

Aisa cast around for words, but nothing came, only the image, deep in her mind, of Da's shadow on the nighttime wall. That was nothing she could tell the Mace about; even if she could explain Da to anyone, there were huge swaths of memory gone, dark patches where Aisa's early childhood had simply disappeared. It would be an impossible tale to tell.

But this place, the Queen's Wing, was safe, a well-lit shelter where they could stay forever. Maman said they were in constant danger here, but Aisa could live with the danger of swords. She understood that it was Maman, Maman's queerness, that had somehow gotten them in here in the first place, but the Queen existed above Maman, a godlike figure dressed in black, and Aisa knew that she would never again have to see Da's shadow on the wall.

She couldn't tell any of this to the Mace. All she could say was, "I'd never do anything to hurt the Queen. I'd kill anyone who tried."

The Mace's arrowlike gaze pierced her for a moment longer, seeming to knife through her body. Then he nodded.

"I'm going to trust you, hellcat. More than that, I'm going to consider this your first test. Swordsmanship is an important quality for a Queen's Guard, but there are other things just as crucial, and one of them is your ability to keep a secret."

"I can keep a secret, sir. Probably better than most adults."

The Mace nodded, pity in his gaze, and Aisa realized then that he must know all about Da. Maman sat right next to the Queen every day, brought her food and drink. They would have found out everything about her, and Da had been no secret in their neighborhood. Even when Aisa was little, no other children had ever been allowed over to their house to play.

"Captain?"

"What?"

"Even if I keep quiet, other people might find out. They might see it in Pen's face, like you did."

"Did you?"

"No, but I'm twelve."

"It's a fair point," the Mace replied seriously. "But let's just say that I see more in men's faces than most. I think the secret will be safe for a while, just between you and me."

"Yes, sir."

"Off to bed, hellcat."

Aisa scrambled up, grabbed her book and candle, and

left. In their family room, she placed the red leather book carefully on her bedside table and climbed into bed. But she couldn't sleep yet; her thoughts were too full of all she'd seen and heard.

Pen Alcott was in love with the Queen. But the Queen couldn't marry one of her Guard—even Aisa knew that, though she could not have said why. So Pen had no hope at all. She tried to feel some sympathy for him, but could only muster up a little. Pen got to stand right next to the Queen every day, his sword protecting her from the wide world. Surely that was reward enough.

Love was a real thing, Aisa thought, but secondary. Certainly love was not as real as her sword.

CHAPTER 7

THE GALLERY

The Mort do nothing halfway.

—ANON.

"Tree."

Tyler held up another slip of paper. The Mace looked at it for a moment, wearing the same irritated, truculent expression that he always wore during these sessions.

"Bread."

Tyler held up another slip, holding his breath. After some dithering, he had decided to throw some difficult words into this batch, for this particular student would not want to be coddled. The Mace stared at the word for a moment, his eyes flickering back and forth between syllables. Tyler had encouraged him to sound out the words, but the Mace refused to do so. He wanted to do everything inside his head. His reading level progressed at a pace that was nearly alarming.

"Difference," the Mace finally declared.

"Good." Tyler put the cards down. "That's very good."

The Mace wiped his brow; he'd been sweating. "I'm still having trouble between C and K."

"It's difficult," Tyler agreed, not meeting the Mace's eyes. Tyler walked a fine line in these sessions, tiptoeing between being encouraging and being solicitous, for if the Mace felt that Tyler was treating him as a child, he would likely beat Tyler senseless. But still, Tyler found himself looking forward to these lessons. He enjoyed teaching, and was sorry that he'd waited until his seventy-first year to discover that fact.

But this was the only enjoyable part of Tyler's days. His leg, which had fractured at the shin, was wrapped in a cast, a constant reminder of the Holy Father's anger. The entire Arvath seemed to know that Tyler was in trouble, and his brother priests had shunned him accordingly. Only Wyde, who was too old to be concerned about his place on the Arvath ladder, seemed willing to be seen in Tyler's company.

The Mace was looking at him expectantly, waiting for more instructions. But Tyler had suddenly lost his enthusiasm for the lesson. He stacked the cards on his desk and looked curiously at the Mace. "How did you get away with it all of these years?"

The Mace's expression tightened, became wary. "What does it matter?"

"It doesn't. I'm only curious. I could certainly never have pulled it off."

The Mace shrugged; he was immune to flattery. "Carroll knew. He wanted my skills in the Guard, and so he helped me to keep it a secret. We had an agreement."

"Why didn't he teach you?"

"He offered." The Mace looked away. "I refused. It didn't

matter then, anyway. Elyssa had about as much use for books as a cat has for a riding crop. But now . . ."

Tyler heard the Mace's unspoken thought easily. Queen Elyssa may not have cared about illiteracy, but Queen Kelsea *would* care, very much. "But the Queen would never kick you out of the Guard."

"Of course she wouldn't. I just don't want her to know."

Tyler nodded, wondering, as he so often did, whether the Mace was the Queen's father. His attitude toward her was often that of an exasperated parent. But the identity of the Queen's father was one of the most closely held secrets of the Guard. Tyler wasn't even sure whether the Queen knew herself.

"What's next?"

Tyler thought for a moment. "Practice stringing individual words together. In the Queen's library are several books by a man named Dahl. Choose one and try to work your way through it. Don't skip the longer words; sound them out, and bring the book with you the next time you come."

The Mace nodded. "I think—"

Three sharp raps sounded on Tyler's door.

The Mace sprung from his chair, a quick, silent movement. When Tyler turned to look behind him, the room was empty, the hidden door beside the desk just swinging shut.

"Come in, please."

The door opened, and Tyler froze as the Holy Father entered the room. Brother Jennings was behind him, his round face curious, but the Holy Father left him outside, closing the door. Tyler grasped the edge of the desk and pulled himself to his feet, keeping his broken leg off the floor.

"Good day, Tyler."

"Your Holiness." Tyler offered him the good chair, but Anders waved it away.

"Sit, Tyler, sit. You, after all, are the one with the broken leg. Most unfortunate, that accident."

Tyler sat, watching Anders's eyes dart all over the room, taking in everything while his face remained immobile. In that way, he did remind Tyler of the old Holy Father, who never missed a single thing. All of Tyler's earlier feelings of bravery seemed to have evaporated, quickly and quietly, and he was acutely aware of his own old age, how fragile he was in comparison to this hearty, middle-aged man.

"I am in a difficult position, Tyler." The Holy Father gave a heavy, melodramatic sigh. "The Queen ... she has laid hands on me, you see."

Tyler nodded. No one was supposed to touch a priest of God's Church—not publicly, anyway—and it was unthinkable for anyone, let alone a woman, to lay hands on the Holy Father himself. It had only been a week, but Wyde, who worked at the homeless kitchens in the morning, said that the entire city already seemed to know what had happened at the Queen's dinner. Wyde had even heard one rumor that the Queen had given the Holy Father a savage beating with her bare hands. These stories were harmful to the Queen, certainly; the devout were scandalized. But the damage to the Holy Father was much greater.

"This won't stand, Tyler. If no consequences fall on the Queen for her actions, then we are all left hanging in the wind. The Arvath's political power will dwindle to nothing. You understand?"

Tyler nodded again.

"But if God's wrath were to fall on her swiftly ... think of it, Tyler!" The Holy Father's eyes brightened, sparkling with a hint of that same terrible glee that Tyler had seen there on the night of Father Seth. "Think of how God's Church would benefit! Conversions would increase. Tithing would increase. Faith has grown slack, Tyler, and we need to make an example. A *public* example. You see?"

Tyler didn't see, not exactly, but he didn't like the turn of the conversation. Anders had halted in his pacing now, right in front of Tyler's bookshelves. He pulled down *A Distant Mirror*, and Tyler tensed, lacing his fingers together at his waist. When Anders opened the book and ran a finger down one of the middle pages, Tyler's flesh crawled beneath his skin.

"The Queen is not vulnerable!" he blurted out. "There is the Mace—and she has magic—"

"Magic?"

In a sudden, sharp movement, Anders wrenched the book down the binding, tearing it in two. Tyler cried out, his hands reaching automatically before he snatched them back. He did not have the Queen's gall; he could not lay hands on the Holy Father. He could only watch as Anders dropped one shredded half of the book and began to rip pages out of the other, one at a time. They drifted lazily, back and forth, toward the floor.

"Magic, Tyler?" Anders asked softly. "And you a priest?"

A soft knock came at the door, and Brother Jennings leaned through the doorway, his avid eyes taking in the entire scene. "Everything all right, Your Holiness?"

"Perfectly so," Anders replied, his gaze fixed on Tyler. "Fetch a few more brothers in here. There's work to do."

Brother Jennings nodded and left. Tyler stared mutely at the books on his shelves. There were so many of them.

"Please," he heard himself beg. "Please don't. They never did you any harm."

"These are secular books, Tyler, and you've been storing them in the Arvath. I'd be well within my rights to burn them."

"They don't hurt anyone! I'm the only one who reads them!"

Brother Jennings knocked and entered. Several other priests followed, including Wyde, who gave Tyler an apprehensive glance as he came through the door.

Anders pointed to the shelves. "Remove the books and their holders to my private apartments."

The younger priests began to move immediately, but Wyde hesitated, staring at Tyler.

"Problem, Father Wyde?" Anders asked.

Wyde shook his head and held out his arms to accept a pile of books from the shelf. He didn't look at Tyler again. While they worked, Anders continued to rip the pages from *A Distant Mirror*. One landed at Tyler's feet, and when he looked down, he saw "Chapter 7" in bold print. Tears filled his eyes, and he had to bite his lip to keep them there. Looking up, he made the unpleasant discovery that Anders was enjoying himself enormously, his eyes sparkling with pleasure. The priests continued to march in and out of the room, until finally the shelves stood empty against the wall. The sight made Tyler want to break down and weep. Brother Jennings levered the bookshelves from the wall and tipped them horizontal, and Wyde snuck Tyler one last apologetic glance as he grabbed hold of a corner. Then they were gone. The wall was blank; only two whitened rectangles remained to show where Tyler's books had been. He stared numbly at them, and now the tears came, beyond his power to hold back.

"Tyler?"

Tyler turned, his heart pounding, to face the Holy Father. For the first time in his adult life, he wanted to do violence to another person. His hands had clenched into fists inside the sleeves of his robe.

Anders reached inside his own robes and came out with a small vial of clear, colorless liquid. He passed it thoughtfully from one hand to another before remarking, "The Queen is not protective of her person with you. I watched you pass her the bread at dinner. Does her drink ever pass through your hands?"

Tyler nodded jerkily. His face had gone cold. "Tea."

"The Mace can't consider you a threat, or he would never tolerate such an arrangement." The Holy Father held out the vial. It looked smooth in his hand, almost oily, and Tyler stared numbly, unable to accept.

"I won't insult your intelligence, Tyler, by explaining what you're to do with this. But I want it done within a month. If not, you will watch me douse every single one of your books in oil and strike a match. I will do it personally, on the front steps of the Arvath, and you will watch."

Tyler cast around for answers, but there was nothing, only the pile of torn pages on the ground.

"Take it, Tyler."

He took the vial.

"Come with me," the Holy Father commanded, opening the door. Tyler grabbed his crutches and lurched forward to follow. Several brothers and fathers had their doors open, and they stared at Tyler as he went by, following the Holy Father down the hallway toward the staircase. Tyler sensed them, but did not see them, his mind utterly blank now. It seemed important not to think of his books, and that meant not thinking of anything at all.

At the end of the corridor, they emerged onto the staircase landing. Tyler tried to keep his eyes on the ground, but at the last moment he couldn't help looking up. Seth was there, sitting on his stool as he had done every day for the past two weeks, his legs spread wide to display the mangled area between them. The actual wound had been cauterized and stitched up somehow, but what remained was almost worse, a charred and seamed landscape of red flesh. Pink streaks radiated outward along Seth's inner thighs, signifying the beginnings of infection. Hung around his neck was a placard with one scrawled word:

ABOMINATION

Seth stared blankly down the hallway, his gaze so fixed that Tyler wondered if they were keeping him dulled with some sort of narcotic. But no, what killed pain would also kill the point of the lesson, wouldn't it? For the first week, Seth's moans of agony had been audible all the way down the hall, and none of them had slept for days.

Tyler closed his eyes and then, mercifully, they were past Seth and down the stairs. Anders began to speak again, his voice pitched low enough to reach Tyler, but not Brother Jennings, who trailed silently several feet behind. "I am not unaware, Tyler, that this must be an unpleasant errand for you. And every unpleasant errand requires not only punishment for failure, but reward for success."

Tyler followed mutely, still trying to push Seth's image from his mind. The Holy Father's talk of reward did not cheer him in the slightest; in his childhood, Tyler had seen village dogs trained in much the same way for the ring. When an animal was beaten hard enough, it would work just to not be beaten, and consider itself well rewarded. The status quo could shift at any time.

My books.

The numbness broke slightly and Tyler felt agony there, waiting, like freezing water beneath thin ice. He focused on walking, feeling each step as an individual ache. The old Holy Father had always used the lift to transport him between floors, but Anders rarely did so. He seemed to enjoy demonstrating his own fitness, and now he was surely enjoying Tyler's discomfort as well. The arthritis had woken up, causing Tyler's hip to throb unhappily. His broken leg snarled with each step, even though Tyler was careful never to let it bump against the ground. He concentrated on each of these discomforts, almost relishing them, easy pains that were entirely physical.

After endless flights of stairs, they passed the ground floor and continued down the steps into the Arvath's basement. Tyler had never been to the basement, which was only a resting place for Holy Fathers deceased. No one came down here except for two unfortunate brothers who had drawn the duty to keep the crypts free of insects and rats. These two, men unfamiliar to Tyler, sprang to their feet and bowed as the Holy Father entered, Tyler following at his heels like a ghost.

Anders took the torch that one of the young men offered and led Tyler into the tombs. It was bone-cold down here, and Tyler shivered in his thin robes. They passed the entrances to many crypts, decorated arches of stone that stretched high above them on both sides. The corpses of Holy Fathers were always embalmed before being laid to rest, but Tyler still thought that he could smell death in this place. Briefly, he wondered if Anders had brought him down here to kill him, and then he discarded that idea. He was needed.

God, please show me the way out.

The crypts were behind them now. Ahead was only a single large stone door, covered with a layer of dust. As they drew up in front of it, Anders produced a simple iron key.

"Look at me, Tyler."

Tyler looked up, but found that he couldn't meet the other man's eyes. Instead, he fixed his gaze on the bridge of Anders's nose.

"I am the only person with a key to this door, Tyler. But if you succeed in your task, I will give this key to you."

He opened the door, though it required several twists of the key to do so. The door squealed miserably as the Holy Father shoved it open; no one had entered this room in a long time. The Holy Father beckoned him inside, but Tyler already knew, somehow, what would be there, and as light from the torch fell over the room, despair wrapped around Tyler's heart.

The room was full of books. Someone had constructed shelves for them, the sort of rough-hewn furniture that had predominated after the Landing, when even simple tools were difficult to come by. Tyler's eyes roamed helplessly across the room: shelf after shelf of books, thousands of them, all the way down to the far wall.

He stepped forward, drawn helplessly, reaching out to touch the books on their shelves. Some were leather-bound, some paper. No one had cared for them, or even bothered to organize them; titles and authors had been thrown together haphazardly, stacked horizontally on the shelves. Everything was covered with a thick layer of dust. The sight hurt Tyler's heart.

"Tyler."

He started. For a moment, he'd forgotten that the Holy Father was there.

"If you succeed," the Holy Father said softly, "not only will you have the key to this room, but you will become the Arvath's first librarian. You will cease to be the Keep Priest, and I will relieve you of all other duties. No one will ever bother you again. Your only task will be to live down here and take care of these books."

Tyler turned back to stare at the room, breathing in the smell of old paper. He could spend the rest of his life in here and not read the same book twice.

"The poison is delayed," the Holy Father continued. "It will take some two or three hours for the Queen to show the first symptoms. This is your window to return to the Arvath."

"They'll come after me. The Mace will."

"Perhaps. But not even the Mace will dare to remove you from the Arvath without my permission. You saw how they had to lure Matthew to the Keep in order to take him. You may never be able to leave the Arvath again, but so long as you make it back, you will be safe from reprisal, and you may live your life out here, with these books."

Thinking of the Mace's uncanny ability to appear and disappear from walls at will, Tyler almost smiled. The Mace would find him, no matter where he went, but Tyler didn't bother to correct the Holy Father. He wondered what the Queen would say if she could see this room.

"What happens after she dies?" he asked, startling himself.

"There will be a bit of squabbling, certainly, but eventually the Tear will become a Mort protectorate."

Tyler blinked. "The Red Queen is a noted unbeliever. Will that not be worse for the Church?"

"No." A smile played at the corners of Anders's mouth. "Everything has already been arranged."

Poor bedfellows, Tyler thought sickly, recalling the Mace's words. "My leg is still weak, Your Holiness. I would like to go back upstairs."

"Of course," Anders replied, his tone solicitous now. "We will go at once."

Anders locked the door behind them and they moved slowly back between the tombs. Tyler's leg had gotten so bad that he was now forced to hobble.

"We will take the lift, Tyler, to spare your leg."

Together, they crowded onto the thick platform of wood that stood beside the staircase, and Anders nodded to the two priests who waited there.

"Brothers' quarters."

Tyler grabbed the railing, slightly sick again, as the lift began to rise.

"This is a test, Tyler," the Holy Father told him. "God is testing your faith, your loyalty."

Tyler nodded, but he felt lost and bewildered. He had lived in the Arvath for his entire adult life, considered it home. But now it seemed a strange landscape, pitted with unknown dangers. When the lift reached the quarters, he wandered away from the Holy Father without a word, past Seth and down the hallway, past the staring eyes of his brothers, past Wyde, who waited beside Tyler's doorway, his eyes downcast.

"I'm sorry," Wyde murmured. "I didn't want to, Tyler, but–"

Tyler closed the door in his face and went to sit on the bed.

The bare walls seemed to glare at him, and he tried to ignore them, tried to pray. But he couldn't escape the feeling that no one was listening, that God's attention was elsewhere. Finally he gave up and pulled the small vial out of his robes, rolling it in both hands, running one thumb over the wax stopper. The liquid inside was perfectly clear; Tyler could look straight through and see a distorted image of the tiny room around him, the room where, not so long ago, he had expected to live contentedly for the rest of his life. He thought of the Queen's library, the way time seemed to disappear as Tyler sat there, everything melting away until he felt that he was part of some better world. He could not do this thing, but he could not leave his books either. There seemed no way out.

Tyler got up and placed his hand on the wall, smoothing a palm across the white stone. There was no help for him in prayer, he saw now, nor could he afford to wait for miracles. God would not single Tyler out. If he wanted salvation, he would have to save himself.

T his is a fool's errand," Mace grumbled.

"You think all of my errands are foolish, Lazarus. I'm not impressed."

They were traveling in near darkness, through one of Mace's many tunnels that seemed to beehive the Keep. The only illumination came from a torch carried by Father Tyler, who limped alongside Pen. In the dim amber light, the priest's face looked paler than ever. Kelsea had asked Mace what was going on in the Arvath, to make Father Tyler so miserable, but Mace, being Mace, had refused to say, remarking only that the new Holy Father was even worse than the old.

It was Father Tyler who had sent Kelsea on this little jaunt. The vision of William Tear had sent her into a kind of frenzy, and in the past week she had torn Carlin's library apart, determined to find some information about Lily Mayhew, about Greg Mayhew, about Dorian Rice, about any of them. When Father Tyler had arrived this morning, Kelsea had been sitting there on the library floor, in a rut of sleeplessness and failure, surrounded by Carlin's books, and she seized on the priest as a last resort. Were there any written histories about the years surrounding the Crossing, the life of William Tear? There had been no actual publishing after the Crossing, of course, but perhaps there was a handwritten history? Someone should have kept a journal, at least.

Father Tyler shook his head regretfully. Many of the original generation of utopians had indeed kept journals, but in the dark period after the Tear assassination, most of them had disappeared. Several fragments had been preserved in the Arvath, and Father Tyler had seen them, but they discussed everyday problems of survival: the scarcity of food, the labor of constructing the fledgling village that would one day become New London. Most of Father Tyler's own knowledge of the Crossing was based on oral history, the same folklore that pervaded the rest of the Tearling. No real writings had survived.

"But there is something, Majesty," Tyler remarked, after a moment's thought. "Father Timpany used to tell stories about a portrait gallery somewhere in the lower floors of the Keep. The Regent would visit the gallery from time to time, and Timpany said there's a portrait of William Tear down there."

"Why on earth would my uncle visit a portrait gallery?"

"It's a gallery of your ancestors, Majesty. Timpany said

that when the Regent was drunk, he liked to go down and scream at your grandmother's portrait."

It turned out that Mace knew exactly where the gallery was: two floors down, on the laundry level. As they descended a twisting staircase, Kelsea could hear many people speaking through the walls. Although she had her own private laundry—Mace, who worried about contact poisons, had insisted on it—Kelsea had kept the Keep laundry open, sending the rest of the Queen's Wing's linen down there. Her uncle's Keep had been stuffed with unnecessary services, but Kelsea couldn't bring herself to put so many people out of work. She had fired the worst of the Keep servants, the masseuses and escorts, those she simply wouldn't have on her payroll. But she tried to make use of everyone else. At the bottom of the staircase, she could see no farther than the tiny, dim circle of torchlight that surrounded them, but she had the sense of a vast, hollow space above her head.

"Who built all these tunnels?"

"They're part of the original architecture, Lady. There are hidden ways all the way from the top of the Keep down to the dungeons. Several passages extend out into the city as well."

Mention of dungeons made Kelsea think of Thorne, who now sat in his own specially constructed cell several floors up. Kelsea didn't trust him in the Keep's dungeons, not even with Elston standing guard over him at all times. She also had a vague idea that Thorne should remain separated from the albino, Brenna. So he remained in isolation, save for a gloating Elston just outside the bars of his cell. Kelsea didn't know what to do about Thorne. Should she put him to trial? For the past six weeks Kelsea and Arliss had been quietly converting the Census Bureau into a tax collection agency, but they had also been pulling the honest men from the Bureau and moving them back into the judiciary. Creation of a justice system was slow going; the Tearling had few laws, and none of them were codified anywhere. Since the Mort had reached the border, Kelsea had found little time to devote to this endeavor, but at her request, Arliss had kept at it, and now New London had five public courts, where anyone could petition a judge for redress of grievances. The Crown could try Arlen Thorne in a public court, but what if he was acquitted? Judge or jury, either one could be bought. Conversely, even if Thorne's guilt was not beyond question, many jurors would condemn him regardless of the evidence. After the Regent, Thorne was the most hated figure in the Tear. There was no real purpose to a trial, and yet Kelsea felt there should be one, all the same.

Mace wanted to simply put Thorne to death. The man was so universally hated that no one would protest a quick execution, particularly not if Kelsea made the execution public. She saw the wisdom of Mace's advice; such a move would gain her throne the diehard support of anyone who had ever watched a loved one put into the cage. Even the Arvath didn't protest against capital punishment these days, and Kelsea certainly had no problem with it. Yet something in her demanded a trial, even a show trial, something to legitimize the act. But there was legal precedent for summary executions: if Father Tyler's folklore was to be believed, William Tear had practiced them, had even carried one out with his own hands.

And so have I, Kelsea thought, suddenly cold. In her mind she saw blood, thick and warm, spurting over her right hand and dripping down her forearm. The outside world assumed that Mhurn had simply been a casualty of the Battle of the

Argive. Mace had allowed that belief to flourish, but Kelsea and the rest of her Guard knew better, and no matter how she tried to dismiss the matter from her mind, the image kept recurring to her: her knife hand, bathed in blood. It seemed so important for Thorne to have a trial.

"Cover your eyes, Lady."

Kelsea shielded her eyes as daylight bloomed in the darkness ahead. She passed through one of Mace's hidden doors and found herself in a long, narrow room with a high ceiling. The light came from a bank of windows on the far wall. Looking out these windows, Kelsea saw that they were at the extreme western end of the Keep; outside, she saw first the rolling foothills of the city and then the tan backdrop of the Clayton Mountains.

"Here, Majesty!" Father Tyler announced from the far end of the hallway.

Kelsea turned and found that the wall they had just come through was lined with portraits. They ran the length of the gallery in both directions. Father Tyler had gone to the farthest portrait and rested a hand on the base of the frame, where there was an engraved wooden plaque. The portrait showed the same man Kelsea had seen in her vision: a tall, severe man with short-cropped blond hair, his face set in businesslike lines. Kelsea's heart leapt. She had known that her visions were real, of course, but it was still an enormous relief to have empirical proof.

"William Tear," Father Tyler announced, placing his torch in the empty bracket on the wall. The sunlight was so bright in here that there was no need of fire. "The plaque says this was painted five years after the Crossing."

Kelsea moved closer, staring up at the first Tear King. He stood in front of a fireplace, but not the sort of grand fireplace that littered the Keep, more like that of the cottage where she had grown up. Even the artist had not been able to disguise Tear's annoyance at having to simply stand still; his expression betrayed extreme impatience. The portrait must have been someone else's idea. Dimly, in the background, Kelsea glimpsed a shelf full of books, but a thick layer of grime had accumulated on the surface of the portrait and she couldn't make out any titles.

"I want a Keep servant to clean these," she told Mace. "Surely they have plenty of time on their hands."

Mace nodded, and Kelsea moved on to the next portrait: a young blond man barely out of his teens. He was good-looking, but even through layers of dust, Kelsea could see the worry that shrouded his eyes. She ran her fingers over the frame, looking for a plaque, and found it coated with dust as well. She polished it with her thumb, wiping her dirty hand on her skirt, and bent down to read the engraving. "Jonathan Tear."

"Jonathan the Good," Father Tyler murmured beside her.

On Jonathan Tear's chest, Kelsea spotted a sapphire, one of hers, dangling on its chain. She looked quickly back to the portrait of William Tear. He wasn't wearing any jewelry, at least not that Kelsea could see. There was a sizable space between the two portraits, William and Jonathan, wide enough that Kelsea wondered if another portrait had once hung there.

"Who was Jonathan Tear's mother?"

Father Tyler shook his head. "That I don't know, Majesty. William Tear had no queen; legend says he didn't believe in marriage. But there's no record of any doubt that Jonathan the Good was his son. The resemblance is marked."

"What was Jonathan so worried about, do you think?"

"Perhaps he feared death, Lady," Coryn replied behind her. "He was twenty years old when he was murdered. That portrait couldn't have been done more than a couple years before."

"Who murdered him?"

"No one knows, but they got through Tear's Guard. The worst moment in our history, that—"

Coryn broke off suddenly, and she knew that he was thinking of Mhurn. Barty had said the same thing about the Tear assassination: the Guard had failed. Regretting Coryn's discomfort, Kelsea swallowed the rest of her questions about Jonathan Tear and passed onward to the next portrait: a woman, very innocent-looking, with a beautiful head of reddish-brown hair that ran over her shoulders like a river, dropping in long streamers down her back. She smiled beatifically from the canvas. Kelsea checked the engraved plaque: "Caitlyn Tear." Jonathan Tear's wife. After the assassination, Caitlyn Tear had been hunted down and slaughtered. Although the woman in the portrait was long dead, beyond any harm, Kelsea's heart wrenched. This woman looked as though she couldn't even conceive of evil, much less endure it.

The next portrait made Kelsea suck in her breath. She would have known this man anywhere: he had stood in front of her fireplace two weeks earlier, the handsomest man in the world. He sat on the Tear throne—the elaborately carved back was unmistakable—smiling an easy politician's smile. But his amber eyes were cold, and by an odd artist's trick, they seemed to follow Kelsea no matter where she moved. Gingerly, she felt along the edges of the frame, but there was nothing, only an odd scarring of the wood that suggested that the plaque, if one existed, had been torn away long ago.

She wondered at the handsome man's presence in this gallery of Tear royalty, but said nothing.

"Handsome devil," Mace remarked. "No idea who he is, though. Father?"

Father Tyler shook his head. "He doesn't match any Raleigh monarch I've ever heard of. He *is* exceptionally good-looking, though; perhaps he was a companion to one of the Raleigh Queens. Several of them never married, but all of them managed to produce heirs. They had an eye for the handsome men."

Kelsea picked that unfortunate moment to look at Pen, and found his eyes on her as well. The night he had rejected her sat between them like a vast gulf, and Kelsea had a terrible feeling that they would never get back to the easy friendship they'd had before. She wanted to say something to him, but there were too many people nearby, and after a moment even the impulse at reconciliation vanished. The eyes of the man from the fireplace were hypnotic, but Kelsea dragged herself away and moved on to the next portrait. They were into the Raleighs now; all of these portraits had their plaques intact, and the engravings became clearer, less worn by the passage of time, as Kelsea moved closer to the present day.

All of the Raleighs wore both sapphires, the jewels appearing changeless from one portrait to the next. These were Kelsea's ancestors, her blood, but she found them somehow less important than the three Tears, less real. Carlin had never admired the Raleighs; perhaps her prejudices in this, as in so many things, had simply trickled down to Kelsea over the years.

In the tenth portrait, Kelsea was confronted with a woman so beautiful that she almost defied description. She had the same blonde hair and bright green eyes as many of the Raleigh queens, but her face was creamy-skinned and flawless, and she had the most gracefully proportioned neck that Kelsea had ever seen on a woman. Unlike the previous portraits, which had focused on one person at a time, this one also portrayed a child, a pretty girl of nearly six years, who sat on her mother's lap. And in this portrait Kelsea noticed a new development: the woman wore one sapphire, the child wore the other. Kelsea bent down to the attached plaque and read, "Amanda Raleigh."

"Ah, the Beautiful Queen!" Father Tyler moved down to join her in front of the portrait. Kelsea's guards, most of whom had been scattered down at the far end of the room, slightly bored, moved closer as well, staring avidly up at the portrait. Kelsea felt irritation bite against her mind, but then she spotted a second child in the portrait, tucked almost behind the Beautiful Queen's skirts. This girl was even younger than the child on the Queen's lap, perhaps no more than three or four, but already she was dark-haired and sullen-looking, and Kelsea was suddenly reminded of her own childhood self, staring back at her in the pool of still water behind the cottage. In the radiance of the Beautiful Queen and her daughter, the girl was easy to miss, and Kelsea realized that this must have been the artist's deliberate choice: to highlight one child and obscure the other.

"The Beautiful Queen had only one child, so I'm told. That must be Queen Elaine on her lap." Kelsea pointed to the little girl who cringed behind the Beautiful Queen's skirts. "So who's this?"

Mace shrugged. "No idea."

Father Tyler considered the girl. "A disfavored child, would be my guess. Amanda Raleigh had a husband, Thomas

Arness. He was Elaine's father. But I've heard that Amanda was hardly faithful to Arness, and there may have been other children. Disfavored children sometimes showed up in royal portraits from the pre-Crossing, but never in positions of prominence. A cruel thing, really, almost worse than not being included at all." Father Tyler studied the portrait for a moment before remarking, "This is the worst case I've ever seen. That child is completely marginalized."

Kelsea stared at the little girl, pity stirring inside her. Unlike the smiling princess on the Beautiful Queen's lap, the hidden girl had dark, unhappy eyes. She wasn't looking at the artist, as the other two subjects did; rather, she was staring up at the Beautiful Queen, her gaze filled with poorly concealed longing. Kelsea suddenly wanted to weep, and didn't know whether it was for the child or for herself.

In the next portrait, the child on the Beautiful Queen's lap had grown up and borne a child of her own. The engraving identified them as Queen Elaine and Crown Princess Arla. Elaine was not as beautiful as her mother—*but who could be?* Kelsea wondered bitterly—but she reminded Kelsea of someone. Andalie? No, for although this woman was a brunette, she didn't have Andalie's pale, ethereal style of beauty. Queen Elaine did not smile for the artist; she, too, looked extremely annoyed at having to sit for a portrait.

"See here, Lady!" Dyer pointed at Elaine's face. "She has your stubborn jaw!"

"Hilarious," Kelsea muttered, but she could not deny that there was a likeness, even now, when so many changes had overtaken her own face. Before Dyer could remark on anything else, she continued to the next portrait.

Arla the Just sat on the Tear throne, no child in sight, both sapphires around her neck and the Tear crown on her head.

Fascinated, Kelsea stared at the crown, a single, elegant circle of silver, set with perhaps four or five sapphires. She tapped her finger against the canvas. "Any luck on finding that thing, Lazarus?"

"None yet, Lady."

Kelsea nodded, disappointed but not surprised, and turned back to the portrait. Queen Arla had not been particularly pretty, but she possessed a magnetic quality that shone clearly through the canvas. She was much older than the other Raleigh women, and Kelsea remembered then that Queen Elaine had lived long, that her daughter had not been crowned until she was nearing her own middle age. Arla had been an autocrat, and the portrait showed her as such, reflected a clear determination to have her own way. Her smile was so contented that it was nearly smug, radiating pride to the point of arrogance. But pride had gotten Arla in trouble in the long run.

Barbarians at the walls, Kelsea's mind whispered, *and she provoked them, just like you.*

She shook the thought off, moved quickly to the next portrait, and found herself staring up at her mother.

Queen Elyssa did not look at all the way Kelsea had imagined. There had been long days in the cottage, lonely days when Carlin had been angry with her, when Kelsea would console herself by picturing the phantom woman who had borne her: a delicate, willowy woman, like something out of a Grimm tale. But the Elyssa in the portrait didn't look frail at all; she was tall, taller than Kelsea, and she radiated health and substance, a striking blonde woman with sparkling green eyes. She stood beside a plain, unadorned table, but she was grinning, the carefree grin of a woman with nothing in the world to worry about. Kelsea, who had almost been pleased with this version of her mother, found herself latching on to that grin. Even if the portrait had been painted immediately after Elyssa took the throne, the Mort would already be tearing their way through the Tear countryside. The Mort Treaty, the lottery, these things couldn't be far away, and the utter carelessness of her mother's expression sharpened Kelsea's resolve, her determination that no one would suffer for her mistakes.

"Lady," Mace murmured.

"What?"

"It does no good to dwell on the past. The future, now . . . that's everything."

Kelsea was annoyed that Mace had read her so easily. But she saw no judgment in his face, only his own brand of hard truth, and after a moment she relaxed, shrugging. "And yet sometimes the answer to the future lies in the past, Lazarus."

Mace turned and barked, "Spread out, all of you!"

Kelsea's guards moved away, to all ends of the room. Kelsea stared at Mace, bewildered, but he only moved closer and murmured, "Is that where you go at night, Lady, on your wanderings? The past?"

Kelsea swallowed, though something seemed to catch in her throat. "What makes you think I go anywhere?"

"Pen missed it, that night last week. He was on the library door. But I was right next to you, Lady. You said, 'There's a better world out there. So close we can almost touch it.' I know those words; there was a song about them in the village where I grew up. A song of the Crossing."

"I was sleepwalking."

Mace chuckled. "You're no more a sleepwalker than Andalie's little one, Lady. I found her in Arliss's office the other night. When Arliss is gone, that office is *always* locked. But Glee got in there, all the same."

"What's your point, Lazarus?"

"That night, for a minute, just before you came out of your fugue, you seemed to . . . fade."

"Fade?" The word chilled Kelsea, but she produced a half-hearted snicker.

"Laugh if you like, Lady, but I did see it." Mace leaned in even closer now, lowering his voice to a whisper. "Do you ever consider, Lady, that it might be better to simply take them off and throw them away?"

Kelsea reached up automatically, taking her jewels in a clenched fist. She didn't know whether they even functioned any longer, or whether something else was working on her now. But everything in her rebelled at the idea of taking them off.

Mace shook his head and then gave her a pained grin. "Well, it was worth a try."

"Look here, Lady!" Coryn announced, pointing to the next portrait.

"Oh, for God's sake," Kelsea breathed. Her uncle's face beamed down at her from the wall: younger than the man she had met, but unmistakably Thomas Raleigh. He carried less weight, and his nose didn't quite have the alcoholic shade of red that it would attain later, but the air of entitle-ment, the sense of being God's gift to the earth, these things emanated from the canvas in nearly visible waves.

"Take that nonsense down!" Kelsea snapped. "He's not a Tear monarch, he never was. Get rid of it."

"I'll take care of it, Lady," Mace replied. "I had no idea he'd put up a portrait. I haven't been down here in years."

"Doesn't anyone use this gallery?"

"I doubt it. Look at the dust."

Kelsea went back to glaring at her mother's portrait. Even if she somehow found a solution to the Mort nightmare on the horizon, it did nothing for the fifty thousand Tear who had already gone to Mortmesne, her mother's gift to the world. This was familiar territory, a problem with no solution.

"May I ask you a question, Lady?" Dyer asked.

"Please."

"I wondered if you had decided what to do with the prisoner Javel."

"I will let him out of prison, certainly, but only once I've thought of a way to keep him from drinking himself to death." Kelsea turned away from the portraits to face her five guards, who stood in front of the sunlit windows like a row of chessmen. "I don't know what to do with the boy, the Jailor, either. He's earned some reward, but for the life of me, I don't know what to give him. Does he have no friends, no one who knows him well?"

Coryn spoke up. "I know his father a little. The old Jailor, retired now. I can ask."

"Do that. I don't want the reward to be meaningless. They gave us a great gift, both Ewen and Javel."

"And what will you do with the gift?" Pen asked. It was the first full sentence Kelsea had gotten in days, but she wished that she could just ignore him. "What about Thorne?"

"I don't know."

"Better decide soon, Lady," Dyer cut in. "The entire kingdom is screaming for his blood."

"Yes, but they scream for the wrong reasons. They want him to suffer because of his years as Overseer of the Census. Yet that was a government position, and as terrible as they were, Thorne's actions as Overseer were legal under the Regency. I can't have a rule of law that bows under public pressure. If I execute Thorne, it must be for his crimes."

"He's guilty of treason, Lady."

"And yet that's not the reason the entire kingdom will line up to watch him hang."

The five guards stared at her, and Kelsea felt more than ever that she was on a chessboard, a pawn facing five power pieces. "You all agree? That I should execute him?"

They all nodded, even Pen, who Kelsea had thought might be a secret holdout.

"I'll make a decision soon, but not yet. I did promise Elston his fun, you know."

Leaving them chuckling behind her, Kelsea moved back down the gallery to have another look at the man from the fireplace. He was even more striking in daylight, and although the portrait was clearly very old, he had not aged a day since. His eyes followed her as she came closer, and although Kelsea knew it was silly, she felt as though he really could see her from a distance.

"Take this one down as well," she said finally. "I don't know who he is, but he's not a monarch. He doesn't belong on this wall."

"Should we get rid of it?"

"No. Bring it upstairs." She peered around her guards until she found Father Tyler, staring out the window. "Thank you, Father. Most interesting, this place."

"Yes, Lady," the priest replied absently. But his bleak gaze remained fixed on the mountains.

What have they done to him? Kelsea wondered again. Her eyes strayed to the cast on his knee. She was surprised by her own protective instinct toward the priest. He was an old man, one who wanted only to sit and read books and think about the past; it seemed a crime for anyone to harm him. On several mornings lately, Kelsea had found Father Tyler asleep on his favorite sofa in the library, as though he no longer wished to spend his nights in the Arvath. Had the Holy Father done something else to him? If he had—

Stop, Kelsea told herself. She couldn't try to assert authority over the inner workings of the Arvath. That path would only lead to disaster. She pushed God's Church from her mind, and as it went, she suddenly had an idea, a possible solution . . . not to Father Tyler, but to another problem.

"Lazarus? Can any of the Guard speak Mort?"

Mace blinked in surprise. "Kibb, Dyer, and Galen, Lady. And myself."

"Do any of them speak it well enough to *pass* for Mort?"

"Only Galen, really." Mace's brow furrowed. "What's on your mind?"

"We're going back upstairs now, but not everyone. Two of you go down to the dungeon and bring me Javel. Try to wake him up a bit."

But an hour later, when Javel entered the Queen's Wing, Kelsea was disappointed to see that his earlier apathy had not changed. He looked around without interest as Coryn escorted him to the foot of the dais, then simply stood staring at the ground. Where was the man who had attacked the burning cage, all alone, with an axe? Kelsea wondered whether she would have seen the real Javel on the day Thorne had broken into the dungeon. Ewen had been very cagey about what had happened down there, but Mace finally got the whole truth from him: if Ewen hadn't intervened, Javel would have beaten Thorne to death with his bare hands. That was the man Kelsea wanted to see.

She was pleased to notice that Ewen had at least left off Javel's manacles. There was no need for restraint; Javel merely stood there, straight and beaten, as though waiting for his own execution.

"Javel."

He didn't look up, only replied hollowly, "Majesty."

"You've done me a great service in the capture of Arlen Thorne."

"Yes, Majesty. Thank you."

"I have pardoned you. You're free to leave the Keep now, at any time, and go your own way. But I would ask you to stay and listen to a proposal."

"What proposal?"

"I'm told that your wife went to Mortmesne in the shipment six years ago. Is this correct?"

"Yes."

"Is she still alive?"

"I don't know," Javel replied listlessly. "Thorne said so. He said he could get her back. But now I think it was all lies, and she's dead."

"Why?"

"She was a pretty woman, my Allie. They don't last long."

Kelsea winced, but plowed forward. "Was your Allie pretty and weak, Javel? Or was she pretty and tough?"

"A damned sight tougher than me, Lady, though that doesn't say much."

"And yet you think she couldn't have survived six years in a Mort knockhouse?"

Javel looked up, and Kelsea was pleased to see a hint of anger in his eyes. "Why say this to me, Lady? Do you wish to make it worse?"

"I wish to see whether you still care about anything at all.

268

Do you think your wife would be happy to see you here now, like this?"

"That's between her and me." Javel looked around him, seeming to notice Coryn for the first time. "You said I was free to leave."

"So you are. The door is behind you."

Javel turned and walked away. Kelsea sensed Mace bridling beside her, but to his credit, he kept quiet.

"What will you do now, Javel?" she called after him.

"Find the nearest pub."

"Is that what your wife would have wanted?"

"She's dead."

"You don't know that."

Javel kept walking.

"Don't you want to find out?"

He halted, perhaps ten feet from the doors.

"I have ended the lottery, Javel," Kelsea continued, staring at his back, willing him to stay still. "No shipment will ever leave this country under my Crown. But that doesn't redress the wrongs of the past, the Tear already in Mortmesne. What do I do about all of them, all of those slaves? The answer is clear: I have to get them out."

Javel remained in place, but Kelsea saw his shoulders heave, once, an involuntary movement.

"Lazarus is thinking that I have other things to worry about," she continued, with a nod to Mace, "and he's right. My people are starving and uneducated. We have no true medicine. On the eastern border is an army that will crush us into dust. These are real problems, and so for a time I've let the others lie. But here is where Lazarus and I differ a bit. He believes that avoiding the wrongs of the future is more important than righting the wrongs of the past."

"So it is, Lady," Mace muttered, and Kelsea threw him a quick, pained grin. She wished that Father Tyler were still here; he would have understood. But he had already gone back to the Arvath.

"Lazarus means well, but he's mistaken. The wrongs of the past are not less significant, they're just harder to fix. And the longer you ignore them in favor of more pressing issues, the worse the harm, until the problems of the past actually create the problems of the future. And that brings us back to your Allie."

Javel turned around, and Kelsea saw that his eyes were wet.

"Let's say, for argument's sake, that your wife is alive, Javel. Let's say that the very worst has happened to her in Mortmesne, the most terrible thing that your imagination can conjure. Would you still want her back?"

"Of course I would!" Javel spat. "Do you think it was easy, watching her carted off in the cage? I would do anything to change it!"

"You can't change it. And since you can't, I ask you again: do you still want her back?"

"I do."

"Then here is my proposal. You will go to Mortmesne with two of my Guard. I will arm and fund you. And if you can get your Allie out, then I'll know it can be done."

Javel blinked, his expression doubtful. "I'm not a particularly good fighter, Lady. I can't even speak Mort."

"And you're a drunk," Dyer remarked from the wall.

"Shut up, Dyer!" Kelsea snapped, thinking of Barty. Barty, she now suspected, had been an alcoholic. There was no way to know for sure, but a thousand tiny hints had been scattered throughout her childhood. "Your drunkenness, Javel, is not my primary concern. I want someone committed to the enterprise."

"I only want my Allie back."

"That's all I'm asking you for."

"I'll go." Javel's eyes gleamed . . . not with life, not yet, but at least with some purpose. "I don't know how it can work, but I'll go."

"Good. Take a few days for yourself, get your affairs in order. Lazarus will be in touch."

Javel's face fell; he had clearly meant to leave right then. Mace stepped forward and growled, "Do yourself a favor, Gate Guard, and stay out of the pubs. This will be a tough trick even with a clear head."

"I can do that."

"Good. Devin, escort him to the Gate."

Javel followed the guard out the door with wandering footsteps, as though unsure of where he was going.

"You're mad, Lady," Mace muttered. "The ways that this can fail . . . I can't even list them. And you want to send two of my best men along with that ass."

"When it fails, they do call it madness, Lazarus. But when it succeeds, they call it genius, and the genius will be yours, for I'm putting this entire operation into your hands. I want to know nothing more about it."

"Thank God for small favors."

Kelsea smiled, but as the doors closed, she whipped around sharply. "Dyer!"

He came forward.

"Your mouth is a fine source of amusement to me, Dyer. But that means nothing if you can't learn when to keep it shut."

"I apologize, Majesty."

"You speak passable Mort, yes?"

Dyer blinked. "I do, Lady. My accent isn't wonderful, but I am fluent. Why?"

Kelsea glanced at Mace, who gave her an almost imperceptible nod. Dyer stared at them for a moment, then groaned. "Oh, Lady, don't tell me."

"You're going, my friend," Mace cut in. "You and Galen."

Dyer looked up at Kelsea, and she was surprised to see real hurt in his eyes. "Am I being punished, Lady?"

"Of course not. This is important work."

"To break a single slave out of Mortmesne?"

"Think bigger, you prick," Mace growled. "*I'm* sending you over there. Do you really think you'll have only one agenda?"

This time, it was Kelsea who blinked, but she recovered quickly. If she was already looking further down the road, it was no surprise that Mace was doing the same. The Mort rebellion, it had to be; Mace had made it something of a pet project in his limited free time. Under his direction, the Crown had already sent several shipments of goods to the rebels in Cite Marche.

"I apologize, Majesty," Dyer said.

"Accepted." Kelsea glanced at her watch. "Is it dinner yet?"

"Milla says thirty minutes, Majesty!" a new man called from the kitchen doorway.

"Call me when it's ready," Kelsea told Mace, climbing off the throne. "All of you have worn me out today."

In her chamber, she found the portrait they had brought up from the gallery, now leaning against the wall beside her fireplace. Kelsea stared at it for a long moment, then turned to Pen.

"Go away."

"Lady—"

"What?"

Pen splayed his hands. "Things can't remain like this forever. We have to move past what happened."

"I have moved past it!"

"You haven't." Pen spoke quietly, but Kelsea heard the low hum of anger in his voice.

"It was a weak moment, and it won't repeat."

"I'm a Queen's Guard, Lady. You have to understand that."

"I understand that you're just like every other man in the world. Get out."

Pen's breath hissed through his teeth, and Kelsea was pleased to see real pain in his eyes for a moment before he retreated to his antechamber. But as soon as he pulled the curtain closed, she collapsed in her armchair, regretting her own words. Here had been a perfectly good opportunity to repair the situation, and she had thrown it away.

Why must I be such a child?

Looking up, Kelsea caught a glimpse of her own reflection in the mirror and stiffened. She wasn't a child anymore; the ground had shifted beneath her again. A pretty—though stern—woman stared back at her from the glass. Even by the soft light of the fire, Kelsea could see that her cheekbones had become more prominent; they seemed to shape her face, pointing it downward toward a mouth that had somehow become lush.

Kelsea gave a croak of laughter. If she had a fairy godmother somewhere, then the old woman must be senile, for she was granting the wrong wishes, those that mattered least. The Tear was in a shambles and the Mort army had begun its assault on the border, but Kelsea grew prettier by the day.

Maybe this is what I wished for, she thought, staring at the mirror. *Maybe this is what I wanted more than any other thing.* A phrase from one of Carlin's books recurred: blood will tell. Kelsea thought of the portrait two floors beneath her, the smiling blonde woman with no care in the world beyond her own pleasure, and felt like screaming. But the face in the mirror remained serene, mysterious, just on the point of deepening into beauty.

"True Queen," Kelsea muttered bitterly, and heard her voice crack. Her reflection blurred for a moment, became indistinct. She blinked, confused, and then found herself fading, that curious sense of incipient otherness, of becoming someone else, which she had experienced before. She should call Pen, warn him that she was starting on one of her fugues, but humiliation overwhelmed her, and for a moment she could not find her voice. The power of this particular memory did not seem to fade with the passage of time; at any moment it could rise like the tide, swamping Kelsea and drowning her in an ocean of shame. Why should she tell Pen what was coming? It would serve him right if she blundered into a wall or a piece of furniture, if she injured herself on his watch.

You are being utterly childish. These aren't real problems. Lily *has real problems.* The Tearling *has real problems. Your little dramas aren't even on the map.*

Kelsea tried to shut the voice out, but it was too right to ignore, and for a moment she loathed the sensible side of herself, that pragmatic core that no longer allowed her even the luxury of throwing a tantrum. The room faded around her, rippling, and Kelsea felt a moment of wonder at how close the two worlds seemed to be. Lily's life and her own . . . sometimes it seemed as though they lay right beside each other, perfectly aligned . . . as though Kelsea could step over some line and simply be in a different time, in the America that was gone.

"Pen!"

He appeared in moments, his face stiff.

"I'm going," Kelsea murmured. The room was fading away now, and as Pen approached, she found that he was fading as well, until she could look right through him, into a sunlit room.

"It's all right, Lady," Pen murmured. "I won't let you fall." His grip on her arm was good, strong and comforting, but Kelsea sensed that, in time, even that would fade.

CHAPTER 8

ROW FINN

The Frewell administration liked to propound the age-old fiction that women were frail and indecisive creatures, badly in need of homes and husbands to give them structure and guidance. But even the most cursory glance at the late pre-Crossing suggests otherwise. American women were extremely resourceful in this period; they had to be, in order to survive in a world that valued them for only one thing. Indeed, many women were forced to create secret lives, lives about which we know very little, and about which their husbands certainly knew nothing.

—*The Dark Night of America*, GLEE DELAMERE

After two days, Lily had run out of books. Dorian was a voracious reader, and she went through Lily's hidden stash like lightning. Lily offered her a pocket reader, but Dorian dismissed it with a contemptuous sniff. "All the e-books are edited and purged. I worked a stretch in a SmartBook factory, and the government people were all over the place, editing content. Stick with hard copies; they're harder to alter after publication. In the better world, there won't be any electronics at all."

The better world. Lily had thought it was only a slogan, something that the Blue Horizon used to make its deeds seem more innocuous. But now she wondered. The tall Englishman, Tear, had seemed so certain that it was real. "There is no better world."

"There will be," Dorian replied calmly. "It's close now . . . so close that we can almost touch it."

That was the same thing Tear had said. The words had the ring of religious rhetoric, but Dorian seemed too practical for that. For that matter, so did Tear. In the past couple of days Lily had done several online searches, but the information was very sparse. There was a birth record for a William Tear from Southport, England, in 2046, and eleven years ago, a William Tear had been awarded the Military Cross for heroism with the Special Air Service. Lily had assumed that the Special Air Service was the British version of the old American Air Force, but after some more research, she found that the American analogue to the SAS was actually the SEALs. Now she was certain she had the right man. She had met plenty of paramilitary types through Greg, and the men always projected an air of invincibility. Tear had given the same impression, but it was combined with something else, something close to omniscience. For a few insane moments there in the nursery, Lily had been sure that he knew everything about her.

There was no other information on Tear, which seemed impossible. Lily could look up her friends' drug prescriptions—the legal ones, anyway—their genealogies, their medical records, tax statements, even their DNA sequences, if she felt like it. But William Tear had been born, had served in the British special forces, and that was all. The rest of his life had disappeared. When Lily searched for Dorian Rice, she found the same thing. The results yielded countless news stories, but they had all been published in the last few days and dealt with the explosion at the airbase. Greg had said that Dorian had escaped from the Bronx Women's Detention Center, but there was no arrest record online. There was no mention of Dorian's family, no birth certificate. It was as though someone had literally wiped Dorian and Tear from history. But only Security had the power to remove things from the net; the days when citizens could edit their own information had vanished with the enactment of the Emergency Powers Act.

Lily longed to ask Dorian about herself, but she didn't want Dorian to know that she'd gone snooping. Dorian had stopped jumping at every little thing, but she still displayed an odd paranoia that came and went. She didn't want to discuss William Tear; whenever Lily mentioned him, Dorian would snap, "No names!" making Lily feel as though she had blasphemed somehow. Dorian was able to sit up now, to make her way across the nursery, but she still froze whenever the phone rang, and she didn't like to be touched. She insisted on doing her own injections.

Tear wasn't the only topic that was off-limits. When it came to the better world, Dorian remained maddeningly evasive, speaking in vague phrases and giving no real answers. Lily couldn't tell whether she was holding something back; maybe Tear's followers didn't understand the better world either, maybe they were just as much in the dark. And yet Lily was desperate to know. The vision she had seen that night with Tear had taken hold in her mind: a vast, open land, covered with wheat and the blue ribbon of river. No guards or walls or checkpoints, only small wooden houses, people moving along freely, children running through wheat.

"When does it arrive, this better world?" Lily asked.

"I don't know," Dorian replied. "But I don't think it's very far off now."

On Sunday Lily had to leave Dorian alone to go to church, and she fretted through the service. She barely heard the priest's lecture on the sins of a childless woman, although, as always, the priest looked right at Lily and the other delinquents in his congregation. Greg put a hand on Lily's back, trying to convey sympathy, she supposed, but the deep gleam in his eyes made her uneasy. Greg was planning something, certainly, and it could be nothing good. For a brief moment she wondered if he was scheming to divorce her; even after the Frewell Laws, the government would still ease the way for rich executives who wanted to shed barren wives. But Lily was beginning to see something now that she had never seen before: to Greg, she was property, and Greg wasn't a man to give property away, not even if it was damaged. Lily wondered if things would change someday, when she became irreparably childless.

Cheerful thoughts, candyass, Maddy whispered, and Lily blinked. Ever since Dorian had rolled over the back wall into the garden, it seemed as though Maddy was everywhere, always ready to offer her opinion. But it was rarely anything that Lily wanted to hear.

After church, Greg directed his driver, Phil, to take them to the club. Lunch at the club was a Sunday routine, but Lily wished she could beg off. The thought of their friends was almost unbearable today. Lily wanted to be back in the nursery with Dorian, trying to unravel the mystery of the better world.

As they pulled out of the church parking lot, Greg pushed the button that raised the partition, blocking Phil out. Lily was alarmed to see his eyes bright with excitement.

"I found a doctor."

"A doctor," Lily repeated cautiously.

"He's not cheap, but he's licensed, and he's willing to do it."

"Do what?"

"Plant you."

For a moment Lily had no idea what he was talking about. The word *plant* made her think of implants, and her mind went automatically to the tag in her shoulder. But no, Greg meant something else. A truly awful idea popped into Lily's mind, and she shrank from it ... but she also knew that it was exactly what Greg meant.

"In vitro?"

"Of course!" Greg took her hand, leaning forward. "Listen to this. The doctor says he can use my sperm, just stick it in another woman's eggs. You have the baby and no one ever has to know."

Lily's mind went blank. For a moment, she considered simply throwing open the car door, rolling out while it was still in motion and fleeing to ... where?

"What if it's not my eggs that are the problem?"

Greg's brow furrowed, and his lower lip pushed out a fraction of an inch. He had expected his idea to be received with enthusiasm, Lily saw now, and the unadulterated contempt that had reared its head on the night of Dorian's arrival (*of the rape*, Maddy reminded her) seemed to multiply and fester inside her. Greg thought that he had come up with a great idea, that having another woman's eggs forcibly implanted inside her would seem like a godsend to Lily. And for the first time, it occurred to her to wonder whether Greg even understood that he had raped her. After Frewell, it was almost impossible to prove rape at all, and spousal rape hadn't been prosecuted in years. What would consent even mean to Greg? The bulk of his sexual education seemed to have come from his father and his frat buddies, and none of them had done him any favors.

Lily cleared her throat, dragging the words up as though with a chainfall. It would be so much easier not to say anything, but she had to know. "The other night—"

"I'm sorry, Lil." Greg took her hand, cutting her off. "I didn't mean to take it all out on you. Even without the bombing, work has been so bad lately."

"You raped me."

Greg's mouth popped open, an expression of such complete surprise overtaking his face that Lily realized she had been right: he didn't know. She turned away, staring out the window. They were just passing through the great stone arch of the New Canaan Country Club, and beyond, the vast greens of the golf course stretched toward the near horizon. Greg cleared his throat, and Lily knew what was coming even before he spoke.

"You're my wife."

Before she knew what she was doing, she laughed. Greg's face darkened, but he didn't know that Lily wasn't laughing at him, but at herself. Frewell's bullshit had worked on her too, because until the other night she had honestly believed that marriage turned men into better people, better protectors. But marriage didn't change anyone. Lily had married a man shaped by his father, the same father who had put a hand on Lily's ass at the wedding rehearsal dinner and asked whether he could get an early slice of the cake. Was she actually surprised, now, that this was where they had ended up? Was she even allowed to complain?

The tag, Lil, Maddy whispered, and she was right. The tag was the great equalizer. Lily couldn't run, because no matter where she ran to, all the money in the world wouldn't keep Greg from finding her there, and Security wouldn't lift a finger to stop him from taking her back; they would fall all over themselves to assist one of their own.

The car pulled up at the entryway, and Lily sensed Greg's relief at the end to the conversation. Coldness had descended on Lily now, a state of nearly frozen calculation. For the first time, she saw that she might have even bigger problems than what had happened the other night. She knew the amount of professional grief Greg was enduring about being childless; it was certainly impeding his career. But she had underestimated how desperate Greg was, how far he was willing to go. They moved through the enormous marble entryway of the club, an edifice that Lily usually admired, but now she barely saw it, her mind continuing forward on its unpleasant track. In vitro fertilization had been illegal since Lily was in grade school, but it was a booming black market among wealthy couples, who saw additional children as an easy way to earn the Frewell tax breaks. If Greg had found an in vitro doctor, would that doctor be able to tell that Lily was on contraception? Was there a way to flush the hormones out of her system somehow? She couldn't ask the Internet; that was the sort of search that got you a visit from Security.

Why don't you tell him you don't want kids?

But that was no longer possible, if it ever had been. She had told Greg so, in tiny ways, for years. It was nothing he was able to hear. And if the other night had proven anything, it was that what Lily wanted wasn't worth a damn. She would have to find a way around the in vitro doctor, just as she had always circumvented the surveillance system in her house. But at the moment she could think of nothing. All of the years of her marriage, years she had spent scrambling, trying to escape this noose . . . and now it seemed to be drawing tight around her neck. Lily estimated that she had less than half an inch of space left.

In the restaurant, the maître d' led them toward their table, where Lily saw several of their friends, the Palmers and Keith Thompson, already seated. Lily didn't enjoy the circle jerk that was lunch with Greg's golf buddies and their wives, but their presence suddenly seemed like a godsend, infinitely better than sitting across from Greg alone. And Keith wasn't too bad, definitely her favorite of Greg's friends. He never leered or groped or shot veiled barbs about Lily's failure to get pregnant. He was a hurried little man who'd risen to become president of his family's grocery chain; his father was the chairman. At one of their dinner parties, Keith had wandered, extremely drunk, into the kitchen where Lily was organizing dessert, and they'd had a long talk, during which he confessed to Lily that he was simply waiting for his father to die. But he was only drinking water today, and his brittle smile telegraphed his displeasure at his lunch companions.

"Mayhew!"

Mark Palmer stood up and Lily saw that he was already drunk; his cheeks were rosy and he had to grab the edge of the table for balance. Michele, beside him, had her own buzz going; her eyes were dull and she merely nodded as Lily greeted her and took a chair. When Dow and Pfizer had merged, the resulting company had kept Mark and fired Michele, but Michele still had friends somewhere in the production line. She sold under-the-counter painkillers to half of New Canaan, and made a good profit. Lily's body still ached whenever she sat down, and for a moment she considered doing a little business with Michele today, but then discarded the idea. She was hiding a terrorist in her nursery, and Greg wanted to haul her off to a back-alley doctor. Painkillers would make Lily as dull as Michele, who was her own best customer, and Lily couldn't afford that. But they would still need to go off to the bathroom at some point, so that Lily could return Michele's books and ask for more.

Greg ordered whisky, shooting another resentful look at Lily as the waiter walked away. She had driven him to drink, that look said. There was no introspection in Greg's gaze; the word *rape* seemed to have rolled off him like water. Lily suddenly remembered a day several years ago, a weekend in college when they had driven up the coastline, not going anywhere in particular, simply cruising, Lily with her right foot stuck out the passenger-side window and Greg with his left hand on her thigh. What had happened to those two kids? Where had they gone?

Lunch was served, but Sarah and Ford did not appear, which was odd. They always lunched at the club on Sundays. Lily hadn't seen them in church either.

"Where's Sarah?" she finally asked Michele.

The table went quiet, and Lily realized that everyone knew something she didn't. Michele gave her a discouraging shake of the head, and Mark quickly began to tell a story about some mix-up at work. A few minutes later Michele jerked her chin toward the lobby, and Lily stood up.

"Where are you going?"

Greg had grabbed her wrist and was looking up at her

with narrowed, suspicious eyes. Lily suddenly realized that she hated her husband, hated him more than she had ever hated anyone or anything in her entire life.

"To the bathroom. With Michele."

Greg let go, giving her arm a small jerk as he did so, and Lily stumbled away from the table. Keith Thompson stared after her with concerned eyes, and Lily wished she could tell him that it was all right, but that seemed extremely optimistic.

In the bathroom, Lily asked again, "What happened to Sarah?"

Michele paused in the act of fixing her eyeliner. "It happened three days ago. How do you not know?"

A fair question. There were no secrets in New Canaan; Lily usually knew the scandals of her neighbors before they even knew themselves. "I've been busy."

"With what?"

"Nothing special. What happened?"

"Sarah's in custody."

"What for?"

"She tried to take out her tag."

Lily said nothing for a moment, trying to connect this information with Sarah, who had once told Lily that her husband only used his fists because he cared so much. Of all of Lily's friends, Sarah seemed the least likely to try something so drastic. "What happened?"

"Don't know." Michele began to fix her lipliner. "She went at her own shoulder with a knife. Missed the tag, but she nearly bled to death. Ford turned her in."

Now that *was* in character. Once, on a family vacation, Ford had left Sarah at a rest stop on the Pennsylvania Turnpike. If Sarah hadn't called him a few minutes later, he might have been all the way to Harrisburg before he noticed she was gone.

"What'll happen to her?"

Michele shrugged, and Lily saw that Michele had already begun to forget about Sarah, to move on. This forgetting was something you learned to do when someone disappeared, the response so ingrained that it seemed like poor taste to do anything else. Lily had not been able to forget Maddy, but that was different. She bore fault.

"I have your books." Lily pulled them from her bag, but before she could hand them over, Michele reeled away, bent over and threw up into the sink. Even before she was finished, the sink's cleaning mechanism began to wipe it away, making small, methodical sweeping sounds.

"Are you all right?" Lily asked, but Michele waved her away. Her voice, when it came, was garbled.

"I'm pregnant again."

"Congratulations," Lily replied automatically. "Boy or girl?"

Michele spat into the sink. "Boy, and a good thing too. If we had another girl, Mark wanted to have it taken care of."

"What?"

"I don't really care, either way."

Lily stared at her. Michele had never talked this way before, and although Lily could imagine that it was no picnic being Mark Palmer's wife, she had always assumed that Michele was like the rest of her friends: happy to be a mother. Michele was always going to soccer games and bragging about her children's grades. Lily tentatively offered her the books again, and Michele shoved them inside her enormous purse. The size of Michele's handbags was a running joke among their group of friends, but she needed the space for all the contraband she had to transport around New Canaan. Michele did many of her dealings in this very bathroom, one of the few places in the city that had no surveillance camera.

"What are you going to do?" Lily asked.

"Have it. What else am I going to do? Mark's already bragging to everyone at work."

"What about the painkillers?"

Michele narrowed her eyes. "What about them?"

Lily pursed her lips, feeling like the unpleasant chaperone at a party. "Aren't they bad for the baby?"

"Who cares? Eighty percent of upper-income mothers are on tranquilizers or painkillers, or both. Did you know that?"

"No."

"Of course you didn't. Drug companies don't want that information made public. People might start asking why." Michele fixed her with a disgusted stare. "And then there's you. Never have to be pregnant, do you? Never have to be a mother."

Lily recoiled. She and Michele had never been good friends, but they had always gotten along . . . and now Lily realized how little that meant.

"Mark laughs at you two all the time . . . Greg and his empty oven. But you'll never have to have four screaming kids hanging off you, will you?"

Lily backed up a step at the sight of Michele's normally pretty face, contorted with hatred and—jealousy? Lily thought it was. But even as she backed away, she felt her temper rising. The picture Michele painted was the stereotype of a poor woman with too many mouths to feed. Lily had even seen the image on government posters whenever a social services bill was up in Congress. But Michele had two nannies to help raise her three children. Some of their friends even had three or four nannies. Michele spent perhaps an hour a day actually being a mother.

Michele had taken out a bottle of pills now, and she swallowed two of them with ease. The digital cleaner had finished, and now the sink was as clean and gleaming as it had been when they came in. Michele splashed some water on her face and dried it with a towel. "We should go back out."

When they sat down at the table, Keith leaned over and asked Lily, "Are you all right?"

She nodded, fixing a pleasant smile on her face. For the rest of the meal, she tried to keep her eyes off Michele, but she couldn't help it. Were all of her friends so miserable on the inside? Sarah had answered that question. Jessa, maybe; her husband, Paul, was a decent enough guy until he drank. Christine? Lily didn't know. Christine's eyes had a constant, glazed shine that could be either drugs or religious fervor; Christine was the head of the Women's Bible Circle at their church. Lily had never trusted any of her friends, but she had thought she knew them.

Over lunch, Lily tried to talk to Keith, who asked after her mother and about her plans for the rest of the summer. But Greg was now staring at Keith as well, with the same narrow, suspicious stare. Lily had seen that look many times growing up, on their dog, Henry, who didn't like to share his chew toys with anyone else. Here was the *real* pig in a poke: she didn't belong to herself anymore. She was a doll, a doll that Greg had bought and paid for.

There are ways around that, Maddy whispered, but it did nothing to alleviate Lily's anxiety. Dr. Davis's clinic was one thing, but finding a doctor who would perform an abortion

. . . that was a whole different level of illegal. She suddenly remembered the heavily pregnant woman in the clinic, the one who had bled all over the chair. Was it possible that Dr. Davis performed abortions as well? Lily had never heard a whisper of that, but of course she wouldn't have. That was something you didn't tell anyone.

Greg was staying at the club to play golf with Mark and a few of their other friends, so Lily went home alone, glad for the quiet emptiness of the backseat. After Phil dropped her off, she made Dorian some broth and took it to the nursery, along with a bottle of water. She had been afraid to feed Dorian anything but broth, chicken and beef, but if Dorian had grown tired of the selection, she didn't say anything. When Lily entered the nursery, she found Dorian on the floor, stretching, reaching for her toes. Her shirt was soaked with sweat. She must be getting better, to be able to stretch that way, but she still looked very pale.

"Won't you tear your stitches?" Lily asked.

"Doesn't matter," Dorian grunted. She had tied her blonde hair up into messy pigtails, and this made her look more like Maddy than ever. "Can't afford to be laid up."

"I'm sure he'd rather you get well first." Out of deference to Dorian, Lily didn't use Tear's name out loud. But she wondered: was the Englishman really so demanding that he would expect Dorian to be up and about two days after being shot? Or did she put this pressure on herself?

"This is a nice nursery," Dorian remarked. "But I don't hear any kids running around."

A wild giggle popped from Lily's mouth. "I don't want kids."

"Me neither."

"No, I mean, I might want them. But not here." She

gestured toward the house around her. "Not like this. I take pills."

She had hoped to surprise Dorian, maybe impress her, but Dorian merely nodded and continued with her stretching.

"Have you ever been married?"

"God, no. I'm a dyke."

Lily recoiled, slightly shocked. "You have sex with women?"

"Sure."

The nonchalance with which Dorian confessed this stunned Lily into silence. Openly confessing a crime to a stranger, especially a serious crime like homosexuality . . . that seemed like real freedom. She pointed to the scar on Dorian's shoulder. "Was that from your tag?"

"Yup. First thing we do is remove that little bastard."

"How?"

"Can't tell you," Dorian replied, panting, as she reached for her toes. "Valuable information if you were ever taken into custody."

"I wouldn't tell."

Dorian smiled grimly. "Everyone tells in the end."

"I mean I'm trustworthy."

"Trust me with a secret, then. Where do you hide your pills?"

Lily showed Dorian the loose tile in the corner, the pile of contraband underneath.

"It's good, well camouflaged. How many hiding places do you have?"

"Just this."

"That's no good. You should always have more than one hiding place."

"I can't hide anything anywhere else. Greg will find

it. He does inspections now. But he never comes in here."

"Jonathan says you fixed the surveillance in this place." Dorian gave her a look of frank admiration. "Where'd a wall lady learn to do something like that?"

"My sister. She was good with computers."

"Well, I'd still get another hiding place. One is never enough."

"How many do you have?"

"When I was a kid, dozens. But I don't have any now." Dorian pushed herself up and reached for the bowl of broth. "In the better world, we won't need to hide anything."

"I don't understand. Is the better world biblical? Are angels going to descend and wipe the earth clean?"

"God, no!" Dorian replied, laughing. "In the better world, no one will need religion."

"I don't understand," Lily repeated.

"Well, why should you? The better world's not for people like you."

Lily recoiled, as though she'd been slapped. Dorian didn't notice; she was busy eating her broth and staring out the glass doors into the backyard. She was waiting, Lily realized now, waiting for the Englishman to come and take her away. Part of her was already gone.

Lily left the nursery, closing the door carefully behind her, and went downstairs. It was all nonsense, she told herself. Tear and his people were probably crazy, the whole lot of them. But all the same, she felt as though they had left her behind.

When Kelsea came back to herself, she heard thunder. She looked up and found the blessed comfort of Carlin's bookshelves, the long rows of volumes, each in its own place. She reached out to touch the books, but then

291

Lily's sorrow echoed in her mind, pulling her back across centuries.

Why am I seeing this? Why do I have to suffer with her, when her story is already done?

The thundering sound came again, and with it, the last of Lily's memories faded away, and Kelsea was suddenly alert. Not thunder, but many feet, moving in the hallway outside. Kelsea turned away from the books and found Pen standing just behind her, listening intently, his manner so grave that Kelsea forgot to be angry at him.

"Pen? What is it?"

"I had a thought to go investigate, Lady, but I'm not supposed to leave you at such times."

Now Kelsea heard a hollow, muffled groan, slightly distant, as though it came from down the corridor. "Let's go and see."

"I think it's Kibb, Lady. He's been sick for two days now, getting worse all the time."

"Sick with what?"

"No one knows. Flu, maybe."

"Why didn't anyone tell me?"

"Kibb didn't want us to, Lady."

"Well, come on."

She led him into the corridor, where nothing was moving, only the flicker of torches. In the dim light the hallway looked twice as long; it seemed to stretch miles from the darkened door of the guard quarters to the well-lit audience chamber.

"What time is it?" she whispered.

"Half past eleven."

The hollow groan sounded again: muffled agony, weaker this time, near the guard quarters.

"Mace won't want you down there, Lady."

"Come on."

Pen didn't try to stop her, which afforded Kelsea some small satisfaction. Weak torchlight gleamed from the open door of one of the chambers near the end of the hallway, and Kelsea walked faster, her feet hurrying her along.

Turning the corner, she found herself in what was clearly a man's bedchamber. Everything seemed to be dark, and there was very little decoration, but Kelsea admired the room's austerity; this was just the way she imagined her guards' quarters.

Kibb lay on the bed, his brow shiny with sweat, naked down to his hips. Bent over him was Schmidt, Mace's doctor of choice for emergencies. Elston, Coryn, and Wellmer were at the bedside, and Mace, crouched at the foot of the bed, completed the tableau. As Kelsea entered the room, Mace's face darkened, but he only muttered, "Lady."

"How is he?"

Schmidt did not bow, but Kelsea did not take offense; there seemed to be no ego to compare with that of the doctor in demand. His voice revealed a heavy Mort accent. "The appendix, Majesty. I would try to operate, but it would do no good. It will burst before I am able to get in there clean. If I perform as quickly as I must, he will bleed to death. I have given him morphia for his pain, but I can do nothing else."

Kelsea blinked, horrified. Appendectomy had been a routine pre-Crossing surgery, so common and simple that Lily's procedure had been done by machines rather than human hands. But the grim resignation on the doctor's face said everything that needed to be said.

"We've promised to take care of his mother, Lady," Mace murmured. "We've made him as comfortable as possible.

There's little else we can do. You shouldn't be here for this."

"Perhaps not, but it's a little late to walk away."

"El?" Kibb asked. His voice was slurred with some kind of narcotic.

"I'm right here, you ass," Elston muttered. "I'm not going anywhere."

Elston was holding Kibb's hand, Kelsea saw. It looked odd, Kibb's small hand buried in Elston's giant fist, but she couldn't even smile. They did everything together, Elston and Kibb, and Kelsea couldn't remember a time when she had seen one without the other. Best friends . . . but now, looking at their clasped hands, at the agony that Elston was trying so desperately to hide, Kelsea's mind came up with a third and fourth piece of information: neither Elston nor Kibb had a woman in the Keep, and their chambers adjoined.

Elston looked up at her dumbly, and Kelsea did her best not to blush. She reached for Kibb's other hand, which lay fisted at his side. His eyes were closed, his teeth clenched against another groan, and cords stood out on his neck. Kelsea could see individual beads of sweat as they rolled down his temples and cheeks to settle in the matting of his hair. At the touch of her hand, Kibb's eyes opened again, and he attempted a smile through gritted teeth.

"Majesty," he croaked. "I am a Queen's Guard of the Tear."

"Yes," Kelsea replied, not knowing what else to say. Her own helplessness had frozen her tongue. She wormed her hand inside his, felt him clasp it gently.

"My honor, Lady." Kibb smiled, a smile of drugs, and his eyes slipped closed again. Elston made a choking sound and turned away, but Kelsea could not. Schmidt was undoubtedly the best doctor Mace could find, but he was only the shadow of a dead breed. There was no real medicine any-more; all of it had gone down with the White Ship, the medical personnel left behind, bobbing in the waves beneath the storm. What Kelsea wouldn't give for even one of those doctors now! She thought of the brutal cold the survivors must have endured, treading water in the middle of God's Ocean until exhaustion made them sink beneath the waves. By the end, they must have been in agony. Frigid air seemed to coalesce around Kelsea and she began to shiver helplessly, her legs cramping. Her vision went dark.

"Lady?"

A great shock slammed into Kelsea's chest, so hard that she gasped. Pen caught her from behind, or she would have fallen backward. She clamped Kibb's hand more tightly, struggling to hold on to him, knowing somehow that if she let go, the spell would be broken and nothing could be done—

Her stomach imploded in pain. Kelsea clamped her mouth shut, but a shriek built behind her lips and her body bucked in rebellion. Unbearable pressure laced across her abdomen and seemed to wrench her muscles, stretching them beyond their capacity.

"Hold her! Get her mouth open!"

Hands were on her arms and legs, but Kelsea barely felt them. The pressure on her abdomen doubled, tripled, going up and up, a feeling that had no comparison for Kelsea beyond the increasing scream of a teakettle. Her body con-tinued to thrash, her heels digging into the chamber floor, but the inner Kelsea was thousands of miles away, struggling in the dark of God's Ocean, trying not to go under. A wave of freezing water broke on her, closed over her head, and Kelsea tasted bitter salt.

Fingers forced her mouth open—somehow, she knew they

were Pen's—and groped for her tongue, but it all seemed very distant. There was only the shredding agony in her belly, and the cold, a paralyzing cold that seemed to have enclosed the entire world. Kelsea breathed in shallow gasps, trying not to gag at the intrusion of fingers pinning her tongue.

"You! Doctor! Get over here!"

Hands on her shoulders now, bruising hands, holding her down with great force. Mace's hands, his face above her torn with anxiety, shouting commands because that's how Mace dealt with crisis, sometimes it seemed that he could do nothing but give orders—

The pain vanished.

Kelsea took a deep breath and lay still. After a few moments, the hands on her relaxed, but didn't let go entirely. She looked up and saw them crouched over her: Mace, Pen, Elston, Coryn, and Wellmer. The ceiling was a mass of incomprehensible tiles over their heads.

With a murmured apology, Pen removed his fingers from her mouth. Kelsea's body felt light, clear, as though her blood had been replaced with water . . . the water that came from the spring near the cottage, so clean that they could prepare food with it directly from the pool. The unnatural cold had gone as well, and Kelsea was warm now, almost drowsy, as though someone had wrapped her in a blanket.

"Lady? Are you in pain?"

Kelsea was still gripping a hard object: Kibb's hand. She sat up, feeling Pen move to support her shoulders. Kibb lay entirely still now, his eyes closed.

"Is he dead?"

Schmidt leaned over Kibb, his hands moving in a rapid, clinical way that Kelsea admired: forehead to pulse, and back to forehead again. He checked these areas with increasing agitation before finally turning to Kelsea, his face blank. "No, Majesty. The patient breathes easy."

He pressed downward on Kibb's abdomen, tentatively, ready to withdraw at any twitch. But there was nothing. Even Kelsea could see Kibb's chest rise and fall now, the deep, even breathing of a man in the darkest part of unconsciousness.

"His fever is finished," Schmidt murmured, pressing hard on Kibb's stomach now, as though desperate to elicit a response. "Really, we should dry and cover him, or he will take a chill."

"The appendix?" Mace asked.

Schmidt shook his head, sitting back on his heels. Kelsea reached up to clutch her two sapphires. They hadn't spoken to her since the Argive, but still their weight was comforting, a solid thing to hold.

"Sir?" One of the new guards was peeking around the doorway. "Is everything all right? We heard—"

"Everything is fine," Mace replied, turning a threatening glare on everyone in the room. "Back to your post, Aaron, and shut the door behind you."

"Yes sir." Aaron vanished.

"He's all right?" Wellmer whispered. His face was pale and young, just as it had been months ago when Kelsea first met him, before life had begun to mature him a bit. Mace did not answer, only turned to Schmidt with a resigned expression, the face of a man waiting for a verdict who knows that he is already condemned.

The doctor wiped his forehead. "The swelling is gone. He appears to be completely healthy, but for the perspiration ... and even that could be explained as the *cauchemar*, the night terror."

Now they all turned to look at Kelsea, all of them except Elston, who continued to stare at Kibb.

"Are you all right, Lady?" Pen finally asked.

"I'm fine," Kelsea replied. She thought of that first night when she had cut open her own arm. She had done so several times since; it was a coping mechanism, and her body was a good place to divert the rage. Her legs were better to cut than her arms, easier to hide. But was this a similar thing, or was it different? If it was her jewels, why didn't they give any sign? Kelsea's shoulders felt like brick. "I'm tired, though. I'll need to sleep soon."

Schmidt's face was a portrait of upset, his eyes moving swiftly between Kelsea and Kibb. "Majesty, I do not know what I have just seen, but—"

Mace grasped the doctor's wrist. "You saw nothing."

"What?"

"None of you saw anything. Kibb was ill, but he took a turn for the better in the night."

Kelsea found herself nodding.

"But—"

"Wellmer, use the brain God gave you!" Mace snapped. "What happens if word goes out that the Queen can heal the sick?"

"Oh." Wellmer pondered this for a moment. Kelsea tried to think as well, but she was so tired. Mace's words jangled in her mind: *heal the sick* . . .

What did I do?

"I see, sir," Wellmer finally replied. "Everyone would have a sick mother, a sick child . . ."

"Kibb!" Mace bent down and shook Kibb's shoulder, then slapped him lightly across the face. Elston winced, but said nothing. "Kibb, wake up!"

Kibb's eyes opened, and by a trick of the torchlight Kelsea thought that the pupils seemed almost transparent, as though they had been cleaned out and replaced with . . . what? Light? She turned her senses inward and examined her own body, her own heartbeat. Everything was moving faster. She shook her head, trying to get rid of the rays that seemed to be shining through her mind. They went, but with a slight twinkle of mischief that did nothing to allay the feeling of unreality that swamped her.

"How do you feel, Kibb?" Mace asked.

"Light," Kibb groaned. "All light."

Kelsea looked up and found the doctor staring at her again.

"Do you remember anything?"

Kibb laughed softly. "I was on the edge of a cliff and sliding. The Queen grabbed me back. Everything was so clear—"

Mace crossed his arms, his jaw clenched in frustration. "He's like a man on an opium binge."

"Will he sober up, Lady?" asked Coryn.

"How would I know?" Kelsea demanded. All of them, even Pen, were looking at her with the same suspicion, as though she had hidden something from them, some long-time secret that had finally come to light. She thought of the cuts on her arms and legs again, but forced the thought away.

Mace grunted in exasperation. "We have to hope he'll come out of it. Leave him in here and post a guard. No visitors. Lady, you should go on back to bed."

This sounded so wonderful to Kelsea that she merely nodded and trudged away, ignoring Pen's nearly silent tread behind her. She wanted to sort things out, but she was too exhausted to think. If she could heal the sick—but she shook her head, cutting off the rest. There was power there, yes, but it was a ruinous sort of power. Even now, she could feel the edges of the idea curdling inside her head.

Heal the sick, heal the sick.

Mace's words rang like bells in her mind, no matter how she tried to push them away.

The next evening, after dinner, Kelsea was in the middle of her daily argument with Arliss when a messenger arrived, bearing the news she'd been dreading: six days ago, the Mort had broken through on the border. Having been frustrated in several attacks by the line of archers in the trees, Ducarte had finally taken the most direct method and simply set the entire hillside on fire. Hall had had the good sense to withdraw his battalion back toward the Almont and avoid direct battle, but nearly all of his archers had been caught in the fire, burning to death in their treetop nests. By now the Mort would be transporting their heavy equipment over the hillside, and the bulk of their infantry would already have moved down into the Almont. On Bermond's orders, the Tear army had pulled back to the Caddell. Fire still raged across the Border Hills; if it didn't rain soon, thousands of acres of good timber would be destroyed.

Kelsea had thought herself prepared for this news; after all, it had been inevitable from the start. But still it hit her hard, the idea of Mort soldiers on Tear land. For the last two weeks a separate wing of the Mort army had been besieging the Argive Pass, just as Bermond had warned her; the Mort Road was a much more convenient route by which to move supplies from Demesne than the rough ground of the Border Hills. But so far the Argive had held, and while the Mort had been pinned inside their own territory, the invasion had seemed somehow less real. The Mort would find no reward in the Almont; the eastern half of the kingdom was nearly emptied now, but for a few isolated farming villages on the extreme northern and southern outskirts whose occupants had chosen to remain where they were. There was nothing for the Mort to pillage, but still Kelsea hated the idea of them out there, moving like a slow dark tide across her land. She crumpled the message in one fist, feeling a new cut open on the inside of her thigh. The cuts kept her anger inside her, kept it from spilling out all over everyone surrounding, but it had grown frustrating, always having to hold back. Kelsea longed for a real target, someone she could actually injure, and this longing then led her to cut herself more deeply, to relish the pain even while she bled. The cuts healed themselves at an incredible rate, sometimes even before a day had elapsed, and so they were fairly easy to hide from everyone . . . everyone except Andalie, who dealt with Kelsea's laundry. Andalie remained silent, but Kelsea knew that she was concerned. Despite the heat of the summer, Kelsea had taken to wearing nothing but thick black dresses with long sleeves, and this only served to deepen her kinship with Lily Mayhew, who had so many things to hide. Kelsea spent long periods of time trying to understand Lily, to understand what possible connection there could be between them, for Kelsea could not believe that she would see anything so detailed, so realistic, for no reason at all. With Father Tyler's help, she had now been through all of Carlin's history books, and there was no record of Lily anywhere. Historically speaking, Lily was unimportant . . . but it never felt that way when Kelsea was with her, bound up inside her life. Still, she had tabled her research, for there was only so much time

she could expend on Lily, on the past. The present had become too terrible.

With Bermond's message still clutched in her fist, Kelsea left Arliss's office and stormed down the hall to her own chamber. Closing the curtain on Pen, she wandered over toward the fireplace. The portrait of the handsome man still leaned on the wall, covered with a dropcloth. Kelsea had found that the picture made her a bit uneasy; the man's eyes did indeed follow her wherever she went, and he seemed to be smirking at her. Andalie, too, disliked the man in the portrait intensely. If she, or Glee, had had any more visions, Andalie kept them to herself, but she treated the portrait like poison, and she was the one who had draped a sheet over the man's face.

Now Kelsea pulled off the sheet and stared at the portrait for a very long time. If nothing else, the man from the fireplace was extremely handsome, enjoyable to gaze at. Andalie said that the man was evil, and he was; Kelsea could sense it even in the portrait, the hint of cruelty in his smile. But, Kelsea realized, that was also part of the draw. She'd had several dreams about the man now, barely remembered dreams in which she had been naked before him on what felt like a bed of fire. Always, Kelsea woke up just before physical contact, her sheets soaked with sweat. It was different from what she felt for the Fetch, who, despite his misdeeds, seemed fundamentally decent. This man's wickedness pulled at her, magnetic. She drew a finger down the canvas, debating. He had said he knew how to defeat the Red Queen. Kelsea had only half believed him, but the Mort were here now, and she could no longer afford not to grasp at straws. The man had said that he wanted freedom. He had said he would come when she called.

Kelsea sat down in front of the fire, crossing her legs beneath her. The fire was strong, and the heat baked her face.

I am only keeping my options open, she told herself firmly. *There's nothing wrong with that.*

"Where are you?" she whispered.

Something seemed to gather darkly in front of the flames, like coal dust compacting, and a moment later he appeared, just in front of the mantel, tall and substantial. Kelsea's reaction to his presence was even stronger now than it had been before, a flurry of pulse and nerves that she fought to force down. Lust made her stupid, she saw now . . . and she could not afford to be stupid with this creature.

Where do you come from? she asked him. *Do you live in the fire?*

I live in dark, Tear heir. I've waited long years to see the sun.

Kelsea pointed to the portrait. *This picture is very old. Are you a ghost?*

He surveyed the portrait, a humorless smile crossing his face. *You might think of me as a ghost, but I am flesh. See for yourself.*

He placed a hand on Kelsea's chest, just above her breasts. Her shoulders hitched involuntarily, but he didn't seem to notice, giving her a searching look. *You are stronger, Tear heir. What has happened to you?*

I want to bargain.

What, no time for pleasantries? He smiled, and Kelsea was alarmed by her own response to that smile. *Pleasure makes life bearable, you know.*

Kelsea shut her eyes, focusing, then hissed as a new slice opened on her forearm. It was a deep one, and painful, but it steadied her, calming her pulse, the ache in her breasts. *You said you knew how to defeat the Queen of Mortmesne.*

So I do. She is not invulnerable, though she would like to be.

How can she be beaten?

What do you offer in return, Tear heir? Yourself?

You don't want me. You want your freedom.

I want many things.

What can a creature like you possibly want in the physical world?

I still take joy in physical things. I must sustain myself.

Sustain yourself on what?

He grinned, though a flare of red sparked in his eyes. *You are quick, Tear heir. You ask the right questions.*

What do you want? Be explicit.

Shall we draw up a bargain, like the treaty that wrecked your mother?

Did you appear to my mother this way as well?

Your mother was beneath my notice.

He meant this as a compliment to Kelsea, she could tell, and it worked, creating a tiny, warm glow inside her. But she pressed on, knowing that she could not afford to be sidetracked. *If we're to bargain, I want the terms clearly defined.*

Fine. You will set me free, and I will tell you of the Red Queen's vulnerability. Have we a bargain?

Kelsea hesitated. Things were moving too quickly. The Mort were hampered by their siege equipment; by Hall's estimates, Kelsea had at least a month before they reached the city. That was not long, but it was enough time to reflect, to make a good decision. And now a new worry struck Kelsea: even if she was somehow able to destroy the Red Queen, would that necessarily translate to defeating her army? Would it die with the head cut off, or would it simply grow a new one, hydra-like?

Too many unknowns here, Kelsea, Carlin whispered, and Kelsea knew she was right.

I will consider it, she told the man before her. He blinked, as though fatigued, and Kelsea realized that he looked less substantial, somehow . . . Squinting, she saw that the fire behind him was clearly visible, flames flickering dimly through both his clothing and the area where his rib cage should have been. His face, too, had turned pale with fatigue.

Noticing the direction of Kelsea's gaze, the man frowned. He closed his eyes for a moment, seeming to solidify right in front of her, becoming more opaque. When he opened his eyes, he was smiling again, a smile of such warm, calculating sensuality that Kelsea took a step back. Her arousal instantly darkened, became tinged with an edge of fright.

What are you?

His gaze darted behind Kelsea, over her left shoulder, and his face compacted into a snarl, lips drawing back from his white teeth. His eyes gleamed red, burning with a sudden, blazing hatred that made Kelsea stumble backward, her feet tangling in her dress. She braced herself to land on her tailbone with a hard thud, but before she could, someone caught her beneath the arms. When Kelsea looked up, the last of the fire had gone out and the man was gone, but arms remained around Kelsea from behind, and she struggled, kicking against the floor.

"Easy, Tear Queen," a voice murmured in her ear, and Kelsea quieted.

"You. How did you get past Pen?"

"He's unconscious."

"Is he all right?"

"Of course. I put him out for a bit, only long enough for us to do some business."

Business. Of course it would be business. "Let me go. I'll light a candle."

The Fetch released her, giving her a firm push up, and Kelsea shuffled her way to the bedside table. Her cheeks were still flushed, and she could feel the blood burning there. She took her time about lighting the candle, trying to get some control back, but as she fumbled around on the table for her matches, his voice echoed behind her.

"Two inches to your left."

So he does see in the dark, Kelsea thought, irritated. When she finally lit the candle and turned to face him, she expected to see the man she remembered, all amused mouth and dancing eyes. But his face was grave in the candlelight.

"I knew he would come here, sooner or later. What did he ask for?"

"Nothing," Kelsea replied. But she knew that the blush on her cheeks would give her away. She had never been able to lie well, and certainly not to the Fetch.

He stared at her for a long moment. "Let me give you some friendly advice, Tear Queen. I have known this creature for a very long time. Don't give him anything. Don't even converse with him. He will only lead you to grief."

"Who is he?"

"Once he was a man, a powerful man. You would know him as Rowland Finn."

The name rang a bell, deep in Kelsea's mind. Carlin had mentioned Finn once, something to do with the Landing . . . what had it been?

The Fetch stepped closer. He was staring at her face, Kelsea realized, cataloguing the changes, and she dropped her chin, peeking up at him as she pretended to study the floor. He looked healthy, if somewhat leaner than the last time Kelsea had seen him. His face was slightly tanned, as though he'd been in the south. He still pulled at her, as much as he ever had, and the pull was accompanied by a sick sense of loss, deep in Kelsea's stomach. All the lust that had governed her body in the last few minutes had transferred easily to the Fetch, and now she realized how hollow her earlier reactions had been; what she felt for this man dwarfed anything she would ever feel for anyone else. She had dreamed of the day when she would see the Fetch again, when she would greet him not as a round-faced girl but as a pretty woman, perhaps even a beautiful one. But she didn't like the way he was staring at her, not at all.

"Who are you, Fetch? Do you have a real name?"

"I have many names. All are useful."

"Why not tell me the real one?"

"A name is power, Tear Queen. Your name was once Raleigh, and now it's Glynn. Did the change mean nothing to you?"

Kelsea blinked, for his question made her think not of Barty and Carlin, nor even of her own mother, but of the Mort Treaty, the signature in red ink at the bottom. The Queen of Mortmesne, her true name hidden from the world. Why did she hide it so closely? Kelsea was Glynn now, but she had also been Glynn as a child, because the entire world was looking for a girl child named Raleigh. But why would a woman as powerful as the Red Queen need to hide her birth name from anyone? Was she so anxious to leave the past behind?

Who is she, really?

The Fetch had wandered over to her desk, fingering the papers there. "You've lost weight, Tear Queen. Don't you eat enough?"

"I eat plenty."

"Then stop trying to hide your face. Let me see what you've done to yourself."

There was no help for it. Kelsea turned for his inspection, keeping her eyes on the floor.

"You have transformed," the Fetch stated flatly. "Is this what you wanted?"

"What do you mean?"

He pointed to her sapphires. "My knowledge of those things is not extensive. But this isn't the first time I've seen them grant a wish. You performed a great feat in the Argive. What else have you been able to do?"

Kelsea firmed her jaw. "Nothing."

"I know when you're lying, Tear Queen."

Kelsea recoiled. His tone was eerily reminiscent of Carlin's when she caught Kelsea committing minor infractions: sneaking an extra cookie from the kitchen, or dodging chores. "Nothing! I have dreams sometimes. Visions."

"About what?"

"The pre-Crossing. A woman. What does it matter?"

His eyes narrowed. "When, in our acquaintance, have you ever been the one to decide what matters?"

Kelsea's composure seemed to buckle beneath her, like a beam made of weak wood. "I'm not a child in your camp anymore! Don't talk to me like that!"

"In my eyes, Tear Queen, you are a child. An infant, even."

Angry tears sprung to Kelsea's eyes, but she fought them, swallowing great gulps of air, the bleak thought recurring in her mind: *This isn't how it was supposed to go.*

"What does she look like, this pre-Crossing woman?" the Fetch asked.

"She's tall and pretty and sad. She hardly ever smiles."

"Her name?"

"Lily Mayhew."

The Fetch smiled then, a slow, genuine smile that undermined Kelsea's anger, washing away its foundations like the tide. "Is there a girl there? A girl with long reddish hair?"

Kelsea blinked. Running quickly through Lily's memories, she shook her head, and was shocked by the disappointment in the Fetch's face. He had needed her to say yes, needed it badly.

"Who is Lily Mayhew?"

The Fetch shook his head. His eyes glimmered, almost with tears, though Kelsea refused to believe that, when she had never seen this man moved by anything. "Only a woman, I suppose."

"If you're only going to ask questions and give no answers, then fuck off."

"The mouth on you, Tear Queen."

"I mean it. Speak plainly or get out."

"All right." He sat down in her armchair and leaned back, crossing his legs, all trace of emotion gone. "There is a protest movement growing in Mortmesne."

"I've heard about it. Lazarus has sent them some goods."

"They need more support."

"Support them, then. My kingdom barely has the cash to arm itself."

"I do support them. I've funneled a considerable amount of my own wealth in that direction."

"Ah. So it is you. Levieux, is it? The old? Did you never think of funneling some of that wealth into the Tear?"

"Until very recently, Tear Queen, I would sooner have invested my money in magic beans. Now I'm committed to these people, who agitate for a more equitable Mortmesne.

But they require victories to keep going. Open support from the Tearling would be good for morale."

"What of Cadare?"

"The Cadarese have already begun to sabotage their tribute to Mortmesne, which is a useful distraction. But the Mort hold the Cadarese in small esteem, whereas you're a figure of much curiosity over there, particularly among the poor."

"I'll consider it. I need to talk to Lazarus."

"You know the Mort have broken through the border."

"Yes."

"What will you do when they come?"

"The entire population will be in New London by then. It'll be a tight fit, but the city can hold them, at least for a time. I have an entire battalion laying in supplies for siege and fortifying the back side of the city."

"They will breach the walls eventually."

Kelsea frowned. "I know that."

"And what will you do?"

She said nothing, kept her eyes away from the fireplace. The Fetch didn't press her further, only leaned his chin on one fist, watching her with clear amusement. "Your mind is a fascinating thing, Tear Queen, always moving."

She nodded, wandering across the room to her desk. She realized that she was trying to put herself front and center, trying to force him to notice her, the way she always noticed him. She suddenly found herself loathsome. She was the same Kelsea she had always been, and he hadn't wanted her before. If he suddenly wanted her now that she had a pretty face and a pretty body, what did that make him?

I can't win. Her old appearance had been genuine, and had gained her nothing. But her new appearance was worse, hollow and false, and anything that she gained by it would carry that falsity like a disease. If this was the work of her jewels, then Kelsea didn't want it anymore.

"You grow pretty, Tear Queen."

Kelsea flushed. The statement, which might have pleased her moments before, now made her feel sick.

"What will you do with your new beauty? Catch yourself a rich husband?"

"I won't share my throne, not with anyone."

"What about an heir?"

"There are other ways to get one."

He threw back his head and laughed. "Practical, Tear Queen."

Kelsea looked toward the curtain, thinking of Pen. If the Fetch's laughter hadn't woken him, he really must be out cold.

"Your guard is fine. I'll wake him on my way out. If it's any consolation, he was a tougher mark than your uncle's guards ever were; at least Alcott stays awake on duty."

Seeing an opportunity to change the subject, Kelsea jumped on it. "I suppose I should thank you for my lawn ornament."

The Fetch's face sobered, turning thoughtful. "Thomas died well, though it galls me to admit it. He died like a man."

Dying well. Kelsea closed her eyes and saw again the Mort coming, crossing the Caddell and breaching the walls. She turned away, staring at the fireplace. Where was the handsome man, Rowland Finn, now? Where had he gone back to?

"Don't think about him, Tear Queen."

She whirled to face him. "Do you read minds?"

"I don't need to. You've never hidden anything from me. I can't stop him from coming here as he pleases, but I repeat

311

my caution: give him nothing. Nothing he asks for, no house room in your mind. He's a seductive creature, I know—"

Kelsea started in surprise, feeling caught.

"—and even I was deceived once, long ago."

"How long?" Kelsea blurted out. "How old are you?"

"Too old."

"Why haven't you died?"

"A punishment."

"What are you being punished for?"

"The worst of all crimes, Tear Queen. Now be quiet and listen."

Kelsea winced. He had used Carlin's tone again, the tone one would take with a wayward child, and Kelsea felt a sudden desperation to prove him wrong, to show him that she wasn't a child anymore. But she didn't know how.

"Row Finn, the man, was a liar," the Fetch continued. "He's a liar still. The Mort Queen gave in; she was a fool. Are you a fool as well?"

"No," Kelsea mumbled, though she knew she was. She had become pretty, and she no longer felt like a child. But she was the worst fool in the world for thinking that these things would make a difference to the Fetch. He was still as far beyond her reach as he had ever been.

"You've impressed me, Tear Queen. Don't ruin it all now." The Fetch stood from the chair, pulling something from his pocket, and Kelsea saw that it was his mask, the same dreadful mask he liked to wear about the countryside. He meant to leave now. This was all she would have.

Good riddance, a voice whispered inside her head. But Kelsea recognized that for what it was: her mind's sad attempt at self-defense. The Fetch would disappear now, leaving her with nothing. She longed for something to hold on to, and on the heels of that longing came anger. She was the most powerful woman in the Tearling, and still this man was able to wreck her with only a few words. Was this really the way it would always be?

Not always. Not forever, please God. Give me some light at the end.

She took a deep breath, and when she spoke, she noted with pleasure that her voice had strengthened, become hard. "Don't ever come here uninvited again. You're not welcome."

"I'll come and go as I please, Tear Queen. I always have. You just make sure I don't have to come for you." He drew the mask over his head. "We made a deal."

"Fuck the deal!" Kelsea snarled. "That creature Finn offers actual aid. What have you ever offered?"

"Only your life, you ungrateful brat."

"Get out."

He gave her a mocking bow, eyes gleaming behind the mask. "Perhaps in time, you'll grow as pretty as your mother."

Kelsea grabbed the book from her bedside table and flung it at him. But it only bounced harmlessly off his shoulder. The Fetch laughed, bitter laughter that emerged hollowly from the mask's mouth.

"You can't hurt me, Tear Queen. No one can. I don't even have the ability to wound myself."

He slipped into Pen's antechamber, closed the curtain behind him, and was gone.

Kelsea fell on the bed, buried her face in the pillow, and began to cry. She hadn't cried in months, and tears were a relief, easing some strand inside her that had been stretched tight. But the pain in her chest wouldn't ease.

I'll never have him. She even murmured it into her pillow, but the Fetch remained there, lodged in her chest and throat like something she'd swallowed, too big for her to contend with. There was no way to make him be gone.

A hand touched Kelsea's shoulder, gently, making her jump. Looking up with bleary eyes, she saw Pen standing over the bed. She put up a hand to convey that she was fine, but he stared at her in quiet consternation, and the anxiety in his face brought on fresh tears.

Here's the man I should have fallen in love with, she thought, and that only made her weep harder. Pen sat down on the bed beside her and placed his hand gently on top of hers, clasping her fingers. The small gesture wrecked Kelsea, and she cried even harder, her face swollen and nose running freely. So many things in this life had proven more difficult than they were supposed to be. She missed Barty and Carlin. She missed the cottage, with its quiet patterns, where everything was known. She missed the child Kelsea, who had never had to make more than a day's decisions, or worry about more than a child's consequences. She missed the ease of that life.

After a few minutes Pen tugged her up from the pillow and wrapped his arms around her, holding her against his chest, rocking her in the same way Barty used to when she'd taken a fall. Pen wasn't going to ask her any questions, Kelsea realized, and that seemed such a gift that her tears finally began to subside into gasps and hiccups. She huddled against Pen's bare chest, liking the feel of it: warm and hard and comforting against her cheek.

It could be a secret, her mind whispered, the thought coming from nowhere, but a moment later Kelsea realized that the voice was correct. It *could* be a secret. No one had to know, not even Mace. Kelsea's private life, her private choices, were her own business, and now she found herself whispering, repeating the thought out loud. "It could be a secret, Pen."

Pen drew back, looking down at her for a long moment, and Kelsea saw, relieved, that he knew exactly what she was offering, that she didn't have to explain.

"You don't love me, Lady."

Kelsea shook her head.

"Then why would you want this?"

That was a good question, but part of Kelsea was annoyed, anyway, that Pen had asked it. *I'm nineteen!* she wanted to snap. *Nineteen and still a virgin! Isn't that enough?* She didn't love Pen and he didn't love her, but she liked the way he looked without a shirt, and it seemed desperately important to prove that she wasn't a child. She shouldn't need a reason for wanting the same things as everyone else.

But she couldn't say these things to Pen. They would only hurt him.

"I don't know. I just do."

Pen closed his eyes, his mouth twisting, and Kelsea recoiled, suddenly remembering the balance of power between them; did he think she was *ordering* him to sleep with her? Pen had principles, and as he had pointed out, he was a Queen's Guard. Maybe it wasn't enough that no one else would know; Pen would know, that was the problem.

"It's entirely your choice, Pen," she told him, placing a hand against his neck. "I'm not the Queen right now. I'm just—"

Pen kissed her.

It wasn't anything like her books. Kelsea barely had time to decide what she was feeling; she was too busy trying not to be inept, trying to figure out where her tongue was supposed to go. *A lot of work*, she thought, slightly disappointed, but then Pen's hand crept up to her breast and that was better, closer to the way she thought it was supposed to be. Kelsea wondered if she should take off her own dress or let Pen do it, and then realized that he was already far ahead of her, half of her buttons undone. The room was cold, but she was sweating, and when Pen's mouth found her nipple, she jumped, stifling a moan. He pulled the rest of her dress off, then froze.

Kelsea looked down and saw what Pen saw: her arms and legs, crisscrossed with wounds in various stages of healing. They didn't look as bad as they would have in the daylight, but even Kelsea, who was used to her own injuries, knew that her limbs were a ghastly sight.

"What have you done to yourself?"

Kelsea grabbed her dress, tugging the sleeves back on. She had botched this, just as she always seemed to ruin things when she tried so hard to behave like an adult.

Pen stopped her, taking her wrist in a light grip, his face unreadable. "You can't talk about it?"

Kelsea shook her head, staring truculently at the ground. Pen ran a light thumb over the scar on her thigh, and Kelsea realized suddenly that she was sitting there nearly naked, a man looking over her body, and she wasn't even blushing. Perhaps she was growing up a bit, after all.

"I see," Pen said. "It's not my business."

Kelsea looked up, surprised.

"You live in a world none of us can see, Lady. I accept that. And your choices are your own."

Kelsea gazed at him for a moment longer. Then she took his hand from her thigh and placed it, gently, between her legs. Pen kissed her, and she suddenly found her hands all over him, as though she couldn't pull him close enough.

"This may hurt," he whispered. "It does, your first time."

Kelsea stared up at him, this man who had done nothing for months but guard her from danger, and realized that the vast majority of her books had been misleading. They painted love as an all-or-nothing proposition. What she felt for Pen wasn't close to what she felt for the Fetch . . . but it *was* love, somehow, all the same, and she placed a hand against his cheek.

"You won't hurt me, Pen. I'm tough."

Pen grinned, his old grin, the one Kelsea hadn't seen in weeks. When he pushed inside her, it did hurt, a stinging burn that made her want to close her legs, but Kelsea would not have let Pen know it for the world, and she pushed up against him, trying to match his movement. The pain deepened, but there was no going back now; Kelsea felt as though she had crossed a chasm, some bridge that lay broken behind her. The Mort were there, waiting . . . Kelsea shook her head, trying to shove the thought away. The invasion shouldn't intrude here, not now. She tried to focus on Pen, her body, but found that she could not rid herself of the image: ahead, waiting, like an awful tide, the Mort.

CHAPTER 9

THE DARK THING

Oh, what may man within him hide,
Though angel on the outward side.
— *Measure for Measure*, WILLIAM SHAKESPEARE *(pre-Crossing Angl.)*

August dawned bright and burning. The city stank with the heat; whenever Kelsea went out on her balcony, she could smell sewage and the less pungent but still unpleasant smell of animal flesh left to rot in the sun. Without grazing fields, many of the animals that the evacuees had brought with them were beginning to die of starvation. After a quick consultation with Mace, Kelsea had ordered that all farm animals in and around the city, save for milking cows and goats, be immediately slaughtered and their meat cured for siege. This decree had earned her no points with the cattle farmers of the Almont, but their anger seemed preferable to the disease that would surely spread if animals died and rotted on the banks of the Caddell, contaminating the city's water supply.

Javel, Dyer, and Galen left for Demesne on the second of August. They departed in the dark of night, quickly and quietly, so quietly that even Kelsea did not know until they were already gone. She was furious, but Mace merely pointed out to her, in his usual laconic manner, that she had put him in charge of the operation, and there was nothing Kelsea could say to that.

On the fourth of August Kelsea found Andalie alone in her chamber and closed the door, leaving Pen outside. She had spent days quietly working up the courage for this, but before Andalie's questioning gaze, she nearly lost her nerve. She and Pen had slept together three more times, and while it had certainly gotten better, each time an unpleasant truth had been weighing more and more heavily on Kelsea's mind.

"Andalie, can I ask you a favor?"

"Yes, Lady."

"When you go to the market, do you . . . do you ever hear of black-market items being available down there?"

Andalie's gaze sharpened. "What is it you're seeking, Lady?"

"I want . . ." Kelsea peeked toward the door, making sure that Pen hadn't somehow slunk back into the room. "I want contraception. I've heard it's out there."

If Andalie was surprised, she didn't show it. "It is out there, Lady. The question is how to distinguish the true from the false. And the true is always very expensive."

"I've got the money. Can you do it? I don't want anyone to know."

"I can do it, Lady. But I wonder if you've considered the consequences."

Kelsea frowned. "You have moral objections?"

"God, no!" Andalie chuckled. "I would've taken the stuff

319

myself, but we never had the money. It was all I could do to feed all of my children two meals a day. I do not condemn you, Majesty. I simply mean that even I have heard the tone of the city. The people want an heir. I don't know what happens if you take a contraceptive and it is discovered."

"Public opinion is the least of my concerns right now. I'm nineteen. This kingdom doesn't own every part of me."

"They will disagree with you on that. But regardless, I can get the syrup, if that's what you want."

"It is," Kelsea replied firmly. "When do you go to market?"

"Thursday."

"I'll give you the gold. I appreciate this."

"Be careful, Lady," Andalie cautioned. "I know all about the wildness of youth, believe me. But regret has a terrible ability to follow you, long after youth has vanished."

"Yes." Kelsea had been looking down at her feet, but now she abruptly looked up at Andalie, nearly begging. "I only want to be able to have a life, that's all. A life, just like any other girl my age would have. Is that so terrible?"

"Not terrible at all, Majesty," Andalie replied. "But though you may wish for an ordinary life, you will not have it. You are the Queen of the Tearling. There are some things you cannot choose."

A few days later, Kelsea finally got up the courage to run an errand she'd been putting off for nearly a month. Gathering up Mace, Pen, and Coryn, she left the Queen's Wing, traveled up three flights of stairs, turned left, then right, then left again, and entered a large, windowless room on the twelfth floor of the Keep.

Elston stood up from an armchair just inside the doorway. For once, Kibb was not with him. Although Kibb appeared to have completely recovered in a physical sense, Mace was still wary, still testing Kibb to see if anything had changed.

"Enjoying yourself, Elston?"

"More than you can imagine, Lady."

The room was lit by many torches, and at its center was a steel cage that stood almost to the ceiling. The bars were thin, but they looked to be extremely strong. In the center of the cage, Arlen Thorne sat in a simple wooden chair, his head tipped back, his gaze focused on the ceiling. The chair was the only furniture in the cage.

"He doesn't even have a cot?" Kelsea asked Mace in an undertone.

"He can sleep just fine on the floor."

"What about a blanket?"

Mace's brow furrowed. "What is this sudden sympathy for Thorne, Lady?"

"Not sympathy, concern. Even worse criminals would deserve a blanket."

"Have you come to gloat, Majesty?" Thorne called from the center of the room. "Or will you merely mumble to each other all day over there?"

"Ah, Arlen. How the mighty have fallen." Kelsea moved to stand ten feet from the bars, and Pen followed, placing himself between Kelsea and the cage. For a moment, she was distracted by Pen's lithe swordfighter's form, which she now saw in an entirely new light; the sex was getting better, and it was difficult, these days, to keep from picturing him naked. But they had agreed to keep this thing in the dark, and in the dark it would stay. "Coryn, can you find me something to sit on, please?"

"Lady."

"How goes the invasion, Majesty?" Thorne asked.

"Poorly," Kelsea admitted. "The Mort are pushing inward from the border. My army won't hold for long."

Thorne shrugged. "The inevitable result."

"I'll give you this, Arlen: at least you don't feign remorse."

"What is there to be remorseful about? I played the hand I was dealt as well as I could. Bad luck is bad luck." Thorne leaned forward, his bright blue eyes piercing in the dim room. "How *did* you find out about my special shipment, Lady? I have always wondered. Did someone talk?"

"No."

"Then how did you know?"

"Magic."

"Ah, well." Thorne sat back. "I have seen magic worked, once or twice."

"Don't you care about anything, Arlen?"

"Care is a liability, Majesty."

Coryn reappeared with a chair, and Kelsea sat down in front of the cage. "What of Brenna? Surely you care for her. Or have I been misinformed?"

"Brenna is a useful tool, and she enjoys being used."

Kelsea's mouth twisted in distaste, but then she remembered the spitting, raging woman down in the dungeon. Perhaps there was something in what Thorne said.

"How did Brenna come to be what she is?"

"Environment, Majesty. My Brenna and I grew up in the worst hell imaginable." Thorne tipped his head toward Mace, his mouth twisting with malice. "You know what I'm talking about. I saw you there."

"You are mistaken," Mace replied tonelessly.

Thorne smiled. "Oh no, Captain of Guard, I am sure it was you."

In the next instant the mace lashed against the bars, a

deafening clatter of steel on steel in the confined space.

"Keep talking, Thorne," Mace said in a low voice, "and I will end you."

"What do I care for that, Captain? You or the rope, it makes no difference to me."

"And what about when I send that pet of yours to Mortmesne, to Lafitte?" Mace grasped the bars, pressing against the cage, and Kelsea was suddenly glad that she could not see his face. Mace never allowed himself to be rattled so easily; Thorne must have touched a very deep nerve. "Albinos are a curiosity, you know. Such women will always draw customers."

"You have no reason to harm Brenna."

"But I will do it, Thorne, if you drive me there. Keep your mouth shut."

Thorne raised his eyebrows. "You support this, Majesty?"

Kelsea was uncomfortable with the turn of the conversation, but she nodded firmly. "I support whatever Lazarus chooses to do."

"See, I knew it. Kelsea the virtuous. Kelsea the selfless." Thorne shook his head, chuckling. "Those poor deluded bastards out there have worked themselves into a frenzy over you, Majesty. They think you'll save them from the Mort. A clever act, yours, but I always knew you were no better than the rest of us."

"I never claimed to be virtuous or selfless," Kelsea snapped back. "And I hardly know how *you* can claim any sort of high ground."

"But I make no secret of what I am, Kelsea Raleigh—I suppose it's Glynn now, isn't it? These delusions the rest of you suffer . . . so much work and architecture to convince yourself that you're better, more pure. We all want what we want, and there's very little we won't do to get it. Call yourself whatever you like, Queen Kelsea, but you're a Raleigh through and through. No altruists in that line."

"I don't want to die, Arlen, but I would lay down my life for any of these men, or they for me. That's a real thing, sacrifice, but you will never understand it."

"Oh, but I do understand it. I have a piece of information that Your Majesty would find valuable, so valuable that I have thought, many times, that I could likely trade it for my own life. But I will not do that."

"What information?"

"First, my price: the life and welfare of Brenna."

Mace began to bark, but Kelsea cut him off. "Define welfare."

"Brenna is known as my charge. When I'm gone, many people will seek to unleash their wrath on her as well. She needs protection."

"Don't try to paint your albino as an innocent, Thorne. She's a dangerous creature."

"She has been unfortunate, Majesty. Brenna and I were raised as animals. But for luck, even your Mace might have turned out just like us."

Mace lunged toward the bars, his big hands grasping for Thorne. Thorne didn't flinch; even Mace's long arms couldn't reach far enough through the bars.

"What?" Thorne asked. "Don't want to reminisce with me? Not even about the ring?"

"Elston." Mace turned, snarling. "Keys."

"Elston, don't you dare."

"Let us have him, Lady!" Elston replied eagerly, moving forward and pulling the keys from his belt. "Please, I beg you!"

"Sit down, Elston! And you, Lazarus, enough. This man will die in front of the people he's wronged. Not you."

Mace had started forward again, but now he stopped. "You will execute him?"

"Yes. I've decided. Next Sunday, in the circus."

"Thorne has wronged me, Lady," Elston said quietly. "My grievance is as good as any in the Tearling. Let me be the one."

"Good Christ, grow up!" Thorne snapped. "It was an accident. I'd no idea what you were. Twenty years later, and you still can't move on with your life!"

"You flesh-peddling—"

"Enough!" Kelsea shouted, losing patience. "Out of here now! Everyone but Pen!"

"Lady—"

"Out, Lazarus!"

Mace had the good grace to look a bit ashamed as he departed, taking Elston and Coryn with him. The door closed with a thump.

"Thank God for small favors," Thorne muttered. He collapsed into the chair, tipped his head back, and closed his eyes.

Kelsea was disturbed. The conversation had taken a sharp turn into uncharted territory. Mace had given her the impression that the albino was an odd remnant of Thorne's past, a fetish that he carried around with him like a good-luck charm. But unless Thorne was playing some deeper game here—and Kelsea couldn't imagine what it might be—what she was seeing now was a wholly altruistic act, one that did not accord with Arlen Thorne at all.

"Where did you grow up, Arlen?"

"You will execute me next Sunday, Majesty. I don't owe you a biography."

"Perhaps not. But if something terrible was truly done to you as a child, perhaps I could prevent it from happening to others."

"What happens to others is their own concern. I only care what happens to Brenna."

Kelsea sighed. The altruism, if that was what it was, would clearly extend no further. "Assuming that I like what you're selling, what is it that you want me to do with her?"

"I want a place for Brenna here."

"In the Keep?" Kelsea asked incredulously.

"There's nowhere else she would be safe, Majesty. You cannot hide her; she's too recognizable. I want her in a safe structure, decently fed and clothed, and protected by a loyal guard who cannot be suborned with bribes."

"Even the most loyal guard can be turned, Arlen. You destroyed one of mine."

"Morphia destroyed Mhurn, Lady, just as it has destroyed so many fools who try to hide from the here and now. I am merely the man who found the corpse, dusted it off, and made of it what I could."

"God, you're cold, Arlen."

"So I'm told, Majesty. But the fact remains that only a fool blames the dealer."

Kelsea took a deep breath and blanked all thoughts of Mhurn out of her mind. "What makes you think Brenna would accept my protection? She doesn't seem to care for me much."

"An understatement, Lady, I'm sure. But she will accept."

"And what do you offer in return?"

"A bargaining chip against the Red Queen."

Kelsea eyed him skeptically.

"Ours has been a long acquaintance, Majesty. No one

knows the Red Queen well, but I venture to say I know her better than most men who live to tell the tale."

"Is your bargaining chip one that would turn her away from us, send her army home?"

"No, Majesty. If it were, we would be dickering for my life as well as Brenna's."

"If your information won't save the Tearling, then what do I care?"

"Only you can say, Lady." Thorne shrugged. "But I myself have never regretted acquiring a piece of leverage. Such things often come in handy when we least expect it."

Kelsea winced, feeling herself maneuvered. This man was a liar, one of the best in the Tear . . . and yet she believed him. He seemed resigned to his fate. And in the scheme of things, what he asked was very small.

"I don't break my word, Majesty, and I've heard tell that you don't either." Thorne's bright blue eyes glimmered through the bars of the age. "I'm not trying to cheat you. An honest bargain: the safety and care of my Brenna for a good piece of information. Do you accept?"

Dealing with the devil, Kelsea thought. She should call Mace in here, get his opinion. But somehow this seemed like a decision that should belong to her alone. She considered for a moment longer, then sighed and nodded. "We have a bargain, Arlen."

Thorne offered a hand through the bars for her to shake, but Kelsea shook her head. "Not a chance. What's your information?"

"Your two sapphires, Majesty. She wants them, more than you can possibly imagine."

"These?" Kelsea looked down, but her hand had already gone instinctively to clutch the sapphires, and now they were hidden from view. "Why didn't she simply demand them from my mother as part of the Treaty? She could have done so."

"I don't think she wanted them so badly in those days, Majesty. At any rate, she wanted slaves more. But she and I have had a long and fruitful business relationship, and while you were in hiding, I saw her longing for those jewels grow like a fever. She was just as desperate for news of them as she was for your head, and each year that your uncle failed to lay hold of them, she held him in more contempt."

"What does she want with them, exactly?"

"She never told me, Majesty."

"Care to hazard a guess?"

Thorne shrugged. "She's a woman terrified of dying, of ceasing to exist. I noticed it often, though it's a quality she tries desperately to hide. Perhaps your jewels would help?"

Kelsea's mind went immediately to Kibb, lying on the sickbed covered in sweat. She thought of Row Finn's offer: a way to destroy the Red Queen. Mace said it had been years since anyone had tried to assassinate her; everyone assumed it could not be done. Was it possible that the Red Queen was still physically vulnerable somehow? But even if Row Finn knew of that vulnerability, what good could such information do Kelsea now? An army of at least fifteen thousand lay between New London and Demesne.

"But this is conjecture, Majesty," Thorne continued. "The Mort have designated her *un maniaque* . . . what we would call a control freak. You, your sapphires, these things are variables, and the Red Queen is not a woman who is comfortable with variables, not even pleasant ones."

Kelsea stared at him, fascinated and disgusted at the same time. "Did you sleep with her, Arlen?"

"She wished me to. She sleeps with a man, and then feels that he is hers, neatly categorized and collected. But I am part of no one's collection."

Thorne stood up and stretched. His arms were so long that he nearly reached the top of the cage. "Why delay my execution until Sunday, Majesty? I'm tired of waiting, and I'm certainly tired of Elston's company. Why not simply do it now?"

"Because even in death, Arlen, you will be useful. Your execution will be a public event, and announcements will go out to all corners of the kingdom. The people want this, and I will give it to them."

"Ah, the pleasure of the mob. It's a wise move, I suppose."

"You don't fear death?"

Thorne shrugged. "Do you play chess, Majesty?"

"Yes, but not well."

"I play a great deal of chess, and I play well. I don't often lose, but it has happened. Always in such games, there is a point at which you realize you will be bested, that checkmate is four or ten or twelve moves away. One school of thought says you should make the best endgame you can, fighting until the bitter finish. But I have never seen any point in that. I have done the math, and I was checkmated from the moment your people grabbed my Brenna. All moves since then have been the pointless scurrying of pawns."

"What is Brenna to you?" Kelsea asked. "Why does she mean so much, when all other people mean nothing?"

"Ah . . . now that story *will* cost you my life, Majesty. Are you willing to trade?"

"No. But I will bring Brenna up here and allow you to say good-bye."

"Not good enough."

"Then we're done." Kelsea stood up from the chair. "If you change your mind, let Elston know."

She made it halfway to the door before Thorne called, "Glynn Queen?"

"Yes?"

"I will not tell you the tale of my life, and neither will Brenna. But your Mace might do so, if you could force it from him."

Kelsea turned, considered him for a moment, then replied, "You are transparent, Arlen. You only want to drive a wedge between us."

Thorne's lips thinned in a smile. "Perceptive, Majesty. But curiosity is a terrible thing. I believe my wedge will burrow deeper over time."

"I thought you were done."

"Even the checkmate phase has its entertainments." Thorne sat back down in his chair, giving her a tiny wave of farewell. "Good day, Glynn Queen."

I ncrease the dosage."

"What?"

"Increase the dosage!" the Queen snapped, doing her best to force her voice through the thick pane of glass.

Medire nodded and hurried around the examination table, on which was strapped a slave from Callae. The slave didn't know it, but she was already dead. The only question was how long it would take. A thin line of reddish foam had begun to work its way from the corner of her mouth, and she gasped for breath, her fingers clenching and unclenching at her sides. The Queen wondered if the woman was making noise; the pane of glass was almost perfectly soundproof, one of Cadare's finest achievements. She checked the watch in her hand and found that nearly seventy seconds had elapsed.

The woman gave a final gasp, her mouth rounding like that of a fish. Then her eyes fixed on the ceiling and she was still. Medire reached for her wrist, monitored the pulse for a moment, and nodded at the Queen, who checked her watch again.

"Seventy-four seconds," she told Emmene, who stood beside her with his pen and paper.

"Better than the last trial."

"Much better. But we should refine it even further if we can."

Oddly enough, the Queen owed this newest discovery to the Tearling. More than eleven hundred soldiers had died of snakebite at Lake Karczmar, and the recovered bodies had arrived in Demesne bloated black, pumped full of toxin. The toxin had been difficult to harvest, and several soldiers had died collecting specimens, but the rewards were worth it. Not only did the venom kill quickly via both injection and ingestion but it also had a sweet taste, easily hidden by wine or mead. So many poisons were bitter; this one would be a valuable addition to the Queen's collection.

"Your Majesty."

Beryll had come in behind her, his soft tread inaudible. He rarely came down to her laboratory; Beryll was the most efficient man the Queen had ever known, but he didn't have the stomach for her experiments. He kept his eyes carefully away from the glass.

"What is it?"

"A rider from General Ducarte. The army has broken the Tear line in the Almont and begun to move down the Crithe. The Tear are in retreat."

The Queen smiled, a more genuine smile than she had produced in weeks. There had been so little good news lately. "Send some heralds out to announce it, here and in Cite Marche. That should stop their squabbling up there."

"The General estimates that he will advance at least three miles per day."

"Ducarte's estimates are always accurate. Send him my congratulations."

Beryll consulted the letter in his hand. "He also reports that the villages in the eastern Almont were evacuated in advance of the army's arrival. There was no plunder; all the army found were a few sick animals left behind. The rest of the Almont may be abandoned as well."

"So?"

"Ducarte's soldiers grow restless, Majesty. Spoils are a part of their compensation."

"I don't care about spoils," the Queen muttered, her voice petulant. Gold, slaves, livestock, lumber . . . these things would matter greatly to the army, yes, but they no longer mattered to her. What she wanted was in New London.

Still, she reflected, this news had not come a moment too soon. Production had slowed in all sectors of the Mort economy, but the hardest hit came in mining, where the casualty rate among slaves had always been high. The Queen's suggestion that the foremen drive their slaves a bit less harshly had been met with thinly veiled ridicule. Mining in Mortmesne was a numbers game, defined by dangerous conditions and heavy turnover. The mill needed grist, and each day it seemed as though a rash of new complaints poured in from the mining communities in the north.

Fingers tapped on the glass behind her. Medire, his eyebrows raised, motioned toward the woman, asking if they were done. The Queen nodded and turned away as he threw a cloth over the corpse. Beryll was still waiting expectantly.

"What?"

"Also a message from Lieutenant Martin in the north. Three more attacks in Cite Marche. His intelligence suggests that rebels are planning to move on to other cities, including Demesne."

"Nothing about the man Levieux?"

"Nothing in the note, Majesty."

"Wonderful." The Queen wondered if she truly had made a tactical error in removing Ducarte to the front. Surely he would have produced some results by now. But it was too late; Ducarte was nearly halfway across the Almont, and he would not take kindly to being yanked back and forth.

"What do I have tonight?"

Beryll closed his eyes, consulting memory. He was over ninety years old, had fallen victim to multiple frailties, but his mind remained strong and regimented. "You have dinner with the Bells, but they won't be here until six. You have plenty of time."

"I need a nap."

"You take too many naps, Majesty," Beryll murmured, in a tone of heavy disapproval.

"There's nothing else to do. I don't sleep at night anymore."

This was true. It was the dream, which never left her lately: the inferno, the man in grey, the girl. The Queen found herself unable to shake a sense of impending disaster.

"Why not take one of Medire's concoctions?" Beryll asked.

"Because then I would need to take them habitually, Ryll. I have no wish to become dependent."

"You are dependent on me, Majesty."

The Queen chuckled. The rest of her servants maintained a formal distance, necessary but often tiresome, but Beryll had been with her since he was seven years old, when she had selected him from a pit of Mort nobles awaiting execution. His parents had already died in the uprising, and the Queen had been moved by the solitary child, his face full of a pain that the Queen recognized and still dimly remembered from her youth: abandonment and loss.

"I do depend on you, Ryll. It has been a long lifetime, you and me."

"I would not have traded it for the wide world, Lady." Beryll smiled, his stiff resolve breaking for a moment, and in the smile the Queen glimpsed the child she had lifted from the blood-puddled pit. She had reached down and extended a hand, and the boy had grasped it . . . the memory hurt. Time seemed to stretch over such an unbridgeable distance lately. The Queen cast around for something to lighten the mood. "At any rate, Medire isn't half the pharmacist he thinks he is. I've heard some ugly rumors about side effects. Rashes and spots."

"It makes the pages uneasy, Majesty, knowing that you don't sleep. Their anxiety then passes further down the chain."

"When we take the Tearling, I'll sleep fine."

"As you say, Majesty," he replied, in a tone that stopped just short of disbelief.

Beryll left her when they reached the top of the stairs, heading off toward the throne room, and the Queen continued slowly on her way, perusing the two messages that Beryll had handed her. Ducarte's note was like the man himself, brief and to the point: the invasion was proceeding as it should, the bulk of the Mort army moving steadily across the Almont Plain. But Martin's words had been written hastily, the tone bordering on panic: three of his interrogators had been snatched off the street and found hung from the city walls four days later. Two Crown armories had burned to the ground. Vallee had taken an arrow in the knee from a sniper. Martin's anxiety would not help matters. As soon as Ducarte reached New London and got his fill of whatever he wanted there, she would put him back on this ... this ...

Rebellion.

Her mind shied away from the word, but after a moment's thought, she was forced to acknowledge its essential truth. She had a rebellion on her hands, and none of her people were equal to quelling it.

In the wide, high-ceilinged corridor that led to her chambers, the Queen found five pages in a cluster, talking in low voices.

"Surely there's something else you could be doing with your time," she remarked acidly, and was pleased to see them jump at her voice. "Go and make yourselves useful."

They left, with quietly murmured apologies that the Queen did not acknowledge. Her pages behaved respectfully, but all of them occasionally betrayed the impudence of youth, impatience at having to wait on a woman they considered old. The Queen paused before entering her chamber, examining herself in one of the floor-length mirrors that stood beside the door. She was not young, no, not like these girls with their wrinkle-free eyes and upright breasts. But neither was she old. She was a grown woman, a woman who knew what she was about.

I am changeless, the Queen thought proudly. Still

vulnerable to weapons and wounds, certainly, but age, that relentless double-edged blade of decay and disease, would never touch her again. The Queen sobered, frowning. She would never grow old, but all the same, time had been growing on her lately: a sense of time as power, as a force that exerted incredible pressure. Her life had been long, but much of it had flown past unexamined. Only recently had the Queen begun to feel the passing years on her shoulders, nothing so simple as mere time . . . now it was history.

She went on into her chambers, closing the door behind her. Beryll would bring her some hot chocolate, and that would put her to sleep for an hour or so, at least. The room was nice and warm, perfect for napping. She would–

The Queen nearly tripped as her feet connected with a dull, lifeless heap on the ground. She looked down and found Mina, one of her pages, sprawled on the floor, her neck wrung so neatly that her head faced backward.

The Queen spun around and stared at the fireplace. A roaring blaze was going, a pillar of flame so strong that she could feel its heat all the way across the room.

"No–," she began, and then a hand clamped around her throat.

"You are faithless, Mort Queen," the voice hissed in her ear.

She tried to scream, but the dark thing's hand had already begun to squeeze, forcing her windpipe closed. She summoned everything she had and forced it away, shoving it across the room, where it landed on a table in the far corner, breaking the wood with a dull crunch.

The Queen darted behind the sofa, trying to force breath down her abraded throat, her eyes never moving from the dark mass that was just beginning to uncoil itself in the corner. Suddenly it whipped to its feet in a strange, unnatural motion, like that of a slingshot, and the Queen shrieked. A painted clown leered at her from the shadows, pale face and lips twisted in a grin. Its eyes were a bright, burning crimson.

The Queen struck again, pushing it back toward the ground. But she could strike no more than a glancing blow. The thing's flesh was strange, shifting; she could not grasp its outline, could not find limbs or organs or tissue. There was nothing for her mind to lay hold of.

A bright jet erupted from the fire, coming straight toward her. She dove to the ground, rolling away toward the wall, and felt a rush of warm air as the sofa burst into flames behind her. The room suddenly stank of scorching fabric. The Queen tried to scramble to her feet, but a hand grabbed her arm and flung her across the room, into the wall. Something crunched deep within her shoulder, and the Queen screamed, a loud, hoarse cry. She sank to her knees and found that she could not push herself back up. Heat baked her face; the enormous carpet in front of the hearth had now caught fire as well. Her shoulder was a thicket of agony.

Fists thudded against the door, and the Queen heard a babble of voices outside. But she could not wait for them, nor could they help. She found it again, coming for her now, moving silently through the smoke. It grabbed her by the hair and yanked her to her feet, and the Queen hissed as strands ripped from her head. The dark thing pulled her up and dangled her on her tiptoes.

"We had a bargain, Mort whore."

"The girl," she gasped. "I can still get the girl."

"The girl is mine already. She was an even easier mark

than you." It smiled wide, shaking her back and forth. She screamed again; her shoulder felt as though it was tearing in half. "She belongs to me, and I have no further use for you, Evelyn Raleigh. None at all."

The chamber door burst open, the lock flying across the room. The dark thing's attention was diverted, only for a moment, but in that moment the Queen suddenly saw it clearly: a shining silver shape in her mind, bones limned in red light. She found its rib cage, grabbed hold, and squeezed, catching its entire midsection in the vise of her mind. The dark thing snarled, but the Queen bore down, tighter and tighter, until it released her hair and dropped her back down to her feet. Its red eyes were only an inch from hers now, and the Queen shuddered at the disdain she saw there: disdain not just for herself but for everyone, all of humanity, whatever might get in its way.

"You cannot kill me, Mort Queen," it whispered, its deep red lips parting in a grimace. Its breath stank of blood, of decayed flesh. "You are not strong enough. The girl will set me free, and I will not need fire to find you."

The Queen sensed her guards bounding through the doorway now, vague shapes against the smoke. Beryll, too; she could feel him, loyalty and anxiety rolled up into one, all the way across the room. The dark thing squirmed within her grasp, a terrible feeling, as though worms were writhing together in her mind. She tried to crush it, but she simply didn't have the force.

"Get the fire out!" she screamed at her guards. "All of the fire! Put it out!"

Her guards obeyed instinctively, rushing over to the bed to grab the linens. The dark thing tried to break free, but she tightened her hold again. Its outline was extraordinarily clear in her mind, but the edges were painful, a current like lightning moving beneath her hands.

Power, the Queen thought dizzily. *How did it acquire so much?*

The dark thing giggled, a lunatic chortle that almost made her lose her grip. "You will never have what you seek, Mort Queen. You will never be immortal."

"I will," she panted. She thought she felt something weakening in its ribs, but could not be sure. The sizzling sensation beneath her hands made everything difficult to judge. "I will."

"I have seen your flight, you know. Pursued by a man in grey, the girl at your side. I have seen the cataclysm behind you."

The Queen closed her eyes, but she could not shut the words out.

"The immortal need not flee, Mort Queen. But you, you will flee, and die, and all the accoutrements of hell will await you. Believe me, Mort Queen, for I have been there."

The Queen bared her teeth as she felt something give inside its body, some small fault cracking open. The dark thing emitted a high screech, and the Queen howled in triumph. Blood trickled from her nose, but she barely noticed. She had hurt it. Only a bit, but that was enough. The dark thing was not immortal either. Perhaps she didn't have enough power to kill it, but it *could* be killed.

Dimly, she sensed her guards bringing the fire under control. But they were ignoring the hearth.

"All of the fire, damn you! The fireplace as well!"

Over the dark thing's shoulder a shadow loomed, a shadow that turned into Beryll, coming toward them with a wooden chair grasped in his hands like a club. He swung it at the dark thing's head, and the Queen felt the impact rico-chet all through her, the dark thing's outline shuddering inside her mind. It hissed, turned its head, and found Beryll.

"No!" the Queen shrieked. But it was too late. Her concen-tration had broken. The dark thing pulled free of her, grabbed Beryll by the throat, and snapped the old man's neck with one quick twist of its hands. Beryll went down without a sound, and at that moment the fire went out, plunging the room into darkness. The bright shape in the Queen's mind flickered, faded, and finally disappeared. She sank to the floor, panting, clutching her dislocated shoulder.

"Majesty!" her guard captain shouted. "Where are you?"

"I'm fine, Ghislaine. Light a candle. Only a candle, mind."

Confusion and stumbling followed her words. The Queen crawled sideways, leaning on her good shoulder and groping with the bad, until she reached Beryll's limp, still-warm body beside the wall. As the thin glow of candlelight began to illuminate the room, she found his wide eyes staring up at her. Beryll had lived a long life, yes, and he was an old man, but the Queen could only see the child she had pulled from the pit: a tall, skinny child with intelligent eyes and a ready smile. Something contracted inside her, and she wanted to cry. But that was unthinkable. She had not shed a tear in over one hundred years.

The Queen looked up and found her guards circled around her, waiting, clearly frightened; they thought they would be blamed for this disaster. Blame needed to be taken, for certain, and after a moment's thought, the Queen real-ized where the culpability lay.

"My pages. Get them in here."

When the five women were all lined up before her, the Queen looked them over, wondering where the treachery lived. Juliette, who came from one of Demesne's best families and clearly intended to be Queen here one day? Bre, who had once taken a whip for ruining one of the Queen's dresses? Or perhaps Genevieve, who liked to make rebellious comments in order to win the approval of the others. The Queen had never felt her own age so heavily as when she saw the five of them in front of her, a solid wall of unrelenting youth.

"Which of you lit the fire?"

She saw many emotions flit across their faces: surprise, thoughtfulness, indignation. All of them eventually settled into exaggerated expressions of innocence. The Queen frowned.

"Mina is dead, but it wasn't Mina. She's never been able to light a decent fire to save her life. You know me, ladies. I am not fair. If no one admits guilt, you will all face punishment. Who defied my express command by lighting a fire?"

No one answered. The Queen felt as though they stood united against her. She looked down at Beryll's body and suddenly realized the truth of things: there was no loyalty anymore. Beryll, Liriane . . . her own people were all dead now, and she was surrounded by grasping young strangers. The bubble of anger inside her head abruptly deflated, lapsing into sorrow and exhaustion, a strange sense of futility. She could punish them all, yes, but what would that prove?

"Dismissed, all of you. Get out."

The guards went, but the five pages merely stood there, their eyes wide and confused. Blonde, redhead, brunette, even a dark, exotic Cadarese named Marina. What on earth had possessed the Queen to choose these women? She should have had men all along. Men came at you directly, with raised fists. They didn't sneak up on your back with a knife.

"We're dismissed, Majesty?" Juliette ventured, in a tone of disbelief.

"Go. Find me a replacement for Mina."

"What of the corpses?"

"Get out!" the Queen screamed. She felt her own control slipping, inch by inch, but there was no way to rein it in. "Get out of here!"

Her pages fled.

The Queen shuffled over to her desk, her movements strangely hunched as she tried to protect her shoulder. It was badly dislocated; probing beneath her skin, the Queen sensed the outlines of the problem, a contortion of the musculature. Setting it straight would hurt like a bastard, but the Queen had bigger problems. The dark thing's face hovered in front of her, eyes bright and gleeful. It thought it had the girl now, and the girl was all it wanted. Worse, it had called the Queen by name.

How could it know? she raged inwardly. No one could know; she had covered her tracks too well. Evelyn Raleigh was dead. But still, the dark thing had called her by name.

Evie! The voice echoed in a corner of her mind, her mother's voice, always a trifle impatient, always exasperated at what was lacking in her daughter. *Evie, where did you get to?*

The Queen sat down at her desk. Moving carefully to spare her dislocated shoulder, she opened a drawer and took out a small portrait in a sanded wood frame. The portrait was the only tangible thing left to remind the Queen of her early life, and sometimes she toyed with the idea of throwing it away. But it had been too important to a young and desperate girl, and it had taken on the quality of a talisman; for a brief time, the Queen believed, the portrait had even kept her alive. Whenever she tried to discard it, something always held her back.

The woman in the portrait was not the Queen's mother, but when the Queen was young, she would have given the world to make it so. The subject was a brunette, heavily pregnant, her skin browned from long hours spent in the sun. This portrait was old; the woman wore clothing too shapeless to be from anything but the Landing era, and a primitive bow was strung across her back. Her face was beautiful, but it was not the easy, careless beauty of any Raleigh queen. This woman had suffered; there were scars on her collarbone and neck, and her face was lined with long-healed pain. But there was no bitterness there. She was laughing, and her eyes radiated kindness. Flowers were woven in her hair. When the Queen was young, she would spend hours staring at this picture, her guts knotted in jealousy . . . not of the woman, but of the child in her belly. She wished she knew the woman's name, but even in the Keep gallery, the picture had never been labeled.

Evie! Why do you make me wait?

"Shut up," the Queen whispered. "You're dead."

Thinking of the past was a mistake. She tossed the picture back in the drawer and slammed it shut. If the dark thing had no use for her anymore, then she held no leverage. She could not prohibit fires forever; sooner or later, what had happened today would happen again. And if the girl actually did manage to set the dark thing free somehow, there would be no defense. The last remnants of memory disappeared from her mind, and she turned all of her thoughts to the present. The girl, the girl was the problem, and no matter what the dark thing said, the Queen did not consider the girl an easy mark. She could not offer Elyssa's bargain, for the girl had refused to send Mortmesne a single slave. For a strange, wistful moment, the Queen wished that she could sit down with the girl, speak to her as an equal. But the jewels made such a friendly discussion impossible. The Queen hesitated for a moment longer, considering, and then pressed the gold button on the wall.

A few moments later Juliette entered the room, her steps hesitant, her eyes pinned to the floor. A smart girl, Julie, not wanting to push her luck. "Majesty?"

"Prepare my luggage for travel," the Queen told her, turning toward the fireplace. She reached behind her back and grasped her left wrist in her right hand. "At least several weeks' worth. You will accompany me. We leave tomorrow."

"For what destination, Majesty?"

The Queen took a deep breath and yanked her left arm backward, snapping her neck and upper torso forward at the same time. The pain was sudden and excruciating, consuming her entire shoulder in fire, and a scream climbed up the back of the Queen's throat. But she kept her mouth shut tight, and a moment later there was the satisfying crack of the musculature popping back into place. The pain quickly faded, retreating into a dull ache that could easily be cured with drugs.

The Queen turned back to Juliette, her smile pleasant, although her brow was wet with perspiration. Juliette's expression was horrified, her face drained of color. The Queen took a step forward, just to see what would happen, and had the pleasure of watching Juliette scuttle backward, almost through the doorway.

"Pack for warm climate and some rough living."

"Where are we going, Majesty?" Juliette quavered. Had the Queen really found her intimidating a few minutes ago? There was nothing to fear, not from one so young.

"To the front, Julie," she replied dismissively, moving to look out the western window. "To the Tearling."

All the way up the stairs, Ewen kept his eyes on the Mace's back. He was scared, but there was no question of not following; Ewen knew that much from Da. When you were summoned by the Captain of Guard, you simply went. The Mace carried a large grey bundle under his arm, and he hadn't even looked at Ewen since they'd left the dungeon. Worse yet, the Mace had left another jailor to take Ewen's place while he went upstairs. The new man was not as big as Ewen, but he was certainly smart, with quick eyes that darted around the dungeon. The one remaining prisoner, Bannaker, had completely recovered from his injuries, and Ewen, knowing that Bannaker would be dangerous when fully healed, had moved him to Cell Two. But the first thing the new jailor did was to walk over to Cell Two and check its locks, and this made Ewen angry: as though he would leave a cell unlocked, with a prisoner inside! The new man then sat down at the desk as though he owned the place, putting his feet up, and at that moment Ewen knew that the Queen was going to remove him from his post. He had been a good jailor for almost five years, but the Queen must have found out that he was slow. With each stair that Ewen climbed, he became more sick to his stomach. Their family had been jailors in the Keep forever, all the way back to Da's grandfather. Da had only given up the job because he could no longer walk. Ewen couldn't bear to tell Da this news. He felt naked without his ring of keys.

But they did not leave the staircase at the ninth floor, the Queen's Wing. Rather, they kept on going, several floors up, and the Mace led him into a large room that was lit up like Christmas, more than a dozen torches lining the walls. Two Queen's Guards, one large and one small, sat in chairs just inside the door, and in the center of the room was a tall cage, but Ewen couldn't make out what was inside.

"Morning, boys."

"Good morning, sir," they both replied, standing up. The smaller man had eyes so light that they seemed white, and they reminded Ewen of the woman Brenna. Three Queen's Guards had removed her from the dungeon several days ago, which had relieved Ewen no end. Bannaker's eyes might plot escape every moment, but still he seemed less dangerous than the woman. A witch, Ewen was sure of it, powerful and terrible, just as Da had always described them in stories.

"El. Keys."

The big guard came forward into the light, and Ewen recognized him now: the man with the scary teeth. He tossed the keys to the Mace, who slammed them against the bars, a metallic clanging that hurt Ewen's ears.

"Wake up, Arlen! It's your big day."

"I'm awake." A ghostly thin shape unfolded itself from the ground inside the cage, and Ewen recognized the scarecrow. But he was dressed differently now, in a white linen shirt and trousers, and even Ewen knew what that meant: it was the uniform of a prisoner sentenced to death.

"Are you going to behave, Arlen?" the Mace asked.

"I've made my bargain."

"Good." The Mace unlocked the cage. "Tie him up."

Ewen was beginning to wonder if the Mace had forgotten

that he was there, but now those sharp eyes found him. "You! Ewen! Over here."

Ewen moved forward, almost tiptoeing.

"Listen carefully, boy, for we haven't much time." The Mace pulled the bundle from beneath his arm and shook it out, and Ewen saw that it was a long grey cloak. "You showed great courage in capturing this man, and the Queen is grateful. So today, you will be a Queen's Guard."

Ewen stared at the grey cloak, mesmerized.

"You and Elston will transport this prisoner to the New London Circus. Elston is in charge. Your only job is to guard the prisoner, to make sure he doesn't escape. Do you understand?"

Ewen swallowed, found his throat almost too dry to speak. "Yes, sir."

"Good. Here." Mace held out the cloak. "Put it on and come help us."

The deep grey fabric was soft, softer than any clothing Ewen had ever owned. He fastened the cloak around his shoulders, trying to puzzle out what was happening. He knew that he could not be a Queen's Guard; he was not smart enough. But they were waiting for him beside the cage, so he hurried over and stood at attention. The short guard had already tied the prisoner's wrists.

"We're taking him out the Gate."

"Christ, they'll slaughter him before she can execute him."

"Maybe, but she wants to give them a show."

Together, the three of them marched the prisoner between them, out the door and down the stairs. Here, at least, was something that Ewen understood, lessons learned from years in the dungeon. He kept his eyes on the scarecrow's back, looking for the smallest twitch, the slightest sign that his prisoner meant to bolt. When the prisoner coughed, Ewen put a quick hand on his arm. As they descended the staircase, Ewen checked the position of his knife, and found it right where it should be, tucked into his belt.

One job, Da had always said, *and one job only, Ew: make sure they don't run. The rest is for someone else.*

At the bottom of the stairs, they came around the corner toward the Keep Gate and Ewen saw a group of people on horses. The Queen was there, sitting atop a brown horse, dressed in a long black dress that draped over the horse's flank. Ewen thought about bowing, then decided not to when the other three guards did not. He might not be a real Queen's Guard, but he could act like one.

"El, tie him down," the Mace ordered. "Make sure no one can pull him off."

Beside the horses was a broad, open wagon. Ewen helped the big guard lift the prisoner into the wagon bed, then climbed in himself, thinking: *No one has ever escaped on my watch.* He held the idea firmly in his mind as the big guard shackled the scarecrow to the wagon. Ewen had never let a prisoner get free, and it would not happen now. Da was right. The rest was for someone else.

The Keep Gate opened before them, bright sunlight splashing the dark walls. But the sound . . . Ewen looked out and saw people, hundreds of them, maybe even thousands, waiting beyond the moat. As the bridge lowered, the roar seemed to double in volume. The sound was frightening, and it hurt Ewen's ears, but then he reminded himself that he was a Queen's Guard, and Queen's Guards were not frightened. He stood up straight, grasping the side of the wagon for balance as it began to roll.

It took Ewen only a few minutes to figure out what all the noise was about: the scarecrow. They screamed his name, Thorne, mixing it in with curses and threats. Many people threw things: eggs, fruit, even a fresh lump of dog shit that narrowly missed Ewen and landed in the bed of the wagon. Ewen wished he had been able to ask Da what the scarecrow had done, but Da was far too sick to visit the dungeons now. Ewen hadn't seen him in several weeks.

They left the Keep Lawn and proceeded down the Great Boulevard. Here, someone had placed wooden barriers to keep people out of the center of the road, but the mob crowded up against the barriers, nearly knocking them over, shrieking at the wagon the entire way. When the procession passed Powell's Sweet Shop, Ewen saw Mr. and Mrs. Powell out front. Powell's had always been his favorite shop, ever since he was little, when Mum used to take him and his brothers every Sunday if they had been good in church. Mrs. Powell was nicer to Ewen than she was to his brothers; she would always stick a few extra pieces of taffy into his bag. But now Mrs. Powell's face was twisted and dark. Her eyes met Ewen's, but she did not seem to recognize him, nor did she stop screaming, high furious cries that meant nothing.

"Hey, Ew! EW!"

Ewen looked around and saw his brother Peter, clinging to the top of a lamppost with one hand, waving wildly with the other. Peter pointed beneath him, and Ewen saw that they were all there: Arthur and David, his two younger brothers, and Da. Even from this vantage, Ewen could see that Da was leaning heavily on Arthur's arm, that he would have fallen over without help. Ewen longed to wave at Da, but he could not; he was a Queen's Guard, and he sensed the Mace watching him, looking for him to make a mistake. Da didn't wave; he was too weak. But his old eyes were gleaming, and he smiled as Ewen went by.

As they left the boulevard and entered the twisting labyrinth of streets that led to the Circus, Ewen finally turned his attention back to the wagon. The crowd followed, screaming blood and murder behind them, but Ewen no longer heard them. He had never imagined that one single moment of life could be so important. He was a Queen's Guard, and Da had seen, and Da was proud.

For the first few minutes, Kelsea had been able to convince herself that the crowd was merely expressing healthy anger. Seventeen years of the lottery required some outlet, and Thorne was the perfect target, for he stood nonchalantly in the wagon, smiling as though he had not a care in the world, as though he were going to a Sunday picnic rather than his own death. The crowd hurled objects at Thorne, howling like animals, and by the time the procession reached the Circus, Kelsea could no longer deceive herself about what was going on here. This was not a crowd, but a mob, and it was only winding itself up as the procession continued.

The Circus was New London's unofficial plaza, a wide oval of broken paving stones at the center of the city. It was a convenient place for meetings, for it stood at the intersection of five streets and its perimeter was dotted with pubs. But today the plaza was dominated by a high wooden structure: a scaffold, built by contractors in the past week. The platform was taller than Kelsea had expected, perhaps ten feet high, and the scaffold itself seemed to loom over the crowd below.

Three long, twisted ropes, ending in nooses, dangled

from the crossbar. Two of them were already occupied, tightened around the necks of Liam Bannaker and Brother Matthew. Kelsea had expected some pushback from the Arvath; technically, only the Holy Father could sentence one of his people to death. But there had been nothing from the Holy Father for days, no complaints or demands. He was waiting for something, Mace said, but if Mace knew what the something was, he kept it to himself.

Kelsea had hoped that the sight of the rope would touch Thorne, even a little, but he continued to smile broadly, and the crowd screamed louder, and their fury fed his smile, and his smile fed their fury, until it sounded as though the world was ending. Everywhere she looked, Kelsea saw clean hate, eyes and faces and mouths burning with it. Even the evacuees—men and women in the thick, patched trousers and loose shirts of the Border Hills and eastern Almont—had come into the city to see Thorne hang. But Thorne seemed not to care.

There must be something, Kelsea thought, her eyes pinned on him. *Something that would break him.*

She turned to Mace, but he was keeping a careful eye on the boy, Ewen, watching to see that he did not get distracted. Mace thought all of this energy expended on Ewen was a waste of time, but there were some things that you could never explain to Mace. For perhaps the thousandth time, Kelsea wondered what had happened to him, to make him so immune to kindness. In this respect, at least, Thorne had won the chess match: Kelsea never really stopped wondering about Mace anymore, about the strange childhood where Mace and Thorne and Brenna had somehow intersected. But if she asked Mace, he wouldn't tell, and if she ordered him, she would be a tyrant and he wouldn't tell anyway. Thorne had refused to speak another word, even to the last, but Kelsea had kept her end of the bargain. Brenna was now installed in the Keep proper—five floors below the Queen's Wing, to Kelsea's relief—and each day one unfortunate guard had to go down, bring her food, and guard her chamber for the day. Mace had begun to treat the duty as a punishment for small infractions by the Guard, and according to him, it had been surprisingly effective. Kelsea could ask Brenna about Mace's origins, perhaps, but she couldn't imagine that the albino would be willing to tell her anything. She had considered bringing Brenna down here today, but in the end decided that such a move would be too cruel. Now she wished she had done it, just to see the look on Thorne's face. Maddening, to have so many questions to which the answers were hidden by a single pitiless mind.

Kelsea was pleased to see that Ewen's size, at least, was an advantage here. After they stopped the wagon, Ewen held Thorne's arms tightly while Elston dealt with the knots. Normally, it would have been Kibb with Elston, as always, but Mace was still testing Kibb, trying to analyze what had changed since his illness. Kibb *was* different, even Kelsea could see it. He sang less, laughed less, seemed more introspective. From time to time Kelsea would catch him staring at her, puzzled, as though trying to decipher some code that only the two of them understood.

At the foot of the scaffold, Kelsea dismounted and headed up the stairs to the platform, surrounded by her Guard. The crowd howled around her, a sound for nightmares, but she no longer minded, for the cacophony fit her mood. After months spent hunting for Thorne, this should have been her day of triumph, but somehow everything had gone wrong. Thorne had not stood trial, and Kelsea could feel Carlin's certain disapproval, like a low headache at the back of her mind. Eight days ago, the Mort had crossed the Crithe, and no amount of ingenuity from Hall or Bermond could hold back their numbers; soon Kelsea would have to evacuate the sprawling camp outside the city and move the refugees inside. Whenever she closed her eyes now, she saw the Mort: a faceless black horde, waiting, at the end of the New London Bridge. What did they wait for? Kelsea shrank from the answer.

She beckoned her herald, Jordan, who had hung back from the group of Queen's Guards in clear discomfort. The guards were not unkind to him, certainly, but there was little doubt that Jordan was a mouse among hawks.

"See if you can get them to settle down."

Jordan moved to the front of the scaffold and began yelling, waving his arms. His deep voice was strong enough to make the wood thrum beneath Kelsea's feet, but still, it took a few minutes for the crowd to fall into an uneasy silence, one broken by hisses and muttering. Elston and Ewen had moved Thorne to the pinnacle of the scaffold, where he stood with bound hands, staring far over the crowd.

"Arlen Thorne, Brother Matthew, and Liam Bannaker." Kelsea was pleased to hear her words ring across the Circus and bounce back again from the wall of pubs. "You are guilty of treason, and the Crown has sentenced you to death. Should you have anything to say before you hang, the Crown is listening."

For a moment, she thought that Thorne might speak. He scanned the crowd, and Kelsea knew without knowing that he was looking for Brenna, for the damnable albino who had such an incomprehensible hold on him.

Speak, Arlen!

But he said nothing, and then the moment was past. Kelsea felt it blow right by her, a cold wind of withered promise.

"Beast!" a woman screamed, and then they all began again, howling and cursing. There was nothing more to accomplish here; Kelsea nodded to Mace and Coryn, who stepped forward without ceremony and shoved both Bannaker and the priest off the scaffold.

Bannaker's neck broke instantly, a quick crack like a slap, and his limp body swung back and forth in decreasing arcs before the crowd. But Brother Matthew struggled, choking, against his noose. The crowd had begun to fling items again, making a game of it now, trying to hit the two dangling men. Most of these objects bounced harmlessly off the wooden facing, but one piece fell near Kelsea with a dull crack: a mis-shapen brick, its edges worn. Beside the brick, a playing card lay facedown on the platform, no doubt left by some worker on break from construction. Not knowing why, Kelsea bent down and picked it up. Turning it over, she saw that it was the queen of spades.

Kelsea stared at the card, transfixed: a tall woman dressed all in black, holding weapons in both hands. The Queen's all-knowing gaze pinned Kelsea where she stood, as though she knew every thought in Kelsea's mind.

But no, Kelsea thought, *that isn't it at all.* The nights of slicing her own flesh open, the incident with Kibb, the steadily growing sense of her own power ... all of it had been narrowing to a point, distilling Kelsea to her essentials. She squeezed her hand into a fist, feeling the playing card crumple inside.

I am her: the tall, dark woman with death in each hand. She is me.

"Be silent!" she shouted.

A hush fell over the crowd, as quick and sharp as a curtain dropping. Brother Matthew still convulsed, gagging, at the end of his rope, but Kelsea didn't mind the counterpoint. She moved up toward the edge of the scaffold, so far out that Pen, close as always, grabbed a handful of her dress. It felt as though there were yards of extra material in the small of Kelsea's back now, where the fabric had always stretched tight for her entire life. She had transformed, become something more than herself, become extraordinary.

The queen of spades.

"You have come to watch this man die!" she announced. "But I know you, people of the Tearling! You do not come to watch a hanging! You come for blood!"

"Aye!" hundreds of voices shouted back.

"Make him bleed, Lady!"

"Give him to us!"

"No." Something seemed to be unfurling inside Kelsea, unfolding stealthily, like a dark pair of wings opening in the night, and she wanted to spread them wide, feel their span. Always she had been a child of the light, loving the warm sun through the cottage windows, when it felt as though all things were right and kind. But the world was also full of darkness, a cold gulf that beckoned. The people hungered for violence, and suddenly Kelsea wanted, more than anything, to give it them.

Corruption. Carlin's voice, a dim echo, long ago in the morning gleam of the library. *Corruption begins with a single moment of weakness.*

But Kelsea was not weak. She was strong . . . stronger than Carlin could ever have imagined. Her entire being seemed to be filled with bright light.

"Arlen."

It was only a whisper, but Thorne jerked around to face her, a marionette pulled by invisible strings.

I own him, Kelsea realized, her mind a dark marvel. *Every cell, every molecule. I could force him to speak. I could force him to tell me everything I want to know.*

But that was nonsense. The time for talk had come and gone.

"Lady?"

Mace touched her arm, and Kelsea turned to see that he was offering the third noose in one hand. But she ignored it, staring at Thorne, memorizing his form, learning his outlines. He watched her placidly, and Kelsea saw that he felt no regret, even now. In the bleak white landscape of his mind, he was certain that he had acted justifiably, that no man would have done any better. Seventeen long years of facilitating the shipment . . . but no, Thorne's role had been even worse. Deep within his mind, Kelsea found a bright flash of memory: a hand holding out a pen, a smooth, persuasive voice, speaking in murmurs. *I'm afraid you have no choice, Majesty. There's no better option.*

Fury coiled inside Kelsea, a sick fury that seemed to come from nowhere, descending like an animal with ragged claws and needle teeth. She tasted blood on her tongue.

A dark slash opened just above Thorne's left eye. He cried out, clapped a hand to his forehead, and Kelsea watched with pleasure as blood spilled between his fingers and ran down his cheek. The crowd broke its silence now, howling in delight, pushing toward the scaffold. Kelsea leaned forward, heedless of Pen's restraining grip on her dress, and grasped Thorne's hair, tipping his head back. Bright blue eyes stared up at her from a face tacky with blood.

"I have news for you, Arlen. We're on my chessboard now."

Another slice appeared across Thorne's cheek, opening all the way from his hairline to the corner of his mouth. Thorne groaned, and Kelsea felt that winged thing inside her growing, heaving, desperate to break its bonds. She slashed at Thorne's neck, dangerously near the jugular, and watched crimson bloom across the white linen of his shirt. Thorne screamed and the sound was music to Kelsea's ears, the crowd's approval roaring around her, lifting her up. She saw herself as they must see her: a beautiful woman, long dark hair snapping in the wind, a figure of great power and ... was it terror? Kelsea hesitated, seeing the scene before her from another angle, as though a third person stood beside her, observing dispassionately. Thorne was bleeding from half a dozen deep wounds. He had fallen to his knees. The crowd had pushed farther up against the scaffold in its eagerness now, some of them shinnying up the supports and reaching for Thorne, their hands grasping at his legs. But they shied away from Kelsea. Even the most eager took care that their hands should not come within range of her, not even to brush the hem of her dress. Terror, yes ... it must be, and Kelsea's mind went out to the black shadow of the Mort army, somewhere in the floodplain between the Caddell and the Crithe.

My kingdom, she thought, and the wings inside her spread wide, prepared for some unimaginable flight. Briefly her mind skipped backward, to that night when Kibb had lain dying, when she had snatched him back. That was power, yes, but it would not save the Tearling. Her kingdom was laid bare, ripe for slaughter, and she had nothing to offer but this darkness. The black wings folded, enclosing Kelsea in their embrace, and she nearly sighed at the relief she found there, a bottomless fathom where no light ever shone, where all choices were easy because all choices were one.

She returned to Thorne, pushing past his skin, seeking the meat beneath. Her mind had sharpened into a killing blade and she launched into the creature in front of her, slashing everything within her reach, feeling a sweeping excitement as tissue shredded away from bone. Thorne howled, his body becoming misshapen as the inner upheaval played out across his skin. Blood gouted from his nose, spattering the hem of Kelsea's dress, but she barely noticed. She was already digging into the meat of his chest, looking for his lungs. She found one, constricted it, and felt it pop with sickening ease. More blood poured from Thorne's mouth, and at the sight of scarlet dripping down his chin, Kelsea felt it again: a fainting sort of pleasure, akin to what she felt when Pen touched her at night. But this was more visceral, like a punch to her core. Thorne's other lung collapsed and he fell forward, writhing, on the scaffold. The crowd screamed with delight, and the sound lifted Kelsea up. Her entire body felt charged, electric.

"I am the Queen of the Tearling!" she shouted, and the crowd immediately fell silent. Looking over them, their open mouths, their wide eyes, all fixed on her, Kelsea felt as though she held the world in her hands. She had felt so before, but could not remember when. She placed her boot on Thorne's neck and pressed down, hard, liking the way he writhed, liking the feel of his neck beneath her boot.

"The price of treachery in my Tearling! Mark and remember it!"

Thorne's neck snapped. He gave a final gagging cough and seemed to seize, his spine arching. Then he was gone. Kelsea felt him go, like leaves in a wind, but the wild darkness inside her didn't diminish. Instead, it pushed harder, demanding that she find another traitor, more blood. Kelsea drove it back, sensing that here was a seductive thing, to be carefully controlled. She looked down at Thorne's corpse, at the muddy mark of her boot on his neck. The darkness in her mind faded to white, then disappeared.

"To the Queen!" a woman's voice shouted.

"To the Queen!"

Kelsea looked up and saw cups upraised all across the crowd. They had come prepared to celebrate when the deed was done. She had given the crowd what they wanted, what they needed . . . but still Kelsea hesitated, a trickle of anxiety fermenting in her belly now.

Who did those things? The queen of spades? Or me?

Mace placed a cup in her hand, and Kelsea suddenly understood that the drinking was a ritual. She raised the cup to the crowd, wondering if there were any specific words she was supposed to say. No; she was the Queen. She could make up her own words, her own ritual, and they would trump everything that had come before.

"The health of my people!" she shouted. "The health of the Tearling!"

The crowd roared the final words back to her and then drank. Kelsea took a sip and realized that although Mace had come prepared, he was no fool; the liquid in her cup was only water. But it tasted sweet somehow, and Kelsea drained it. When she turned to give the cup back, she found Mace still holding the noose in his other hand. Although his face was blank, Kelsea sensed disapproval beneath.

"Well, Lazarus?"

"You've changed, Lady. I never thought to see you bow to the will of the mob."

Kelsea flushed. The realization that Mace could still do that, make her feel ashamed with a single cutting remark, was unwelcome. "I bow to no one."

"That I can well believe."

Mace turned away, and Kelsea grabbed his arm, desperate to make him understand. "I haven't changed, Lazarus. I've grown older, that's all. I'm still me."

"No, Lady." Mace sighed, and the sigh seemed to pass through Kelsea, a breath of doom on cold wings. "Tell yourself whatever pleasing stories you want, but you're not the girl we took from the cottage. You've become someone else."

— CHAPTER 10 —

FATHER TYLER

Always, we think we know what courage means. If I were called upon, we say, I would answer the call. I would not hesitate. Until the moment is upon us, and then we realize that the demands of true courage are very different from what we had envisioned, long ago on that bright morning when we felt brave.

—Father Tyler's Collected Sermons, FROM THE ARVATH ARCHIVE

The Arvath staircase was made of solid stone, bleached white stone that had been mined from the rocks around Crossing's End. But with each step, Tyler became more careful, tormented by an irrational certainty that the stone staircase would squeak beneath his feet. He climbed slowly, dragging his broken leg.

Occasionally he passed one of his brothers going down the staircase, and they gave him only the most cursory glance before moving on. Tyler's position as Keep Priest gave him latitude, made it plausible that he might be invited up to the Holy Father's private quarters so late at night. But Tyler had to count the landings in order to know where he was. He had never climbed so high in the Arvath. He did not know whether he would be coming back down.

When he reached the ninth floor, he darted away from the staircase, concealing himself in a recess that stood across the hall. The opulence of his surroundings made Tyler dizzy, for the decor on this level was a far cry from the plain stone walls and handwoven rugs that graced the brothers' quarters downstairs. Gold and silver shone in the torchlight: candlestands, tables, statuary. The floors were Cadarese marble. The walls were draped with red and purple velvet.

The hallway continued for perhaps fifty feet before it turned left toward the Holy Father's private quarters. There was no one in sight, but Tyler knew that around the corner he would surely find guards and acolytes, at least several of them, near the Holy Father's door. It was just after two o'clock in the morning. If Tyler was lucky, the Holy Father would be sleeping, but it seemed too much to hope for that his guards and servants should do the same. Even on tiptoe, Tyler's shoes made a scuffling sound that seemed deafening in the cavernous hallway.

I will grab my books and be gone, he repeated to himself. Only ten books; Tyler had already chosen them, so that he would not be tempted to exceed his capacity. He liked the historical significance of the number 10, the symmetry with the Crossing. Books were one of the few personal items William Tear had allowed his people, ten books apiece. If they tried to sneak other items aboard, he left them behind. It was only arcana, one of thousands of tiny pieces of information about the Crossing that Tyler had picked up during his lifetime. But he had never forgotten a single one.

If I survive this, Tyler decided, *I will write the first history of the Crossing. I'll bind it myself, and present it to the Queen for printing.*

That was a good thing to tell himself, a grand dream. But the Queen's ambition to create a printing press had come to naught so far. No one in the Tearling had any idea how to begin building such a thing. There was no mechanism for broad distribution of the written word.

There will be.

Tyler blinked. The voice was implacable. He believed it.

Peering around the corner, he saw that fear had made him overly cautious. Only two men stood in front of the Holy Father's door, and they were acolytes, not the well-armed guards who accompanied the Holy Father whenever he left the safety of the Arvath. If Brother Matthew had still been the Holy Father's right hand, this would be much more difficult, but Brother Matthew had been executed Sunday past, and these two on the door appeared young and soft, perhaps not yet taken into the Holy Father's confidence. They looked up sleepily as he approached.

"Good evening, brothers. I must speak to His Holiness."

The acolytes exchanged nervous looks. One of them, a boy barely out of his teens with a catastrophic overbite, replied, "His Holiness is not receiving visitors this evening."

"The Holy Father told me that I was to come to him with this news immediately."

They shot each other another uncertain glance. Indecisive, these two, and poorly trained. It was another marked difference between Anders and the old Holy Father, who never let his people represent him to the world until they were as competent as himself.

"Surely it can wait until morning?" the second youth asked. He was even younger than the first, still young enough for pimples to dot his face in small clusters.

"It cannot," Tyler answered firmly. "This is news of the most vital importance."

They turned away from him and held a huddled conference. Despite his anxiety, Tyler was amused to hear the two of them begin a game of rock, paper, and scissors to decide who would go in. After three tries, the young man with the overbite lost and slipped, white-faced, through the great double doors. The other acolyte did his best to appear professional while they waited, but he yawned continually, ruining the illusion. Tyler could only pity him, this boy growing up directly under Anders's eye and tutelage. He could not imagine how the boy would conceive of his Church, his God.

"I should check your bag," the boy ventured after a few moments.

Tyler held out his satchel and the acolyte peered inside, but all he saw was Tyler's old Bible, a heavy hardcover given to him by Father Alan on his eighth birthday. The acolyte handed the satchel back, and Tyler replaced the strap over his head, settling the bag across his body. Sometime in the last few minutes, his fear had begun to ebb, leaving something electric in its wake. His heart seemed too big for his chest.

The other acolyte's head appeared from the doorway, and Tyler could not mistake the look of relief on his face: Tyler was wanted. "Please come in."

He opened the door wide, and Tyler followed him into what was clearly a common room of some sort, an enormous chamber with high ceilings and thick rugs. Oil paintings covered the walls, and velvet sofas were scattered throughout the room. The acolyte did not look at any of these things, keeping his gaze straight ahead. But Tyler, who glanced around the room in curiosity, let out a startled gasp. To his right, a woman lay sprawled on a low sofa, completely naked, her limbs thrown every which way to conceal nothing. It was the first time in his life that Tyler had seen a woman's bare breasts, and he turned away quickly, embarrassed both for her and for himself. But the woman seemed entirely oblivious of their presence, her eyes wide and unfocused.

"Please wait here," the acolyte told him, and Tyler halted abruptly as the boy continued onward toward a large, arched doorway at the far end of the room. Left alone, Tyler was unable to stop staring at the woman on the sofa, at her breasts and the dark triangle between her thighs. Although he felt no lust—his age had moved him past that particular indignity—the sight of these things was fascinating. The woman had long, dark hair that fell in ribbons over the edge of the sofa, and she returned his gaze without shame. As Tyler's eyes adjusted to the dim candlelight, he spied a syringe within the crease of her elbow, the head of a needle still buried deep in her arm. Having seen this, he could not help seeing other things: a vial of white powder, still uncapped, on the low table between them; a spoon, bent and twisted through long misuse; deep bruising that went halfway up the woman's other arm. She was not young, this woman, but her body was still lithe, and to Tyler's eye, the needle in her arm seemed a ruinous thing, a perversion of potential.

"Who are you?" she asked Tyler, her voice wet and slurred. "Never seen you before."

"Tyler."

"You a priest?"

"Yes."

She straightened a bit, propping herself on one elbow. Her gaze had sharpened slightly. "Never seen a naked woman before, eh?"

"No," Tyler replied, dropping his gaze to stare at the ground. "I'm sorry."

"Don't be sorry. I don't mind if they look."

"Who's they?"

"Oh . . ." The woman looked off into the corner, her eyes turning vague again. "All of them. Other priests. The ones who visit. They never stop at looking."

Something turned over in Tyler's stomach.

"You won't touch, will you?"

"No."

"Want a hit?"

"No, thank you." Tyler pulled the ancient Bible from his bag, fingering the edges of the cover, touching the pages. It felt very solid in his hand. "What's your name?"

"Maya."

"Tyler! What brings you to me so late at night?"

But the Holy Father already knew. His face radiated good humor. He wore a hastily tied robe of black silk, and his hair was mussed, but he made no attempt to repair his appearance, and Tyler remembered suddenly that there was a second woman here, that the Holy Father kept two. He had forgotten to include the women in his calculations, and their presence would make his enterprise more dangerous. For a moment Tyler considered begging off, lying to the Holy Father and then simply leaving the Arvath under the cover of night. But then, thinking of his books, he screwed up his courage, set his face in grim lines, and announced, "It's done, Your Holiness."

"The Queen took the substance?"

"Yes."

"So late?"

"The Queen sleeps little these days, Your Holiness."

This, at least, was true. Tyler, who had spent several recent nights on his favorite sofa in the Queen's library, had been awakened more than once by the Queen herself, touring her bookshelves, touching each book in turn. She wandered the wing, trailed doggedly by Pen Alcott, but always she came back to her library for solace. She and Tyler were alike that way, but whatever the Queen was looking for, she did not find it. Except for the times when she fell into her strange catatonic states—and thank God the Holy Father knew nothing of those—she seemed to sleep very little. "She took it in tea, perhaps an hour ago."

"Well, this is splendid news, Tyler!" The Holy Father clapped him on the back, and Tyler had to fight not to shrink away. Maya was staring at the two of them now, her eyes narrow and sharp.

"My books, Your Holiness?"

"Well, I think we'll wait and make sure the deed is done, Tyler. You understand." The Holy Father grinned, a predator's grin that consumed his whole face.

Tyler's hands tightened on his Bible, but he nodded. "May I not even have a glimpse of my books, Your Holiness? I have missed them."

The Holy Father stared at him, a moment that seemed very long. "Certainly, Tyler. Come with me. They're in my bedchamber."

From the corner of his eye, Tyler saw Maya's mouth drop open in dismay. Her presence could wreck everything, but there was no turning back now. The moment the Holy Father turned away, Tyler swung the Bible with all of his strength, the way a woodsman would swing an axe. The heavy book connected solidly with the Holy Father's head and knocked him sprawling, but the blow had not been enough; the Holy Father pushed himself to his hands and knees, drawing deep breath, preparing to shout.

"Please, God," Tyler breathed. He limped forward, raised the Bible, and brought it straight down on the back of the Holy Father's head. The Holy Father dropped soundlessly to the rug, and this time he lay still.

Tyler looked up and found Maya staring at him with wide eyes. He tucked the Bible back into his bag, raising his hands to show that he meant her no harm. "My books. He was lying, wasn't he? They're not here."

"They took them out a week ago. Down to the basement."

This, more than anything else, told Tyler that the promise of a reward had been a lie. If he'd done the deed, the Holy Father would have . . . what? Killed him? Tyler considered the man on the ground for a moment—he was breathing, Tyler noticed gratefully—before he saw the clear path, the smart move: the Holy Father would have handed him over to the Mace.

"Thank you, God," Tyler breathed, "that I did not do it."

"You're the Queen's priest," said Maya.

"Yes." Tyler edged toward the door, listening, but there was no noise from outside. Still, he should leave now, before the Holy Father regained consciousness, before the woman raised the alarm. He grasped the handle, but her voice stopped him.

"Is the Queen good?"

Tyler turned and saw that Maya's eyes had filled with alarming need. He had seen similar desperation long ago, out in the country, when dying parishioners would ask a still-unordained Tyler to take their final confessions. For some strange reason of her own, Maya needed him to answer yes.

"Yes, she's good. She wants to make things better."

"Better for who?"

"For everyone."

Maya stared at him for a moment longer, then scrambled up from the sofa. Tyler was no longer embarrassed by her nakedness; in fact, for a few moments he had forgotten all about it. Maya hurried over to the Holy Father's prone body, reached beneath him, and pulled a chain over his head. On the chain was a small silver key.

"I need to leave," Tyler told her. He did not want to abandon her here, she was so terribly troubled, but he could not take her with him, even if she wished to flee. Adrenaline had departed, and was rapidly being replaced by the full realization of what he had done. His leg was even worse than he'd thought; going up the stairs had strained it badly. The journey downward would be terrible.

"My mum was a pro, priest."

"What?"

"A pro. A prostitute." Maya crossed the room and crouched down in front of a glossy oak cabinet, her movements sure. Tyler barely recognized the languid addict of a few moments before. "Mum used to talk to us about the thing she would do someday, the one important thing that would wipe out all the years before. You only got one moment, Mum said, and when it came, you had to jump, no matter the cost."

"I really need to—"

"He tells us about the invasion. Soon the Mort will be at the walls, and there are too many to hold back. It will take a miracle." The lock clicked, and Maya opened the cabinet, then looked up at him, her face suddenly shrewd. "But they say the Queen is full of miracles."

When she stood, she held a large wooden box that had been burnished within an inch of its life; the sides gleamed deep cherry in the torchlight. "You have to give it back to her. It's wrong for him to keep it here."

"What is it?"

She opened the lid, and Tyler stared at the Tear crown, which sat before him on a deep red cushion. Silver and sapphire glittered, sparkling reflections against the open lid of the box.

"This is my moment, priest," Maya told him, shoving the box into his hands. "Take it and go."

Tyler considered her for a moment, thinking again of the farmers he had known in his youth, dying in their huts, desperate to confess, and he wished that he could suspend time, even for an hour, to sit and talk to this woman who had never had anyone to listen. Her dark eyes were entirely clear now, and Tyler saw that they were beautiful, despite the lines that shrouded them like hoods.

"Andy?" A woman's voice drifted from beyond the darkened archway, sleepy and confused. "Andy? Where'd you get to?"

"Go, priest," Maya ordered. "I'll try to hold her, but you have very little time."

Tyler hesitated a moment longer, then took the box and tucked it alongside the Bible in his satchel. For a moment, grief over his books threatened to overtake him, but he would not give it space, was ashamed to even feel it now. He had lost his library, but the woman before him was risking her life.

"Go," she told him again, and Tyler limped for the doors,

opening one of them just wide enough to let himself through. His last glimpse of Maya was fleeting, a quick flash of her staring at the vial on the table before he shut the door behind him. The two acolytes leaned against the wall on either side, so casually that Tyler wondered if they had been eavesdropping. Overbite eyed him narrowly, then asked, "Does the Holy Father want us?"

"No. I think he means to retire for the rest of the night." Tyler turned and started down the hall, but he only made a few steps before a hand fell on his shoulder.

"What's in the bag?" Overbite asked.

"My Bible."

"And what else?"

"My new robes," Tyler replied, amazed at how easily the lie came to him. "The Holy Father has granted me a bishopric."

Both of them drew back, trading anxious glances. In the hierarchy of the Arvath, the Holy Father's personal aides, even the acolytes, carried more weight than any priest. But a bishop was another matter; even the least powerful of the bishops' college was no one to argue with. As if by mutual consent, the two acolytes bowed and back away.

"Good night, Your Eminence."

Tyler turned and limped down the hallway. He guessed he had two minutes, at most, before they realized that his story was absurd. The Holy Father didn't keep spare sets of bishops' robes around to hand out like candy. And the other woman might raise the alarm at any time.

Tyler paused at the top of the staircase, looking down at its concentric squares as one would face a mortal enemy. His leg was already throbbing, bright flashes of pain that traveled like a current from hip to toe. He wished he could take the lift, which ran a limited service at night to serve the Holy Father's level. They might agree to lower him down to the brothers' quarters. But he would have to wait for the lift to come—the platform was stowed on the lowest floor of the Arvath at night—and if the alarm was raised while he was still on it, he would be stuck, held between floors until Anders's guards came to take him. No, it would have to be the stairs, and considering the way Tyler's leg felt at the moment, he wouldn't get far before he had to hop.

Tyler grimaced, clenched his tongue between his teeth, and started downward, leaning heavily on the handrail. His satchel bounced against his hip with each step, rhythmic drumming that did nothing to help his arthritis. One floor down; he clutched the bag, trying to keep it still, and felt the sharp contours of the wooden box inside.

I am part of God's great work.

This thought had not crossed his mind in a long time. He thought of the woman, Maya, and felt a wave of sick guilt crash through him. He had left her there, in front of a table full of morphia, to endure whatever punishment Anders might mete out. Two floors down. Now Tyler was hopping in earnest, holding his bad foot suspended in midair and clutching the handrail for dear life, using a tiny leap to propel himself down each step. His good leg was beginning to ache as well now, long-unused muscles threatening to cramp. He didn't know what would happen if the leg seized before he finished the staircase. Three floors down. Both of his legs bellowed in protest, but he ignored them. Four floors down. The adrenaline had returned now, blessedly, singing all through his bloodstream as he began the final set of stairs, and against all odds, Tyler found himself grinning like a boy. He was a bookkeeper and an ascetic ... a year ago, who would have guessed that he would be here, hopping like a bunny rabbit down the stairs? Rounding the second corner of the staircase, he caught a glimpse of slumped shoulders two flights down, a man's nearly bald head. His grin died in its tracks.

Seth.

Tyler paused, hearing a muffled sound high above. One moment more, and then the silence shattered in a deep thrum of bells. The alarm. Shouts echoed down the staircase, and now Tyler could hear pounding feet several floors up. They had not wanted to wait for the lift either. Tyler began hopping again, rounding the corner to the final flight of stairs. As he came closer, he saw that Seth was asleep but perspiring, his skin waxy in the dim light. Seth was not healing. He was not meant to. Once every priest in the Arvath stopped having nightmares, once Seth had outlived his usefulness, the Holy Father would simply have him removed, as neatly and cleanly as he had removed Tyler's books. Tyler reached the landing, and now he was confronted by the placard around Seth's neck: "Abomination." The word seemed to reach deep into Tyler, opening a broad vista of things that should not be. When God's Church had sprung up after the Crossing, it had been a hard church, a reflection of its times, but a good church. It did not achieve its ends through hatred, through shame. And now—

"Seth," Tyler whispered, not knowing that he would speak until the words were out. "Seth, wake up."

But Seth continued to dream, his lips fluttering in the half-light.

"Seth!"

Seth woke with a jerk and a low cry. He looked up with bleary eyes.

"Ty?"

"It's me." Tyler grabbed the placard and pulled it over Seth's head. Footsteps thundered above them; the Holy Father's guards could not be more than two floors away now. Tyler threw the placard over the edge of the railing, where it fluttered downward for a moment before disappearing from sight.

"Come on, Seth." He got an arm around Seth's waist and pulled him off the stool. Seth hissed in pain, but did not draw away.

"Where are we going?"

"Away from here." Tyler pulled him down the hallway. "I can't carry you, Seth. My leg's bad. You have to help."

"I'll try." But Seth firmed up his own arm behind Tyler's back, lending support as the two of them limped along. Tyler's mouth stretched in a grim smile.

What a pair we make. Old, lame, and mutilated.

But even this bit of gallows humor pricked at his memory, and now Tyler recalled something from his childhood, an illustration from one of Father Alan's tapestries: Jesus Christ, King of the Jews, on the road to Galilee, leading the blind, helping the lame, offering comfort to the leper. Tyler used to sit and stare for long minutes at that tapestry, the only art in Father Alan's house that did not depict a God of wrath. The Jesus in the tapestry had been mild and benevolent of face, and though the miserable of the world were crowded around him, he did not turn away.

This is my God, Tyler had realized, and now, hobbling down the high stone hallway more than sixty years later, he felt exalted at the memory. His broken leg buckled beneath him and he thought he would pitch forward, bringing Seth down with him, both of them tumbling over the flagstones until they fetched up against the wall. But then Tyler felt them: invisible hands gripping his legs, bolstering his knee, helping him to run.

"Seth!" he gasped. "Seth! He's with us!"

Seth gave a choked laugh, his hand clenched tightly on Tyler's thin ribs. "What, even now?"

"Of course now!" Tyler began to laugh as well, his voice high and hysterical. "Great God, only a little farther!"

The shouts behind them grew louder, and now Tyler could feel the footsteps of their pursuers beneath his feet, vibrating against the stone floor as they poured from the staircase. In every doorway there seemed to be a brother just roused from sleep, staring at Tyler and Seth with wide eyes, but no one moved to stop them in their clumsy progress down the hallway. The invisible hands were gone now and the two of them were supporting each other, their shuffling, limping gaits somehow finding symmetry, a three-legged race that carried them along. When they reached Tyler's door, they both limped inside, and Tyler shot the bolt.

It took the Holy Father's guards nearly two minutes to find a piece of wood solid enough to break down the door. When the heavy oak rectangle finally tore free of its hinges, several guards crashed into Father Tyler's quarters, falling over each other in their haste and ending up in a pile on top of the busted door. They were quick to recover, to straighten up and look around, swords drawn, ready to meet resistance.

But all they found was an empty room.

Kelsea dragged herself up the last flight of steps, trying not to pant. She was carrying less weight, but the miraculous change to her exterior had not gotten her into good condition. Mace was beside her; Pen had gone on leave for the weekend. Kelsea had had no opportunity to speak privately to him before he left, but she couldn't help wondering whether he would go to see the other woman. It was none of her business, Kelsea told herself, and yet five minutes later she would find herself thinking about it again. She had wanted this thing to mean nothing to either of them, but was quickly discovering that it didn't quite work that way.

She reached the top of the stairs and found herself gazing over the high wall that bordered New London's eastern side. From here, she could look out across the Caddell and over the Almont, now mottled green and brown in the late summer.

Beneath the city's walls, just on the far side of the Caddell, lay the refugee camp: more than a mile of tents and hastily built shelters spread across the banks of the river. From this distance the people in the camp were antlike, but there were more than half a million of them down there. The Caddell provided plenty of water, but sewage was becoming a problem, and despite the huge stores that Mace had brought in, the camp would soon run out of food. It was the height of harvest season, but no one was farming the Almont. Even if the Tearling somehow made it through the invasion, fruit and vegetable stores would be decimated for years. Some families in the north, near the Fairwitch, had elected to remain and take their chances, and so had a few isolated villages on the Cadarese border. But most of the Tearling was now crammed in and around New London, and Kelsea sensed the kingdom before her as a vast wasteland under a grey sky, nothing but deserted villages and empty fields, haunted.

Perhaps ten miles distant, sprawled near the horizon, was

the Tear army, a cluster of tents that had faded from long use. The army was massed on the banks of the Caddell, at the point where the river suddenly bent to begin its twisting journey around New London. Her army appeared unimposing, even to Kelsea, and it was not helped by comparison with what lay on the horizon: a vast, dark cloud, the subtle haze reflected from many miles of black tents, black banners, and the innumerable hawks that now soared over the Mort camp at all times. Hall had caught the Mort napping beside Lake Karczmar, but that would never happen again, for now the Mort had come up with some sort of sentinel species to overfly their camp. Unlike most Mort hawks, which would not cry out, these birds emitted an ungodly shriek whenever any of Bermond's soldiers tried to approach. Several scouts had been caught in this manner, and now Bermond was forced to keep an eye on the Mort from a distance, but not for long. They were coming, and they were coming fast. Hall's missives came without judgment, but Bermond's were a constant stream of reprimands, and Kelsea knew that he was right. She had made a great mistake, one that her entire kingdom would suffer for, and although she was not certain that all other options would not have been greater mistakes, this one seemed to demand punishment. Every day she came out here to watch the Mort approach, to see the black cloud on the horizon draw nearer. It seemed no more than what she deserved.

"They're trying to cut the Caddell," Mace remarked beside her.

"Why? There's nothing on either side now."

"If they come up the bank and try to cross the river in front of the city, they would lose considerable numbers to our archers. But if they hold both banks, they can come with defenses ready, be impervious to arrows. Then they can simply focus on scaling the walls and taking the bridge."

Even Mace was a pessimist now. There was no hope anywhere, unless Kelsea could make it herself. The thought sickened her. When she looked in the mirror this morning, a beautiful brunette stared back at her, but not just any brunette. Lily's hair, Lily's face, Lily's mouth . . . the two of them were not identical, not by any means, but individual pieces were beginning to match. Kelsea and Lily were sharing a life; now it seemed they would share a face as well. But Kelsea's eyes had never changed; they were still Raleigh eyes . . . her mother's eyes, twin spots of deep green carelessness that had brought down an entire kingdom.

"Glory to the Queen!"

The shout came from below, from the bottom of the inner wall, where several members of her Guard had blocked the stairwell. Kelsea peered over the edge and found a crowd of people gathered at the foot of the stairs. They waved furiously, a sea of upturned faces.

They think I can save them. Kelsea dug up a confident smile and waved back, then returned her attention to the Almont. She had never had any options, but that fact would earn her no leniency. When she was judged—as she surely would be, by history if nothing else—there would be no mitigating circumstances. She stared at the dark sprawl on the horizon, not allowing herself to look away. Almost without thinking, she opened up a new wound on her calf, feeling a grim satisfaction as blood trickled down toward her ankle.

Punishment.

"Sir!"

Mace leaned over the edge of the staircase. "What?"

"Messenger from General Bermond."

"Send him up."

Kelsea turned away from the Almont as Bermond's messenger reached the top of the stairs. Army messengers really were extraordinary; the man had run up five flights of stairs, but he was barely even out of breath. He was young and lithe, a sergeant by the copper pin at his collar, and his eyes widened as he caught sight of Kelsea. But this effect was no longer gratifying, if it ever had been. She signaled the man to speak, then turned back to the Almont.

"Majesty, the general wishes to report that the Argive Pass has fallen."

Mace grunted beside her, but Kelsea kept her gaze pinned on the black cloud on the horizon, trying not to blink.

"The Mort have already begun to bring supplies through the Argive; this will cut their resupply time considerably. Last night over a thousand reinforcements also came down the Pass. They will reach the Mort line by tomorrow. The entire Mort army has now crossed the Crithe and taken the north bank of the Caddell, and the vanguard will soon push the Tear away from the southern bank as well. The general estimates that this will happen in no more than three days. He believes they mean to follow the Caddell all the way to New London."

The messenger paused, and Kelsea heard the gulp of his Adam's apple bobbing up and down.

"Continue."

"General Bermond wishes me to report that the Tear army has now lost over two thousand men, more than a third of its forces."

Kelsea's eyes refused to stay open any longer, and she blinked, momentarily blotting out the horizon. But when she opened her eyes, the cloud was still there.

"What else?"

"This is all I have to report, Majesty."

No good news. Of course not. "Lazarus, how long until the Mort reach the walls?"

"My guess, less than a week. Don't let the distance deceive you, Lady. Even with Bermond doing all he can, the Mort are capable of advancing two or three miles a day. They'll be here by the end of the month, no later."

Kelsea looked down at the refugee camp, that sprawling mess of hardship, inadequate shelter, the beginnings of starvation. That responsibility lay at her feet as well. She turned back to the messenger. "Advise Bermond that we'll move the refugees inside the city. It will take at least five days. Bermond is to hold the Mort off the camp until evacuation is complete, then retreat and hold the bridge."

The messenger nodded.

"Well done. Dismissed."

He scampered down the stairs and out of sight. Kelsea turned back to the Almont. "Arliss should be in charge of evacuating the camp. His people know names and faces down there."

"Lady, I assure you—"

"Did you really think I wouldn't find out, Lazarus? His little minions are all over that camp, dealing narcotics like there's no tomorrow."

"There *is* no tomorrow for these people, Lady."

"Ah. I knew it." Kelsea turned to face him, feeling her temper grind into terrible life. But beneath was something even worse than anger: shame. She craved Mace's approval, always had, in the same way she had always longed for accolades from Barty. But Barty had approved of her without reservation. Mace made his approval more valuable, forcing

Kelsea to earn it, and the knowledge that she had failed cut very deep. "I knew that sooner or later you would tell me that I fucked it all up."

"Done is done, Lady."

This was worse; not only did Mace not approve, he didn't even want to discuss it. Kelsea's eyes watered, but she forced the tears back, furious. "I suppose you think I'm just like her."

"You spend too much time dwelling on your mother, Lady. That's always been a weakness of yours."

"Of course it has!" Kelsea shouted, mindless of the guards nearby. "She overshadows everything I try to do here! I can't make a move without being hampered by her mistakes!"

"Perhaps, Lady, but don't deceive yourself. You make your own mistakes as well."

"Is this about Thorne?"

His gaze slid away from hers, and Kelsea narrowed her eyes. "You cannot be serious."

"Listen to me, Lady. Listen very carefully." Mace's face had paled, and Kelsea suddenly realized that the granite expression she had mistaken for resignation was actually anger, a deep, quiet anger that was somehow worse than the blustering rage she had seen from Mace once or twice before. "You have done many things that I would not have done. You are reckless. You do not consider all consequences, nor do you take advice from people who are more informed than you. And yet I have never condemned any of your actions, until now."

"Why?" she hissed. "What makes Thorne so important?"

"*It's not Thorne!*" Mace roared, and Kelsea shrank back. "Stop being a child for once! It's you, Lady. You have changed."

"This?" Kelsea ran a hand down her face and neck. "*This* is what concerns you?"

"I wouldn't care if you transformed into the Beautiful Queen herself, but your new face is not the issue, Lady. You are *different*."

"Less naive."

"No. More brutal."

Kelsea's jaw clenched. "And what of that?"

"Think it over, Lady. There are worse things than becoming your mother."

Kelsea's temper snapped, and for several seconds, she hovered within inches of picking Mace up and heaving him over the wall. She could do it, she knew. . . . Thorne's execution had awakened something inside her, some creature that stalked through her daily life, looking for any excuse to spring. This creature was predatory, implacable, and it did not want to go back to sleep.

Mace stepped forward, reaching out to take her shoulder. Mace never touched her unless there was a security issue, and Kelsea was so surprised that she stilled immediately, feeling her anger retreat.

"Take your jewels off, Lady," Mace pleaded. "Let them go. For all the good they've done, it's not worth what's happening to you. I'll hide them away. No one will ever find them. Build your throne, your legacy, on something else."

For a moment, Kelsea wondered whether he was right, whether the jewels were the real problem. The dreams, the voices, Lily's inexorable invasion . . . some part of Kelsea's own life seemed to have gotten lost en route. The way her guards eyed her now, when they thought she wasn't looking: tentative, suspicious, sometimes even fearful. The feeling of helplessness when she looked in the mirror and found Lily's face staring back at her. Everything had gone bad somehow, and Kelsea wasn't even sure when it had happened.

But the sapphires . . . what Mace asked was impossible. It didn't even matter that the sapphires did nothing anymore, that they seemed to be lifeless. They were *hers*, and now Kelsea found herself staring a hard truth in the face: she had her own narcotics. They merely took a different form.

"No," she finally replied. "You can't ask me for that."

She felt his eyes on her, their weight nearly physical.

"Are we going to have a problem, Lazarus?"

"I suppose that depends on you, Lady. I'm a Queen's Guard. I'm sworn."

A throat cleared behind Kelsea, and she whirled, furious that anyone dared to interrupt. But it was only Coryn, standing at the top of the steps.

"We'll continue this at a later time," she told Mace.

"I can hardly wait."

She gave him a sharp glance, feeling her temper trying to awaken again, but then it subsided. It was only Mace, after all, Mace who always said the true thing that Kelsea didn't want to hear. She put one hand to her temple, which was suddenly throbbing, clamoring for attention. She felt as though her mind was being pulled in two directions, past and future lying opposite each other on a straight track. At one end lay Lily Mayhew and the strange Englishman who had brought them all to the new world, built a colony, and given the kingdom its name, and at the other end was the Mort army, breaking the walls of her city. Kelsea could see each step clearly: the breach of the wall, the black masses pouring in, the orgy of slaughter and violation and brutality that would follow. Men, women, children . . . no one would be spared. The Sack of New London, they would call it, a horror that would decimate the Tearling for generations. How could there be no alternative? Could she destroy the Mort army as she had destroyed Thorne? She could try, but the terrible consequences if she failed . . . Kelsea turned back to the horizon, and though it was only her imagination, the black cloud seemed closer. Madness beckoned, and Kelsea felt that it would embrace her, if she allowed it . . . a deep, dark nothingness that would wrap her like a cloak and take all dilemmas away.

"What is it, Coryn?"

"We've had word from the Cadarese. They will not offer assistance. Further, the King's offer of marriage is withdrawn."

Kelsea felt a bitter smile stretch her lips. "Is Kattan here?"

"No, Lady."

"Kattan's the First Ambassador," Mace told her, "the man for happy times and sweet offers. When they want to cut and run, they send some poor bastard who may or may not survive the trip."

"The Cadarese messenger did leave a present, Lady," Coryn added.

"What is it?"

"A stone bowl. For fruit."

Kelsea began to giggle. She couldn't help it. Mace was smiling now, too, but it was a tired smile, worlds removed from his normal grin. "The Cadarese are isolationists, Lady. This is their way."

"I suppose there will be no good news," Kelsea replied, her laughter subsiding. "It just isn't that kind of day, is it?"

"Nor that kind of month, Lady."

"No, I suppose not." Kelsea began to wipe a tear from her cheek and saw that her hand was bleeding.

"Are you all right, Lady?"

"I'm fine. We should arm everyone in the city who's fit to hold a sword."

"We don't have the steel."

"Wooden swords, then, anything. Just give them weapons."

"To what end?"

"Morale. People don't like to feel defenseless. And when the refugees come in, I want all the families with children moved to the Keep."

"There's not enough room."

"Then do the best you can, Lazarus." Kelsea rubbed her temples. Lily was calling her, tugging at her mind, but Kelsea didn't want to go back, didn't want to watch Lily's life play out inside her head. The present was bad enough.

"We should get you back inside, Lady. You have a fugue coming on."

She turned to him, surprised. "How do you know?"

"Just the look you get. We know the signs now."

"When is Pen back?"

Mace gave her an inscrutable look. "His leave is over tonight, but he likely won't be back until after you fall asleep."

"That's fine."

"Be careful, Lady."

She whipped around, meaning to snap at him: it was none of his business whom she slept with! But she kept quiet. Pen did not belong to her, after all. If he belonged to anyone, it was to Mace.

"Lady!"

"Christ God, Coryn, what? Another messenger?"

"No, Lady." Coryn raised his hands. "It's the magician now. He says he must speak to you."

"Who?"

"The magician who performed at your dinner. Bradshaw."

But the man who emerged from the staircase was not the impeccably neat performer that Kelsea had seen at dinner that night. Bradshaw had been badly beaten. Both of his eyes were puffed with dark bruising, and there were red scrapes across his cheeks.

"Majesty," he panted. "I must beg you for asylum."

"What?"

"The Holy Father has placed a price on my head."

"You're joking."

"I swear to you, Majesty. One hundred pounds. I have been on the run for days."

"I have no love for the Holy Father, Bradshaw, but it seems unlikely that he would place an open bounty on a man's head."

"I'm not the only one, Majesty! The old priest, Father Tyler. The Holy Father offers a bounty for him as well."

Kelsea felt her stomach sink, a slow roll, as she realized that she had not seen Father Tyler for several days. Arliss and his siege preparations had kept her far too busy to notice, but now she counted backward and found that it had been at least three days since Father Tyler had last come to the Keep.

"Where is he?" she asked Mace.

"I don't know, Lady," Mace replied, his face troubled. "This is the first I've heard of this."

"Find him, Lazarus. Find him right now."

Mace went to confer with Coryn, and Kelsea was left with the magician. Mace had left her unguarded, she realized suddenly, and this was perhaps the truest indication that he knew the real score: Kelsea was in no physical danger from anyone anymore. Her Guard was only a polite fiction. An idea glimmered at the edges of her mind for a moment, something to do with the Mort, but when she reached out to grasp it, the idea was gone, subsumed in worry over Father Tyler. The magician had been able to outrun his pursuers; what could Father Tyler do? He was an old man with a broken leg.

"Does the Holy Father have some prior grievance with you?" she asked the magician.

"No, Majesty, I swear to you. I never saw him before that night at the Keep. Word in the Gut is that the Holy Father has excommunicated all performers of my trade. But I'm the only one for whom he offers a bounty."

So this was not about Bradshaw. The Holy Father might hate magicians, but the bounty was a slap aimed directly at Kelsea.

"How much danger are you really in?"

"Less than another might be without my gift of vanishing. But I can't outrun them forever, Majesty. I'm too well known in the city. I swear to you, I will be of use to you."

Kelsea laughed and gestured over the wall. "Look out there, Bradshaw. I have no need of an in-house performer now."

"I understand, Majesty." The magician stared at the ground for a long moment, then squared his shoulders and spoke quietly. "I'm no performer."

"What does that mean?"

Bradshaw leaned closer. If Mace had been nearby, he would never have allowed it, but he was still deep in conference with Coryn, and so Bradshaw was able to hunch over Kelsea, hiding her from the rest of her Guard.

"Look."

Bradshaw raised his right palm and held it perfectly still.

After a moment, the air above his palm began to shimmer, as cobblestones did in high heat. The shimmer solidified into a knife, a silver knife with an old and intricate handle.

"Try it, Majesty."

Kelsea grasped the knife, found it solid in her hand.

"They say you have magic, Majesty, in your jewels. But there is other magic in the Tear. My family is full of such gifts."

Kelsea snuck another quick look at Mace. He would not like it, she knew; he distrusted magicians, all of their ilk. And yet the man had meant no harm that night; Kelsea had hired him to perform. There were larger considerations here, too: the Holy Father might have paid off the nobles of New London, but the truly devout would never tolerate something as prosaic as a bounty from the Arvath.

"I will take you in," she told the magician. "But the Queen's Wing won't be a safe haven for very long. When the Mort come, you may wish you had simply disappeared for good."

"Thank you, Majesty. I will take no more of your time."

Bradshaw whirled, with his unnatural acrobat's grace, and was off toward Mace before Kelsea could tell him that she was not busy, far from it, that she had nothing better to do than stare out at the horizon and watch a ghastly destruction play out over and over in her mind. That cloud on the horizon belonged to her. She was the one who had brought it here. She shivered, sensing again the tickling fingers of Lily's mind, nearly a physical thing, worming its way inside her own. Lily's life was hurtling toward some calamity, and she needed something from Kelsea, something Kelsea could not see yet. And now Kelsea saw that there was no difference which vision she lived in. Past or future, in either direction lay only terror. She turned back to the horizon and restarted the count of her own mistakes, preparing to suffer through them again, one at a time. Preparing to scourge.

Bastards aren't worried about us anymore, that's for sure," Bermond muttered. "No real sentries out there, just the hawks."

Hall grunted in agreement, but didn't look up from his helmet. A sword had grazed his chin two days before, slicing the helmet's clasp clear off. Hall had rigged a substitute by sewing on an extra piece of leather, but now the fit was imperfect. The helmet kept threatening to slide off his head.

Still, it could have been worse. He would have a scar, but his winter beard would easily cover it. The stupid clasp had probably saved his teeth, if not his life. The clasp seemed like something Hall should have kept, a good-luck charm to carry in his pockets, but it was lost now, perhaps three miles up the Caddell.

"Stop fucking with that thing, Ryan, and have a look."

With a sigh, Hall dropped his helmet and pulled out his spyglass. He hadn't slept in three days. The last two weeks had been a blur of pitched battles and retreat as the Mort army pushed them inexorably southwest, across the Crithe and back toward the lower Almont. Sometimes Hall couldn't tell whether he was asleep or awake anymore, whether the war he fought was real or merely taking place inside his own head. The Mort had taken both banks of the Caddell several days ago, and now the river was crossed with several portable footbridges, ingenious mechanisms that Hall could not help admiring, even while he schemed ways to bring them down. The footbridges allowed the Mort to hold not only both sides of the river but the water itself, to move straight up the riverbed without effectively dividing their forces. The bridges appeared to be made of solid oak, reinforced with steel in the center to keep them from snapping under the army's weight, but they disassembled quickly for transport. Someone in Mortmesne was a hell of an engineer, and Hall wished he could speak to him for just a few minutes, even now while the world came down around their ears.

Hall's spyglass caught and held on a flag on the south side of the Caddell. Most of the Mort camp was either black or a deep stormcloud grey, but this flag was bright scarlet. Hall stood up from his crouch, disregarding the threat of Mort archers, and focused the lens. The red flag was planted on top of a deep crimson tent.

"Sir. Ten o'clock on the south side of the river."

"What? Oh hell, look at that." Bermond set down his spyglass and rubbed his temples. He hadn't slept in days either. Even the blue plume on his helmet, a sign of rank to which Bermond was ridiculously attached, hung limply in the hazy sunlight. "All we need now."

"Maybe it's not really her, only a ruse by the Mort."

"You think it's a ruse?"

"No," Hall replied after a moment's thought. "She's here, come to finish what she started."

"Morale's hanging by a threat already. This might snap it."

Hall turned his spyglass west, toward New London. The Queen's refugee camp sprawled in front of the city, a vast acreage of tents and tarps, and now it was a frenzy of activity as Census people evacuated the last occupants into New London. Stone walls ringed the city, a perimeter set just off the edge of the Caddell, some ten feet high. But these walls had been hastily constructed on soft riverbank ground; they would not stand up to assault. Everything was a holding action. One more day to finish the evacuation, and then Bermond would pull the army back to New London, and they would all settle in for siege. A thick cloud of smoke hung over the city; they were slaughtering and roasting all of the animals, curing the meat for the long haul. The army had also been hoarding water, knowing that once the Mort reached the walls, the Caddell would be cut off. Good preparations, but still, a holding action. There was only one way for a siege to end.

"Still, Mort morale might be weak as well," Bermond mused hopefully. "The Mort like their plunder, lad, and we've given them none. I hate to admit it, but the Queen had a good idea with her evacuation. There must be some grumbling going on in their camp by now."

"Not enough," Hall replied, and gestured toward the crimson tent. "If they were grumbling, she'd put a stop to it."

He didn't want to mention the Red Queen by name. An old superstition from his childhood on the border, where every child knew that if you spoke of the Red Queen, she might appear. Names made a thing real, far more real than that distant spot of scarlet . . . and yet once his men spotted the tent, Hall knew that the fear would sweep through the remainder of the Tear army like an evil wind.

Bermond sighed. "How do we keep them off for one more day?"

"Pull back. Mass at the entrance to the bridge and build a barricade."

"They have siege towers."

"Let them try. We have oil and torches."

"You're in fine form today. What did you do, sneak off to Whore's Alley last night?"

"No."

"Then what?"

"I had a dream."

"A dream," Bermond repeated, chuckling. "About what?"

"About the Queen," Hall replied simply. "I dreamed that she lit a great fire that wiped the land clean. The Mort, the Red Queen, the wicked . . . all of the Tear's enemies were swept away."

"Never knew you to be a man for portents, Ryan."

"I'm not. But all the same, it put me in a good mood."

"You place far too much faith in a naive child."

Hall did not reply. Bermond would never see the Queen as anything but an upstart, but Hall saw something else, something he could not quantify.

"They're coming again," Bermond muttered. "Put your helmet on. See if you can push them down toward the muddy part of the bank. Their footwork isn't nearly as fearsome as their steel, and they'll have trouble on soft ground."

Hall signaled to the men behind him to get ready. A detachment of Mort had emerged from the camp, spreading out along the north bank of the Caddell. Time and time again they had pushed the Tear back with flanking maneuvers, an easy business with overwhelmingly superior numbers. This would be no different. Hall spared a final glance for the refugee camp behind him, the antlike frenzy of the final stages of the evacuation.

One more day, he thought, then drew his sword and led his men down the knoll toward the river. Bermond remained on the hilltop; his limp didn't allow him to engage in close combat anymore. Hall's men caught him up as he ran, surrounding him on both sides, Blaser right beside him. Blaser had taken a nasty wound to the collarbone on the shores of the Crithe, but the medics had stitched it up, and now Blaser was bellowing as they reached the bottom of the hill and ran into the Mort line. Hall felt the impact of an iron sword against his, all the way down his arm, but the pain was muted, as it always was in dreams. He regarded the assailant across from him, slightly bewildered, wondering for a moment what they were actually fighting about. But muscle memory was a powerful thing; Hall heaved the soldier away and sliced downward, finding the join between wrist and glove. The man shrieked as his hand was nearly severed.

"Hawks! Hawks!"

The shout had gone up behind Hall, on the knoll. He looked up and found at least ten hawks speeding over his head. Not sentries, these; they cruised the sky, spread equidistant, flying westward in silent formation. Specially trained, but for what?

There was no time to ponder it. Another Mort soldier came at him, this one left-handed, and Hall forgot about the hawks as he fought the man off. His helmet fell backward again, off his head, and Hall cursed as he threw it to the ground. Fighting without a helmet was a good way to die, but even death seemed like an acceptable outcome at this point. At least there would be sleep waiting there. Hall jabbed at the Mort, felt his sword clang harmlessly off the man's iron breastplate. The damned Mort armor! A scream came from behind him, but Hall could not turn around, not even when warmth soaked the back of his neck.

Someone launched into the Mort from the side, knocking him to the ground. Blaser, grappling with the soldier for a moment before clubbing him across the face. When the man lay still, Blaser got up and grabbed Hall's arm, pulling him back toward the Tear line.

"What is it? A retreat?"

"Come, sir! The general!"

They pushed their way back through, knocking aside several Mort along the way. Hall moved along in a dream. Everything seemed muted somehow: the sunlight, the sounds of battle, the stench, even the screams of the dying. But the waters of the Caddell were clear and sharp, a bright and sparkling red.

Atop the knoll ahead, a group of soldiers were clustered, their faces grave. Something about this tableau shook Hall awake for the first time in days, and he began to run, Blaser at his side, heedless of the battle at the bottom of the hill.

Bermond lay facedown in a heap. No one had dared touch him, so Hall squatted down and rolled him over. A collective groan went up from the assembled men; Bermond's throat had been torn out, leaving only shreds of flesh that dangled on either side of his neck. His chest had been protected by his armor, but all four of his limbs had been shredded to pieces. His left arm was barely attached at the shoulder. His eyes gazed blankly at the sky from a face wet with blood.

A few feet away, in the grass, Hall spotted Bermond's helmet with its ridiculous blue plume. A silly affectation, that helmet, but Bermond had loved it, loved riding the Tearling with the plume waving jauntily in the breeze. A general for peace, not wartime, and Hall felt his throat tighten as he closed Bermond's eyes.

"Sir! We're losing ground!"

Hall straightened and saw that the Tear line was indeed weakening. At several points, the Mort had pushed the Tear neatly inward, like a pin in a cushion. Hall stared at the men around him—Blaser and Caffrey, Colonel Griffin, a young major whose name he didn't know, several infantry—feeling at a loss. Promotion of a general required a formal procedure, approval by the Queen, a ceremony. Hall had stood right beside Bermond, years ago, when Queen Elyssa had invested him with command. At this moment the Queen was miles away, but when Hall looked around, he saw that all of them, even Griffin, were looking to him, waiting for orders. Queen or no, he was the general now.

"Caffrey. Fall back to the next knoll."

Major Caffrey took off in a dead sprint down the hill.

"You, Griffin. Pull the remainder of your battalion back and head for New London. Take the leftover material from the deserted areas of the refugee camp and barricade the bridge."

"A barricade of old furniture and tents won't hold up for long."

"But it has to. Ask the Queen for extra lumber if you need to, but get it done. We'll meet you there as soon as the evacuation's complete."

Griffin turned and strode away. Hall returned his attention to the battlefield and saw that the Tear had already begun to retreat, inching up the gentle slope at the bottom of the knoll. He looked down at Bermond's corpse and felt sorrow and exhaustion heave up inside him, but there was no time for either. The Mort were slowly creeping up the slope, accelerating the retreat. A deep voice bellowed orders behind the Mort line, and Hall knew, somehow, that it was General Ducarte, close to the battle now. Ducarte wasn't one to hang back and keep his hands clean. He had come to see blood.

"You." Hall pointed to the two infantrymen. "Go with Griffin. Take the general's body back to New London."

They lifted Bermond's body and carried it down the other side of the knoll, toward the horses. Hall followed their passage for a moment, then lifted his eyes to the refugee camp. Defenseless people, an entire city.

One more day, he thought, watching the Mort mass at the weakest point of the Tear line and charge, swords and freshly polished armor gleaming in the sunlight. They went through the Tear easily, breaking the line even as Hall's soldiers scrambled to get back up the hill. Tear soldiers swarmed in, bolstering the gap, but the damage was done; there was a hole in Hall's formations now, and they would have no time to regroup. The Mort pressed their advantage, massing at the weak point, forcing the Tear to fall backward and accommodate them. Bermond was dead, but Hall could still feel him somewhere, on the next hill perhaps, watching and evaluating, waiting to see what Hall would do next. The sun broke through the clouds and Hall drew his sword, relieved to find new life in the muscles of his arm, to find himself more awake than he had been in a long time. The Mort tore through the Tear line, a black mass that could not be defeated, and General Hall charged down the hill to meet them.

CHAPTER 11

BLUE HORIZON

In the decade before the Crossing, the American Security appa- ratus took thousands of alleged separatists into custody. The sheer number of detainees convinced the American government, as well as the public, that Security was winning the war on domestic terrorism. But this single-minded focus on demon- strable results also blinded the government to the real issue: an enormous fault beneath the American surface, unseen, that was finally beginning to crack.

—*The Dark Night of America*, GLEE DELAMERE

Dorian was gone.

Lily stood in the doorway of her nursery, blinking. Dorian was gone, and so were the medical supplies, the extra clothes that Lily had given her. The nursery was still as always, full of tiny dust motes that floated in the late-morning sun. No one would know that Dorian had ever been there.

Of course Lily hadn't expected her to say good-bye, but she had thought there would be more time. Now William

Tear had come in the night and taken Dorian away. Lily turned and walked back down the hall, all of her pleasure in the morning suddenly evaporated. What was she supposed to do now? She was supposed to play bridge later, with Michele and Christine and Jessa, but she saw now that she would have to call that off. There was no way she could sit there at the table with the three of them, gossiping and drinking whatever cocktail Christine favored this week. Something had shifted, and now there was no way for Lily to return to the world of small things.

Two days later, the news sites announced that simultaneous terrorist attacks had taken place in Boston and Dearborn, Virginia. The terrorists in Boston had broken into one of Dow's warehouse facilities and stolen medical equipment and drugs, nearly fifty million dollars' worth, a huge coup that was splashed all over the top of every website. But the attack in Virginia, though less spectacular, was more interesting to Lily because it made no sense. Some ten or twelve armed guerrillas had broken into a billionaire's Dearborn horse farm and stolen most of his breeding stock. The guerrillas came prepared, with their own trailers for the horses, but they took nothing except the animals and some equipment for their care.

Horses! Lily was baffled. No one actually used horses for anything anymore, not even farming; they were a rich man's vice, only valuable for harness racing and the gambling that went with it. Lily wondered briefly if the tall Englishman was crazy—for she was certain, somehow, that this was Tear's work—but that wasn't the impression she had received. Rather, the entire thing seemed like a puzzle, one that was missing several pieces. Horses and medical equipment stolen, jet facilities destroyed. Each day Lily moved these pieces around a board in her mind, trying to understand. She felt sure that if she could only fit them together, assemble the puzzle, then it would somehow clarify everything, show her the Englishman's real plan, the clear outlines of the better world.

Three days after the Virginia attack, Lily was back in the hospital. It started very simply: a shirt Greg wanted to wear happened to be at the dry cleaner's, and when Lily couldn't produce the shirt, Greg slammed her fingers in the bedroom door. It didn't even hurt at first; there was only the door, held tight against her hand so that no sensation traveled. But when Greg opened the door a few seconds later, the pain came roaring in, and when Lily screamed, Greg did something he had never done before and punched her twice in the face. On the second shot, Lily felt her nose break, a thin, crisp snap, like stepping on a twig in winter.

Greg was already late for his meeting, and so it was Jonathan who took Lily to the emergency room. He said nothing, but she could see his set jaw and narrowed eyes in the rearview mirror. Whom did he disapprove of? Both of them? She hadn't spoken to Jonathan since that night in the living room; he was clearly determined to pretend that it had never happened, so Lily did the same. Sometimes she wished that she could talk to him about it, but Jonathan's reserve kept her from opening the discussion. She concentrated on her nose instead, working hard to keep blood from dripping to the seats.

It turned out that Lily had two broken fingers in addition to the broken nose, and she could only stare groggily around the brightly lit room as Jonathan responded to the doctor's questions. When it was time to repair her nose, they knocked her out. She spent the night in the hospital, in the charge of two nurses, and when she woke up and heard their voices, kind and mothering, Lily wished that she could stay there forever. There was pain in the hospital, and sickness, but it was a safe place. Greg had said it wouldn't happen again, but he had been lying; several times since that day at the country club, Lily had woken up with Greg's fingers inside her, shoving painfully, almost scraping. Broken bones were bad, but that was infinitely worse, and the hospital felt so safe compared to home.

Five days later the power went out all over New England. It was a brief outage, only twenty minutes, and there was no real damage done except for a few traffic accidents. But still, the incident caused a flurry of panic in Washington and on the stock exchanges, because such an outage was supposed to be impossible. In a world where everything was run by computers, safeguarded and backed up eight ways to Sunday, the system wasn't supposed to have room for failure. Greg said that the hardware had been defective, but Lily wondered. She thought of Dorian, of how a woman without a tag had been able to get through Security at a naval base. She thought of the thousands of soldiers, like Jonathan, who had come back from serving in Saudi Arabia to find that there were no jobs, no market for their skills. And now she began to wonder: how many separatists were there, really? The news sites spoke of the Blue Horizon contemptuously, describing the cell as a few disorganized, dissatisfied groups of mentally unstable individuals. But the evidence didn't bear that out. Lily thought of Arnie Welch, the Security lieutenant who had once admitted, over too many drinks, that the terrorists were both efficient and organized. William Tear had said that there were ways through every barrier, and the questions swirled in Lily's head, maddening. Just how big was the Blue Horizon? Did they all answer to Tear? What was the better world?

The next weekend Greg had Arnie Welch over to dinner, along with two of Arnie's underlings. Greg always invited Arnie on the rare occasions when he was in town; they had been fraternity brothers at Yale. Greg said it was useful to be friends with a Security lieutenant, and even Lily saw the sense in that. But this time, when Arnie walked through the door, Lily didn't see Greg's parking tickets or a quick travel visa for vacations or even the Security helicopters that Arnie would sometimes loan as a favor when business was slow. Instead, she saw Maddy being hustled out the school doors, the last flash of her blonde pigtails, a picture so clear that Lily swayed momentarily on the threshold, and when Arnie tried to put an arm around her shoulders, she ducked away toward the kitchen.

For once Arnie didn't drink during dinner, and he glared at his two flunkies when they showed signs of reaching for the whisky. Greg heckled him about it, but Arnie merely shrugged, saying, "I can't afford a hangover tomorrow."

Lily was just as happy to have Arnie stay sober. He got pretty handsy when he drank; once he'd actually tried to worm his hand between her legs at the table. Lily could never tell whether Greg noticed these advances; as possessive as he had become, he seemed to have achieved a level of deliberate blindness when someone was in a position to be useful to him. But Lily had seated Arnie on the far side of the table, just in case.

Although her nose was almost back to normal, Lily still had noticeable bruising under her right eye, but she was not surprised when Arnie didn't ask about it. She found that she could barely eat. Her healing fingers, both of them still encased in temporary splints, made it hard to manipulate the knife and fork, but that wasn't really the problem. She had spent most of her married life telling lies, but ever since Dorian toppled over the back wall, there had been a shift in the foundation, and it was becoming harder to dissemble, harder to force each individual lie out. She was afraid of her husband, but the fear was less important now. She sensed a wider world out there, a world not run by people like Greg, and sometimes, even though she understood nothing, she knew exactly what Dorian meant: it was so close she could almost touch it.

Pigs, she thought, watching Greg and the military men snort and chuckle and snuffle their food. *Pigs, all of you. You have no idea about the better world.* Lily didn't understand the better world either, true, but she thought she was beginning to at least see the outline now. No poverty and no greed, Tear had said. Kindness is everything. People like Greg would be entirely irrelevant. Yesterday he had told her that he'd made contact with an in vitro doctor. They would go on Monday. Lily couldn't imagine what her life would look like on Tuesday.

She had her doubts that Arnie could really stay sober throughout dinner; even among Greg's normal set of dinner invitees, Arnie was a consummate boozehound. The whisky bottle sat on the table right in front of him—Greg's idea of a good joke—during the entire meal, but somehow Arnie ignored the bottle, sticking strictly to water. He was nervous and jumpy, constantly checking his watch. His two underlings weren't much better, though they still found time to nudge each other and grin at Lily during the meal. She was used to this kind of thing, and ignored their comments, even when she heard herself referred to as a nice piece of snatch.

"What's got you so twitchy?" Greg finally asked Arnie. "Are you on drugs?"

Arnie shook his head. "Stone sober. I have a long day tomorrow, that's all."

"Doing what?"

"It's classified."

"I'm cleared."

Arnie looked uncertainly across the table at Lily. "She's not cleared."

"Oh, fuck her, she's not going to tell anyone." Greg turned to Lily with narrowed eyes. "Are you?"

She shook her head automatically, keeping her eyes on her plate.

"So come on, man, give," Greg begged, and Lily suddenly saw something she had never seen before: Greg was jealous of the military men across the table. Greg worked for several defense contractors, yes, but his was a desk job. Arnie was trained to fire weapons, to interrogate, to kill people, and Greg thought that made Arnie a better man. "Tell us what you've been up to."

Still Arnie hesitated, and Lily felt a tiny alarm go off inside. Clearance or not, Arnie was always telling Greg things he shouldn't, and it usually didn't take much alcohol to make it happen. She kept her eyes on her plate, trying to make herself as invisible as possible, waiting for him to speak. But after a few moments, Arnie merely shook his head again. "Sorry, man, no. It's too big, and your wife's not cleared."

"Fine, come on upstairs. We'll talk in my study."

"You two go down and wait in the car," Arnie told his two

flunkies, then wiped his mouth and threw his napkin on the table. "Thanks, Lily. That was great."

She nodded and smiled mechanically, wondering if Arnie had noticed the splints on her knuckles. The flunkies left, and Greg and Arnie disappeared upstairs. Lily stared at her plate for a moment, considering, then grabbed the edge of the table with her uninjured hand and levered herself upward. Leaving the dirty dishes scattered all over the table, she hurried through the kitchen and into the small guardhouse that housed their surveillance equipment. Jonathan was supposed to be on duty tonight, but Lily was hardly surprised to find the alcove empty. She wondered how many nights the house had been left unguarded while Jonathan was out running errands for the Blue Horizon.

Tapping at the screen, Lily brought up Greg's study, a dark, mahogany-filled room that tried too hard to be masculine. The walls were paneled with bookshelves, but they held no books, only Greg's old football trophies and pictures of Greg and Lily with important people at various events. The walls were covered with plaques; Greg liked to show off his awards.

Arnie was sitting in one of the big armchairs in front of Greg's desk, and Greg was behind the desk, with his leather executive chair tilted back. Both of them were smoking cigars, and the haze had drifted up toward the camera, making Greg's features indistinct.

"The building blew and collapsed," Arnie said, "just like it was supposed to. They clearly had an escape plan, but it got botched somehow. I've got to hand it to Langer; much as I hate that bastard, he pulled off a pretty good trick. It looked like all of them died, but Langer managed to grab one alive, some guy named Goodin. They've been working on him for the past four days, and he finally broke last night."

"What broke him?" Greg asked, his voice crawling with eagerness, and Lily closed her eyes. How long would it have taken them to break Maddy? Forever, Lily thought, but deep down, she knew that wasn't true. She wiped her forehead and her hand came away wet.

Arnie looked uncomfortable too. "I'm off duty now, man. I don't want to talk about that shit."

"Yeah, I suppose not," Greg replied grudgingly. "So what did he say?"

"He wasn't high up or anything, but he gave us a lot." Arnie's face became animated again. "The leader of the Blue Horizon is some guy who calls himself Tear. A Brit, if you can believe it."

"I do believe it. The UK and their fucking socialist experiment."

"Well, this Tear is apparently the big money. The separatists think he's some kind of god. Blue Horizon sprang up out of the old Occupy movements, but you know they didn't know what they were doing. This Tear, though, he's a trained guerrilla. That's why they've been such a pain in the ass the last few years." Arnie lowered his voice, and Lily thumbed the volume control on the screen. "They're holed up in an abandoned warehouse down on Conley Terminal."

"Where's that?"

"Port of Boston. I've spent all day looking at maps. That warehouse has been condemned for at least ten years, but Frewell's boys took all the money Boston was supposed to use for a new container facility and put it into some God crap or another, so all the containers have just been standing there. Goodin said they're using the warehouse as a head-quarters. We're going in at dawn."

Lily stared at the screen, frozen.

"They've put Langer in charge of the whole thing; it's his baby now, and he wants prisoners. We have to surround the Terminal on land and water, which is no easy trick ... lots of boats and lots of men. My division is supposed to provide a secondary perimeter tomorrow morning." Arnie sighed and stubbed out the remains of his cigar. "So no booze."

"Want to play some poker? I've got a game downtown."

"Can't, really. I have to be in Boston in two hours. My cop-ter's waiting down at the pad."

Greg nodded, though his lip had pushed out in that little pout that Lily had come to know so well lately. "Fine. I'll walk you out."

Lily shut off the screen and hurried back into the dining room, where she set the washer to begin clearing plates. When Greg and Arnie's voices had disappeared out the front door, she dug her phone from her purse and called Jonathan, but he didn't pick up; there was only his dry, deep voice, a generic greeting. Lily couldn't leave him a real message; her calls were monitored. Trying to keep the panic from her voice, she demanded that he call her back immediately. But she couldn't escape the feeling that wherever Jonathan was, he wouldn't get back to her in time. She could see it now: the darkened warehouse, Dorian inside with William Tear. Dorian had said that she wasn't going back into custody, not ever again. The Boston waterfront. The Blue Horizon. Lily closed her eyes and saw the tiny group of wooden houses beside the blue river, bathed in sun.

I have to do something.

And what can you do, Lil? Maddy asked, her voice jeering.

You've never had the courage to do anything in your entire life.

I did, Lily insisted. *When Dorian fell into the backyard, I did.*

But deep down, she knew that Maddy was right. Dorian had been a low-risk decision, almost a game, insulated in the relatively safe environment of the nursery. What Lily was contemplating now was something else entirely. She formulated a plan, rejected it, formulated another, rejected that, formulated a third and examined it, turning it over for flaws. It was a stupid plan, no doubt. It would probably get her arrested, maybe even killed. But she had to do something. If the better world was real, it was also unutterably fragile, and without Tear, there would be nothing.

"Arnie's gone."

Lily focused on the window again and found Greg reflected behind her, though she could not read his expression in the glass. She said nothing, looking ahead now, toward Boston. There was no place for Greg in that journey. He would only get in her way.

"Are you excited, Lil?"

"About what?"

"About Monday."

Lily's hand clenched on the handle of a pot, and for a moment she very nearly turned and flung the pot at his head. But her mind cautioned patience. Her aim might not be good enough. Greg had six inches and nearly a hundred pounds on her. She would have one shot only, and she could not afford to miss. She cast along the counter, and her gaze fixed on a large, heavy picture frame, nearly a foot tall, that stood on the windowsill. Photos of their wedding day flashed endlessly over the screen in sparkling pixels; Lily saw herself, only twenty-two years old, covered in yards of white satin, getting ready to cut an enormous tiered cake. Even though her hair was beginning to come down from its elaborate coiffure and Greg's wretched father stood beside her, she was laughing.

God, what happened?

Greg took a few steps forward, so close now that Lily could feel his breath on the back of her neck. She reached out to touch the picture frame, grasping its edge in her good hand.

"Lil?"

If he tries to fuck me now, she thought, *I will go insane. It will be very easy; I'll just float off, and then none of this will matter, not William Tear or the Blue Horizon or a warehouse down on the Boston port. None of it.*

"Lil? Are you excited?"

His hand settled on her shoulder, and Lily whipped around, bringing the frame with her, swinging it sidearm as she would a tennis racket at the club. The frame crunched into the side of Greg's head, tiny plastic shards flying everywhere, peppering Lily's hand and arm, and Greg fell sideways, banging his head on the marble counter on the way down, a deep *thunk*. Lily raised the frame again, ready, but Greg was down for the count, sprawled on his side on the kitchen floor. After a moment, blood began to trickle down his face from his scalp, tiny red dots dripping onto the white tile.

"Well, that's done," Lily whispered, unsure whom she was talking to. She thought about checking Greg's pulse, but couldn't bring herself to touch him. Moving slowly, as if in a dream, she went upstairs to their bedroom. She pulled out her oldest jeans, the ones she never wore when Greg was around, and a faded black T-shirt. These clothes were still nicer than anything poor people would wear outside the wall, but they were better than nothing and might offer some camouflage. She covered them with a beaten leather jacket she'd had since she was fifteen, a remnant of better times that Lily refused to give away. The Mercedes was an automatic; after a moment's thought, Lily removed her splints and left them on the dresser. She tapped at the wallscreen, examining maps of the Port of Boston while she dressed. Conley Terminal was a big container facility down near Castle Island, tucked into one of the thousand inlets that seemed to make up the Massachusetts coastline. Public roads, it would be have to be, Highway 84 to the Mass Turnpike. The private roads would be full of Security checkpoints, particularly at night, and when they scanned her chip and found out that she had left her husband behind, it would raise more questions. Lily would have a better chance on public roads . . . if she even managed to get outside the New Canaan wall at all.

After a bit more searching, she found that condemned property was the province of the Department of the Interior. There were two condemned buildings located on Conley Terminal; only one looked like a warehouse, but Lily mapped each location carefully and sent the maps on to the Mercedes. Belatedly, she realized that these searches were probably going to trip an alarm somewhere at Security, and she had a quick moment of panic before she realized how small a problem that really was, with her husband lying bleeding on the kitchen floor. Even if Greg wasn't dead, women had been executed for less. Lily went downstairs and grabbed the small codekey with the Mercedes emblem off the hook on the wall. The Mercedes was their third car, the fancy one for emergencies or important visitors. When she held the key up to the light, she found that her hands were shaking. Her driver's license was still valid, but she hadn't driven a car since she was eighteen.

"Like riding a bike," she whispered. "Just like riding a bike, that's all."

She spared a final glance at Greg, who still lay sprawled in the same position on the kitchen floor. Blood had begun to pool beneath his right ear now, but he was still breathing, and for a moment Lily wondered at her own coldness, until she isolated its source: it didn't really matter whether Greg lived or died, or whether she did herself, only that she got to Boston. The better world, the small village beside the river, these were the things which mattered, and they burned inside Lily's head, searing through the fear, lifting her up.

She turned and headed down the hallway toward the garage.

No one had driven the Mercedes in a while, but it didn't seem any worse for disuse. Jonathan must have been taking care of it; he liked tinkering with cars, kept the BMW and Lexus in good working order. The Mercedes had a full tank, and its headlights cut easily through the night as Lily turned off Willow Avenue and onto the checkpoint road. Ahead of her the wall loomed: twenty feet of solid steel polymer, topped with laser edging, blocking off the horizon. Something inside Lily seemed to freeze at the sight, and a low, panicked voice began to babble inside her . . . the voice of her marriage, Lily realized now, its tone craven and helpless.

You'll never make it through, not in a million years, and when they find Greg—

410

"Shut up," Lily whispered. Her voice shook in the darkness of the car.

The checkpoint appeared out of the fog: a fifteen-foot break in the wall, lit by bright fluorescent lamps. A small guardhouse, also walled in steel, stood off to the left, and as Lily approached, two guards in Security uniforms emerged. Each of them carried a gun, the small laser pistols that Security seemed to favor these days. Greg had a gun, Lily suddenly remembered, a tiny thing that he kept in his study. She could have grabbed it, and this made her wonder what else she had forgotten. But it was too late.

"Evening, ma'am," the first guard said as she lowered the window. He squinted at her for a moment, then smiled wide. "It's Mrs. Mayhew, isn't it?"

"Yes, John. How are you tonight?"

"Fine, ma'am. Where you heading?"

"Into the city to see friends."

"All by yourself at this hour? Where's that black bodyguard of yours?"

"He had to run an errand for my husband."

"Just a moment." He walked around the hood and disappeared back into the guardhouse. The other guard remained on the right side of the hood, a dark silhouette against the fluorescent lamps. Lily kept a pleasant smile on her face, but her fingers had clamped on the steering wheel. The guard had gone to call Greg, and now her mind produced a clear picture: the kitchen, Greg lying there motionless, but his phone rang on and on. The muscles in her thighs were shaking. Outside the bright circle of fluorescence that bathed the car, everything was pitch-black.

"Ma'am?"

Lily jumped; the guard had silently reappeared at the other window.

"We're not getting any reply from your husband, ma'am."

"He's ill," she replied. "That's why he's not coming with me."

The guard consulted a tiny handheld, and Lily knew that he was scrolling through the details of her life. Greg's position, the fact that they were not under surveillance, would weigh in Lily's favor. Lily had never been in trouble, and that would help too. Maddy would be in there, certainly, but so would the information that Lily had been instrumental in turning Maddy in.

"Does your husband always let you go into the city at night by yourself?"

"No. This is the first time."

The guard stood staring down at her, and Lily had the disturbing certainty that his eyes were crawling, even though her breasts were encased in the thick leather jacket. But she kept the smile plastered on, and after a moment the guard raised something black and gleaming. For one panicked moment, Lily thought it was a gun, but then she saw that it was only a scanner. She offered her shoulder and waited for the scan to register with a soft beep. The guard waved Lily forward, and she depressed the gas pedal. Too hard, for the Mercedes leapt forward with a growl. She stomped on the brake, gave an apologetic smile out the open window. "I haven't driven in a while."

"Well, be careful, ma'am. Stay off the public roads. And don't open your door for any strangers."

"I won't. Have a good night."

Lily pressed the gas again, gently this time, and rolled the car forward, out of the bright circle of light.

When Lily was in the car, Jonathan used the private highway. But there had been a few times when the highway was down, blocked by debris dragged onto the roadway or sabotaged by explosives. Even Security couldn't repair a badly damaged highway in less than a week, and at such times Jonathan always turned onto a small back road a few miles outside the wall, a dirt track that headed north for a few minutes through the woods before it joined with Highway 84. No matter how hard Security worked to keep the public off the private roadways, they always found a way through, cutting new paths through the woods and digging tunnels beneath fences. This idea, which would have alarmed Lily a few weeks ago, now seemed oddly comforting. Jonathan's back road might have allowed William Tear to get close to New Canaan before slipping over the wall, might have allowed Dorian to evade Security as she fled from the base. It took Lily several U-turns before she spotted the small break in the undergrowth. When she guided the car through, she could hear the scrape of brambles along the paint.

"The better world," she whispered as she guided the Mercedes forward through the woods, feeling the sharp thump of rocks beneath the tires. Trees surrounded the car, ghostly white pillars in the glare of the headlights. "It's out there, so close we can almost touch it."

She kept an eye on the side windows and rearview mirror; there were probably some people living out here somewhere, though they'd need some serious weaponry to break into this car, which had steel-reinforced windows and was built like a tank. But she saw no one, and after twenty minutes of carefully crawling along, she emerged onto the public highway. Highway 84 was much wider than the private

413

roads, its northern span stretching six lanes across, and without the ten-foot walls that bordered most private freeways it felt very wide, almost limitless in its emptiness, remnant of a bygone era when everyone could afford cars and gas. Signs on Lily's right advertised the speed limit as sixty-five, but Security never bothered to police the public highways anyway, and sixty-five seemed ridiculously slow, almost like standing still. Lily sped up, then sped up further, easing the car over eighty-five and up toward ninety, finding a pure pleasure in going fast, in watching the miles fly by.

Several times she saw the remains of old barricades on the highway shoulder: piles of trash, blown tires and tree branches that had simply been cleared to one side and left for wind and time to disperse. She couldn't fathom the purpose of such barricades, and this, more than anything else, drove home to Lily how little she knew about life outside the wall. Even as a child, she had always used the private roadways, always had temperate weather, never needed to worry about starving.

Occasionally she saw fires lining the sides of the road, large bonfires surrounded by the silhouettes of many people. The poor, moving out of the cities and into the forests . . . safer, most likely, but also harder to survive. Lily couldn't slow down to take a closer look; armored or not, a Mercedes rolling at street speed was an open invitation. But she couldn't help staring at them in the rearview mirror, all of those human shadows standing around the flames. She couldn't help imagining the lives they led.

"The better world," she whispered, repeating it every time another mile ticked off the odometer and into the night at her back. Green exit signs flew by, some of them so worn that Lily could barely read the white letters announcing their

414

towns. Vernon, Tolland, Willington. Some of these were undoubtedly ghost towns, while others were alive but given over to lawlessness. Lily dimly remembered hearing Willington mentioned on a news site a few months ago, something about a cult. But she couldn't remember, and then Willington was behind her. She was halfway to Boston now, only seventy-five miles to go.

Her phone beeped, and Lily gave a small croak of fright, certain that Greg had woken up, that he had gotten hold of a phone. She could barely bring herself to look at the screen, but when she did, she saw the word *Jonathan* shining against the bright blue background.

"Answer . . . Jonathan?"

"Where are– Mrs. M.?" His voice crackled with static, dropped out. But of course, cell service would be wretched outside the walls. People like Lily weren't even supposed to be here. With the advent of panic buttons in cars, no one even used a phone for emergencies anymore.

"I'm on my way to Boston."

"What's in Boston?" She might have been imagining it, but even under the static, Lily sensed a sudden, guarded quality about Jonathan's voice.

"The warehouse! The port! They're in trouble, Jonathan. Mark had Arnie Welch over for dinner–"

"Mrs. M.? Can– hear you. Don't–" Now the static cut in for a long moment, "Boston!"

"Jonathan?"

The call dropped.

Lily redialed, but she knew already that it was an empty gesture. She didn't even get Jonathan's voicemail this time, only a dead and empty silence. Peering down at her phone, she saw that she had no service. Too late, she realized

Erika Johansen

that the brief call had surely been recorded by Security.

"Fuck," she muttered. Jonathan had told her not to go to Boston, she was sure of it. But Jonathan didn't know what she did, and inertia had taken over now. She was already in trouble. There was no turning back.

At Sturbridge, she switched over to the Massachusetts Turnpike. For the first fifteen miles of the Pike there were no freeway lights at all, not even the old arc-sodiums; the highway was completely dark except for the faint glow of moonlight, and Lily was forced to slow down to forty-five, which felt like crawling after the pure, open speed of 84. She navigated on intuition rather than sight, squinting for the outline of things ahead, knowing that she should have turned back long ago. She breathed a sigh of relief as she passed Auburn and spotted the thin orange glow of lights in the distance.

"The better world," she whispered, watching another green digit trip forward on the odometer. "So close we can almost touch it."

She was only forty miles away.

When Lily was growing up, Boston had still been a good place to visit for a day. Mom and Dad would take her and Maddy; even though Dad had grown up in Queens and was a diehard Yankee fan, he had a secret admiration for Boston. Mom liked to see the sights and shop, but Dad's bent was historical; he took Lily and Maddy to Boston Common, to the Kennedy Library. Once they had even gone to the docks, to the site of the Boston Tea Party, and Dad explained what had happened there, quite a different story from the one Lily had heard in school. Maddy said that Dad's version might get him in trouble, so Lily had never repeated

416

it, but it had been a struggle in tenth grade not to raise her hand and tell the teacher he was wrong. Whenever Lily thought of Boston, she always remembered standing on the docks and looking down at the water.

Now Boston was buried under a haze of smog. The last few times Lily had been here with Greg, in the daytime, there had been no sunlight, only a thin, sickly luminescence, and now, in the middle of the night, the sky over the city was bright orange, reflecting the streetlights below. When Lily rolled down the windows, the air tasted foul. When was the last time she had breathed outside air? She couldn't remember, she was so used to scrubbed air, the purifiers that covered New Canaan.

As soon as she passed the Washington Street exit, Lily's phone chirped happily to let her know that service had been restored. If Greg had woken up, he would be able to track her by her tag, but that would take some time in the middle of the night. Her phone, though, was in Greg's name, and he would be able to look up its location himself. After a moment's thought, Lily chucked the phone out the window.

She took the exit for Massport Haul Road and began to wind her way down Summer Street, heading toward the vast black emptiness that signified water. She had never been down to this part of the port; Dad had taken them up to the Congress Street Bridge and—in those days—the many child-friendly amusements up at Boston Harbor. But here at Conley Terminal, the waterfront was a sea of containers, and Lily was struck by the ghostly outlines of the container cranes, an endless row of storklike apparatuses towering over her head. They would be different colors, probably, but in the yellow light they all took on varying shades of jaundice. The terminal seemed empty; Lily saw no people walking across the seamed pavement, no cars or movement of machines. Security was down there, she knew, probably hidden in the shadows of buildings and containers. What if they stopped her on the way in?

She parked the car on the edge of an enormous parking lot, behind several dumpsters in a lonely clump around a small outbuilding that looked as though it might once have taken tickets. For a moment, Lily simply sat there, feeling the adrenaline of the drive fade away. Her muscles felt as though she'd run a marathon.

According to her map, the first condemned building was about half a mile to the north, a corrugated behemoth that looked like it was ready to collapse. The walls were covered with enormous patches of rust. Lily had brought along a plain black baseball cap, and now she gathered her hair up and tucked it inside the cap before getting out of the car. Someone might find the Mercedes and break into it while she was gone, but there was nothing to be done about that. A last look around revealed no one visible, and Lily darted across the poorly lit pavement, the stench of asphalt and chemicals burning her nose.

The port had appeared deserted on the way in, but with each step Lily became more convinced that she was being watched. Several times she ran across port rats, big as kittens and not frightened of Lily at all. Most of them merely glanced at her as she passed by, but one actually stood its ground, squeaking in outrage, and Lily was forced to go around it, watching it with a wary eye, realizing anew how far out of her depth she really was.

She finally reached the south wall of the warehouse and crouched against it, breathing hard. She had a stitch in her side. There were no doors on this wall; she would have to move around the corner to the east wall, the long side of the warehouse. Huddling close to the corrugated tin, she sidled down the wall until she reached the corner. She was just leaning forward to peek around it when something hard pressed against the side of her head.

"Hands above your shoulders."

Lily obeyed. She had never even heard him approach.

"She can't be Security," another man said.

Lily raised her voice and spoke clearly. "I need to talk to Dorian Rice, William Tear, or Jonathan." She felt like an idiot; she didn't even know Jonathan's last name.

"No names." The man's hands were all over her now, but it was an impersonal search, feeling for weapons. Lily was glad she hadn't brought Greg's gun. She forced herself to remain still, though the man knocked her cap off so that her hair fell down her shoulders and into her face.

"Pretty lady down here, unarmed . . . you must be out of your fucking mind."

"William Tear, Dorian Rice, Jonathan. I need to speak to one of them."

"Do you now? And what about?"

"Just give her to us," another man's voice floated out of the darkness behind Lily. "She's wall bait, it's all over her."

A hand groped beneath Lily's shirt, running across her naked shoulder. "Yup. Still tagged too."

"Turn around," the first voice ordered.

Lily turned and found a short, powerfully built black man in green army fatigues. Behind him were several other shadowy figures, their silhouettes barely visible through the fog that had begun to creep across the port. The man pressed a gun against her temple, and Lily willed herself to be calm, breathing slowly and easily, in through her nose and out through her mouth.

"You're right, she's from inside the wall. But trying to dress like outside." The man leaned closer, breathing heavily in Lily's face. "What are you doing here, wall lady?"

"I need to see one of them," Lily repeated, hating her own voice. She sounded like a child stamping her feet on the floor. "You're all in danger here."

"What danger would that be?"

"Enough!" one of the shadows snarled. Lily couldn't see his face. "My boss said to kill anyone who approached the building. Just hand her over. We haven't had wall bait in a long time."

"This is our territory. My leader decides what happens to an intruder." The black man shook his head disgustedly before turning back to Lily. "You picked a bad night to wander down here, wall lady."

"Please!" Lily begged. Time was ticking by, seconds rolling by constantly, impossible to get back. "Please. The better world."

"What do you know about the better world?"

"I know that it's close now. So close we can almost touch it."

He blinked and then studied her for a moment, his dark eyes moving rapidly across her face. Lily felt herself being dissected from the inside out.

"What's your name, wall lady?"

No names, Lily almost replied. But then her mother's voice echoed through her head, a constant phrase from Lily's childhood: *Now is not the time to be smart.*

"Lily Mayhew."

The short man tapped at his ear. "Come back."

He began to chatter rapidly in a language Lily didn't recognize. It sounded vaguely like Arabic, but she couldn't be sure. Her own name passed through the conversation, but Lily barely noticed; she was too busy watching the shadows who stood behind the man's shoulder. Panic was trying to swarm in her head, which created multiple scenarios faster than she could ignore them: gang rape, torture, her own lifeless body floating in the Inner Harbor. The short man was with Tear, Lily felt certain, but at least some of these others were not, and they loomed out of the darkness, seeming ten feet tall in the fog. They made Lily think of Greg, and she suddenly saw him, clear in front of her, sitting up from the kitchen floor and opening his eyes. The image made Lily jump, as though someone had prodded her with something sharp.

"We're taking her in," the black man announced.

"In there?" One of the shadows detached itself and resolved into a tall man with messy blond hair, dressed in a flamboyant woman's jacket of bright blue silk. The rest of his clothing was utterly destroyed, and as he drew nearer, Lily realized that she could smell him, a high stink of something rotten. She didn't like his eyes either; they had a bulging, manic look that Lily recognized from grade school, where several kids in her class had already been addicted to meth. When the man spoke, she saw that his teeth were a black-stained ruin. "She's not going anywhere near my boss. She could be wired."

The black man shook his head wearily. "They'll scan her for IEDs."

"Not good enough."

"You're in our house." The black man produced a second gun. "That means my leader's orders stand. When we come

421

down to Manhattan, you can make the decisions." He turned back to Lily. "Lace your hands on the back of your head."

Lily did.

"Walk to your right. Stay close to the building, and keep walking until I tell you to stop. Try anything creative and I won't think twice before I shoot you in the head."

Lily nodded jerkily.

"Blue Horizon my ass," the man in the silk jacket muttered. "Bunch of pussies."

The black man ignored him, prodding Lily forward. "Move. Now."

Lily walked forward, concentrating on the ground ahead so that she didn't stumble or stagger. The man with the two guns wasn't bluffing; he had the air of the war vet about him, a quality Lily recognized from Jonathan. This man would do whatever needed to be done, even if that meant shooting Lily in the head and throwing her body into the harbor. She wondered what time it was, checked the instinctive motion to look at her watch. She was halfway down the corrugated side of the warehouse when the man said, "Stop."

Another group had emerged from the fog on her right. The leader was hooded, carrying some kind of assault rifle on a strap over one shoulder. But as they neared, the hood came down, and Lily recognized those blonde Goth-girl knots with no trouble at all.

"Rich lady. You're kidding me."

Lily had stopped, but now the gun prodded her forward again. "I couldn't reach Jonathan. They're coming here. At dawn."

Dorian's face was marked up with black paint, but Lily still saw her brow furrow. "Who?"

"Security. All of them. You have to get out of here."

"Is she nuts, coming down here?" the black man asked. "I didn't want to take the chance."

"Not nuts, no," Dorian replied slowly.

"I'm not," Lily blurted out. "I swear I'm not. Please . . . you have to get out of here."

"We can make her talk," the man in the blue jacket offered, and the eagerness in his voice made Lily's stomach turn.

"Not a chance," Dorian replied, and Lily heard real hatred in her voice. "I know your methods, you prick."

"You and your precious better world, where everyone's equal to everyone else. But they aren't, are they? You and your boss still treat our people like shit."

"Your people *are* shit. Shooting up and whoring each other out and killing each other for the clothes off your backs."

Lily heard a dry click behind her. Dorian looked past her and raised her gun. "Don't even think about it."

"I'm thinking about it, cunt."

The men behind Dorian moved forward and Lily saw that they were all armed with the same weaponry: gleaming black cylinders that looked like some sort of military hardware. Lily had never heard of a separatist attack on a federal armory . . . but of course, she wouldn't have. Security would never release that information to the public.

"We're wasting time!" the man in the blue jacket snapped.

Dorian ignored him, turning cold eyes back to Lily. "Consider what you're doing here, Mrs. Mayhew. Because if I find out that you're here to fuck us over, I'll watch you die slow."

"I'm not," Lily insisted, trying not to let hurt creep into her voice, for she suddenly realized the staggering level of her own arrogance. In those few days in the nursery, she had convinced herself that she and Dorian had built up some sort of trust. But the divide between them was vast, and any dream of bridging it was a rich girl's fantasy. "Security's already surrounded this place, water and land. They're coming in tomorrow."

"How would a wall bitch know something like that?" asked one of the men behind her.

"This one might," Dorian replied thoughtfully. "She married into the DOD."

Lily blushed. Dorian's tone made it sound as though Lily had married her cousin and joined a family of inbred lunatics in their shack.

"Scan her and bring her inside."

Lily held still for the body scanner, though the black man gave her an extra sharp prod in the stomach. The scanner made her wonder, again, where they had gotten all of this hardware. Security equipment was supposed to be tagged upon manufacture. Had the Blue Horizon figured out a way to remove the tracking chips from equipment as well as people? When the scan was done, Dorian chattered the strange language into her own headset for a moment and then prodded Lily with the tip of her rifle.

"Inside."

Lily went through the warehouse door, her hands still laced behind her head, and blinked as light assaulted her eyes, blinding her for a few moments. When she recovered, she found herself in a large room with corrugated metal walls. A small table was set up in the middle of the room, two men seated there. Lily first spotted Jonathan, standing behind a chair at the far end, and in the chair sat William Tear, staring with narrowed eyes at the man opposite. Dorian prodded Lily in the back with her rifle, and Lily marched forward. Several more guards moved to surround her now, though she was relieved to see that they only had pistols. Two of the guards were women, which surprised Lily; she had somehow assumed that Dorian was unique.

Tear looked up in annoyance as they approached, but as he spotted Lily, his face changed, became unreadable, and he stood up from his chair. The man at the near end of the table turned around, and Lily fought not to recoil. He had lost most of his face to acid, or something worse. Red, angry tissue covered his cheekbones and crawled over his forehead. His teeth were just as bad as those of the man outside.

"Nice, Tear," the burned man rasped. "Your people let a Security agent through."

"No," Tear replied coldly. "Not sure what she is, Parker, but she's not Security."

"Look at her clothes. Whatever she is, she's wall meat, and she's seen my face."

Parker came toward Lily. His disfigurement made him look simultaneously ancient and rapacious, and Lily shrank back. He reached out and grabbed her breast, roughly, wrenching it to the left, and Lily clamped her lips shut on a groan.

"Take your hands off her." Tear's voice had turned to ice now.

"Why should I?" Parker grabbed at Lily's other breast, and her hand balled into a fist. But then she felt Dorian's hand slide over her shoulder and clamp there, a warning. Lily closed her eyes, forced herself to be still.

"Because if you don't, Parker, I break that hand and throw you out of here with nothing, none of my toys. How would you like that?"

Parker's face twisted angrily, but he finally let go. Lily

backed up, clutching her aching breast, until she bumped into Dorian's rifle again. These people, Parker and his men, were what Lily had always pictured when she thought about life outside the wall: violent and careless, with none of the fundamental decency she sensed from Tear and his people. So what were they doing here?

Tear left the table and Jonathan followed, keeping close, in the same way that he did with Lily. His eyes constantly landed on Tear and then flitted away, anxious, looking for threats, and at that moment Lily realized that Jonathan had never really been her bodyguard. He was Tear's man, and Lily had only been an incidental stop on the way.

Tear halted in front of her, and she was struck again by his military posture: straight, with the heels together. Time seemed to be slipping away again; she wished she could check her watch, but she kept her hands up. It would be long past midnight now. How many hours until dawn?

"Mrs. Mayhew. Why are you here?"

Lily took a deep breath and repeated the entire evening's events, everything since Arnie Welch had shown up for dinner. She omitted nothing except Greg and the picture frame; when the moment came, she found herself unable to tell that story in front of all of these people. Tear's gaze never wavered from her as she spoke, and Lily found that she had been right, that night in the nursery: his eyes were not grey but silver, a bright and glimmering silver. Lily had to fight not to look down.

"She's lying," Parker announced flatly, when Lily had finished.

Jonathan leaned over to whisper into Tear's ear, and Tear nodded. "We did lose Goodin a week ago. Several bodies were burned beyond recovery in that explosion."

"That's an easy piece of bullshit for Security! They could have identified your man by dental records and then sent this whore in to tell a story."

"Security doesn't have any medical records on my people."

"Someone else talked."

"How did she know where to find us, then, Parker?" Tear's voice thinned with contempt, but he turned to Dorian. "Dori. Take your boys out and have a look around. Thirty minutes."

The gun barrel withdrew from Lily's spine, and she shivered. Dorian's hand squeezed her shoulder one last time, then left.

"So what to do with the whore?" Parker asked. His men had moved up to surround him, and Lily saw that they carried only knives or pistols, antiquated guns that must have been at least twenty years old, none of the heavy weaponry that Tear's people were holding. Tear's people seemed cleaner as well, as though they had access to plumbing. Here and there Lily saw crooked teeth, but none of them seemed to be rotten. The Blue Horizon clearly had their own doctors; did they have a dentist as well? Clothes, teeth, weapons . . . everything about Tear's people seemed to be newer. Better.

What can he possibly want with these people?

"This is our house, Parker," Tear replied. "The woman belongs to us. Jonathan, take her in the back and have a good time. Afterward, we might pass her around." He sat back down at the table and gestured Parker into the other chair. "Let's finish up."

Jonathan grabbed Lily's arm roughly and began dragging her toward a door at the far end of the room.

"Fight me," he muttered. "Put on a show."

427

This was actually a godsend. Lily's nerves, frayed almost bare, suddenly sprang to life, and she hauled back and punched Jonathan in the face. He took a fistful of her hair and dragged her toward the door. Lily pawed ineffectually at his shoulder, and then they were through the door and Jonathan slammed it shut, then stood her up in front of him.

"Scream. As loud as you can."

Lily drew a deep breath and screamed. Jonathan let her go on for perhaps two seconds and then clamped a hand over her mouth, muffling the scream into a grunt. He released her, and Lily moved over to perch on the arm of a puffy, misshapen chair that sat against the wall.

"Sorry about that, Mrs. M. It's all these people understand."

Jonathan hurried over to a door that stood open on the far side of the room. He shut the door, but not before Lily glimpsed something enormous in the warehouse space beyond: long bars of wood crisscrossed with horizontal beams that extended out of her range of vision. Lily had the impression of a massive skeleton, wooden goliath, half finished.

The skeleton of a ship.

She stared at Jonathan for several long minutes, her thoughts jumbling together around this new puzzle piece. Horses and medical equipment stolen. Transcontinental jets destroyed. Satellites brought down from the sky. A wooden ship being built by hand. The river-covered land that Lily had only glimpsed in her mind, a land where there was no Security, no surveillance, nothing.

And then she understood.

"You're leaving. All of you are leaving."

"I can't talk about it, Mrs. M."

428

The door slammed behind them and Tear stalked into the room. "It's set. September first."

"Parker gone?"

"No. He thinks he'll get a crack at Mrs. Mayhew here. Animals, the lot."

"What's the word on the DOD feed?"

"Those three destroyers are still sitting a few miles outside the harbor. They're not moving, just waiting."

Lily's mouth dropped open, and she stared at them, staggered. How could Tear have gotten into the Department of Defense?

The same way they can bring the satellites down from the sky and put out the power, her mind whispered. *Technology is only as good as the people who supervise it.*

"There's radio silence all around the edge of the terminal," Jonathan continued.

Tear nodded. "Hard to say when they'll come, but I'm betting soon."

Lily groaned, the truth tumbling into her stomach like a pile of rocks. "You already knew."

"Yes."

She sat down in the chair, covering her face with her hands. All of this . . . the entire journey, Greg . . . she had done it for nothing. She looked up at Jonathan, her cheeks blooming with furious color.

"I tried to save you the trip, Mrs. M."

Another whoop came from the room outside, and Tear rolled his eyes. "That's long enough, I suppose. Go and tell some heroic rape stories. Get them all ready to move as soon as Dori comes back. We'll send Parker and his bunch out by the surface tunnels."

Jonathan left, and Tear collapsed into an armchair near

the door, perching his arms on his knees. The silver eyes gleamed at Lily, even from across the room. "I'm sorry for all of this. I'd like to shoot them as dogs, but I need them."

"Why?"

"Because my people are valuable, Mrs. Mayhew. They're intelligent and well trained. Brute force would be a waste of their talents."

"What happens on September first?"

"Nothing you want to know about. How did you get here?"

"I drove."

"Husband let you out in the middle of the night for a romp, did he?"

"I think I killed him."

Tear looked up sharply.

"I bashed him on the head and left him there." Lily didn't want to keep talking, but it was like that night in the nursery; the words tumbled out. "He wanted to me to have a baby. He wanted to take me to an in vitro doctor. It didn't matter what I wanted."

Tear nodded. "It's a problem. Women are selling their eggs for the price of a small bag of meth, but the rewards on the other end are enormous."

Lily considered for a moment. "I wanted to kill him."

"Well, you'll be facing a world of hurt when you get home, one way or another."

Lily nodded.

"Leave your car here. Security's ringed the port; there's no way you got in without their notice. They've seen your car and marked it as belonging to my people. Leave it here and Jonathan will take you home. You can claim you were carjacked and called him to come get you."

"My tag will show I've been here."

"That's true," he replied, and Lily saw that he'd only been trying to make her feel better.

Three quick knocks and Jonathan came back in. "Dori's back, sir. Nothing new out there. I told Parker we're leaving soon."

"Is the gear all packed?"

"Five minutes."

Tear gestured toward the closed door on the far side of the room. "Pity we didn't have more notice. I hate to leave her here."

"When?" Lily blurted out. "When are you leaving?"

"What makes you think we're leaving?"

"You are," Lily muttered, her throat hoarse with tears. "On a ship."

"And where do you think we're going?"

"To the better world."

Tear leaned forward. Lily was struck again by his silver eyes, which seemed to reflect even the dim glow provided by the fluorescents. "Why did you come here, Mrs. Mayhew? This has nothing to do with you, and you took an enormous risk. Why?"

Lily couldn't answer. As a child, she used to pick a single item and stare at it for as long as possible, until her eyes had dried out and her gaze had lost all focus. She remembered taking a vast pleasure in having her gaze so captured, in being transfixed, and now she could not take her eyes from William Tear. She followed each of his movements, even the small ones: the rapid flicker of his eyes across her face, the tap of his fingers on one knee, the clench of his jaw. All things seemed to center on Tear, to hinge on him.

I believe it.

In that moment, Lily believed it all. There was a better

431

world out there, somehow, and it was close . . . almost within their reach. The wheat, the bright blue river, the endless trees. If Tear asked her to die for the better world, she would do it. She wouldn't even need to think. And if he asked Lily to die for *him*, she would do that too. She had never felt anything so deeply in her life.

Her eyes had watered again; Lily tore her blurry gaze from Tear and wiped her arm across her face. When she looked up, she found Jonathan watching her, a small smile on his face. He reached out a hand and Lily clasped it in both of hers, gripping tightly. She didn't want to let go; she thought she might drown.

"The better world," she gasped. "I see it. All the time."

"We all see it, Mrs. M."

Tear reached beneath her chin and tipped her face up with one finger. His eyes were so brilliant now that they seemed to glow in the dim light. "What do *you* see, Lily?"

"Water," Lily stammered. "Blue water, then cliffs, then land. Yellow land, covered with wheat. And there's a village on a hill, next to a river. Children."

"What are they doing?"

"I don't know," Lily admitted. "But they're free. They're all free."

Tear smiled and released her chin. "This is the Blue Horizon."

Lily began to cry.

"Five years ago," Tear continued, "when we asked to secede, I had planned to create the better world myself, to take a small corner of America and remake it. Despite its blight, this country is an incredible creation, and a piece of it would have served us well. But it's just as well they turned us down, for it would never have worked. Parker, people like him, they're built to spoil things. They would never have left us alone. If not them, it would be your government, finding seller's remorse ten or fifteen years down the line. If we made the better world in a place where others could reach it, they would only try to tear it down."

Lily wiped away her tears. "There's no more land. Where can you go?"

"The world is bigger than you think."

"Why do they get to come along?" she asked. "Those people outside?"

"Parker's people?" Tear chuckled bitterly. "Parker's people sell their children and trade women for food. They don't get anywhere near the better world."

"Sir," Jonathan muttered from the door. Listening, Lily heard voices raised in argument outside, then a quick, light hum that she thought might be silenced laser fire. Tear gestured for her to stand, and she pulled herself from the chair. She didn't know how tired she was until she tried to stand up.

"I apologize, Lily, but there's no way around this. Hold still and close your eyes."

Lily shut her eyes. Her head rocked back as a short, sharp blow landed on the corner of her mouth. There was very little pain, but she tasted blood. Tear smeared the blood across her chin, then tore the neck of her shirt in two places. "Just for show; it'll heal quickly. Don't forget to limp."

Jonathan opened the door and Tear dragged Lily outside. Dorian was blocking the doorway, her rifle trained on Parker and his men. They reminded Lily of wolves who had treed an animal.

"This bitch is out of her mind!" Parker shouted. "Tell her to stand down!"

"Security has ringed us. We need to get out of here now."

"We didn't see anyone."

"Wonderful." Tear's voice was acid. "You have access to satellite imagery, do you?"

"Fuck you."

"Fine. Stay and wait for them."

Parker's one good eye gleamed with hatred. "How do we get out?"

Tear bent to the floor and swung up a trapdoor, revealing steps that descended into darkness. Parker gave Dorian one last furious look, then squatted to peer down the stairs.

"Flashlights?"

"No flashlights. Our heat signature will be risky enough. It's a straight shot through the tunnels into downtown Boston."

"What about the wall bitch?"

"Jonathan likes her. He wants to take her with."

Parker stared at Lily for a moment. "Ah well. Not long now, anyway."

He made for the trapdoor, but Tear stopped him with a hand on his chest. "We have an agreement, Parker. September first."

"September first," Parker replied, grinning, and Lily saw so much pure evil in that grin that she had to close her eyes for a moment. She called up the real world and realized that it was now the early morning of August 30. "September first, and we have our carnival."

Tear's mouth twitched in disgust, but he nodded. "Into the tunnel. Look for a ladder beside a blue emergency light; it'll bring you out beside Fenway."

Parker and his men went first. Perhaps thirty of Tear's people had returned to the warehouse and gathered around the trapdoor; most of them carried guns, like Dorian, but several had nothing, only small receivers tucked into their ears and tiny metallic threads coiled around their index fingers. Computer techs.

"Radio silence until you get outside the city," Tear ordered. "We'll meet at home."

So Arnie had been wrong; this wasn't their headquarters after all. Lily followed Jonathan down the stairs and then they were into blackness, nothing but scraping footsteps and the jingling of straps that held the guns. Dorian was somewhere behind her, Lily knew, and she took some comfort from that. Occasionally she heard squeaking sounds somewhere near her feet, but even the scurrying proximity of rats wasn't particularly frightening. These were safe people, and Lily trusted them to keep her safe, no matter where they were going.

But what happens on September first? her mind asked, its tone plaintive. *What's the carnival?*

After perhaps half a mile, someone coughed in the darkness ahead and Jonathan grabbed Lily's arm, bringing her up short. Parker and his men kept on moving, up the corridor, the sounds of their passage growing fainter, diminishing into silence.

Jonathan pulled her to the right, whispering, "Stairs."

Lily felt her way down another staircase. She had gotten a second wind for a while, but it was wearing off now, and she thought that soon she might simply collapse. But she kept going, determined not to slow them down, not to be—what had they called her?—a wall bitch. It was an eerily apt term; Lily applied it to most of her friends and found that it fit.

"Hold," Tear announced, an eternity of time later. Lily paused, heard them all come to a halt around her.

"Bang."

A deep thrumming echoed above their heads. The tunnel shook, concrete dust sifting down to land on Lily's hair and face, getting into her eyes. A great breath of heat pushed against her back, and for a few moments, the tunnel was filled with a hollow roar of sound. Then it faded, and they stood once more in the quiet dark.

"The better world," someone murmured.

"The better world," they repeated, and Lily repeated it with them, liking the sound of her voice with theirs, hoping that no one would mind.

After a moment, as though by collective consent, the entire group began walking again. They were moving through a labyrinth of tunnels now, sometimes going up staircases, sometimes down, sometimes slipping through narrow crevices that made Lily feel claustrophobic, trapped. She kept going, focusing on the present, for the future was not to be considered. She couldn't imagine what was waiting for her at home.

Perhaps twenty minutes later, she followed Jonathan up a ladder and emerged through an open manhole into a dark alley, where she found herself surrounded by dumpsters that clearly hadn't been emptied in years.

"Help Dori up when she comes," Tear told Jonathan. "She won't want help, but do it anyway. That bullet hasn't quite finished with her yet."

Lily tucked her arms around herself. The air was warm in late August, but she was wet through with perspiration, and wind seemed to sneak up beneath her jacket.

What happens on September first?

"Get your fucking hand off me!" a voice hissed from the manhole.

"Shut up, Dori." Jonathan hauled her up from the hole, rifle and all. "Everyone knows how tough you are."

"I could put you down, South Carolina."

"Sure you could."

"We need to move." Tear was staring at the mouth of the alley. Lily could see nothing, but she believed him; he reminded her of a dog on point, scenting danger that was invisible to the eye. After ten people had emerged from the manhole, Jonathan replaced the cover, and Lily remembered something Arnie had said once: that the Blue Horizon liked to split its forces to prevent losses. The rest must have moved on in the tunnel.

"Come on, Mrs. M."

They went one at a time from the mouth of the alley, vanishing in all directions. Dorian touched Lily's shoulder in passing, but when Lily turned, she was already gone. Tear tugged at her arm and they both followed Jonathan up a street that Lily didn't recognize. Office buildings, long derelict, reared above both sidewalks. Each window seemed to tell its own story of breakage, and Lily heard the telltale sounds of people inside, shuffling and muttering, but she couldn't see anyone. The glow of smog above their heads was beginning to dim with approaching dawn.

"Get the car," Tear said, and Jonathan moved off into the mist. Lily swayed on her feet and Tear grabbed her elbow, steadying her.

"You're in a lot of trouble, Mrs. Mayhew. Tell as good a story as you can about the car, but Security will eventually think to look up your tag. They'll want to know what you were doing here."

"Have you ever been in custody?"

"Yes."

"What happens?"

"You try to live through it."

"And what happens on September first?"

Tear's jaw tightened. "I can't tell you."

"In case they torture me?"

"Yes."

Lily considered this for a moment, feeling her stomach knot up. She closed her eyes, tried to think of the better world. But all she saw was the school doorway, Maddy's tousled head disappearing forever. A car pulled up in front of them, and it took Lily a moment to recognize her Lexus, Jonathan at the wheel. The car's sleek, black frame seemed alien, grotesque on this broken street.

"Get in. Jonathan will take you home."

"Can't I . . ." Lily took a deep breath. "Can't I stay here, with all of you?"

Tear looked at her for a long moment. "No, Mrs. Mayhew. I'm sorry. There are already too many. A lot of good people will be left behind."

Lily nodded, trying to force a smile, but Dorian's voice rang in her head: *The better world's not for people like you.* She got into the car, barely registering the plush leather seats. Tear began to close the door, and she grabbed his wrist, almost in desperation. "I don't know how I get through this."

Tear put a hand on her cheek. Warmth seemed to sink into her skin, bringing her back from the cold place in her head. "I promise you, you will get through it."

"You can't promise that."

"Yes, I can. Believe me, you're tougher than you imagine."

"How do you know?"

He withdrew his hand, straightening up. The silver eyes

glimmered. "I know, Lily. I've known you all my life."

The door slammed in her face and a fist thumped twice on the roof. Jonathan floored it, and Lily was thrown back in her seat. She twisted around, wriggling until she could look out the back windshield and see William Tear staring after them, his tall frame standing military-straight under the lights of Boston.

They were halfway back to New Canaan before Jonathan said a word. Lily had spent the journey looking out the window, trying to think of a more plausible story for Security. She had nothing. With each mile, her stomach tightened, then tightened further, knots seemed to coil in on themselves until she thought she might be sick.

"Don't worry, Mrs. M."

Lily jumped. She had forgotten that someone else was in the car. She looked up and found Jonathan's eyes on her in the rearview mirror.

"I think I killed him, Jonathan."

"You had cause."

Lily blushed. This was the closest they'd ever come to talking about that night ... about any of the nights. "Security won't care about that."

"We look out for each other, Mrs. M. We take care of each other. Without that there's nothing."

"Won't you be in trouble too? If they track this car?"

"I fixed the tag on this car a long time ago. It was in the garage most of the night, until you called and I came to pick you up."

Lily nodded slowly. It boggled her mind, the world of hidden things that had undoubtedly been going on around her for years. Outside the window, another green sign flashed by: Tolland. The horizon was lightening, blush pink eating its way into the dark sky overhead. Lily stared at the pink haze, wishing she could see much farther east, all the way to the Atlantic, where the sun would already be up. She leaned against the window, enjoying its coolness on her cheek, and behind her eyes she saw the half-finished ship. There must be many more ships, she realized, hidden . . . where? All over New England? She thought she knew, now, what would happen on September first: they would leave, Tear and his people, and more than anything, Lily wanted to go with them, to that wide-open place covered in water and trees. In the distance, outside the glass, she heard a voice.

"Kelsea."

Lily shook herself awake, but it was a losing battle. Half of her body was already fast asleep.

"Kelsea."

"Mrs. M.?"

"Who's Kelsea?" Lily murmured. The glass felt so cool, pillowing her cheek. She wanted to stay there forever, wanted—

Kelsea!"

She opened her eyes to a moving world, Pen shaking her shoulders. The hallway jumped wildly around her. For a moment she was back in the car, then she was back with Pen. Her head throbbed wildly. She felt sick.

"Lady, I had to wake you. It's important."

"What time is it?"

"Eleven in the morning."

Kelsea shook her head, trying to clear it, trying to get her bearings. She was standing in the hallway, just outside the balcony room. The early sunrise was still bright in her mind, bruised pink. She could feel cool window glass on her cheek. "Well, what couldn't wait?"

"The Mort, Lady. They've reached the walls."

Kelsea's heart sank. "We knew this was coming."

"Yes, but Lady—"

"What?"

"The Red Queen. She's come with them."

BOOK III

CHAPTER 12

NIGHT

You cannot bargain with the tide.
—Tear proverb of unverified origin, generally
attributed to the Glynn Queen

The Mort army covered both sides of the Caddell, spread north and south across the Almont and even curving around the southern edge of New London. Dusk was coming down on the city, and in the fading light the Mort camp was an impenetrable dark sea.

In front of the black tents stood more than fifty neatly ordered lines of soldiers. To the naked eye, they seemed to be covered in glittering iron. It was an ostentatious display, clearly designed to frighten Kelsea, and it worked. She was terrified, both for herself and for the people behind her, almost her entire kingdom now crammed inside New London's walls. How could they resist the force assembled down there? Behind the tents, Kelsea glimpsed a line of siege towers, and somewhere out there, hidden from view, were the cannons. Assuming that the cannons worked–and

Kelsea did—the Mort wouldn't even need their siege towers. They could simply smash the walls of New London to rubble.

Glee stirred in Kelsea's arms, making her jump. The child was so easy to hold that Kelsea had forgotten she was there. Andalie had opted to come on this outing, and Kelsea had taken the girl to give her a rest. But the people in the streets had murmured in astonishment when they saw the small child in Kelsea's arms, and now Kelsea worried that she might have called too much attention to both Andalie and Glee. They were valuable, just as Andalie had said, and their best hope seemed to be in anonymity. Glee had fallen asleep on the way to the wall, but now she was awake, staring up at Kelsea, her gaze contemplative. Kelsea put a finger to her lips, and Glee nodded solemnly.

Mace had picked Andalie's other daughter, Aisa, to accompany them. She remained several feet behind Kelsea, almost like a second Pen, holding a knife in her hand. Mace had taken a liking to the girl, but then so had many of the Guard. Coryn said she had the best knife hand since Prasker—whoever that was—and Elston deemed her a tough piece of business, which was the highest praise he could give. Aisa was taking this expedition very seriously, never loosening her grip on the knife, her thick brows lowered over a face that was both solemn and grim. The heroism of her small, determined form, now, when it could make no difference, only made Kelsea feel worse.

Scanning the Mort camp, Kelsea finally found what she was looking for: a crimson tent located near the center. Though it was only a tiny speck of red among all that black, something tolled inside Kelsea like a funeral bell. The Red Queen was leaving nothing to chance this time; she had come herself, just to make sure the job was done right.

Torches surrounded the tent, but after a moment Kelsea noticed something odd: these torches were the only fire she could see in the Mort camp. It was just after dinner, but the perimeter was dark. Kelsea considered this fact for a moment before tucking it away.

"Did everyone make it inside the city?" she asked.

"They did, Lady," Mace replied, "but the army was decimated in the last attempt to hold the Mort from the bridge."

Kelsea's stomach roiled, and she peered down at the New London Bridge, cursing her poor eyesight. "What keeps the Mort off the bridge?"

"A barricade, Lady." Colonel Hall stepped forward, emerging from a group of army men farther down the wall. A thick bandage swaddled his right arm, from which the sleeve had been cut away, and he had taken a nasty wound across the jaw. "It's a good barricade, but it won't hold forever."

"Colonel Hall." Kelsea smiled, relieved to see him alive, but sobered at the sight of his injuries. "I'm sorry for the loss of General Bermond, and your men. All of their families will receive full pensions."

"Thank you, Lady." But Hall's mouth twisted wryly, as though acknowledging how little a pension meant in this moment.

Mace poked her lightly in the back, and Kelsea remembered. "I formally invest you as general of my armies. Long life to you, General Hall."

He threw his head back and laughed, and though Kelsea did not think the laughter was meant to be unkind, it rang in her ears. "Above all, let us have niceties, Lady."

"What else do we have now?"

"Glory, I suppose. Death with honor."

"Precisely."

Hall came a bit closer, paying no attention to Pen, who moved to block him. "May I tell you a secret, Lady?"

"Certainly." Kelsea patted Glee's back and set her on the ground, where the child wrapped an arm around Kelsea's knee.

Hall lowered his voice. "It's a real thing, glory. But it pales in comparison to what we sacrifice for it. Home, family, long lives filled with quiet. These are real things too, and when we seek glory, we give them up."

Kelsea did not reply for a moment, realizing that Bermond's death must have hit Hall harder than she had expected. "Do you think I sought this war?"

"No, Lady. But you are not content with the quiet life."

Mace grunted beside her, a soft sound that Kelsea recognized as agreement, and she fought the urge to kick him. "You don't know me well enough to say that."

"This entire kingdom knows you now, Queen Kelsea. You've brought us all to disaster, to satisfy your own notions of glory. Of better."

"Be careful, Hall," Pen warned. "You don't—"

"Shut up, Pen," Mace growled.

Kelsea swung around, furious. "Have you turned on me for good now, Lazarus?"

"No, Lady. But it's not wise, particularly in wartime, to silence the voice of dissent."

Kelsea's face burned, and she turned back to Hall. "I didn't end the shipment for glory. I never cared about that."

"Then prove me wrong, Majesty. Save the last remnants of my men from an unwinnable fight. Save the women and children—and the men as well—from the nightmare they will surely face when the Mort break the walls. You cut a man to pieces, rather than watch him die a simple death by the noose. Prove me wrong and save us all."

Hall turned back to the edge, dismissing her in a single movement. Kelsea's face had gone numb. She felt alone suddenly, alone in a way she hadn't been since her earliest days in the Keep. She looked over the faces of her Guard, clustered around the stairwells that fed the inner wall. Mace, Coryn, Wellmer, Elston, Kibb . . . they were loyal, they would lay down their lives for her, but loyalty wasn't approval. They thought she had failed.

"Look, Lady." Mace gestured over the edge.

The regimented lines of Mort had not moved, but as Kelsea squinted in the dying light, she saw that there was movement down there, a clutch of figures in black cloaks darting through the lines, bearing torches, wending their way toward the front.

Mace had pulled out his spyglass. "The one in the middle is the Red Queen's personal herald. I remember that little bastard."

The herald was a wisp of a man, so slight that he could easily have blended into the night in his cloak. But his voice was a thick bass that echoed off the walls of the Keep, and his Tear was perfect, without even the slightest Mort accent.

"The Great Queen of all Mortmesne and Callae extends greetings to the Heir of the Tearling!"

Kelsea gritted her teeth.

"My message is as follows. The Great Queen assumes that you realize the futility of your situation. The Great Queen's army will find it an easy matter to break the walls of your capital and take whatever it wishes. No Tear will be spared.

"However, if the Tear heir removes the barricade to the New London Bridge and opens the gates, the Great Queen promises to spare not only her, but twenty members of her entourage as well. The Great Queen gives her word that these twenty-one will not be harmed."

Someone's hand was on Kelsea's wrist. Glee, clutching too tightly, her tiny nails digging in, but Kelsea barely felt it. *Save us all*, Hall had said, and now Kelsea saw that if she could not save them, they would not be saved. She focused on the herald, the men around him, calling up the terrible thing inside her. It woke easily, and Kelsea wondered whether it would always be there from now on, ready to spring out at any opportunity. Could she even live that way?

"The bridge is to be cleared and the gates will be opened by dawn," the herald continued. "If these terms are not met, the Great Queen's army will enter New London by any means necessary, and lay your city to ruin. This is my—"

The herald broke off, then suddenly doubled over and blew apart in a spray of blood. So great was Kelsea's anger that it seemed to ripple outward, to encompass the rest of them, knocking some men backward and flattening the rest. It spread throughout the regimented ranks of Mort, gathering speed and power like a hurricane wind.

And then it simply met a wall.

This sudden obstacle was so unexpected that Kelsea stumbled backward, as though she had run into the wall herself, headlong. She nearly knocked Glee over, but Andalie caught the girl easily, and Pen took Kelsea's arm and kept her upright. Her head throbbed, a sudden, vicious headache that seemed to have come from nowhere.

"Lady?"

She shook her head to clear it, but the headache had clamped down like a vise, waves of pain that made it nearly impossible to focus.

What was that?

She took her spyglass from her pocket. The light was almost entirely gone now, but Kelsea could still see the damage she'd wreaked down there, at least several hundred dead in the front of the Mort lines. Gruesome deaths all, some of them reduced to little more than piles of bloody tissue. But beyond, she still sensed that impenetrable barrier, no less real for the fact that it could not be seen. The crimson tent caught her eye again; its entrance had been drawn, and now Kelsea glimpsed someone beneath the awning. It had grown too dark to make out a face, but the figure was unmistakable: a tall woman in a red gown.

"You," Kelsea whispered.

Someone was tugging at her skirt. Kelsea looked down and found Glee's tiny face looking upward.

"Her name," Glee lisped. "She doesn't want you to know."

Kelsea put a light hand on Glee's head, staring at the red-clad figure. She was less than a mile away, but that distance seemed infinitely vast. Kelsea tested the barrier, trying to slice into it, the same way she would cut into her own flesh. She could not make a dent.

The Mort lines had hastily recovered and reassembled in front of the camp, and now a new man stepped forward, a tall figure in a bulky black cloak.

"I speak for the Queen!"

"Ducarte," Mace murmured. Kelsea focused her spyglass and found a balding man with close-set, bestial eyes. She shivered, for here she sensed a pure predator. Ducarte's gaze roved the city's walls with unconcealed contempt, as though he had already opened a breach and begun the sack.

"If the gates of New London are not opened by dawn tomorrow, none will be spared. These are the Queen's terms."

Ducarte waited a moment longer, until even the last echo of his words had died away. Then he put up the hood of his cloak and reversed his journey through the ranks of Mort, leaving the dead behind, heading back to the camp.

"Arliss."

"Queenie!" He looked up in surprise, his wizened face breaking into a smile, the perennial stinking cigarette clamped between his teeth. "What brings you to my door?"

"I need you to do something for me."

"Well, sit down."

Kelsea settled herself on one of the ratty armchairs Arliss used for conducting business, ignoring the miasma of cigarette smoke that clung to the upholstery. She didn't care for Arliss's office, a filthy warren of desks and loose papers, but she had the beginnings of a plan now, and she needed him.

"Pen, leave us alone."

Pen hesitated. "Technically, he's a danger to your person, Lady."

"No one's a danger to my person anymore." She met his eyes for a long moment, and found an odd thing: although they had slept together several times since that first night—and it had improved exponentially, at least from Kelsea's end—that night was the one that would always be there, between them. "Go, Pen. I'm perfectly safe."

Pen went. Kelsea waited until the door closed behind him before asking, "How's the money?"

"Slowed to a trickle. The minute the Mort came out of the hills, every noble took it as a license to stop paying tax."

"Of course."

"I'd hoped to clean up a tidy profit on the sapphire those miners bring back from the Fairwitch, but no one's heard a peep. I'm guessing they took those bonuses you gave them and disappeared."

"Money is tight, then."

"Very. There are fortunes to be made in wartime, Queenie, but not in good government. Personally, I think we're all fucked."

"You're nothing but sunshine, Arliss."

"This is a dead kingdom walking, Queenie."

"That's why I'm here."

Arliss looked up sharply.

"I need you to do something for me, and I need you to keep it a secret."

"A secret from whom?"

"From everyone. Especially Lazarus." Kelsea leaned forward. "I need you to draft me a Bill of Regency."

Arliss leaned back in his chair, watching her narrowly through the haze of smoke. "You plan to give up your throne?"

"For a time."

"I take it the Mace doesn't know."

"He can't know."

"Ah." Arliss tilted his head, considering. "I've never drafted a Regency bill before. Your uncle is dead, Queenie. Who's the Regent?"

"Lazarus."

Arliss nodded slowly. "That's a wise choice."

"Can you get hold of an old copy of my mother's bill?"

"Yes, but I've seen that bastard; it's fifteen pages long."

"Well, take the essential language. I don't want it open to interpretation anyway. Only a page long, and as many copies as you can write. I'll sign them all, and they can go out to the city tomorrow after I'm gone."

"And where is it you're going?"

Kelsea blinked and saw the New London Bridge, the Mort waiting in the hills beyond. "To die, I think. I hope not."

"Well, now I see why the Mace can't know." Arliss tapped his fingers on his desk. "This will change things."

"For you?"

"For me . . . and my competitors. But it's always good to be in the know first."

"I have to do something."

"You don't *have* to do anything, Queenie. You could take her offer, save the women and your core Guard."

"That's what my uncle would have done. But I can't."

"Well, that's the bitch of choice, isn't it?"

She glared at him. "Choice has been very good to you lately, Arliss. You've been coining money from drug sales to the refugees. Did you think I wouldn't find out?"

"Let me tell you something, Queenie . . . my drugs are the only reason you haven't had panic or widespread suicide down in that camp. People have to cling to something."

"I see. You're an altruist."

"Not at all. But it's foolish to blame the dealer for catering to his market."

"That's Thorne talking."

"Yep. Thorne was a little shit all his life, but he was always right about that."

Kelsea looked up, suddenly forgetting the drugs, and even the Regency bill. "You knew Thorne when he was young?"

"Lord yes, Queenie. He'll tell you that no one knows where he came from—"

"He's dead."

454

"—but there are a few of us, if you take the trouble to look."

"Where did he come from?"

"The Creche."

"I don't know what that is."

"Deep under the Gut, Queenie, there's a warren of tunnels. God knows what they were built for; they're too deep to be sewers. If you want something too fucked even for the Gut, and you know the right people, you go down to the Creche."

"What was Thorne doing there?"

"Thorne was sold to a pimp when he was barely born. Lived his entire childhood down there . . . such as it was."

"How do you know?"

"Don't look at me like that, Queenie. I had to go down there on business once or twice, early in my career. They need a fairly steady supply of narcotics, for obvious reasons, but I got out of dealing down there a long time ago."

"You got out."

"Yes, I did. It's a bad place, the Creche. Kids for sex, for—"

"Stop." Kelsea held up her hand. "I see."

"A bad place," Arliss repeated, shuffling the papers on his desk. "But Thorne was smart and quick. He was practically a king down there by the time he was eighteen."

"Was Lazarus there too?"

"He was, though he'll not admit it if you ask him."

"What was—" Kelsea's voice died, and she swallowed, feeling the words slip around a dry place in her throat. "What was he doing down there?"

"The ring."

"Explain."

"Children fighting children."

"Boxing?"

"Not always. Sometimes they gave them weapons. There's value in variety."

Kelsea's lips felt as though they'd frozen solid. "Why?"

"Gambling, Queenie. More money changes hands over kidfighting than any other betting matter in this kingdom, and the Mace was one of the greatest contenders they'd ever seen, a juggernaut." Arliss's eyes gleamed with memory. "He never lost, even in his early years. Lazarus isn't even his real name, you know, just a nickname his handlers came up with when no one could bring him down. The odds got so high by the time he was eleven or twelve that I nearly stopped taking bets on him at all."

"You took bets?"

"I'm a bookie, Queenie. I take bets on anything where I can calculate the odds."

Kelsea rubbed her eyes. "Didn't anyone try to put a stop to it?"

"Who would, Lady? I saw your uncle down there several times. Your mother too."

"How did they decide who won?"

Arliss met her gaze steadily, and Kelsea shook her head, feeling ill. "I see. Lazarus never told me."

"Of course he didn't. If some comes out, it all comes out."

"Meaning what?"

"Meaning that the Mace was almost an animal by the time he was done. No one could wrangle him, except maybe Carroll; it was Carroll who got him out of the Creche for good. But the Mace was still a danger to others, long after his days in the ring were over. He's ashamed of his deeds. He doesn't want anyone to know."

"Then why are you telling me?"

Arliss raised his eyebrows. "I don't answer to the Mace,

Queenie. You're a fool if you think I do. I don't even answer to you. I've reached the good time of life now, the time where I've made my money, and if someone is fool enough to threaten me, I don't need to care. I do and say as I please."

"And it pleases you to be *here*? *Now*? Why haven't you fled to Mortmesne? Or Cadare?"

Arliss grinned. "Because I don't want to."

"You're a pain in the ass." Kelsea got up from the armchair, wiping off several puffs of dust that had settled on her skirt. "Will you draft my bill?"

"Yes." Arliss sat back, crossing his arms over his chest, and eyed her speculatively. "So you're going to die tomorrow?"

"I think so."

"Then what in the happy Christ are you doing sitting here talking to me? You should be out getting drunk, getting laid."

"With whom?"

Arliss smiled, a sudden and gentle smile that sat oddly on his twisted face. "You think we don't know?"

"Shut up, Arliss."

"As you like." He pulled a blank sheet of paper from the stack at his left hand, and his next words were muttered down at the desk.

"What did you say?"

"Nothing. Don't throw in the towel yet, Queenie. You're a clever piece of business . . . smarter even than your grandmother, and that's saying something. This is a gutsy thing you mean to do."

"Mad, perhaps. I'll be back to sign the bills before dawn."

Leaving Arliss's office, she wandered up the hallway, feeling lost, not knowing what to do now. Tomorrow morning she would walk out of here, and chances were that she wouldn't be coming back. She wondered whether Arliss was right, whether she ought to simply spend the entire night in bed with Pen.

Kelsea.

She halted in the middle of the hallway. The voice was Lily's, not words but a pleading grab for help. It felt as if a drowning woman were grasping at the edges of Kelsea's mind.

Kelsea.

Lily was in trouble. Terrible trouble. Kelsea stared at the asymmetrical pattern of stones on the floor, her mind racing, moving from point to point. Lily had called, and Kelsea had heard her. In the span of history, Lily Mayhew's life meant nothing; she was not even a footnote. Whatever was happening to her, she was long dead and buried now, but Kelsea couldn't turn away. Yet she didn't know how to reach Lily. They were separated by three centuries, an endless gulf. Kelsea had always thought of time as a solid wall behind her, blocking out everything that had already passed . . . but the world she now inhabited was greater than that.

Was it possible to *create* one of her fugues?

Kelsea stilled, arrested by this idea. The distance might be vast in time, but Kelsea no longer lived in pure time, did she? She had moved in and out of it for months. Could she step off the edge of one age and into another, as neatly as pre-Crossing passengers would have boarded a train? She called up the outlines of Lily's world: the dark storm-filled horizon, much like the Tearling, threaded through with inequality and violence. A burst of fire seared through Kelsea's chest, sending her staggering against the wall.

"Lady?"

Pen, behind her, his voice muffled as though Kelsea were swimming in deep water.

"Pen. It's going to be a long night, I think. I need you to watch out for me when I fall."

"Fall?"

Kelsea's vision had blurred now. Pen was a kind shape in the torchlight. "I don't know where I land."

"Lady?" Pen grabbed her arm. "Is it your fugue?"

"I don't know."

"We'll get you to your chamber."

Kelsea allowed him to lift her along, barely even noticing. Her mind was full of Lily: Lily's life, Lily's fright. What had been waiting for her when she got home from Boston?

"What's wrong?"

Elston's booming, bearlike voice, but now Kelsea heard it from a great distance. Pen was carrying her, she realized, and she had no idea when it had happened.

"Fugue," Pen muttered. "It came on fast. Help me get her to bed."

"No," Kelsea whispered. "Can't afford to sleep the night. Just stay with me and don't let me fall."

"Lady—"

"Shhh." Kelsea was dreaming now, awake and dreaming at the same time. Lily had called, and Kelsea had heard her. Everything had darkened; Kelsea groped blindly in the shadows, seeking the past. If Kelsea could only reach them, Lily and William Tear. She could picture them standing before her, their eyes kind . . . but all around them swirled a maelstrom of violence. Lily—

Lily."

She spun around, hearing a whisper behind her, certain it was Greg. But there was nothing, only early sunlight streaming through the living room windows. The nearly silent motors of the house's internal processes hummed along inside the walls. Had her house ever seemed so small before? The furniture she had bought, the carpet she had chosen . . . there was a falsity to these things, a sense that she could push them aside and see chalk markings, a bare stage.

Greg was not in the house. The kitchen floor had provided no answers, only a large smear of dried blood. Had Greg gotten up, called an ambulance? There was no way to know. The stain on the kitchen floor had the thick, viscous look of menstrual blood, and it reminded Lily that she had forgotten to take her pill the night before. She headed for the nursery, leaving Jonathan in the kitchen. Did she have anything to do today? Yes, lunch with Michele and Sarah, but that could be canceled. If Security came for her, it would be better to have it happen here than downtown or at the club. Lily didn't kid herself that she would hold up well under questioning, but she thought she had the parameters clear now. She would break, one way or another; her job was simply to make sure that she didn't break until September first. Could she do that? She closed her eyes, looking for the better world, but instead she found William Tear, standing beneath the streetlights.

The nursery faced eastward, a wash of light in the early sun. Lily darted over to the loose tile, suddenly aware of the sun moving, of the fact that Greg, or Security, could show up at any time. After she took her pill, she would run upstairs and take a shower, put on a good dress and some makeup. Security would come, and when they did, the way she looked would matter. She would appear as respectable as possible, a woman who couldn't possibly be involved in midnight journeys, in separatist plots. She would—

The space beneath the tile was empty.

Lily rocked back on her heels, staring in disbelief. Yesterday she'd had ten boxes of pills in there. Cash too, over two thousand dollars, her emergency stash. Lily's stomach seemed to contract in on itself as the meaning of the empty hole socked home. Her pills were gone.

"Lose something?"

Lily croaked in fright and nearly fell over, clutching the arm of her sofa for balance, as Greg emerged from behind the nursery door. The left side of his head was caked with dried blood; it had matted his hair and trickled down his neck to stain the shoulder of his white shirt. He was grinning.

"Where've you been, Lily?"

"Nowhere," she whispered. She wanted to speak up, to be strong, but she seemed to have no voice. When Greg wasn't around, he became diminutive in her mind, but in real life, he wasn't small at all. In the light, airy space of the nursery, he seemed about ten feet tall.

"Nowhere," Greg repeated smoothly. "Just out and about, all night, outside the wall."

"That's right. I got carjacked too, in case you care."

"All night, outside the wall," Greg repeated, and Lily shuddered. His eyes were wide and empty, dark orbs that seemed to reflect no light. "My dad was right, you know. He said all women are cunts, and I said no, Lily's different. And look here!"

Greg held up a box of her pills, pinching them between two fingers, the way he would something diseased. And now something utterly unexpected and wonderful happened: at the sight of her pills, Lily's panic melted quickly and silently away. She straightened, took a deep breath, and tipped her head to one side, cracking her neck, as he loomed closer. She

Erika Johansen

had to fight the urge to jump up and grab the small orange box out of his hand.

"All the bullshit I had to listen to, all the jokes they made at my expense. Do you know what I've had to put up with because of you? I lost out on a promotion last year because I didn't have a son! My boss calls me Blank-Shooting Greg."

"Catchy."

Greg's eyes narrowed. "You want to be careful, Lily. I could turn you over to Security right now."

"Do that. Better them than you."

"No." Greg's mouth twisted upward in a wide, spitless grin. "I think we'll keep this just between us. Where were you?"

"None of your business."

He slapped her, and her head rocked backward on her neck, a flower bobbing on its stalk. But she kept her feet.

"You need to learn to watch your mouth, Lily. Where were you last night?"

"Sucking Arnie Welch's cock."

She didn't know where that had come from; it was merely the first thing to pop into her mind. But she watched, amazed, as Greg's eyes narrowed into tiny slits and his cheeks turned white.

He believes it!

For a moment Lily teetered on the edge of hysterical laughter. An image popped into her head: kneeling in front of Arnie Welch, poor old Arnie who was as dumb as a bag of hammers, and Lily began to laugh. She barely felt Greg grab hold of her hair—*should have put it up*, her brain remonstrated—and draw her up, making a square target. She giggled at the sight of his face, the tiny burning red spots in his white cheeks, the bared teeth, even the emptiness of his eyes.

"*Stop laughing!*" he shouted, spraying spittle across her face, and of course this only made Lily laugh harder.

"Weak," she giggled. "And you know it too."

Greg clouted the side of her head, sending her flying. Lily glimpsed a wall of sparkling sunlight in front of her and then she went through the patio doors, shattering both panes of glass. A million pinpricks seemed to needle into her arms and face. She pinwheeled for balance on top of the patio, then fell, rolling down three brick steps to land in the grass of the backyard.

"How weak am I, Lily?" Greg asked, his voice closing, following her down the steps. Lily's arms had been sliced open, her head ached, and it felt like her ankle was twisted. Greg kicked her in the ribs, and Lily groaned and curled up, trying to protect her sides. As she rolled, she saw something that made her go cold: the fly of Greg's pants had tented outward. Lily hadn't taken a pill in more than thirty-six hours, and the old Lily, the careful one, had read every word of the insert that came inside the orange box. The math came out bad. If he raped her now, she could get pregnant.

She rolled over and lashed out with both legs, kicking Greg's feet out from under him. Bright pain exploded in her bad ankle, but the move worked; Greg went down, an expression of almost comical surprise on his face. Lily tried to get up, but he had bruised her ribs, if not something worse, and her left arm wouldn't respond to commands. She couldn't get herself off the ground. She began to crawl, leaning on her right side, dragging herself sideways across the grass toward the kitchen door. In the center of the kitchen island sat a polished wooden block, and its gleaming surface hid more than a dozen knives. Picturing the smoothness of the big butcher knife, its weight in her hands, Lily felt a nearly dizzying excitement, and began to pant as she dragged herself along. Right arm out, as far as her shoulder socket would allow, and then drag her body to catch up. But her arm was already starting to ache. Lily had never been so conscious of her own physical weakness; she remembered Dorian doing pushups despite her stitches, thought longingly of the tough ripple of muscle along Dorian's arms. She tasted blood.

A hand grabbed her bad ankle, making her squeal in pain. Lily peered over her shoulder and saw that Greg had hit something when he fell; fresh blood covered his chin. But he was still grinning, even with the bright red stream slavering from his mouth. He squeezed her ankle, and Lily screamed as she felt something grind together in there: muscle or bone, it didn't matter which, it was all mixed up in a bright implosion of pain. She tried to kick Greg in the face, but there was no leverage while she was lying on her side. She yanked her foot from his hand and pulled herself closer to the kitchen door, thinking only how good the handle of the big butcher knife would feel, how smooth in her hand ... if she could reach it. But she only made it a few more feet before Greg grabbed her again, by the calf this time, his fingers digging in.

"Where you goin', Lily? Where the fuck you think you'll go?"

His voice came thickly, almost bubbling behind her. Lily wondered if he had broken a tooth. She tried to wriggle forward again, but he worked a hand beneath her hip and flipped her over, neatly as a pancake, before crawling on top of her. He put a hand between her legs and squeezed. Lily screamed, but her screams were muffled against his shirt. She took a deep, gasping breath, filled with the sandalwood of his cologne, and felt vomit begin to work its way up her throat. And now, incredibly, Greg was muttering, "Say you love me, Lily."

He had managed to pin both of her wrists over her head with one hand. Lily hawked back and spat, feeling thin pleasure as he recoiled.

"I hate you," she hissed. "I fucking *hate* you."

Greg punched her in the face. His fist missed her still-healing nose, but the bridge tingled with warning pain. Greg unbuttoned her jeans and Lily struggled harder, screaming, furious that it could still be this way, right here, with her husband's broad shoulders and thick arms pinning her down.

"Get off her. Right now."

Greg froze. Lily peered over his shoulder and saw Jonathan, his dark eyes wide and furious, holding a gun to the back of Greg's head.

"Up, asshole."

Greg eased off her, sinking back to rest on his knees, and Lily scrambled away, panting hoarsely. She could already feel heavy pressure high on the ridge of her cheekbone, the beginnings of a shiner. She fumbled with her jeans for a moment before she got them buttoned.

"What are you doing, Johnny?" Greg asked, blinking up at Jonathan as though trying to place him. Lily pushed herself to her feet, but found that her ankle would take no weight. She balanced on the other foot, tottering awkwardly.

"You all right, Mrs. M.?" Jonathan asked, never taking his eyes from Greg.

"Fine. My ankle's broken, I think."

"Whatever you think you saw," Greg began, "marital

disputes are resolved between husband and wife, Johnny. That's the law."

"The law," Jonathan repeated, and his mouth twisted up into something that might have been a smile.

"Why don't you go back to the house, and we'll forget this ever happened? I won't even report it."

"That right? You won't?" Jonathan's words were beginning to broaden, southern twang showing up between each carefully spoken consonant. Dorian had called him South Carolina, Lily remembered, in an early morning that already seemed like years ago. She stared, transfixed, at the gun barrel pressed against the back of Greg's skull.

"Come on, Johnny. You know me."

Jonathan grinned wide, a rictus that showed all of his white teeth. "Yes, indeed, Mr. Mayhew. We have boys like you where I come from. Three of them took my sister for a ride once."

He turned to Lily. "Go inside, Mrs. M."

"No."

"You don't need to see this."

"Of course I do."

"Johnny, put the gun away. Remember who you work for."

Jonathan began to laugh, but it was hollow laughter, and his dark eyes blazed. "Oh, I do. And I'll tell you a secret, Mayhew. The man I work for wouldn't even think twice."

He shot Greg in the back of the head.

Lily couldn't stop a small shriek as Greg's body fell forward to land at her feet. Jonathan leaned down, planted the gun at Greg's temple and fired another shot. The reverberation was very loud, bouncing off the backyard walls. Security would come now, Lily thought, whether they had found the Mercedes yet or not.

Jonathan wiped the gun barrel on his dark pants and put it away. At Lily's feet, half of Greg's head was blown away, leaking steadily into the bright green perfection of the lawn. Lily looked down and found herself covered with gore, but most of the blood was hers, from the cuts on her arms.

"You need a doctor," Jonathan told her.

"I have bigger problems now," Lily replied, then reached out and grasped his shoulder. "Thank you." The words were not enough, but she could think of nothing better, and now she heard the first siren, still distant, somewhere downtown. Someone must have called Security when Lily went through the glass doors. "They're coming. You should go."

"No." Jonathan's face was resigned. "We take responsibility."

"You can't stay here!"

"Sure I can."

"Jonathan. They'll never listen. Even if I told them everything, they wouldn't listen. They'll kill you."

"Probably. But I had to do it."

Lily nodded, trying to think. Even now, at the strangest of all times, the better world was in her head, crowding out all else, every other consideration. It was the river that held her, she saw now, the river with its deep blue water. She had failed in Boston, but here was another chance.

"Give me the gun."

"What?"

"Give me the gun and get out of here."

Jonathan shook his head.

"Listen to me. They'll be coming for me anyway, sooner or later. I can tell the same story, and I have better evidence. Look at me; I'm a mess."

"You won't do any better, Mrs. M.; Security is Frewell's

organization, right down to its bones. They'll look at your face and arms, believe every word you say, and find you guilty, all the same."

"He won't let me go, Jonathan. On the ship. I asked and he said no."

"I'm sorry."

"But you have to go." Lily looked down at Greg's corpse, wishing she were as brave as the rest of them, but she knew she was not, and she needed Jonathan to leave, now, before she lost her nerve. "We take care of each other, yes? You did this for me. Now I want you to go."

"They execute wives who kill their husbands."

"I'm dead anyway," Lily retorted, taking a shot in the dark. "On September first, right?"

Jonathan swallowed.

"Isn't that what's going to happen?"

"Mrs. M.—"

She reached out and grasped the barrel of the gun. Jonathan resisted for a moment, then let it slide bonelessly from his fingers. The sirens were louder now, leaving downtown and entering the quiet maze of streets that had made up Lily's adult life.

"Go. Think about him, not me. Help him."

Jonathan's dark face had gone pale. "They'll check your hands. For powder. Fire a shot into the ground."

"I will. Go."

He hesitated a moment longer, then headed for the wall and climbed it, in almost the exact spot where Dorian had fallen down. Even in the midst of her terror, this symmetry pleased Lily; she felt that she had now come full circle, completed the journey from the woman she had been pretending to be to the woman she really was. At the top of the wall,

Jonathan turned and gave Lily a last reluctant look, but she waved him away with the gun, relieved when he dropped soundlessly into the Williamses' yard, out of sight.

Lily planted herself, aiming the gun at the ground several feet away. She knew that guns recoiled, but she was still unprepared for the force of the shot, which sent her sprawling backward. The gunshot echoed around the garden, and as it faded, Lily heard the squeal of tires turning onto her street.

I killed my husband. He was beating on me and I shot him.

How did you get the gun?

I took it from Jonathan the last time he drove me down-town. Tuesday.

Bullshit. He would've noticed it was gone.

That was true. Lily tried again. *What if I tell them it was Greg's gun?*

The gun's tagged. They'll only need to scan it to know it was Jonathan's.

She couldn't think of a response. Jonathan was right; the story was too flimsy, no matter who did the telling. Greg was dead, shot by two bullets from Jonathan's gun. Last night, Lily had gone outside the wall alone and come back with Jonathan. They would either think that Jonathan had killed him, or that she and Jonathan had done it together. No one would care about Lily's black eye, the cuts on her face and arms. It was all over now; she was a woman who had killed her husband. She thought of the executions that played regularly on the giant screen in the living room: men and women turning pale as the poison hit their veins, drowning them in their own lung fluid. Their agonized gasping always seemed to go on forever before they finally succumbed, and Greg would laugh at Lily when she tried to cover her ears.

They died with bulging, pleading eyes, like fish in the bottom of a boat.

Lily dropped the gun and closed her eyes. When Security burst into the backyard, she was standing on a high brown hill, miles of grain all around her, staring down at the deep blue river that ribboned the land below. She didn't hear them speak to her, didn't understand their questions. She was caught by the world around her, Tear's world, Tear's creation, the sights and sounds of the land, even the smell: freshly turned earth and a tang of salt that reminded her of childhood trips to the Maine shore. Lily didn't feel them pin her arms behind her back and march her toward the front door. She didn't feel anything at all, not even when they pushed her into the back of the truck.

For the first time, Kelsea opened her eyes and found herself not in her library, but in the arms room.

"There you are, Lady."

She blinked and found Pen on one side, Elston on the other.

"What am I doing here?"

"You wandered in." Pen released her. "You've been all over the Queen's Wing."

"What time is it?"

"Almost midnight."

Less than two hours gone. Lily's life was moving faster now. Kelsea blinked and saw, as if through a thin veil, the dark tin box of the Security truck, its armored inner walls. It was night again; flashes of street lighting spilled intermittently through the small slats near the ceiling, fleeing over her hands and legs before it disappeared. Lily was right there, not centuries away, not over the borders of unconsciousness, as she had once been, but *right there* inside Kelsea's mind. If she wanted to, Kelsea could reach out and touch her, make Lily scratch her forearm or close her eyes. They were bound.

"Only crossing," Kelsea whispered, clutching her sapphires. Who had said that? She couldn't remember anymore. "Only crossing."

"Lady?"

"I'm going back, Pen."

"Back where?" Elston asked crossly. "Sooner or later, Lady, you'll have to sleep."

"Back under, I think," Pen replied, but his voice was already distant. Dimly, Kelsea remembered something she was supposed to do, something about the Red Queen. But Lily took precedence now. Another flash intruded: Lily being pulled from the truck and marched down a long staircase, her eyes blinded by glaring fluorescent light. A wave of nausea broke over Kelsea like a wave, and she remembered that Lily had hit the double doors headfirst. Did she have a concussion? "You stay, Pen. Don't let me fall."

"Go, El."

"I'll get the Captain," Elston muttered. "Christ, what a mess it all turned out to be."

He said the last bit quietly, as though hoping Kelsea wouldn't hear. But if she could have found her voice, she would have agreed with him. It *had* all gone wrong, but where was the tipping point? Where had all of her good intentions fallen apart? Lily's feet tangled on the stairs, and Kelsea lurched forward. She grabbed for the armrail, found there was none, and stumbled.

"Get the fuck up!"

"Lady?"

G et the fuck up!"
Lily pushed herself off the wall and regained her feet. These were not the polite guards of the New Canaan Security station. Four men surrounded Lily; three carried small oblong objects, some sort of electrical prod, while the fourth carried a gun.

Lily needed a doctor. None of the cuts on her arms had been very deep; they were already beginning to scab. But she had taken an ugly slice on her scalp when she went through the glass doors, and blood was steadily oozing through the hair on the right side of her head. From time to time nausea beset her; the last attack had been so bad that she nearly collapsed. But she fought it, hard, because those taser-type weapons looked well used. As a child, Lily had once stuck her finger into the socket of a desk lamp that was missing its bulb, and she would never forget the brief, burning agony that had taken her hand in that moment. The four men who surrounded her didn't seem the sort to think twice before giving her a jolt.

They had kept her at the New Canaan station until early afternoon, in a dingy cell that was still years removed from the terrible conditions Lily would have imagined. There was no one else in the cell with her; it was dirty from disuse, not overuse. New Canaan's Security probably never hosted prisoners; there was no petty crime there. Lily was in the cell for hours, but she never spotted so much as a single roach. She hadn't slept in more than thirty hours, and she was exhausted. Hungry too, but the sharpness of that hunger quickly began to fade against her thirst. She didn't know if they would have given her water at the station, but she had forgotten to ask. Now her throat felt as though someone had gone at it with sandpaper.

When the sun was just beginning to set, they had taken her from the cell and loaded her onto another truck. Lily didn't know how long the journey had been, only that night fell long before they came to a halt, and when they pulled her from the truck, she found herself in a wasteland of bright fluorescence and asphalt. The better world had never seemed farther away than it did in that moment, Lily freezing cold from the long journey in only her T-shirt and jeans, blinded by the bright lights and the slow trickle of blood from her scalp. She tried to remember why she was here, but at that moment William Tear and his people seemed infinitely distant. Tracking backward through her memory, Lily realized that it was still only August 30, that September first was still two days away. Two days until the carnival, Parker had said, but Tear would never let a creature like Parker into his better world. So what was the carnival?

What does it matter now?

But no matter how many times Lily had asked herself this question during the interminable truck ride, she remained unconvinced. Carnivals were excess and abandon, doing anything you liked. Lily was no extraordinary empathist, but it took only a few minutes for her mind to slip into Parker's, conjure an image, and spread it out before her like a mural. Parker's carnival would be the same as any other: excess and abandon, brought now into the limitless range of the monstrous, troubled world they all lived in, a world of walls that separated the privileged from the deprived. And the deprived were angry. Lily's mind created the pictures faster than she could push them away, and by the time they reached the Security compound, she had seen the end of the world inside her head, a bacchanal of rage and revenge. Parker's glee was easy to understand now; he might be too debased for the better world, but on the first of September, Tear meant to turn him loose in this one.

I should tell Security, Lily thought. *I should warn someone.*

But that was impossible. Even if anyone would believe her, there was no way to tell them about Parker without also telling them about Tear. They were going to ask her about Tear anyway, no doubt, and despite Tear's words, Lily suspected that she wouldn't last long under interrogation.

I can't tell them anything. Lily steeled herself against another wave of nausea. *I keep quiet until the second of September. That's my job. It's all I can do for them now.*

One of the guards opened a plain black metal door and stood back. "Find her an empty room."

They marched Lily down a dark, narrow corridor filled with doors. Lily was swamped with sudden déjà vu, so strong that it crashed over her mind like a wave, obscuring everything. She had been here before. She was certain of it.

They sat her down in a small room whose fluorescent light barely provided enough of a thin, sickly glow to illuminate a steel table and two chairs that were bolted to the ground. The man with the gun cuffed Lily to the chair, and then she was left, staring blankly at the wall, as the door closed behind them.

Greg was dead. Lily kept this idea firmly in front of her, for despite her current predicament, there was comfort in it. No matter what happened now, it would not be Greg, not ever again. She fell asleep and dreamed that she was back in the backyard, trying to crawl toward the kitchen door. Something terrible was behind her, and Lily knew that if she could only reach the door, there would be solace there. She was searching for the door handle when a hand grabbed her ankle, making her scream. The backyard blew apart and now she was in the long, door-filled corridor again, stumbling along, lost. The light was a dim orange: not fluorescents, but torchlight, and Greg was no longer important, Greg was nothing, because she held a great fate in her hands, the fate of a country, the fate of–

"The Tearling," Lily muttered, jerking awake. The dream dissolved, leaving her with the confused afterimage of a torch behind her eyes. Someone had just doused her with water. She was soaking wet.

"There you are."

The back of the chair seemed to have dug claws into her spine, and Lily groaned as she straightened. She felt as though she had slept for hours. It might even be morning, but there was no way to tell inside this tiny, cramped room.

Across from her sat a thin blade of a man with a pointed face and wide dark eyes punctuated by arching, neatly sculpted black eyebrows. His legs were crossed, one on top of the other, his hands folded on his knee. His posture was very prim, but somehow it fit the room around him. Beneath his dark Security uniform, the man looked like an accountant with several secret nasty habits. He had brought up a screen on the table beneath him, and Lily saw her own upside-down face peering at her from the steel surface.

"Lily Mayhew, née Freeman. You had a busy day."

Lily merely stared at him, her face blank and bewildered, though the sense of futility struck her again. She couldn't act for shit.

"Where is this place?"

"You don't care," the accountant answered pleasantly. "All you care about is how you can get out, isn't that right?"

"I don't understand."

"Oh, you do, Mrs. Mayhew. One of the qualities that

gained me my present position is a great talent for sniffing out a member of the Blue Horizon. You have the same look as the rest of them, something around the eyes . . . you all look like you'd seen Christ himself and come back to tell the tale. Have you seen Christ, Mrs. Mayhew?"

Lily shook her head.

"What did you see?"

"I don't know what you're talking about," Lily replied patiently. "I thought I was here because of my husband."

"You are, certainly. But national security trumps local crime, and I have a lot of latitude in such matters. It could go either way, really. On the one hand we have Lily Mayhew, the brutally battered wife whose life was in danger, who acted to defend herself. And on the other, we have Lily Mayhew, the cheating cunt who screwed her black bodyguard—a *separatist* black bodyguard, just to add to the fun—and then convinced him to help her murder her husband."

He leaned forward, still smiling the pleasant smile. "Latitude, you see, Mrs. Mayhew. It really could go either way."

Lily stared at him, unable to reply. Everything inside her seemed to be frozen.

Screwed Jonathan? Did he really say that?

"Now, me, I'm not interested in your husband. In fact, I too thought Greg was an asshole. But I am extremely interested, one might almost say obsessively interested, in what you were doing down at the Port of Boston early yesterday morning."

"I wasn't," Lily replied. A frog was in her throat, and she coughed it out. "I was heading that way, but I got carjacked on Highway Eighty-Four, just over the state line into Massachusetts."

The accountant's smile widened, and he shook his head. "A tragedy! Do go on."

"I called my bodyguard to come and get me, and he brought me home."

"That is very neat." His fingers played over the steel surface of the table, and a moment later Lily heard her own voice, echoing from speakers on her left.

"Jonathan?"

"Where are you, Mrs. M.?" The static that had covered the call was entirely gone now, Jonathan's voice crystal clear.

"Mrs. M.?"

"I'm on my way to Boston."

"What's in Boston?"

"The warehouse! They're in trouble, Jonathan, all of them. Greg had Arnie Welch over for dinner—"

"Mrs. M.? I can't hear you! Don't come to Boston!"

"Jonathan?"

The call broke off.

"Your tag tells a better story than you do, Mrs. Mayhew. Last night, you traveled up to Boston, to Conley Terminal, and you were there most of the night." The neat little man in front of Lily smiled again, and Lily noticed that he had a real mouthful of teeth, white and square and neat, too neat to be anything but implants. "There are only two ways for this to play out. You can tell me what you know, in which case I will be tempted—though I promise nothing—to paint you as Lily Mayhew, the sympathetic battered wife. It's a terrible crime, to kill your husband, but there are ways around that, even when your husband was Greg Mayhew, Defense Department liaison and all-around Good Citizen. I'm not God, so you'll likely serve a couple of years, but they will be soft years, and when you get out, your husband's money, your beautiful house in New Canaan, your three cars, all of it will be waiting for you. You can start a new life."

His words made Lily think of Cath Alcott, who had gotten into her car one night with her three children and simply vanished. She wondered if Cath had had any money. It changed everything, money. It was the difference between vanishing without a trace and simply dying in some dark place with no one to know or care. Lily thought of the group of people she had seen hunched around the bonfire beside Highway 84 . . . and then the man's voice jerked her back.

"If you say nothing, we go to work on you, and you tell anyway. Don't even kid yourself that you'll be able to stay silent. There's never been a member of your little group that I couldn't break. But if you waste my precious time and delay my investigation, I guarantee that you'll be Lily Mayhew, the cheating whore who shot her husband, and after I'm done with you, you'll die by the needle."

Lily held silent during this speech, though his words made her stomach twist into thick, ropy knots. She was no good with pain, never had been. She feared the dentist, even a cleaning. It was all she could do to drag herself into Manhattan once a year to allow Dr. Anna to poke the horribly uncomfortable speculum between her legs. But the thought of Dr. Anna steadied Lily as well, reminded her that William Tear wasn't the only one who could be hurt if she opened her mouth.

"I'll give you thirty minutes to think it over," the accountant told her, rising from the table. "In the meantime, I'm sure you're hungry and thirsty."

Lily nodded miserably. She was thirsty, so much so that she could feel each individual tooth throbbing in its own dry socket. He left the room and she bent to lay her head on the table, feeling the sting of tears behind her eyes. She searched for the better world, but there was nothing now; she could not call it up in her imagination as she had so many times before. The better world was gone, and without it she wouldn't last long.

Am I really this weak? She thought that the answer might be yes. There had always been something flimsy inside her. Greg must have sensed it; in fact, Lily saw now, Greg might have understood her better than anyone else ever had. All of Lily's bravery only kicked in when there was little risk involved. When the chips were down, she folded. She thought of being alone in their enormous house, of having all of that space to herself, to do as she pleased, without Greg's shadow lurking around every corner. It would be an amazing thing.

Bullshit, Maddy whispered. *They're never going to let you go. And even if they did, you think they'd let a single woman keep all of that money, do as she pleases? In New Canaan? In any city?*

Lily smiled gently. Maddy was right, it was a pipe dream. The little accountant had looked straight through Lily and seen what she wanted more than anything—freedom, the ability to live her own life—and then dangled it in front of her like a cheap toy. Lily Mayhew, née Freeman, had been weak all of her life, but she had never been dumb.

"I won't break," she whispered silently into her crossed arms, into the wetness of tears. "Please, just this once, let me not break."

The door opened with a hollow clang, and a hulking man with a soldier's buzz cut came in, carrying a tray. Lily sat up eagerly, hating herself, but she was too hungry and thirsty to stage a hunger strike. She guzzled the water, then attacked the meat, a cold lump of unidentifiable off-white gristle that didn't seem to taste like anything at all. The food only made her more hungry, and then it was done. She pushed the tray to one side, staring at the grey cement walls around her. The accountant had told her to think it over, but now she could think of nothing but all of them: Tear, Dorian, Jonathan. Where were they now?

With the ships, her mind answered. *Wherever the ships are, that's where they'll be.*

Lily felt certain that this was true. Tear would let Parker loose, and now Lily saw exactly how Parker fit in with the program: he was a distraction, a smokescreen for Security. While Parker was wreaking havoc, Tear's people would board the ships, and then they would leave.

Leave for where? There's nowhere to go! Do you really think he'll sail off the edge of the earth and straight into paradise?

Lily did. The image was eerily persuasive: an entire flotilla of ships, all of them heading toward an unknown horizon where the sun was just beginning to rise. This vision didn't feel like Lily's; rather, it was as though someone else was dreaming inside her head. Did any of them know what was on the other side of that horizon? No, Lily felt certain they had no idea. They would probably end up sinking in the middle of the ocean. Did she really want to face everything that the accountant threatened for that?

Tear. Dorian. Jonathan.

The door clanged open again. The accountant had returned, and he stood over her, smiling broadly, his hands tucked behind his back.

"Well, Lily, what's it to be?"

She looked up at him, sweat misting her brow, her guts sick with anticipation. But the words came out strong and clear, not her own words, and Lily suddenly felt as though there was another woman inside her, someone trying to hold her together, to get her through.

"Fuck it. Let's go."

CHAPTER 13

SEPTEMBER FIRST

Faustus: *Come, I think hell's a fable.*
Mephistopheles: *Ay, think so still, until experience change thy mind.*

—*Doctor Faustus*, CHRISTOPHER MARLOWE *(pre-Crossing Angl.)*

When Kelsea broke free this time, Mace was with her. Both of his arms were locked around her waist, dragging her back, and Kelsea saw that she'd been heading toward the great double doors at the far end of her audience chamber.

"Was I going somewhere?"

"God knows, Lady."

I was. But where?

The answer came: her mother's face, beautiful and thoughtless. Mace released her and she gestured toward the door. "Come on, Lazarus. Let's go down to the portrait gallery."

"Now?"

"Now. Just you and me."

Pen's face stiffened, but at a nod from Mace, he faded back toward the hallway. Kelsea couldn't afford to worry about Pen's feelings now; she checked her watch and found that it was past one in the morning. She was running out of time.

By unspoken consent, they did not take Mace's tunnel this time. Instead, Kelsea marched out her front door, down the long hallway that fronted the Queen's Wing, and into the Keep proper. They had run out of extra rooms long ago, and now even the corridors were lined with people, most of whom seemed to be wide awake. The smell of unwashed bodies was dreadful. As Kelsea went by, they bowed, murmured, reached to touch the hem of her dress, and she nodded in acknowledgment, barely seeing them, secure in the knowledge that if anyone tried anything, she could end him in an instant. An old woman blessed Kelsea as she went by, and Kelsea glimpsed an ancient rosary wrapped around her gnarled fingers. The Holy Father would scream if he knew that one of those was still knocking around; no one in the Arvath wanted sinners to be able to tell their own grace. Seeing the milky cataract that covered one of the woman's eyes, Kelsea reached out and grasped her hand before moving on. The flesh there felt bone-dry, like scales, and Kelsea was relieved to let go.

"May Great God protect and keep you, Majesty," the woman rasped behind her, and Kelsea felt something turn over inside her. Did they not know that she was going to die today? How could they not know that? She quickened her steps, determined to reach the portrait gallery before Lily took her again. She could feel Lily's need now, Lily's pain, eating into the edges of her mind, trying to drag her back, and for a moment she resented Lily, wondered why she couldn't pile her sorrows on someone else.

"Has there been word of Father Tyler?" she asked Mace.

"No. All I could find out is that he and a brother priest vanished from the Arvath several days ago, and the Holy Father is livid. He's offering a thousand pounds for Father Tyler, alive."

Kelsea halted for a moment, leaning against the wall. "If he hurts Father Tyler, I'll kill him, Lazarus."

"You won't need to, Lady. I'll kill him."

"I thought you didn't like priests."

"Why am I here, Lady? You no longer need protection. I could drop you in the middle of the Dry Lands and you'd likely walk out unscathed. These people are no danger to you. Why have you brought me along?"

"We started out together." They rounded a corner and began to descend a new staircase, this one smaller than the Main Stair and circular where the Main was square. People had crowded onto both the top and the bottom of the staircase, but they scrambled out of the way as Kelsea approached.

"You started off with all of us."

"No. That morning with the hawk, you remember? That's when I first knew I was the Queen, and it was just you and me."

Mace glanced sharply at her. "What are you planning, Lady?"

"What do you mean?"

"I know you. You scheme."

Kelsea veiled her thoughts, willing them out of her face. "When the sun comes up, I mean to go down to the bridge and try to parlay."

"The terms were nonnegotiable."

"Nothing is nonnegotiable, Lazarus, not if I have something she wants."

484

"She wants this city and all of its goods in plunder."

"True, it may not work. But I have to try. I'll take only four guards with me, including yourself and Pen. Choose the other two."

"Perhaps not Pen."

She halted, turning to face him. They were near the bottom of the staircase now, only a few turns to go, and Kelsea lowered her voice, mindful of the people who were undoubtedly below. "Something to say, Lazarus?"

"Come now, Lady. A besotted man makes a poor close guard."

"Pen's not besotted."

The corners of Mace's mouth twitched.

"What?"

"For a woman with remarkably clear vision in most areas, Lady, you are stone-blind in others."

"My private life is not your business."

"But Pen's professional life is, and just because I'll tolerate some things in the safety of the Queen's Wing doesn't mean I'll tolerate them elsewhere."

"Fine. It's up to you whether he comes or not." But Kelsea winced at the thought of Pen's reaction to being left behind. Was Mace right? Was Pen in love with her? It seemed impossible. Pen had his woman, and although Kelsea had her occasional possessive moments, the woman served a purpose, allowed Kelsea to feel as though she was doing no harm. She didn't want Pen invested in their arrangement. She wanted it to be private, something that never needed to be dragged into the light of day. She wished Mace had not said anything.

No point in fretting over it, she reminded herself. *Everything ends in a few hours.*

The portrait gallery was full of people, at least several families sleeping on the stone floor. But a few sharp bellows from Mace did the trick; parents scrambled to their feet, grabbed their children, and were gone. Kelsea shut the door at the far end of the gallery, and then it was just the two of them again, Mace and Kelsea, the way it had been at the beginning.

Kelsea went to stare at her mother's portrait. If her mother had been standing before her, Kelsea would have grabbed her by the throat, torn her hair out by the roots until she screamed for mercy. But how much of their current nightmare was really her mother's fault? Kelsea thought longingly of those early days in the Keep, days when blame had been clear-cut.

"Why did she give me away, Lazarus?"

"To protect you."

"Bullshit! Look at her! That's not the face of an altruist. Sending me away for fostering was utterly out of character. Did she hate me?"

"No."

"Then why?"

"What is the point of this little expedition, Lady? To whip yourself with your mother?"

"Ah, hell, Lazarus," Kelsea replied wearily. "If you're not going to talk to me, then go back upstairs."

"I can't leave you down here."

"Of course you can. As you pointed out yourself, no one here can harm me."

"Your mother thought the same thing."

"Queen Elyssa! Nothing but trash in the finest silk. Look at her!"

"Call her all the names you like, Lady. She still won't be the villain you wish her to be."

Kelsea whirled to stare at him. "Are you my father, Lazarus?"

Mace's mouth twisted. "No, Lady. I wish I was. I wanted to be. But I am not."

"Then who is?"

"Has it ever occurred to you that you might not *want* to know?"

No, that had not occurred. For a moment, Kelsea pondered the worst people it could be: Arlen Thorne? The Holy Father? Her uncle? Anything seemed possible. And did blood really matter so much? She had never cared about her father's identity; her mother was the important one, the one who had wrecked a kingdom. Kelsea stopped pacing, looked up, and found the portrait of the Beautiful Queen staring down at her. The favored child sat on her lap, smiling brightly, no dark corners, and behind the Beautiful Queen's skirts was the other, the dark child, the bastard, not loved and not special. Parentage *did* matter, Kelsea realized, even if it shouldn't. Pain stabbed into her vitals and she cried out, doubling over. It felt as though someone had kicked her right in the guts.

"Lady?"

Another blow, and now Kelsea shrieked, cradling her stomach. Mace reached her in two steps, but he could do nothing.

"Lady, what is it? Are you ill? Injured?"

"No. Not me." For Kelsea suddenly knew: somewhere, centuries away, Lily was paying the price for her silence. Lily needed her now, but Kelsea shied away, cowering inside her own mind. She wasn't sure she could face Lily's punishment. She didn't know how she would come out of this thing on the other side. Would she have to feel Lily die? Would she die herself?

"Lazarus." She looked up at Mace, seeing both sides balanced in equal measure: the angry boy who had emerged from the unimaginable hell beneath the Gut, and the man who had given his life in service to two queens. "If something happens to me—"

"Like what?"

"If something happens," she overrode him, "you will do several things. For me."

She paused, gasping. Bright, searing pain scorched her palm and Kelsea screamed, clenching her hand into a fist and pounding it against her leg. Mace moved toward her and she held up her other hand to halt him, gritting her teeth, fighting through it, blind with tears.

"What's doing this to you, Lady? Your sapphires?"

"It doesn't matter. If something happens to me, Lazarus, I trust you to look after these people and keep them safe. They fear you. Hell, they fear you more than they fear me."

"Not anymore, Lady."

Kelsea ignored his comment. The pain in her palm had lost its sharp edge now, but it still throbbed hotly in time with her pulse. Kelsea closed her eyes and saw a small metal rectangle gleaming in the bright white light, recognizable only through Lily's memories: a cigarette lighter. Someone had held Lily's hand to the flame.

Not someone, Kelsea thought. *The accountant.* A man of whom Arlen Thorne would have thoroughly approved. And Kelsea wondered suddenly whether humanity ever actually changed. Did people grow and learn at all as the centuries passed? Or was humanity merely like the tide, enlightenment advancing and then retreating as circumstances shifted? The most defining characteristic of the species might be lapse.

"What else, Lady?"

She straightened and unclenched her fist, ignoring the mouth of seared flesh that seemed to open up in her palm. "If he's still alive, you will find Father Tyler and keep him safe from the Arvath."

"Done."

"Last, you will do me a favor."

"What's that, Lady?"

"Clean out and seal off the Creche."

Mace's eyes narrowed. "Why, Lady?"

"This is *my* kingdom, Lazarus. I will have no dark subbasements here." Through Lily's eyes, Kelsea saw the warren of fluorescent hallways inside the Security compound, the endless doors, each of them hiding agony. Her palm throbbed. "No secret places where awful things go on, things that no one wants to acknowledge in the light of day. It's too high a price, even for freedom. Clean it out."

Mace's face twisted. For once, Kelsea read his thoughts easily: what she was asking would be terrible for him, and he didn't think she knew. She put a hand on his wrist, clutching the leather band that held several small knives. "What's your name?"

"Lazarus."

"No. Not the name they gave you in the ring. Your *real* name."

He stared at her, stricken. "Who—"

"What's your name?"

Mace blinked, and Kelsea thought she saw a bright sparkle in his eyes, but a moment later it was gone. "My first name is Christian. I don't know my surname. I was born in the Gut, to no parents at all."

"Fairy-born. So the rumors are true."

489

"I will not discuss that phase of my life, Lady, not even with you."

"Fair enough. But you will clean the place out." The room wavered before Kelsea's eyes, torchlight becoming electric for a moment before fading back. She wanted to see . . . she didn't want to see . . . she heard Lily screaming. Kelsea clenched her fists, willing the past away.

"You talk like one condemned, Lady. What do you mean to do?"

"We're all condemned, Lazarus." Kelsea's head jolted as a blow landed across her face. Lily was beginning to lose hope; Kelsea could feel despondency creeping in, a deadened numbness that echoed all through her mind. "You might need to take me back up, Lazarus. I don't have long."

"We can go back through the tunnels." Mace played with the wall for a moment, opening one of his many doors. "Where do you go in your fugues, Lady?"

"Backward. Before the Crossing."

"Backward in time?"

"Yes."

"Do you see him? William Tear?"

"Sometimes." On her way through the door, Kelsea reached up to touch her mother's canvas, the painted hem of her green dress, feeling rogue regret surface in her mind. No matter how hard she tried to hate the smiling woman in the portrait, she would have liked the chance to speak to her, at least once. "You knew my mother well, Lazarus. What would she have thought of me?"

"She would have found you too serious, Lady. Elyssa wasn't one to feel anguish on behalf of others, let alone of circumstances that couldn't be changed. She surrounded herself with similar people."

"Was my father a good man?"

A pained expression darted across Mace's face, then was gone, so quickly that Kelsea might have imagined it. But she knew she had not. "Yes, Lady. A very good man." He gestured into the darkness. "Come, or I'll end up carrying you. You've got that look about you."

"What look?"

"Like a drunk about to pass out."

With a last glance at her mother's portrait, Kelsea followed him into the tunnel. Through the walls, she could hear the murmur of many voices, even in the middle of the night, people too worried to sleep. They were all in equal danger now; lowborn or highborn, the army outside the wall would not make distinctions. Kelsea tried to picture the coming dawn, but could get no further than the end of the New London Bridge. Something was blocking her vision. Burning fire spread through Kelsea's arms, a tingling pain that moved on to her chest before attacking her legs. The pain intensified, and Kelsea halted in the darkness, unable to move. She had never felt anything like this; each nerve in her body seemed to have opened up wide, become an infinite conductor.

"Lady?"

"Make it stop," she whispered. She squeezed her eyes shut, feeling tears leak beneath the lids. Mace fumbled for her in the dark and Kelsea grabbed his hand, clung like a drowning man. "I don't want to see."

She couldn't hold herself up; it felt as though her nervous system had collapsed. All muscle control had gone from her legs. Mace grabbed her, lowering her softly to the ground, but the pain didn't stop. Every cell seemed to be on fire, and Kelsea screamed in the darkness, writhing on the rough stone.

"Take them off, Lady!"

Kelsea felt him tugging at the chains around her neck, and she slapped his hand away. But she didn't have the strength to fight him off. None of her muscles were working correctly, and the pain controlled everything. She tried to roll away, but could only wriggle helplessly on the floor.

"Quit, dammit!" Mace dug a hand beneath her neck and lifted her head from the floor. Strands of hair ripped from her scalp.

A warning, the dark part of her mind whispered. *That's all he needs.*

She concentrated on the hand that held the sapphires, first pressing, then digging. Mace grunted in pain, but did not let go, so Kelsea clawed at him now, opening up scratches.

"I know how valuable your hands are, Lazarus. Don't make me take them from you."

Mace hesitated, and she pressed even harder, digging inward toward the muscle until he swore and scrambled away.

Kelsea pulled herself into a sitting position, then rested her head on her knees. The pain had begun again, in her legs this time, and she realized now that she had no choice. Lily's time was an open doorway, and there was no going halfway through.

"Lazarus," she croaked into the dark.

"Lady?"

"I'm going back. I can't stop it." She stretched out on the floor, feeling the blessed coolness of stone against her face. "Don't try to take them off while I'm gone, either. I'm not responsible for what might happen."

"Keep telling yourself so, Lady."

She wanted to snap at him, but now Lily was upon her,

Lily's mind slipping inside her own the way a hand would slip inside a perfectly fitted glove. The pain had faded again; Lily had taken refuge in her own imagination, her vision of the better world, fields and a river seen from atop a hill. Kelsea recognized the view: the Almont, as it looked from the hills of New London, and the Caddell stretching into the distance. But there was no city yet in Lily's dreams, only the wide-open land running toward the horizon . . . a clean slate. Kelsea would have given anything for that land, that opportunity, but it was too late.

"Had enough yet?"

Kelsea barked laughter, a helpless doglike sound. She looked up and saw the grinning, sharklike face of the accountant, and the laughter died in her throat.

I said, have you had enough?"

Lily blinked as sweat ran into her eyes, stinging and blinding. She had found that once she answered an innocuous question, it became that much easier to answer a question that mattered. Now she held silent.

"Ah, Lily." The accountant shook his head sadly. "Such a waste of a pretty woman."

Bile collected in Lily's throat, but she swallowed it down, knowing that if she got sick, it would make everything hurt more. She blinked the sweat from her eyes and shot a glance at the assistant who controlled the box, a tall, bald man with dead, watery eyes that seemed to focus on nothing. The assistant had come and gone many times, bringing pieces of equipment, or notes which the accountant would read quickly, his eyes advancing and then returning in a precise typewriter fashion before handing the note back. Then the assistant would leave again. But now he appeared to be here for good, his finger on the console that made agony travel all over Lily's body. Tiny wireless electrodes seemed to be strapped everywhere; they hadn't put one between her legs yet, but Lily felt certain that they would get there in time.

She had no idea how long she had been in this room. There was no time, only the lulls that the accountant gave her, she felt sure, to contemplate what he might do next. She could have asked him for the date, but even that seemed like it might alert him that something was going on, that time mattered somehow. She was trying to hold on until the first of September, but in truth, it could already have been the fifth or the sixth for all Lily knew. Her muscles throbbed, her hand throbbed. They had stitched the wound in her scalp, but no one had tended to her hand, and the burning hole in her palm had blackened and then crisped over with pus, like a crust on a filthy pie. The assistant's comings and goings were the only way to mark the passage of time. Sometimes the accountant would leave the room as well, shutting off the lights. Another purposeful maneuver, Lily was sure, leaving her alone in the dark.

And yet she was not alone. With every hour that went by, Lily became more aware of the other woman. She came and went, sometimes merely flickering on the edge of Lily's consciousness and sometimes right there. The feeling was nothing Lily could explain to anyone, even herself, but nevertheless the woman was there, just beyond a thin veil, feeling Lily's pain, her fright, her exhaustion. And this woman was *strong*; Lily could sense that strength, like a great lamp shining in the darkness. She was strong the way William Tear was strong, and that strength buoyed Lily up, kept her from opening her mouth and screaming out the answers the accountant wanted to hear. As the hours went on, Lily became more and more certain of something else: this woman knew about the better world. She had seen it, understood it, longed for it with all her heart.

Who are you? Lily wanted to ask. But then the assistant pressed the button again and it was all she could do to cling to the other woman, like a child to its mother's knees, begging for solace. When the electricity was on, Lily forgot all about the better world. There was only pain, white-hot agony that flared beneath her skin, wiping everything else away ... except the woman. Lily tried to think of Maddy, Dorian, Jonathan, Tear, but she could feel herself wearing down. Several times, the pain had ceased just when she was at the point of begging them to stop. She thought of her old life, when she used to be afraid of bee stings, and the thought made her giggle, a dark and senseless giggle that died on its way to the walls of the room, this room that was the only thing left.

"Keep on laughing, Lily. You can end this at any time."

The accountant's voice betrayed irritation. He was growing tired, Lily thought, and this gave birth to new hope: at some point, wouldn't he have to go away and sleep? They could give her to someone else, of course, another interrogator, but the accountant didn't strike her as the sort who would let go. He was a hunter, waiting patiently for the moment when she would break, and he wouldn't want the satisfaction of that moment to go to anyone else, not when he had done so much to loosen the lid.

The pain stopped, and Lily's entire body sagged with relief. Earlier, she had been trying to think of positive things to cling to, and at this odd moment, one occurred to her: she didn't have children. If she had, these people would certainly have made use of them by now. She wondered whether

Mom was in some kind of custody, whether they had come to the nice suburban neighborhood in Media and hauled Mom away.

"Come on now, Lily. You know you'll give it up sooner or later. Why prolong this? Wouldn't you like some food? Wouldn't you like me to let you sleep?"

Lily said nothing, noting with relief that the assistant was standing up and leaving the console. The accountant was a busy man; his assistant was constantly fetching him messages, and Lily thought he must have many other projects. But God help her, she had his full attention now. Behind the glasses, those round, birdlike eyes pinned her where she sat.

"Tell me a little something, Lily, and I'll give you a break for a while. Just tell me *why* you went to Conley Terminal the other night."

Lily felt her consciousness beginning to waver. Her vision had blurred again. There could be no harm in answering the accountant's question . . . after all, he already knew, didn't he?

Focus!

Lily's mind sharpened for a moment. Those words were not Dorian's, not Maddy's. And now she realized that she was actually hearing the other woman, her thoughts inside Lily's mind, so tightly wrapped that Lily might have mistaken them for her own.

The other night.

It definitely wasn't August 30 anymore. Had William Tear and his people gotten away? Lily would have given her life for the correct date, but she couldn't ask.

The assistant left the room, the door booming closed, and for no reason at all, Lily suddenly thought of her father, who had died years ago. Dad had hated President Frewell, hated the proliferation of Security offices in each city and town. But there was no organized resistance then. Dad had been a fighter with nothing to fight for, no one to fight with.

Dad would have liked William Tear, Lily realized now, her eyes stinging with tears. *Dad would have fought for him.*

"Last chance, my girl." There would be no respite; the accountant had moved over to the man to console himself. Lily clenched her toes in preparation, grabbing the arms of the chair. The accountant sat down and smiled pleasantly at her, a predator's smile in a bureaucrat's face, then clucked in mock concern.

"Tell me, Lily . . . whatever turned a nice woman like you into a cunt like this?"

He reached for the console, and the lights went out.

For a long moment, Lily could only hear her harsh, frightened breathing in the darkness. Then she heard shouts and cries in the hallway outside, muffled by the metal door. Beneath her feet, the ground trembled, and Lily was seized with joy, a fierce joy that bordered on ecstasy in the dark.

September first! her mind exulted. She knew, suddenly, that it had come, the end of the old, diseased world. *September first!*

Somewhere, far away, an alarm began to squawk. More muffled screams echoed from the hallway. The accountant's chair scraped back, and Lily drew up into a ball, expecting him to find her at any moment. She could hear the grating crunch of his feet on the concrete floor, but whether he was near or across the room, Lily couldn't tell. She began to feel her way around the arms of her chair, looking for a sharp edge, a nail, anything, tugging as hard as she could against the short reach of the handcuffs. This was her only chance, and if she didn't take it, if they managed to get the lights back on, the pain might go on forever.

The door thrummed, a deep metal gonging sound, and Lily jumped, banging her head against the back of the chair. Several sharp beeps punctuated the darkness: a gun being loaded. Lily could find no sharp edges on the arms of the chair—*of course not,* she thought, *of course there wouldn't be*—and so she began to work on one of the handcuffs that bound her to the chair's arms. She was fine-boned, with thin wrists, but no matter what she did, the cuff wouldn't slip off the protrusion below her thumb. She continued to pull at it, not stopping even when she felt the first trickle of blood. Sometime in the last forty-eight hours, Lily had discovered the great secret of pain: it thrived on the unknown, on the knowledge that there was a greater pain out there, something more excruciating that might yet be reached. The body was constantly waiting. When you took away the uncertainty, when you controlled the pain yourself, it was infinitely easier to bear, and Lily yanked at the handcuff, gritting her teeth, hissing the pain away through pursed lips.

The door boomed again, a much deeper sound, metal hitting metal, and a moment later the hinges burst apart, emitting a silver rectangle of light from some sort of halo device. When Lily was little, they used to take such lights camping, but this one was infinitely brighter, turning the door into a rectangular sun in the darkness. Lily threw up a hand to cover her eyes, but it was too late; she was already blind, her eyes burning, leaking salt. The room was full of gunfire, quick sharp clicks and the metallic ping of bullets bouncing from metal walls. A thin slice of pain tore across Lily's bicep. The backs of her eyelids seemed to be on fire.

"Mrs. M.!"

A hand clasped her shoulder, shook her hard, but even when Lily opened her eyes, all she could see was white fire.

"Jonathan?"

"Hold still for a minute."

Lily held still. There was one sharp crack of metal, then another, impacts that reverberated all the way up her arms.

"There, you're out. Come on."

"I can't see."

"I can. But I can't hold you up. You need to walk."

Lily let him pull her to her feet, though pins and needles awoke roaring in her feet and calves. She stumbled along, Jonathan's arm tucked behind her shoulders. To her left, she heard a gagging rattle, the sound of someone choking. She could see shadows now, bright beams of flashlights in the darkness. The choking intensified, becoming a loud gargling sound that made Lily wince, and then it ceased.

"We have to go!" a voice squealed, so high and panicky that Lily couldn't tell whether it was a man or a woman. "They're bringing the secondary backups online! The power's already on in Building C!"

"Keep your pants on," a woman drawled, and Lily swung toward the voice, though all she could see was another bright blue shadow.

"Dorian?"

"Come on, Mrs. M." Jonathan took her arm, pulling her along. "Gotta move, time is short."

Is it September first? But there was no time for her to ask. They hustled her out the door—Lily skinned her elbow on the busted frame on the way out, but said nothing—and down the hallway, which was still dark. Lily blinked continuously, trying to force her sight back. Scattered light arced across the hall—flashlights—and Jonathan's hand urged her to go faster. Lily heard pounding on the doors as they passed; people were still trapped in there, behind magnetic locks, and now Lily understood Jonathan's urgency. All Security facilities were supposed to have several sources of emergency power in case of a failure; Dorian and Jonathan must have sabotaged more than one, but they had not killed them all. Beneath her feet, buried deep in the stone, Lily felt intermittent thumps as someone tried to bring the building back online.

A figure stepped into the flashlight beams, some ten feet in front of them, and Lily halted, recognizing a Security uniform. The man was big and rangy-looking, and he held up a huge black machine rifle, one that could fire either bullets or darts; Greg used something very similar whenever he went deer hunting with his cronies in Vermont.

"Where are you going with her?"

Behind Lily, someone snarled, a soft sound that made the hairs stand up on the back of her neck.

"She's being transferred to Washington."

Lily knew that voice: it was the accountant's assistant, the bald man who had spent most of the night with his hand on the console. He was on Jonathan's other side, still in his uniform, but when Lily screwed up her eyes to focus, she saw that his face was a grotesque white mask of panic. She was beyond surprise now, beyond reaction; the presence of the assistant merely registered, poking the bubble of her mind with a soft finger, then retreating.

"On whose orders?"

"Special orders from Major Langer." But the assistant's voice was unsteady, and the guard wasn't buying it, even Lily could tell. Dimly, outside the glow of their flashlights, she spotted someone moving down the hallway wall, a sliding shadow in the darkness.

"Where is Langer?"

"He's writing his report." The assistant licked his lips, and Lily heard the dry rasp of his tongue. "I'm supposed to take her outside to the car."

"Who are these others?"

The shape on the wall launched itself onto the guard, knocking him to the ground. The gun chattered as the guard went down, bullets pinging off the walls and floors. Jonathan's arm dropped away from Lily's back, and she heard the thud of his body hitting the ground. Jonathan's flashlight had fallen to the concrete, and in the dim light she saw William Tear, his knee planted in the guard's stomach, both thumbs jammed into the man's eyes. Lily grabbed the discarded flashlight and shone it around until she found Jonathan's feet. The guard screamed, making her jump, and the light jigged crazily around the hallway. For a moment Lily was back in her nightmares, in that other hallway with its endless doors.

"Shine it up." Dorian grabbed the flashlight from her, focusing it on Jonathan's stomach. "Ah, damn."

A narrow trench of blood, sparkling almost black, stained Jonathan's shirt just above his belt buckle. Lily's vision crystallized, the warm bubble around her mind evaporating.

"Help me pick him up."

Lily wrapped an arm around Jonathan's waist and helped Dorian haul him from the floor. Ahead, in the darkness, the guard's screams ended suddenly, a strangled sound that cut off in a grunt.

"Move!" William Tear shouted.

"Jonathan needs a doctor," Dorian panted. "Gutshot."

"There's no time. Parker's people will already be started."

"I'm fine," Jonathan wheezed, his breath whistling against Lily's neck.

"Come on, South Carolina." Dorian hauled him forward and Lily followed suit, trying not to jostle him.

"You, Salter!" Tear snapped. "Get the door open!"

The assistant rushed past Lily, his flashlight bobbing with each stride, toward the door at the end of the hallway. Just as he reached it, the lights came back on in a bright flash, blinding them all. Lily stumbled, nearly pitching Jonathan forward to the floor.

"Move!" Tear roared. "We're out of time!"

The assistant had the door open. Lily and Dorian hauled Jonathan forward, out into the cool night, and up the long metal staircase. It seemed like years since Lily had arrived at this place, and for a moment she wanted nothing so much as to sink down and fall asleep on the steps, better world be damned. But then she felt resistance, even from her own limbs: the other woman was there, pushing her up the steps.

At the top was a parked car, a sleek silver Lexus with the Security shield on the hood. The rest of the buildings in the compound were still dark, but even as Lily watched, one bank of lights came back on, far across the pavement.

"Boss," Dorian muttered. "She's still tagged."

"We'll deal with it in the car. Get Jonathan in."

The assistant, Salter, was waiting by the open passenger-side door, his face both terrified and pathetically eager. As they approached, he bugled, "The better world!"

"Shut up!" Tear hissed.

"I helped!"

"So you did." Tear passed Jonathan to Lily. She saw the

glint of murder in Tear's eyes, but said nothing, merely opened the rear door and helped Dorian maneuver Jonathan into the backseat. "You helped us at the eleventh hour, wanting to get to the better world."

"Yes!"

In one quick movement, Tear grabbed the back of Salter's head and smashed his face into the hood of the car. When he pulled Salter back up, the man's features were nothing but a bloody mask.

"Think on them, Salter," Tear murmured. "All of my people you've helped to break over the years. I wouldn't let you within a hundred miles of the better world."

He flung Salter away. Lily looked across the compound, at the miles of fencing that seemed to surround everything. If the power came back on, how were they going to get out?

"This was going to be a trick, even with Jonathan behind the wheel." Tear shook his head, biting at the inside of his cheek. "I need to work on Jonathan, take out her tag. Dori, can you drive?"

"I'll get us there."

"Get in." Tear slipped into the backseat. Lily opened the passenger door, then froze as an explosion ripped through the tree line on her left, several miles beyond the Security compound. An orange fireball bloomed in the dark, illuminating the silhouettes of infinite trees before they were consumed in flame.

"Into the car, now!"

She got in and slammed the door. Dorian floored it, and the Lexus roared forward across the pavement. Tear turned on the overhead light.

"Twenty degrees left, Dori. The fifth segment from the end."

"I know, boss, I know." Dorian nudged the wheel to the left. Another bank of lights came on above them, and Lily saw that they were heading toward the perimeter fence, doing forty now, their speed still increasing. Lily thought of electrocution, then dismissed it from her mind. Tear would take care of these things, the way he seemed to take care of everything. Metal hammered behind her: bullets, puncturing the trunk and back bumper. The car skewed, and Dorian fought with the steering wheel, cursing, a steady slew of profanity that would have made Maddy proud.

A groan came from the backseat. Tear had produced his little black bag and was kneeling on the floorboards, bent over Jonathan's midsection. Lily was glad she couldn't see the wound, for she already sensed how things would play out. Jonathan had saved her—twice now—and in return, she had gotten him killed.

"It's bad." Tear shook his head. "Have to wait until we're on the highway, until we're steady." He moved Jonathan's legs and perched on the seat. "Lily. Lean forward."

Lily started, realizing that he had used her first name, carelessly, just the way he would speak to Dorian or Jonathan. She wanted to smile, but then she felt Tear rip her shirt down the back.

The car hit the fence. All Security fences were supposed to be titanium, but this section seemed to crumple away from the posts, as though it had been weakened somehow. Dorian yanked the wheel left and the car peeled sideways, skidding, and then they were on the egress road, speeding away. Lily turned and saw the compound through the rear windshield, a wide wash of light and stone and steel, shrinking behind them. Then she jumped, startled, as something cold was smeared across her shoulder blade.

"I usually give a local for this, Lily, but I'm going to need my whole supply for Jonathan. Can you be brave?"

Lily giggled, but it came out as a croak. Brave had been many, many hours ago. She didn't know where she was now, wandering in uncharted territory. She gritted her teeth, readying herself, and tried to think of something else. "Why did you kill the assistant?"

"Salter? You know men like Salter, Lily. He's the sort who can think of an excuse for almost anything he's done. Salter thought that one good deed could make up for a lifetime of terrible acts."

"Can't it?" Lily shut her eyes, tight, as something thin and cold pierced the skin of her shoulder blade. She didn't know why they had rescued her. Would they let her come with them to the better world? She hadn't even done one good deed, not really. The pain was bad, but she pursed her lips—what if even a small wrong move could tip the balance?—holding them shut.

"Depends on the deed and the lifetime. In this case, no. Salter's been Langer's right-hand man for nearly twenty years."

Major Langer, Lily realized. The man in charge. The accountant.

"No roadblocks yet," Dorian remarked, her gaze pinned straight ahead. "That's something. But there's a lot of fire."

"Parker," Tear replied dismissively. "That bunch is ridiculously impressed by loud noises." The sharp instrument worked inside Lily's shoulder. She couldn't stop a small moan from escaping her throat.

"Not much longer, Lily." A spray can hissed, and burning cold spread across her open shoulder. "Thank Christ Parker and his crew never knew what else we had. But I'd bet a hundred quid most of the eastern seaboard's on fire before the night is through."

"Why?" Lily gasped, as another sharp point sank into the muscle of her shoulder. "Why would you let him do that?"

Tear grunted. "Hold very still, Lily. Tricky fucker." Lily thought he had ignored her question, but a moment later he replied, "This country is diseased. The fortunate celebrate on the backs of the starving, the ill, the terrorized. The law affords no recourse to the disadvantaged. That's a historical sickness, and there's only one cure. But I won't lie to you, Lily; we need the diversion as well." Tear left her shoulder for a moment, and there was a clink of metal. "Little fucker's buried deep in the muscle. Inept doctor . . . must have hurt like mad when they put it in."

Lily blinked in surprise, realizing that she didn't remember having her tag implanted. It had been done sometime during her childhood, she knew, but now the tag seemed like something that had always been there, a natural part of her anatomy. She had *learned* to be tagged, in the same way they had all learned to be under constant surveillance, not to speak of the disappeared.

A historical sickness.

"Why did you get me out?"

"The better world's not free, Lily. I test my people. Dori, keep it steady here."

"Sir."

There was a final deep stab into Lily's muscle, and she screeched against her clamped teeth. Another cold tug, and the invasion finally withdrew. Tear presented the tag for Lily's inspection: a tiny piece of metal, so tiny that it would have fit comfortably on her pinkie fingernail. Marveling, Lily held out her hand, and Tear dropped the tag into her palm.

"Controls your whole life, Lily. Do us a favor and toss it out the window."

After staring at the tiny metal ellipse for another moment, Lily rolled the window down and threw her tag into the night.

"Feel better, Mrs. M.?"

She turned to stare at Jonathan, ignoring the fierce pain in her shoulder. He was smiling, but his face was pale beneath its dark skin, and his entire shirtfront gleamed with blood.

"I'm so sorry."

Jonathan waved his hand. "I'll be fine."

But Lily knew better. Saying sorry again seemed ridiculously inadequate, and so she didn't repeat it, only turned to stare out the windshield, hating herself. The night landscape bloomed with fire from horizon to horizon, many towns burning behind their walls. Something else was different, but it wasn't until they got on the freeway, heading south, that Lily was able to pinpoint the difference: she hadn't seen a single electric light since they'd left the Security compound.

"You shut down the power."

"Every cell," Tear replied, digging in his medical bag. "It's not coming back on, either. The east is dark, all the way from New Hampshire to Virginia. How's our time, Dori?"

"Ten minutes ahead of schedule."

"Stay on public highways. With any luck, Parker's people will be looking for bigger game on the private roads." Tear began to bandage Lily's shoulder, applying some sort of salve. It stung, but Lily barely noticed. She was too busy staring out the window, her eyes full of orange flame.

Carnival, she thought. She didn't want to imagine what was happening out there, in the world beyond this car.

Everyone she knew lived behind a wall, her mother, her friends . . . Lily suddenly felt that she was staying afloat atop a pile of corpses, that this guilt would stay with her, with all of them, even Tear, poisoning what it touched . . . poisoning the better world.

None of us escape, Lily realized bleakly, then shut her eyes, wincing at the sounds from the backseat, as Tear went to work on Jonathan.

None of us is clean.

Kelsea woke to find herself in the dark, lying on a cold stone floor. Her shoulder was aching, but whether it was Lily's memories or her own old wound, she didn't know. She felt cheated. How could she be here now, without seeing the end of the story?

"Lazarus?"

There was no answer. Kelsea scrambled to her feet and then fell down again, scraping her knees on the stone. The darkness felt as though it stretched forever around her.

"Lazarus!" she screamed.

"Thank fucking Christ!" Mace shouted. His voice was distant, muted by dead space. "Keep talking, Lady!"

"Here!"

The glimmer of a torch appeared, far off, and Kelsea pulled herself to her feet, wandering toward it, her hands outstretched against obstacles. But there was nothing, only the vast dark space around her. As Mace approached, she saw that his face was white and strained, his eyes wide in the torchlight.

"I thought I'd lost you, Lady."

"What?"

"One moment you were on the ground, making a racket,

and the next you were just gone. I've been looking for you for at least half an hour."

"Maybe I rolled away in the dark."

Mace laughed bitterly. "No, Lady. You were *gone*."

Then why am I back? she nearly asked, but held quiet, recognizing the selfishness of the question. She was back because there were things to do before the morning, before she walked into death.

"Only crossing," she whispered, taking comfort in the words, though she didn't know what they meant.

It was time to talk to Row Finn.

All was quiet as they approached the Queen's Wing. Kelsea hoped that everyone had gone to bed, for it would make this easier if she only had to say good-bye to the night guard. But here she was mistaken, for when the double doors opened, she found her entire Guard, more than thirty of them, still awake, with Pen in front. Andalie was waiting, too, as neatly put together as though she'd had a full night's sleep. Even Aisa was there, though Kelsea noted that she did not stand with her mother. She stood with the Guard.

Kelsea took a deep breath. The rest of them would be easier to lie to than Mace, but she worried about Andalie, who always saw through everything.

"At dawn, I'm going down to the bridge, to try and open negotiations with the Mort."

"With what, Lady?" Coryn asked. "You have nothing to offer."

"Lazarus will decide who comes with me," she continued, ignoring him. "Four guards, no more."

"Elston," Mace announced. "Myself." His eyes roamed the room for a moment before fixing on Aisa. "And you, hellcat. The Mort are tricky bastards. I want your knife."

This was nonsense, but seeing the way Aisa's face lit up in the torchlight, Kelsea said nothing, recognizing Mace's words as a gift, a kindness, just as she had shown to Ewen. She scanned the rows of guards and found Ewen stationed near one end. She had been prepared to send him back down to the dungeon if Mace demanded it, but he had not. The Guard could have reacted to Ewen in many different ways, but they had taken him in, much in the manner of a mascot, giving him responsibility in minor matters, innocuous errands where he could do no harm. Venner clapped Aisa on the back and murmured in her ear, and she scampered off down the hallway.

"And Coryn."

Several guards gasped. Pen stared at Mace, his face turning pale. Kelsea's heart ached for him, but she understood that she could not get involved in this. More, as Pen began to argue with Mace in furious whispers, she saw that she was being handed an opportunity. She turned and hurried down the hall to her chamber, relieved when no one tried to follow, and bolted the door shut behind her.

The fire in her chamber was still going; Andalie, thorough as ever, had tended it throughout the night. Kelsea sat down on the hearth, staring into the flames, willing Row Finn to come. But where would he come from? Kelsea wished she understood, for it seemed like it might matter. She felt exhausted, as though she had traveled countless miles, the weight of Lily's life on top of her own. She longed to go back to Lily, to see the rest of the story, but there was no time. It was four fifteen, and dawn was coming. Kelsea balled her hand into a fist, digging the nails in until thin blood emerged beneath their crescents, until she felt vaguely awake.

Tear heir.

She looked up and found him standing beside the fireplace. He was not so pale as she remembered; now his cheeks were ruddy and his eyes gleamed with a sparkle that seemed unnatural. Her earlier dreams recurred: this man, buried inside her, while all around them the fire burned and burned . . . Kelsea stood up, wiping her bloody hand on her dress.

"You want your freedom."

Yes.

"Speak!" she snapped. "I'm tired of silence."

"I want my freedom."

"How do I kill the Red Queen?"

"Are you ready to bargain, Tear heir?" His eyes gleamed redly. A trick of the light, Kelsea had once assumed . . . and now she remembered Marlowe's old fool, who had decided to make a bargain with the devil. But even the lessons of a good book could not stand up against the weight of the tide that stood outside the city walls. The Mort were the only issue; all other considerations had become secondary.

"I'm ready to bargain."

Finn approached, and Kelsea saw hunger burning in his eyes, a great excitement held in check. Whatever freedom meant to him, he had waited a long time.

"What do I do?"

"Take your sapphires in your hand."

Kelsea did.

"Now say, 'I forgive you, Rowland Finn.' "

"Forgive you for what?"

"Does it matter?"

"Yes."

"You are difficult, Tear heir."

"How is it true forgiveness, if I don't know what I'm forgiving you for?"

Finn paused, his face thoughtful, and Kelsea felt a moment's satisfaction. For months she had been flying blind in regard to her sapphires. Finn might know more than she did, but he didn't have all of the information either.

"Perhaps you're right," he admitted. "I will tell you, then: long ago, I did your family a great wrong."

"What wrong?"

Finn blinked, and Kelsea realized, astonished, that each word was costing him something. Was it possible for this creature to feel remorse?

"I betrayed Jonathan Tear."

This wasn't what Kelsea had expected. "The Fetch said you were a liar."

His eyes narrowed. "Let me tell you something about the man called Fetch, girl. I see your wish to wound him, and believe me, he is vulnerable. Ask him about *his* role in the Tear assassination. See if he has any defense."

Kelsea recoiled.

"I grow weary, Tear heir. Do we have a deal, or not?"

"You first," she replied, forcing the Fetch from her head. "How do I kill the Red Queen?"

"Give me your word that you will set me free afterward. I have watched you for a long time, Tear heir. I know your word is good."

The words reminded her of Thorne. There was something wrong here, something Kelsea was missing. If Finn had been involved in the Tear assassination, what did that have to do with Kelsea? All of the Tears were dead.

The Mort! her mind insisted. *Think of the Mort!* She needed time, time to make a good decision, but all time had run out. If there was even a possibility of killing the Red Queen, didn't that outweigh whatever threat this creature might represent? Kelsea wondered if it had been this way for her mother: two terrible options, the Mort at the very gates, and Elyssa, blinded by the immediate danger into making the worst decision possible.

I see, Kelsea whispered silently, the words falling into some dim corner of her mind. *I see, now, how it was for you.*

"I promise to set you free."

Finn smiled, vulpine. "A good bargain, Tear heir. Your Mort Queen came to me a long time ago, nearly a century now. She was not seeking me, but found me by accident, and once she realized what I was, she begged me to help her."

"Help her do what?"

"Become immortal. She was a young girl then, barely a woman, but already her life had been terrible, and she wished to be so strong that nothing could harm her again ... not man, not fate, not time."

Thorne had been right, Kelsea realized. "You helped her, then?"

"I did. She has distant Tear blood, and for a long time I thought she was the one I was looking for. But she is . . . flawed. Her early years left too deep a mark on her, and she focuses only on her own safety and her own gain. Your heritage is much clearer, undiluted. Sometimes I can even see him, just there, in the expressions of your face."

Who? Kelsea wondered. But she could not afford diversions. "You said she could be killed."

"So she can. She has a bit of your family's talent, and I taught her to refine it: to manipulate flesh, to cure herself when her body failed her. You know these lessons, Tear heir; you have been teaching them to yourself. But the Mort Queen is still vulnerable. Her *mind* is vulnerable, because deep inside her mind will always be that young girl who came to me, frightened and starving and alone. She cannot eradicate her childhood, as hard as she might try. It defines her."

Kelsea twitched, suddenly angry. She did not want to think of the Red Queen as a vulnerable child, like Aisa. Kelsea wanted her to be the figure of great power and terror that she had always imagined. She felt as though Finn had made everything more difficult.

"How is this useful to me?"

"The woman cannot be killed, Tear heir, but the child can. She knows this, and so she must have your sapphires."

"What do they have to do with it?"

"Time, Tear heir, time. Surely you must have realized by now that you hold much more than two pretty necklaces. There are many magic gems out there, but Tear's sapphire is unique. You must have discovered this, no?"

Kelsea said nothing.

"There are many things the Red Queen would like to change in her own history. She believes your jewels would allow her to do so, to wipe away the past that makes her weak. She wants them very badly."

So Thorne had told the truth about that as well. For a moment Kelsea pictured the bleeding man, writhing in agony at her feet . . . then she thrust the image away. "How would someone else make use of that past, though? Surely anyone she might fear from childhood is dead now."

"Not necessarily, Tear heir. She fears me. But even more, she fears you."

"Me?"

"Oh, yes. She may not admit it, even to herself, but she fears you, and fear is a monstrous weakness that an industrious woman like yourself might use. The Red Queen has many defenses, but if you find the child, you find the vulnerability." Finn splayed his hands. "Have I fulfilled my end of the bargain?"

"I'm not sure. What if you've lied?"

Finn chuckled bitterly, his handsome face twisting. "Believe me, I learned a long time ago not to play at truth with your family. The lesson came at a bitter cost."

"All right."

"Your end of the bargain, Tear heir."

"What do I do?"

"Let me see your sapphires."

Kelsea held them out, but he recoiled. "No closer. I can't touch them."

"Why not?"

"Punishment, Tear heir. The worst punishment imaginable."

The worst punishment imaginable. Someone else had used those exact words with Kelsea, not long ago. The Fetch, of course, standing in almost the exact spot where Row Finn was standing now.

"Take both sapphires in your hand—"

"Wait a minute," she interrupted. "You said you had done *my* family a wrong. The Raleighs. What wrong?"

He smiled. "The Raleighs, the grasping Raleighs . . . you may have their blood, but you're no Raleigh. You're a Tear."

"The Tears were slaughtered. None survived."

"Are you so dense, child? Look in the mirror!"

Kelsea turned and looked. From old habit, she expected to see a girl there, but instead she found a woman, tall and lovely, her expression grave, her face prematurely lined with sorrow.

Lily.

For a moment, Kelsea thought it must be a trick, some illusion concocted by Finn to sway her. She raised her hand, watched her reflection do the same. She might have been Lily herself, standing in front of the floor-length mirror that stood in the front hallway of the New Canaan house. Only Kelsea's eyes were still her own, deep green rather than Lily's cool blue.

"Was my mother one of the Tear line, somehow?"

"Elyssa?" Finn giggled, a sound that chilled Kelsea.

"Do you know who my father was?"

"I do."

"Who?"

He shook his head, and in his eyes, Kelsea saw the most alarming thing she had seen during this entire nightmare evening: a thin vein of pity. "Believe me, Tear heir, you don't want to know."

Mace had said the same thing, but Kelsea pressed onward. "Of course I do."

"Too bad. That isn't part of the bargain." Finn gestured toward the sapphires. "Keep your end, Tear heir."

She clasped both sapphires in her right hand. So bad that she wouldn't want to know . . . which of the rogue's gallery in her mother's generation could it be?

"I forgive you, Rowland Finn," he prompted.

Kelsea closed her eyes. Her mother's face swam up before her, but Kelsea ignored it and spoke clearly. "I forgive you, Rowland Finn."

In the dark of her tent, less than five miles away, the Queen of Mortmesne woke screaming.

Finn smiled wide, showing bright, sharp teeth. "Do not even consider revoking your forgiveness, Tear heir. You gave it on your sapphires, and oathbreakers are punished, badly."

"Ah." Kelsea sat back, staring at him. "I see. What was your punishment, then? Different, I'd imagine, from that of the Fetch."

Finn stared at her for a moment, then shrugged. "I am going to pay you a great compliment, Tear heir. Always, I come to the women with this." He circled his perfect face with one hand. "It pleases them, and flatters them, and muddles their thinking. But you're too clever to be distracted, and you're too honest to be flattered."

Kelsea wasn't sure of that. Her pulse had elevated, as it always did when Finn was near. But if he had been fooled, then so much the better.

"You asked, so I will show you my punishment. See who I really am."

Finn's face began to change, the color bleeding away. His hair thinned, became a ragged patchwork on his scalp. His skin whitened, the lips reddened, the eyes grew their own dark hoods. The face was that of a clown, perhaps the joker in a deck of cards, but there was no humor in those eyes, only a killing joy that embraced everything and nothing. Kelsea nearly screamed, but she clapped her hand over her mouth at the last moment, realizing that it would only bring her entire Guard running.

"It burns," Finn rasped. "All the time it burns."

"What happened to you?"

"I have been alive for more than three centuries. I have wished for death many times, but I cannot inflict it on myself. Only on others."

Kelsea had backed up until her knees met the bed, and now she sat down, staring at him.

"Do not be frightened, Tear heir. I am dangerous, infinitely so, but I have no immediate business with you. My hatred lies east, with the Mort Queen. If you fail, I will succeed."

He moved toward the fireplace, and Kelsea felt relieved, but just at the hearth, he turned back to her, his red eyes burning.

"I have no feeling, Tear heir, not for any living thing in this world. But at this moment, you have my gratitude, and perhaps even respect. Do not get in my way."

"That depends on where your way leads you. Stay out of the Tearling."

Finn's smile widened. "I promise nothing. You have been warned."

He retreated back into the fireplace, damping the flames, and Kelsea's stomach knotted in anxiety as she watched him go. Finn's form faded until there was nothing, only the sinking sense that she had not avoided Elyssa's Bargain after all, that the deal she had just made might turn out to be even worse.

Too late now. It was nearly dawn. Kelsea wondered where Lily was now, what she was doing. Had they launched the ships? To where? How had Tear been able to protect his tiny kingdom of travelers from the collapsing world around them? The pre-Crossing earth had held more than twenty billion people, but no one had followed them to the New World. How had Tear gotten away?

"Only crossing," Kelsea whispered again, savoring the words like a talisman. Finn had said that Tear's jewel dealt in time; had Tear been able to see the future, anticipate obstacles? No, that was too simple. An undiscovered landmass in

518

the middle of the Atlantic? That seemed unlikely, if not impossible. Yet they had sailed thousands of miles, crossing God's Ocean to land on the western shores of the New World.

Time, Tear heir, time.

Finn's voice echoed in her head, and Kelsea looked up, startled, as a vision took shape before her. There were no certainties here; there never were where her sapphires were concerned. But she thought she understood, if only dimly, what had happened. Tear's people had traveled thousands of miles across the ocean, yes, but the real journey was not in distance.

The real Crossing was time.

An hour later, cleaned up and dressed, Kelsea went to Arliss's office, where he handed her a sheet of paper without comment. She turned it over and found, charmed, that Arliss had taken some pains with his handwriting, pushing his normally straggling letters into upright legibility. He hadn't waited for her approval of the language; beside him was a steadily growing stack of copies.

Bill of Regency

Her Majesty, Kelsea Raleigh Glynn, seventh Queen of the Tearling, hereby relinquishes her office and places it in the hands of Lazarus of the Mace, Captain of the Queen's Guard, his heirs and assigns, to act as Regent of Her Majesty's Government. Should Her Majesty die or become incapacitated while this Bill of Regency is in effect, the aforementioned transfer of office shall become permanent and the Regent shall be declared ruler of the Tearling. All acts by the

Regent will be taken in Her Majesty's name and according to Her Majesty's laws—

"That's good," Kelsea muttered. "I forgot to tell you that."

—but any such acts may be repudiated by decree of Her Majesty upon resumption of her throne.

Kelsea looked up at Arliss. "A resumption clause?"
"Andalie told me to put it in."
"How did Andalie know?"
"She just knew, Queenie, same as she always does."
Kelsea looked back down at the bill.

At such time as Her Majesty may return and resume her throne, this Bill will be declared null and void. The Regent will relinquish all powers of office to Her Majesty, or Her Majesty's heirs upon sufficient evidence.

Kelsea shook her head. "A resumption clause is a bad idea. It weakens Lazarus right out of the gate."
"You need one, Queenie. Both Andalie and that little sibyl of hers say you'll come back."
She looked up, startled. "They do?"
"The little one seemed particularly sure of it. Vastly changed, she said you'll be, but you will come back."
Kelsea didn't see how this could be. If she tried to kill the Red Queen, she would either succeed or fail, but either way, it seemed unlikely that she would live long after the attempt. But it was too late to change the bill now; they needed

enough copies to distribute throughout New London. Kelsea sat down in the chair opposite Arliss and began to sign her way through the stack. The work was soothing, but monotonous, and Kelsea's mind wandered back to the conversation with Row Finn. Again, the nagging question recurred: who had fathered her? If the Tear line had survived somehow, it could only be because someone had been hidden during the bloody period after Jonathan Tear's assassination. A secret that old would be nearly impossible to discover . . . but Kelsea's paternity might provide a start.

"Lady."

Mace was in the doorway. Kelsea straightened automatically, drawing her arm over the bill she was signing. But Arliss was far ahead of her; he had already whisked the entire stack of copies out of sight.

"What is it?"

"I need you to weigh in on something."

Kelsea got up from the desk, heard a slither of paper behind her as Arliss made her bill disappear as well. "What is it?"

Mace closed the door behind him. "Pen insists on accompanying you this morning. I've said no, but he won't listen. I could have him restrained when we leave, but I don't wish to do that."

"What's the question?"

"Do you think he should come?"

Kelsea nodded slowly. "It would be cruel to leave him behind."

"All right." Mace lowered his voice. "But when we get back, Lady, you and I will have to talk about Pen. He cannot be your close guard and your paramour, all at once."

Paramour. It was such an antiquated concept that Kelsea almost laughed, but after a moment's thought, she realized that Mace had chosen the right word. Paramour . . . that was exactly what Pen was.

"Fine. We'll discuss it."

Mace looked over her shoulder. "What goes on here?"

"We're going over the tax situation."

"That so?" Mace fixed his keen glance on Arliss. "Taxes a crucial issue right now?"

"Whatever Queenie wants to talk about is the issue on my desk, Mr. Mace."

Mace turned back to Kelsea. He stared at her for a very long time.

"Spit it out, Lazarus."

"Why not tell me what you're planning to do, Lady? Don't you think I could help?"

Kelsea looked down, blinking, suddenly near tears. He would not understand, she thought, not until it was all done, and at that point it would be too late to ask his forgiveness. But Mace was a Queen's Guard right down to his core. He would knock her unconscious, if necessary, to keep her from her intended course, and so she could not explain to him, nor to the rest of the Guard. She would not be able to say good-bye to any of them. She thought of the day they'd all ridden up, tired and impatient, to collect her from the cottage. That departure had been terrible, just as this one would be. And yet the world had opened wide, from that day onward. She remembered riding down the length of the Almont, farms all around her, the Caddell still a blue twinkle in the distance. How she had been struck by the land, its vastness, its sweep . . . and remembering, she felt a tear slide down her cheek.

I can't fail, or everything is lost.

"Get the other three together, Lazarus. It's time to go."

Later, thinking on that ride, Aisa would only remember that it should have been raining. Rain would have been fitting, but instead the sky was a deep, clear blue, blushed with pinkish-orange clouds in the coming dawn, the light just bright enough to reveal the ocean of people on either side of the Great Boulevard. New London was bursting at the seams, and although it wasn't yet six in the morning, the entire city seemed to have crowded into the streets.

Despite the three guards with her, Aisa felt very small and alone, and she was frightened, not of death but of failure. Last month the Mace had given her a horse, a pretty young stallion that Aisa had named Sam, and Fell had been teaching her to ride. But riding a horse was much more difficult than working with a knife or sword, and Aisa did not deceive herself that she was proficient. At any moment, she felt, Sam might throw her, and she would rather die than have that happen now, in front of all of these people, in front of the Mace, who had chosen her to come along on this dangerous errand. Aisa's weapons were currently stowed in her belt, but if anyone so much as made a move in the direction of the Queen, she could be off the horse with her knife ready in two seconds flat.

The Queen rode tall and straight between the four of them, the dim light of dawn gleaming dully off her silver tiara. She looked very regal to Aisa, very much as a Queen should when going out to negotiate with her enemy. But the Queen's hands were clenched on the reins, her knuckles fiercely white, and Aisa understood that all was not as it seemed. Before they left the Keep, the Mace had drawn the three of them aside, speaking in a low voice.

"She's up to something. Watch her close. You see any sign

that she's going to bolt, raise the alarm and grab her. She can't take all four of us at once."

Aisa didn't know what to make of this order, or, truly, of the Queen herself. She knew from Maman and the Guard that the Queen sometimes went into a trance, but nothing could have prepared her for last night: the Queen shambling from one room to another, her eyes sometimes closed, sometimes open, as she staggered forward, holding conversations with no one, even bumping into walls. The Mace had cautioned them not to worry, to simply let her be, and left her in the care of Pen. But Aisa *did* worry. In her own way, the Queen reminded her of Glee, who would wander in the same manner, following things that weren't there, tormented by some other world that none of them could see. Sometimes Glee herself wasn't entirely there, and Aisa had thought more than once that one day Glee might simply disappear, vanishing into her unseen world. Perhaps the Mace was worried that the Queen might do the same.

"Queen Kelsea!" a man shouted, and Aisa swung that way automatically, putting her hand to her knife. But it was only an old man standing near the front of the crowd, waving at the Queen. His was the first voice they'd heard raised above the murmur of the crowd; the city seemed to be stunned, all of them staring at the Queen with wide, lost eyes. After perhaps ten minutes of riding, Aisa also noticed another anomaly: they had passed many thousands of people, but she had not seen a single glass of ale, not even when they passed the Cove, New London's notorious run of pubs.

Why, they're scared sober! Aisa realized. They didn't know that the Queen was going out to parlay, but Aisa suspected that it would have made no difference. She, like everyone, had seen the massive force spread across both banks of the

524

Caddell. What could the Queen offer to counter? Aisa thought this was a fool's errand, but she was proud to be chosen, proud to be with them. When the Mort came, she would not stand there defenseless, her eyes lost. She would fight to the end to keep them from reaching the Queen. As the Cove ended, her heart froze; for a moment, she thought she had seen Da, his tall form and black eyes burning, in the center of the crowd. But when the people shifted again, he was gone.

The Boulevard took its final turn and the New London Bridge appeared, a long stretch of stone before them. The vast crowds of people on either side began to melt away, and Aisa finally relaxed as the five of them guided their horses onto the bridge.

Ahead reared the barricade. Aisa was no engineer, but she saw the problem immediately: the barricade was nothing more than a hastily constructed mess of furniture and what appeared to be planks of lumber piled on both sides of the bridge. A thin aisle ran down the middle, so narrow that it would allow passage only in single file. But the entire structure was unwieldy; the low walls that bordered the bridge would not support the barricade's height. The Mace said that the Mort had brought battering rams, and from the look of things, one good blow from a ram would send half the barricade straight over the sides of the bridge and into the Caddell.

The Queen had clearly come to the same conclusion, for she chuckled darkly at the mess before them. "Not going to hold, is it?"

"Not a chance, Lady," the Mace replied. "There's only one way to properly defend a bridge. Hall's done his best with what he had, but a stiff breeze will take his barricade down."

Aisa wondered what the one way could be, but General Hall had emerged from the barricade now, and she kept quiet. Hall had been in and out of the Keep several times in the past week, and Aisa liked to hear him speak: business-like and to the point, with no nonsense or extraneous words. The Mace said that Hall had done hero's work to hold the Mort back until all of the refugees were inside the city. For a moment, Aisa worried that the general would ask what she was doing here with the Guard, but his eyes merely noted her before moving on to the Queen.

"Majesty."

"General. I've come to open negotiations with the Mort."

"There's a contingent of them waiting on the far end of the bridge, but they're not dressed for embassy. They have two rams and they're ready to begin."

"Is Ducarte there?"

"Yes. He commands."

The Queen nodded for a moment, her face deep in thought, then turned and looked back over the city walls behind them. Following her gaze, Aisa saw that every available surface of the boundary wall was packed with people, all of them staring at the bridge. The Queen scanned the wall for a long moment before looking down again, and Aisa knew that she had been searching for someone, a face she did not find. The Queen sighed, her eyes full of sorrow, a sadness that Aisa recognized: she had seen it in Maman's eyes more times than she could number.

"I'm sorry."

The Mace jerked at his horse's reins with one hand, reaching out for the Queen with the other, but then they both froze, horse and rider. A moment later Aisa felt her own muscles seize, an odd, sick feeling, as though a mild cramp had spread across her entire body. From the corner of her eye, she saw that Pen and Elston too had frozen, Pen already off his horse and in the very act of charging forward. Aisa had been part of late-night discussions among the Guard, had heard their recountings of the strange power the Queen wielded; each guard seemed to have his own conjecture on what the Queen's magic meant, how far it could go. But Aisa had never heard of anything like this. She tried to speak, found that her throat would not even allow her to make a sound.

"I'm sorry," the Queen repeated. "But none of you can protect me where I'm going."

She dismounted, walked over to Mace, and looped the reins of her mare around his outstretched hand. The Mace stared down at her, immobile, but his eyes were terrible, twin pools of hurt and fury.

"Forgive me." The Queen grasped the Mace's motionless hand for a moment, smiling sadly. "I'm the Queen, you see."

The Mace's mouth twitched, but nothing came out.

"You're my Regent, Lazarus. It's been arranged. I trust you to look after these people and keep them safe."

The Queen stared at the Mace for another long moment, then turned to the three of them, Aisa and Elston and Pen. "You can't guard me any longer. So do this for me: guard my Regent."

Aisa stared at her, bewildered, for the idea of anyone guarding the Mace seemed laughable. The Queen moved over to General Hall, and for a moment Aisa thought that the general might be able to stop her, but then she spotted the cords standing out on his throat and understood that he was held immobile as well.

"Retreat from the bridge immediately, General, and

prepare for siege. If the Mort don't come, you will know that I succeeded."

Now she moved toward Pen, whose pleasant face had frozen in a rictus of agony. The Queen placed a light hand against his cheek for a moment; Aisa saw her shoulders heave with a single deep breath, and then she turned and darted into the shadows of the barricade.

In the Queen's wake, the guards could do nothing but stare at each other. Aisa thought that she was the only one who remained calm; the eyes of the other three were wide with panic. Pen appeared to be the worst of all; he would have followed the Queen anywhere, Aisa knew, and the Queen had known too. There were other soldiers in the barricade; surely they would be able to stop her . . . but then, staring at the maze of debris, Aisa realized how foolish that hope was. The Queen was powerful, more powerful than Maman, maybe even as powerful as the Red Queen herself. No one would stop her, not if she didn't want to be stopped.

Beneath Aisa's feet, the ground began to shake. A moment later, she realized that she could move again, that the strange hold on her muscles had released. But the ground was now heaving so violently that she lost control of Sam and fell from his back, landing with a painful thud on the cobbles.

"We can still catch her up!" the Mace shouted. "Come on!"

Pen was already gone; he had left his horse behind and charged into the barricade. Aisa pushed herself up from the ground, aware now of a deep, distant cracking, like thunder, to the east. She followed the Mace and Elston into the barricade, trying to keep up with the grey of their cloaks, pulling her knife as she went. As always, the knife was a cold comfort in her hand, and only now, in her extremity, did Aisa realize where that comfort sprang from: the hope that she would meet Da. She hated Da, and she loved him, but someday, somehow, she hoped to meet him with a knife in her hand.

Another deep roll of thunder slammed the bridge, jarring the stone beneath Aisa's feet. She passed soldiers, tucked into crevices in the debris, but there was no time to really see them. They were not important, not in the way the Queen was important. Aisa pushed through, dodging the outthrust points of wood and chair legs. At last she emerged from the shadowy overhang of the eastern end of the barricade to find Mace, Pen, and Elston standing at a flat halt. Aisa drew up beside them and gasped.

At least a hundred feet of the New London Bridge had vanished, leaving a cracked lip of rock, then nothing. Peering over the edge of the precipice, Aisa saw several massive chunks of white stone far below, partially submerged in the rich blue waters of the Caddell. Their edges were ragged, as though a giant had torn the stone off in pieces with his bare hands. There was now an enormous gap in the bridge, stretching from the jagged edge at their feet all the way to the last column of support.

Aisa spotted the Queen, standing on the eastern edge of the precipice. Aisa had good vision, and even from here, she could see that the Queen's face was bone-white, that she looked ready to faint. The sun was just beginning to rise behind her, a nimbus of light playing around her head, and the Queen seemed very small. Aisa wasn't a real Queen's Guard yet, but she thought she could understand, if only dimly, how the other three must feel. She hated seeing the Queen standing across that gulf, unprotected and alone.

"Damn you, Lady!" Pen shouted. Aisa gasped, but the Mace didn't say anything, so she knew she was supposed to pretend that she had not heard.

"I am damned, Pen!" the Queen shouted back.

Aisa snuck a cautious glance at the Mace, and winced at his expression. For the first time she thought he looked old, old and used up. Only three days ago he had taught her how to take a sword to an attacker's knees, and applauded when she got it right. How could everything change so quickly?

"I had no options, Lazarus!" the Queen called across the chasm. "I never had any! You know that!"

She splayed her hands, then turned and walked away toward the eastern toll gate, beyond which a wave of black uniforms stood motionless and waiting. The Queen strode into the middle of them, as though into a hive of bees, and was engulfed. The four of them could do nothing but watch silently, and a few minutes later, when the Mort lines reformed, the Queen was gone.

CHAPTER 14

THE RED QUEEN

Fortune favors the bold, history tells us. Therefore, it behooves us to be as bold as possible.

—*The Glynn Queen's Words*, AS COMPILED BY FATHER TYLER

Ever since they had left the Keep, Kelsea had been fighting Lily off with a stick. She would begin going over her lines, what she would say to the Mort at the far end of the bridge . . . and then Lily would intrude, her grasping fingers of memory weaving through Kelsea's thoughts until the two seemed indistinguishable. Distant pops of gunfire. Visions of a burning skyline and the screams of the dying. But despite these things, Kelsea wished she could simply sink back into Lily's life. It was a troubled time that Lily lived in, troubled and terrible, but her choices were not Kelsea's. Lily's life demanded nothing but endurance. Kelsea looked up and saw white sails, riggings . . . a ship, people standing at the helm. She shook her head, but the vision remained in front of her, blurred slightly, as though overlaid with a veil of the thinnest material. For a moment, Kelsea felt as though she could reach out and tear that veil away, step through the centuries to stand beside Lily. To become Lily.

Could I do *that?* she wondered, blinking up at the ship, its billowing sails, white shadows in the night. *Could I simply cross, and not come back?*

For a moment, this idea was so seductive that Kelsea had to battle it, the way she would have battled an opponent with a knife. She looked down at her sapphires, feeling as though she were really seeing them for the first time. For months she had operated under the assumption that her sapphires were dead, but why? The dreams, the steady transformation of her own appearance, the cuts on her body, Lily's pain, Lily's *life* . . . these things had not come out of a vacuum. Kelsea took her jewels, one in each hand, and held them up to the light. Physically, they were identical, but she sensed great difference between them. If she only had time to sort it out! The sun was rising, but still she hesitated.

"You're not dead," she marveled, staring at the jewels in her hands. Lily's world pulled at her again, demanding that she return, that she watch the end of the story, but Kelsea dropped her jewels and began walking. The vision of the sails finally dimmed as she reached the toll gate at the eastern end of the bridge. The toll tables were all empty now; no one had entered or left New London via the bridge since the army took it over. Kelsea should have been exhausted, but she felt wide awake.

The knoll beyond the toll gate was covered with Mort soldiers, all of them armed for battle, with swords and several knives at the belt. Even now, the sight of all of that good steel hurt Kelsea deep inside. Her army—what remained of it, anyway—had so few good weapons. At the head of the Mort column stood a man in full armor, partially balding, with sleepy eyes that threw Kelsea off for a moment. But the eyes behind the drooping lids were shrewd and pitiless, just as she remembered them through her spyglass. She greeted him in Mort.

"General Ducarte."

"The Queen of the Tearling, I presume." His eyes darted over her shoulder, toward the bridge. "Have you come to beg my mistress for leniency? You will not get it."

"I've come to speak to . . . your mistress." It was a strange term to use, and Kelsea realized that Carlin's Mort lessons, good as they had been, might have skipped something in the way of idiom.

Ducarte's heavy-lidded eyes blinked toward the fallen bridge again and then blinked away. "She will not see you."

"I think she will." Kelsea stepped closer, and was astonished when he took a half step back, several of the soldiers behind him doing the same. Could it be possible that they were *afraid* of her? It seemed ludicrous, with the might of the Mort army lying just over the hill.

Ducarte shouted in rapid-fire Mort. "Andrew! Run and tell the Queen what goes on here!"

One of the men in the line turned and sprinted away, over the crest of the hill, where the sky was rapidly turning from pink to orange. Dawn was here, and Kelsea suddenly found this delay intolerable, worse than the idea of her own death. Ducarte did not want negotiation, she saw now, not even if it would benefit Mortmesne or his mistress. Ducarte wanted to march into New London, wanted to lay waste to all he found there. He was looking forward to the sack, looking forward to—

Carnival.

That was the right word. The man in front of her might as

well have been Parker, anticipating the fall of the world. William Tear had said something about men like Parker— that they were built for this, built to spoil things. And Kelsea suddenly saw that, at all costs, she must keep this man out of her city. She had broken the bridge, but that was not enough. On the other side of the hill were siege towers, rams. New London was not built to withstand assault, and the Mort army was hungry for plunder. Once they started, they would not stop.

"You want to let me pass, General."

"That's for my mistress to decide."

But Kelsea could not wait. She had already begun to probe at Ducarte, browsing through him, in the same way she would have looked through Carlin's library. Here was a man who was not afraid to die, like Mace, but nothing else was similar. This man was cold, not one to be swayed by pleas or pity. Only pain and self-preservation would buy him, Kelsea decided, so she found the soft meat of his groin and dug in, hard.

Ducarte cried out. Several of the men behind him stepped forward, but Kelsea shook her head. "Don't even think about it. Not unless you want a piece of the same."

They backed away, and Kelsea saw that they were indeed afraid. She turned back to Ducarte, loosening her hold for a moment. "The longer you make me wait here, General, the more I feel a need for such diversions."

Ducarte stared at her, wide-eyed. Kelsea suspected that he had never been held powerless before. A famous interrogator, Ducarte . . . and that made her think of Langer, the accountant. Such people did not do well on the other side of the table.

"I have business with your mistress. Let me pass."

"She will not negotiate," he gasped. "Even I won't defy her. She is terrible."

"Let me tell you a secret, General. I am worse."

She gave his testes another hard squeeze, and Ducarte screamed, a high, womanish sound. Kelsea was almost enjoying herself now, a low, dirty sort of pleasure, just as she had felt during Thorne's execution. How easy and pleasant it was, to punish those who deserved punishment. She could reduce this man to meat, and her own death would almost be worth it.

Kelsea, Carlin whispered behind her. The voice was so close that Kelsea turned her head, half expecting to see Carlin standing just over her shoulder. But nothing was there . . . only her city, standing behind her, wide open, in the blue light of early dawn. The sight shook Kelsea, reminded her that she did not belong to herself. Even the magic she used now, magic that she had essentially taught herself, was not hers. It belonged to William Tear, and Tear would never have allowed anything to divert his attention from the main prize . . . the better world.

"Take me to her, General, and I will stop."

All of the blood had drained from Ducarte's face now. He looked up and over the hillside behind him, his gaze frustrated, at the battering rams that stood ready. Kelsea saw the tenor of Ducarte's thoughts now, his ambitions, and she had to stomp down her anger, to leash it as one would a dog.

"Take me to her now, General, or I swear to you, you will not be able to enjoy your siege. You will no longer be equipped to do so."

Ducarte swore, then turned and began tromping back up the hill. Kelsea followed, surrounded by six of Ducarte's men, a group that had the feeling of a guard. This gave Kelsea pause: did Ducarte really need a guard in his own encampment? He was not a man who inspired loyalty, but it seemed extraordinary that he could be that hated. Even this picked guard, Kelsea noticed, made sure to steer well clear of her, traveling perhaps twenty feet out to the side.

They topped the hill, and Kelsea halted briefly, stunned by what she saw. Looking down at the Mort camp from the walls of New London was a very different proposition from seeing it up close. Black tents seemed to stretch for miles into the distance, and Kelsea's first thought was to wonder how they kept from overheating when the sun was up. Then she noticed the sheer, almost reflective nature of the fabric, and her earlier anger recurred. Always, Mortmesne had something new.

As they entered the camp, the six men tightened up around her, and Kelsea saw the reason soon enough. The path they were traversing passed between many tents, and the men lining either side looked at her like hungry dogs. Kelsea tried to prepare for violence, but didn't know what good it would do. The invisible wall she had sensed the other day was still there, protecting the camp; did the woman never sleep? As they moved farther toward the center, whispering became hissing, and the hissing gradually resolved itself into discrete comments that Kelsea wished she could unhear.

"Tear bitch!"

"When our lady is done with you, I'll use you until you break!"

Ducarte made no sign that he had heard them. Kelsea straightened her shoulders and stared straight ahead, trying to remind herself that she had been threatened before, that people had been trying to kill her all of her life. But this, the hostility and bile raining down from all sides, some in Mort and some in broken Tear, this was very different, and Kelsea was afraid.

"She'll make you beg for death!"

So much hate . . . where does it come from? Kelsea wanted to weep, not for herself but for the waste, the thought of how many extraordinary things could have been accomplished in the new world. She could not close her ears to them, so she searched for Lily and found her, just beneath the surface, staring up at the night sky, the white sails in the moonlight. But the sails were billowing now, as though stirred by a strong wind.

I missed it, Kelsea realized sadly. She had missed the launch. But Lily had made it. Lily was on board one of the ships. Grief threatened to overwhelm Kelsea, but she battled it, thinking of William Tear, of the main prize.

They turned another corner, and now Kelsea glimpsed a hint of scarlet through the mass of black. The Red Queen . . . soon Kelsea would stand in front her, face-to-face. In all the long, blurred night past, this was the one thing she had avoided thinking about. A piece of discarded metal caught her left foot, and Kelsea nearly fell in the mud, landing heavily on her ankle. The jeering of the men seemed to double in volume. Her body was exhausted from more than a day without sleep, and it was beginning to show. But her mind . . . her mind felt bright and sharp, sure of its course, if she could only hold herself together a bit longer. The crimson tent loomed ahead, and Kelsea was frightened, but there was relief as well, a sense that her approaching fate was now so final that it could not be averted.

She was nearly done.

The Queen was nervous. She didn't know why; all things were proceeding better than she could have devised. The girl was coming—actually delivering herself!—when the Queen had thought that they would have to fight tooth and nail to get into the Keep. She was wearing both jewels; Ducarte's runner had been very definite on that point. This development simplified matters enormously, but the Queen didn't trust it, for it seemed too easy. She had not seen the Tear sapphires in more than a century, and even as a child, she had never been able to study them as she would have liked. Elaine never took the Heir's Necklace off, and the Queen's mother had never let her close enough. The sapphires would be the last piece of the puzzle, the Queen was sure of it, but all the same her heartbeat was up and her left leg twitched madly, tapping and tapping beneath her skirts.

How to get hold of them?

From the dark thing, she knew that she could not simply snatch the things off the girl's neck, not without suffering a terrible consequence. The dark thing had been working on the girl, that much was obvious, but the Queen had no idea how far that work had progressed, what the girl could do. Did she present an actual threat? It seemed unlikely, not with her crown city under the knife. But the dark thing was an extraordinary liar, one of the best the Queen had ever encountered. Who knew what the girl might have learned, what she believed? The Queen couldn't know, and not knowing tormented her. She had few vulnerabilities left, but in this moment, she was excruciatingly aware of those which remained, and it seemed unfair that they should come to the forefront now, when she was so close to holding the solution in her hand.

Now she heard a new sound: the gathering roar of her

soldiers. What could the girl hope to accomplish by coming here? Did she seek martyrdom? The girl had already demonstrated a marked weakness for the grand gesture, although such demonstrations were so revealing that the Queen felt they constituted weakness in themselves. The din outside grew louder, and the Queen drew herself up straight, casting around the tent to make sure that everything was ready. Ducarte had procured a low table for her to eat meals on, an extravagance that would now come in handy. She would kill the girl, certainly, but first they would have a conversation. There were so many things the Queen was curious about. For a moment, she considered drawing the flaps of her tent, so that she could watch as the girl approached. But no: the girl was coming as a supplicant, and the Queen would treat her as one. She remained standing, hands at her sides, though her heartbeat kept climbing and her leg went like mad beneath her dress.

"Majesty!" Ducarte called.

"Come!"

Ducarte pulled back the flap of the tent, creating a doorway, and the girl ducked through. The anxiety that had been growing on the Queen in the past ten minutes suddenly crystallized, and when the girl straightened, revealing her face to the light, it took all of the Queen's years of control to keep from taking a step backward.

Before her stood the woman from the portrait. Everything was the same: hair, nose, mouth, even the lines of deep sorrow around her eyes.

Is it a trick? the Queen wondered. But how could that be? She had smuggled the portrait from the Keep more than one hundred years ago. Her eyes dropped to the girl's stomach and she was relieved to notice at least one difference: this girl was not pregnant. But otherwise, the detail was exact, and the Queen felt suddenly as though something had been stolen. The portrait, the woman, these things were hers alone; the girl had no right to stand here wearing the woman's face. She stood straight, her posture defiant, with no hint of begging about her, and this deepened the Queen's unease, her sense that something had been tilted askew.

"The Queen of the Tearling," Ducarte announced, rather unnecessarily, and the Queen flicked her hand toward the door.

"Perhaps I should stay, Majesty."

"Perhaps not," the Queen replied. She had spotted another difference now, and this one steadied her, lessened her sense of disorientation: unlike the woman in the portrait, the girl had deep green eyes, the same Raleigh eyes that the Queen had once wished for with all her heart. Both sapphires lay on the girl's chest, just as Andrew had reported, and once the Queen had noticed them, she could not tear her gaze away.

"Majesty, the New London Bridge—"

"I know all of this, Benin. Go."

Ducarte left, dropping the flap of the tent behind him.

"Please, sit." The Queen offered the far chair, and after a moment's hesitation, the girl stalked forward to take it. Her eyes were bloodshot, and the Queen wondered at this. What did the girl cry for? Not herself, surely; she had already proven that she had no interest in her own safety. Perhaps she was merely tired, but the Queen thought not. Grief sat on her plainly, like a raven perched on her shoulder.

The girl was studying the Queen now, staring at each of her features in turn, as though trying to dissect her face and put it back together. *She recognizes me*, the Queen thought for a fearful moment. But how could she? How could anyone?

This wasn't the woman from the portrait. This girl was only nineteen years old.

"How old are you, really?" the girl asked abruptly, in Mort. Good Mort, hers, with only the barest hint of an accent.

"Far older than you," the Queen replied steadily, pleased to hear that her voice betrayed none of the upheaval in her thoughts. "Old enough to know when I have won."

"You *have* won," the girl replied slowly. But her eyes continued to dart across the Queen's face, as though seeking clues.

"Well?"

"I've seen you before," the girl mused.

"We all have visions."

"No," the girl replied. "I've *seen* you. But where?"

Something tightened in the Queen's chest. *Only nineteen*, she reminded herself. "What can it possibly matter?"

"You want these." The girl held the sapphires up on her palm. Even in the diffuse light that filtered through the fabric of the tent, the jewels sparkled, and the Queen thought she could see something, far in their depths . . . but then the girl shook them, and whatever she believed she had seen was gone.

"They are pretty jewels, certainly."

"They come with a price."

"Price?" The Queen laughed, although even she could hear the slight edge in her laughter. "You're in no position to bargain."

"Of course I am," the girl replied. Her green gaze speared the Queen with bright intelligence. Sometimes one could look in the eyes and simply see it, in the focus of the pupil, the sharpness of the gaze. "You can kill me, Lady Crimson. You can invade my city and lay it waste. But neither of those things will get the sapphires from around my neck. I'm sure you know what happens if you try to take them by force."

The Queen sat back, discomfited. The girl did have a bargaining chip, after all . . . and the Queen wondered who had talked. Thomas Raleigh? Thorne?

"I can simply order some other poor soul to kill you and take them off," the Queen replied after a long moment. "What do I care?"

"And that will work, will it?" the girl asked. The arrogance in her voice staggered the Queen. Most information concerning the Tear sapphires was myth and legend; no one had tried to take them by force since the death of Jonathan Tear. But the dark thing had said it could be done. And now the Queen had a truly terrible thought, one that hit her right in her solar plexus: what if the dark thing had lied to her, so long ago? What if it had only needed her to procure the sapphires, do its dirty work and take the punishment?

"Good." The girl nodded. "Think on these things. Because I tell you, anyone who tries to take them against my wishes will suffer agony. And if your hand merely guides them, my vengeance will find you as well."

"I have been cursed before. You don't frighten me." But the Queen was unsettled, all the same. She had overcome the awful idea that the woman from the portrait had come to life before her, but still the girl's face mocked her, raising the ghost of the past. She could not be sure that the girl was bluffing . . . and the stakes if she guessed wrong! "Those jewels have had no proper owner since William Tear."

"Wrong." The girl bared her teeth again, her eyes burning with a fierce emotion, something like jealousy. "They're *mine*."

The Queen was appalled to find herself believing this

nonsense. So little was known about the magic of jewels . . . several special pieces had come out of the Cadarese mines over the years, but nothing with power even remotely comparable to that of the Tear sapphires. The Queen had never heard of a jewel bonding with a specific owner; so far as she knew, possession was everything in this game. But she also didn't think the girl was lying; her gaze was too clear for that, and she didn't strike the Queen as much of a liar to begin with.

I don't know, the Queen admitted to herself, and that was the crux of the problem. Uncertainties abounded here. She wanted to ask the girl about the dark thing, try to glean some further information about her abilities. But she was afraid to raise either issue, afraid to give the girl any more leverage. She was no fool, this one. She had come here with a plan.

"I do know you."

The Queen looked up, found the girl's eyes bright with revelation.

"In the portrait." The girl tipped her head to one side, fixing the Queen with a critical stare. "The disfavored child. The bastard. She was you."

The Queen slapped the girl across the face. But she had only a moment to admire the welt she had made before she was seized, as though with invisible hands, and thrown across the room to land on the thick, sumptuous pallet she used as a bed. She had not been pushed so much as flung, and if she had landed with equal force against something of iron or steel, she would probably be dead. She sprang up, ready to fight, but the girl had remained at the table, motionless, the Queen's handprint ugly and stark on her cheek.

I am in danger, the Queen realized suddenly. The thought

was so novel that it took a moment to become frightening. Somehow the girl had reached right inside her, right through the defenses that the Queen kept around her person at all times. How had she done that? The Queen rallied herself; she should return to the table, but something had shifted now, and even with her defenses up, the Queen found that she did not want to cross the room.

"You don't like being recognized," the girl mused. "Was life with the Beautiful Queen really so bad?"

The Queen snarled, an animal sound that lashed through her teeth before she could hold it back. She had forgotten about the damned portrait. It must still be lying around the Keep somewhere, their last family moment before all hell had broken loose. But the Queen had shed that sad child as though she were emerging from a chrysalis. The girl should never have been able to connect the two. The Queen thought about calling for Ducarte, but she couldn't seem to open her mouth.

"I have poor vision," the girl remarked. "But my jewels are useful. Sometimes I *see*. I simply see, where other people might notice nothing." She stood up from the table and approached the Queen slowly, her gaze appraising and, worse, pitying. "You're a Raleigh, aren't you? A bastard Raleigh, unloved and unwanted and always forgotten."

The Queen felt her guts twist. "I am not a Raleigh. I am the Queen of Mortmesne."

But the words sounded feeble, even to her own ears.

"Why do you hate us so much?" the girl asked. "What did they do to you?"

Evie! Come here! I need you!

The Queen shuddered. The woman's face, her mother's voice . . . one was bad, but both were too much to bear. She tried to gather herself, to find some of the control she'd had when the girl first entered the tent, but whatever she took hold of seemed to melt in her hands.

Evie!

More impatient now, her mother's voice, a bit of steel showing through. The Queen clapped her hands to her ears, but that did no good, for the girl was already inside her head. The Queen could feel her there, reading the Queen's memories as though they were a novel, running through them, flipping the pages, pausing on the worst moments. The Queen stumbled away, but the girl followed her across the tent, across her *mind*, leafing through the past and discarding it behind her. Elaine, her mother, the Keep, the portrait, the dark thing . . . they were all there, called up suddenly, as though they had been waiting all along.

"I see," the girl murmured, her voice laced with sympathy. "She traded you away. They all did. Queen Elaine got everything."

The Queen shrieked, wrapping her arms around herself and clawing at her own skin.

"Don't do that." The girl pulled up the sleeve of her dress, and the Queen saw that her left arm was a mess of welts, some new, some healing. The sight was so shocking, so contrary to what the Queen thought she knew about the girl, that her hands dropped away from her own arms.

"I do it too, you know," the girl continued, "to control my anger. But it does no good in the long run. I see that now."

Ducarte burst through the doorway of the tent, his sword drawn, but the girl whirled toward him and suddenly Ducarte was doubled over, choking, his hands clasped around his throat.

"Don't interfere, Monsieur General. Stay over there, and I will allow you to breathe."

Ducarte backed toward the far wall of the tent.

The girl turned back to the Queen, her green eyes contemplative. The Queen's mind ached, a feeling of terrible violation, as though everything she kept locked away had been laid out in the open under a corrosive sunlight. She could still feel the girl in there, somehow, looking her over, picking through the debris. The Queen tried to summon anything, any of the thousand small tricks she had wielded over the course of her life. She had not felt so powerless since she was a small girl, trapped in a room. The past was supposed to be past. It should not be able to reach up and drag her down.

"What is your name?" the girl asked.

"The Queen of Mortmesne."

"No." The girl walked up and stood right in front of her, only a few inches away. Close enough for the Queen to wound, but the Queen couldn't so much as raise a hand. She felt the girl's mind again, prying at hers, running fingers over everything, and now she understood that the girl might be able to kill her. No weapon would have done the job, but the girl had found her own knives in the Queen's mind. Each little piece of history that she touched was sharpened to a fine point, and the Queen felt her entire psyche shudder at the violation of that, of having another person handle her identity so easily. The girl had found her answer now, and the pressure in the Queen's mind finally eased.

"Evelyn," the girl murmured. "You're Evelyn Raleigh. And I am sorry."

The Queen of Mortmesne closed her eyes.

When Aisa and the other guards entered the Queen's Wing, they found the rest of the Guard standing at attention. Even the night shift, who were now well past their bedtimes, had not retired. Bradshaw, the magician, was leaning against the wall, idly making a scarf vanish and then reappear. Maman was there too; Aisa spotted her standing at attention at the mouth of the hallway, as she always did while waiting for the Queen to come home. The sight of her made Aisa want to cry.

The Mace stomped over to the dais, the grim cast of his face forestalling all questions. Aisa followed him, as quickly as she dared, keeping her hand on her knife. It was ridiculous, a twelve-year-old girl guarding the Mace, but the Queen had charged her to do so, and Aisa would never forget that moment, not if she lived a hundred years. Elston had taken the Queen's charge seriously as well; he followed the Mace closely, alert for threats, and when he spotted Aisa doing the same, he gave her a jagged, approving grin. Pen was no help; he wandered behind the Mace as though lost. He had not wept, as Aisa would have expected a lovesick man to do. But he was not with them either.

It was Wellmer who finally dared to ask, "Where's the Queen?"

"Gone."

"Dead?"

The Mace searched the room until he found Maman at the entrance to the hallway. She shook her head.

"Not dead," the Mace replied. "Just gone."

Arliss was waiting at the foot of the dais. As the Mace approached, Arliss handed him a sheet of paper, and waited while the Mace read. Even when the Mace looked up at him with murderous eyes, Arliss did not flinch.

"You knew."

Arliss nodded.

"Why the hell—"

"I don't work for you, Mr. Mace. I serve the Queen. On her orders, nearly a hundred copies have already gone out. The thing's done; you're the Regent."

"Ah, God." The Mace dropped the piece of paper and sat down on the third step of the dais, burying his head in his hands.

"What will they do to her?" Wellmer asked.

"They'll take her to Demesne."

The voice was unfamiliar; Aisa whipped around, drawing her knife. Five hooded men stood in a group, just inside the closed doors of the Queen's Wing.

The Mace pulled his head from his hands, his keen eyes fixing on the leader. "Kibb! How did these men get into the wing?"

Kibb splayed his hands. "I swear, sir, we shut the doors behind you."

The Mace nodded, returning his attention to the speaker. "I know your voice, rascal. So you do walk through walls, as the stories tell."

"We both do." The leader shook back his hood, revealing a pleasing, dark-haired face and a tan that spoke of the south. "She's valuable. The Red Queen won't kill her."

Aisa wondered how the stranger could be so certain. What value could Queen Kelsea have to the Mort? They could ask for ransom, certainly, but what ransom? Maman said the Tear was poor in everything but people and lumber, but the Mort had their own forests, and the Queen would never agree to a trade for people.

"It would be a smart move to kill the Queen," the Mace

replied. "Leave the Tear without an heir and throw us into chaos."

"All the same, she will not."

The Mace stared at the speaker for a long moment, his eyes measuring. Then he popped to his feet. "Then we need to start today."

The stranger smiled, and it transformed his face from merely pleasant to handsome. "You need people in the capital. I have many. You will have all the help I can give you."

Aisa peeked at the rest of the Guard and was shocked to see Pen smiling, though his eyes were filled with tears.

"We need to get a message to Galen and Dyer in Demesne. And Kibb!" Mace shouted across the room. "You get down into the Wells and find that baker's boy. Nick. Time to call in that favor."

Kibb nodded, a small smile creasing his face. "Going to be an undertaking, sir. You're the Regent now."

"I can do both."

"Sir?" Ewen had stepped forward, his friendly face bewildered and his cheeks wet with tears. Aisa's heart seemed to contract for him. Everyone knew that Ewen worshipped the Queen, and it seemed likely that he did not understand what had happened.

"What is it, Ewen?" the Mace asked, his voice betraying only the slightest touch of impatience.

"What are we going to do, sir?" Ewen asked, and Aisa saw that she had been wrong: he did understand.

The Mace descended the dais, clapping Ewen gently on the back. "We're going to do the only thing we can do. We're going to get her back."

I'm sorry," Kelsea repeated. She could feel that terrible side of herself, hovering, gleeful, waiting to be unleashed on the woman who stood before her. A different Kelsea, that one, a Kelsea who saw death as the most complete and effective solution to all problems.

She expected the Red Queen to fall to her knees, but she did not, and a moment later Kelsea realized that this was a woman who would never beg. It was easy to see, to browse through the woman's life in much the same way she browsed through Lily's, to see patterns forming. Evelyn Raleigh, the child, had begged, and it had gained her nothing. The woman would never beg again. Many memories sailed through Kelsea's mind: playing with a set of toy soldiers on the ruined flagstones of a floor; staring with longing at the blue pendulum of a jewel as it rested on a woman's chest; watching from behind a curtain as well-dressed men and women danced in a room that Kelsea recognized easily as her own audience chamber. Evelyn Raleigh had been desperate to be noticed, to matter to others . . . but in all of those childhood memories, she was alone.

It was the adult memories that Kelsea shrank from. In fragments and pieces, she saw a terrible story: how the disfavored child had risen from obscurity into her own conception of greatness, channeling all of that hurt and disappointment into authoritarianism. Row Finn had helped her, taught her to do her own form of magic, but Kelsea also sensed an innate emptiness in the grown woman before her, a certainty that an accident of birth had deprived her of greater opportunities, and the loss of the sapphires was a particular sore spot. There was a portrait there, too, in the jumble, and though Kelsea glimpsed it for only a moment, she recognized Lily with no difficulty at all. The Red Queen didn't know Lily from Adam, but she felt a deep connection to her, all the same, and now Kelsea saw that Thorne and Row Finn had only been partly correct. The Red Queen did wish for immortality, but she did not need to live forever. She did not fear death. She only wanted to be invulnerable, to decide her own destiny without being subject to the whims of others. The child, Evelyn, had enjoyed no control over her own life. The Red Queen was determined to control it all.

Kelsea took a step back, trying to disengage from this. A greater understanding of others was always valuable, so Carlin said, but understanding the Red Queen would not make the task at hand any easier. For the first time in several weeks Kelsea thought of Mhurn, whom she had effectively anesthetized before his execution. She had no drugs for the Red Queen, but she could at least make it a quick death, not the protracted nightmare she had inflicted on Thorne.

But even as Kelsea tried to pull away, she caught and held on a memory: the young Evelyn, perhaps only eleven or twelve, standing in front of a mirror. This memory was closely guarded, so closely that when Kelsea began to examine it, the Red Queen's entire body jerked in refusal, and she leapt at Kelsea, her hands hooked into claws. She went right for the sapphires, but Kelsea ducked and shoved her away. The Red Queen flew across the room, bouncing with a hiss off the wall of the tent. Kelsea followed her, still digging, for she sensed the pain that surrounded the memory, exacerbating it, like a wound that had never been cleaned. Evelyn stood in front of a mirror, staring at herself, in the throes of a terrible revelation:

I will never be beautiful.

Kelsea recoiled, feeling as though she'd been bitten, slapping the memory away from her as though it were a pernicious insect. But Evelyn's pain did not go easily; Kelsea felt as though it had embedded hooks in her mind. The woman in front of her was beautiful, as beautiful as Kelsea was now . . . but she had created that beauty, cobbled it together somehow, just as Kelsea had. Deep down, the plain girl still reigned supreme; the Red Queen had never been able to outdistance her, to leave her behind, and in this, Kelsea saw a terrible phantom outline of her own future.

The Red Queen was leaning against the wall of the tent now, her breathing labored. But she looked up at Kelsea with furious eyes. "Get out. You have no right."

Kelsea withdrew, disengaging from the woman's mind. The Red Queen sagged to the ground, huddling there, her arms wrapped around her knees. Kelsea wanted to apologize, for she saw, now, the great ugliness of what she had done. But the Red Queen had closed her eyes, dismissing Kelsea somehow; the clear certainty that she would die had permeated the woman's thoughts, calming the tides that lapped there. The Red Queen had lived a long and terrible life, defined by her own casual brutality, and it would be easy, so easy, to dismiss the child who wandered inside her. The dark side of Kelsea wanted to ignore that child; murder hovered in her mind, ravenous, like a dog straining to be let from the leash. But Kelsea paused, suddenly confronted by a nuance she had never considered. The woman in front of her deserved heavy punishment for the acts she had committed, the terror she had inflicted on the world. But the child Evelyn was not responsible for what had been done to her, and the experiences of the child had forever shaped the woman. Kelsea's mind clamored, hectoring, demanding that she do something, that she *act*. But still she hesitated, staring at the crouching woman before her.

The problems of the past. Her own voice echoed in her mind, and Kelsea wished Mace were there, for she felt that she could finally explain this particular conundrum, present him with a concrete example of how the problems of the past, uncorrected, inevitably became the problems of the future.

I can't kill her, Kelsea realized. An army surrounded them, an army that would enter New London and lay it waste. This was Kelsea's only option, her only chance ... but she could not bring herself to do the act. Compassion had ruined everything.

"Open your eyes," Kelsea commanded, and as she spoke the words, she felt the dark shadow inside her crumple and limp away, its wings tattered. It might circle her mind forever, seeking advantage, but at that moment, Kelsea knew that it would never control her again.

The Red Queen opened her eyes, and the rage Kelsea saw there made her flinch. She had intruded where she had no right to be, and this woman would always hate her for what she had discovered there. Again Kelsea considered apologizing, but the memory of William Tear intruded.

The main prize!

"I propose a trade. I will give you my sapphires."

"In exchange for what?" After a moment of initial surprise, the Red Queen's face smoothed over, and Kelsea felt unwilling admiration. So she, too, had the power to wipe away the past when it served no purpose, when it would only be a distraction. Kelsea would earn no points for sparing the Red Queen's life, that expression said; this woman would drive a hard bargain.

"Autonomy for the Tear."

The Queen chuckled, but sobered quickly when she saw Kelsea's expression. "You are serious?"

"Yes. I will give you the necklaces, take them off willingly, and you will withdraw your army and not return for five years. During this time, you will not place one toe in my kingdom. You will demand nothing. You will leave my people alone."

"Five years' worth of lost profits from the shipment? You must be out of your mind."

But beneath the smooth face of the hard bargainer, Kelsea read a different story. Here, at least, Thorne and Finn had been right: the Red Queen wanted the jewels very badly.

"I promise you, if you refuse to trade with me, you will never have my sapphires. I may rot and wither to nothing, and you will still never be able to take them off me without facing the consequences. They belong to me."

"Five years is too long."

"Majesty!" Ducarte blurted out. Kelsea had forgotten he was there, crouched in the far corner of the tent. "You cannot!"

"Shut up, Benin."

"Majesty, I will not." Ducarte stood up, and Kelsea saw that he too was furious . . . but not with her. "The army has been incredibly patient with the lack of plunder, but it cannot last forever. New London is their reward, poorly defended, full of women and children. They have earned that."

"You'll get your ten percent, Benin. I'll pay you out of my own pocket."

Ducarte shook his head. "You will, Majesty, but that will not solve the issue. The army is already angry. To be withdrawn at the moment of victory—"

Kelsea was on the point of silencing him; she did not need his interference, not when she sensed her opponent weakening. But there was no need. The Red Queen turned to him and Ducarte blanched, falling silent.

"You think my army would defy *me*, Benin?"

"No, Majesty, no," Ducarte backpedaled. "But they are already discontented. Poor morale makes poor soldiers, this is established."

"They will tamp down their discontent, if they know what's good for them." The Red Queen turned back to Kelsea, her eyes gleaming, dark pupils flicking between Kelsea's face and the sapphires. "Two years."

"You must not want them very badly."

"Five years is too long," the Red Queen repeated, a hint of sullenness in her voice. "Three years."

"Done." Kelsea held the jewels out, but kept the chains around her neck. "Take hold of them."

The Red Queen eyed her warily. "Why?"

"It's a trick I learned from our mutual friend." Kelsea smiled at her. "I need to make sure you won't back out of the deal."

The Red Queen's eyes widened, suddenly fearful, and Kelsea saw that she had meant to do exactly that. Ah, she was smart, this woman, clever enough to drive a hard bargain on a promise she meant to break.

"I know you now, Evelyn. Three years, that's the honest bargain." Kelsea lifted the sapphires, offering them. "Promise to leave my kingdom alone."

The Red Queen took the sapphires on her palm, and Kelsea was relieved to see a myriad of conflicting emotions cross her face: lust, anger, anxiety, regret. She knew about Row Finn, then. Perhaps she had even seen his real face.

"Majesty!" Ducarte hissed. "Do not!"

The Red Queen's face twisted, and a moment later Ducarte

was curled in a fetal position, moaning, on the floor. The woman's eyes were fixed on the sapphires now, and when Kelsea hunted for her pulse, she found it ratcheted sky-high. Lust had overtaken judgment. The Red Queen paused, clearly framing her words before she spoke.

"If you give me both Tear sapphires, freely, of your own will, I swear to remove my army from the Tearling, and to refrain from interfering with the Tearling for the next three years."

Kelsea smiled, feeling tears spill down her cheeks.

"You leak like a faucet," the Red Queen snapped. "Give me the jewels."

Three years, Kelsea thought. They were safe now, all of them, from the farmers in the Almont to Andalie's children in the Keep, safe in Mace's good hands, and that knowledge allowed Kelsea to reach up and pull the chains over her head. She expected the necklaces to fight her hand, or inflict some terrible physical punishment when she tried to remove them, but they came off easily, and when the Red Queen snatched them away, Kelsea felt almost nothing . . . only a small pang for Lily, for the end of Lily's story that she would never see. But even that loss was drowned under the great gain of this moment. Three years was a lifetime.

The Red Queen put on both necklaces and then turned away, huddling over the sapphires like a miser with his gold. It occurred to Kelsea in that moment that she might escape; Ducarte was still incapacitated, and she could duck out of the tent, perhaps take them all by surprise. But no, the jewels were lost to her now, and without them she was just an ordinary prisoner. She would make it no more than five feet before getting killed, or worse, and anyway, the bridge was broken. Kelsea had done it as a defensive measure, but now she wondered if she hadn't really been trying to ensure that there was no going back.

The Red Queen turned, and Kelsea braced herself for the triumph on the woman's face, the vengeance that would surely follow. The Tearling was safe, and she meant to die a queen.

But the Red Queen's eyes were wide with outrage, her nostrils flaring. Her outstretched fist had closed around the jewels, squeezing so tightly that her knuckles had turned white. Her mouth worked, opening and closing. Her other hand had clenched into a claw, and it reached for Kelsea, clutching madly.

And then, somehow, Kelsea knew.

She began to laugh, wild, hysterical laughter that bounced off the gleaming red walls of the tent. She barely felt the bruising grip of the woman's hand on her shoulder.

Of course it didn't hurt when I took them off. Of course not, because—

"They're mine."

The Red Queen screamed with fury, a wordless howl that seemed as though it should shred the walls of the tent. Her hand ground into Kelsea's shoulder so hard that Kelsea thought it might break, but she couldn't stop laughing.

"They don't work for you, do they?" She leaned toward the Red Queen until their faces were only inches apart. "You can't use them. They're *mine*."

The Queen hauled back and slapped Kelsea again, knocking her to the ground. But even this couldn't stop Kelsea's laughter; indeed, it seemed to feed it. She thought of the long night past . . . Lily, William Tear, Pen, Jonathan, Mace . . . and it suddenly seemed that they were there with her, all of them, even the dead. Kelsea had hoped to emerge victorious, but here was an outcome she had never imagined. The jewels were lost to her; she would never find out how Lily's story had ended. But neither would anyone else.

Rough hands were on her shoulders, pulling her from the ground. Men dressed in black, like the soldiers outside, but by now Kelsea recognized close guards when she saw them, and she shut her eyes, preparing for death.

"Get her out of here!" the Red Queen shrieked. "Get her out!"

One of them, clearly the captain, pinned Kelsea's wrists behind her back, and she felt irons cuffing them into place. The irons were too tight; they pinched her skin as he snapped the clasps. But Kelsea still couldn't stop laughing.

"You lost," she told the Red Queen, and knew that she would never forget the woman's face in that moment: the face of an enraged child denied dessert. Kelsea barely felt the guards' hands tighten on her arms, yanking her out of the tent. The Tearling was safe, her people were safe. The sapphires belonged to her, no one else, and Kelsea roared with laughter, even as they hauled her away.

AND AT THE END

The Crossing

Lily clutched a line of rope on the railing, trying not to fall to the deck. The ship rocked wildly; the water was roiling, stirred by wind and the thunder of explosions on land. Above them, storm clouds were highlighted against the night sky, a swirling purple bruise. Lily had been on ships before, but those had been powerboats, yachts that cut so smoothly through the waves that they barely felt as though they were moving at all. This was different, a terrible funhouse feeling, the ship's deck literally rocking beneath her feet as she clutched the rope, trying desperately to support Jonathan with her other arm. Jonathan was barely conscious; Tear had removed the bullet and stitched him up in the car, but by the time he was done, the backseat was covered in blood, and Tear's grim expression had said it all.

Far behind them was the skyline of New York, a

smoldering orange wreck of dark buildings whose windows gouted flame into the black night. But Lily and the other people on the ship were not looking at the skyline. Their gazes were fixed on the sea behind them, on the two huge ships that had materialized from nowhere. From the shouted reports on deck, Lily also knew that there were several submarines out there, rapidly closing beneath the surface. They had been all right as they sailed down the Hudson and entered the lower bay, but then a siren had gone off, and now, as they moved out into the Atlantic, Security was closing.

"Five minutes!" William Tear shouted from the prow of the ship. "All we need!"

He is insane, Lily realized. Oddly, it didn't seem to matter much. They weren't going to make it, and Lily was sorry for that, sorry that she would never get to see the deep, clean river beneath the bright sun. But these ships were free, and Lily was going to die a free woman, and she would not have been anywhere else at this moment for the wide world, submarines or not.

"Ready!" Tear shouted, and the computer tech near Lily began to chatter into his earpiece in their strange language.

A hollow boom echoed on Lily's left, followed by distant screams. When she craned her neck to see over the beams that covered the deck, she found that one of Tear's ships was on fire, its back end flaming, gouts of black smoke billowing up into the night.

"Torpedo!" someone cried. A second explosion echoed, and then the ship wasn't even half a ship anymore, only a smoldering ruin on the heaving ocean. Everyone on the deck of Lily's ship had run to the railing, but Lily could not leave Jonathan, so only she saw William Tear turn away, clutching something in his outstretched right hand, all of his attention focused on the eastern horizon.

"We're not even armed!" a woman cried.

The destroyers were closing now, less than half a mile away. Lily wondered why they hadn't fired as well, but after a moment's consideration, she knew: they meant to take the rest of Tear's ships, to board them. Security loved its prisoners, after all. Lily's burn wound throbbed, even though her palm had scabbed over with a dark crust, and she knew that whatever happened, she wasn't going back.

Bright light suddenly engulfed the ship, blinding. Lily threw her hands over her eyes, a low squeal escaping her throat, thinking of the halo device that Tear's people had used in the Security compound. Terror suddenly overwhelmed her, the terror that it had all been a dream, that she would wake up and find herself back in that room, facing the accountant, the box. But when she peeked through her fingers, she saw that this light wasn't electric. It was plain old daylight, a soft glow on her arms.

Lily turned toward the light and screamed.

There was a hole in the eastern horizon. Lily had no other way to describe what she saw. The black shawl of night still covered the sky above her head, but as it dipped east, the shawl tore open, its jagged edges surrounding the hole like a broken portrait frame. Inside the frame was day, a pink and orange horizon above the azure water, as though the sun were about to rise. The light bathed everything, and Lily could see all of the other ships around her now, clearly, their flying sails stained orange in the dawn.

Thunder boomed behind them, shaking the deck.

"Get down!" a man cried, and Lily ducked, covering her head. But the whistling shot went right over them, over all of the ships, toward the hole in the horizon. Hatred blazed inside Lily, so strong that if any Security officer had appeared in front of her in that instant, she would have torn his heart out with her bare hands. They were trying to close whatever doorway Tear had opened . . . trying to take the better world.

"Tell them to get through!" Tear shouted from the prow. "We don't have long!"

Their ship was in the lead, nearing the hole, and now Lily could feel warmth on her arms, the heat of sunlight against her skin. A cacophony of screams rang across the deck, wild screams from the people at the railing, and now Lily was screaming herself, feeling as though her entire body were tethered to that open horizon. As they passed through, she let go of the rope and hoisted Jonathan up, shaking him awake.

"The better world!" she shouted in his ear. "The better world!"

But Jonathan did not open his eyes. All around her, on the deck and on the other ships, Lily could hear them, her people, their cries of jubilation echoing across the open ocean. Behind them, the hole still remained, a dark stain through which nothing was visible against the western horizon. At least fifteen ships had made it through, but now the edges of the hole were collapsing inward, its circumference beginning to shrink. Lily didn't know if the last ships would make it. Turning back to the east, she found William Tear clutching the railing, his face white as a sheet. For a moment, his entire body seemed to glow pure blue against the rising sun, and then he collapsed to the deck.

Lily turned to tell Jonathan, but Jonathan was dead.

L ily."
     She looked up, squinting in the dim moonlight, and scrambled to her feet.

Tear looked exhausted. Lily hadn't seen him in two days, not since that night, and she was relieved to see him up and about; the longer he was absent from the deck, the more certain Lily became that he had somehow killed himself performing his miracle, that he, like Jonathan, would not wake up. Lily had asked Dorian about Tear, but Dorian was noncommittal. Lily had tried to make friends with several of the other passengers and found them kind but cautious; no one knew who she was. A younger woman, perhaps Dorian's age, had patched her wounds, but for the past two days there had been nothing for Lily to do but sit by herself, watch the horizon, and wait for Tear.

"Are you all right?"

"I'm fine," he replied, but Lily still had her doubts. He looked like a man who had suffered some sort of wasting illness. "But I need your help. Come with me."

She followed him toward the stern, trying to tiptoe quietly among the sleeping people who covered the deck. Tear, as always, seemed to make no noise at all, and he led her down the ladder to the deep hold belowdecks. The hold had a strange medieval feel, for only lamps and firelight lit all of its rooms; no electric lights anywhere. A broad, dormitory-like area lined with empty cots took up the bulk of the hold. There were over a hundred people on this ship, but most of them didn't want to spend time inside. They preferred to stay on deck, their eyes scouring the horizon. Tear had prepared for this eventuality; at the far end of the dormitory was a room that contained not only plenty of food and water but about fifty gallons of sunscreen. Lily thought this room was where they were going, but Tear bypassed it for the next, which was understood to be private, for his use only. As they walked in, Lily saw that the room's walls were lined with bookshelves, each of them filled with hundreds of books. But Lily had no time to marvel at these. In the center of the room, Dorian was standing over a table, staring down at what could only be a body wrapped in a sheet, the shroud sewn together by hasty fingers.

"It's time, Dori."

She looked up, and Lily saw, even in the dim glow of firelight, that her eyes were reddened from long crying. She looked a question at Lily.

"He would want her here," Tear replied. He levered an arm beneath the corpse's shoulders, hauling it up. "Come on. All together."

Dorian grasped Jonathan's waist, leaving Lily to take the legs. Together, they heaved the body off the table, balancing it carefully on their shoulders. Lily could smell the corpse now, a hint of decay that seeped right through the sheet, but she ignored it, thinking of Jonathan, who had thought she was worth saving, who would never see the better world. Her eyes watered, and she wiped at them savagely, stinging her corneas, as they started up the stairs.

On deck, everything was quiet except for the waves lapping gently at the sides of the ship. In the moonlight Lily could just glimpse the other ships on either side of them, not too far off, keeping pace. In the end, only seventeen of them had made it through; three were lost, sunk forever in Hudson Bay. From overheard conversations, Lily knew that not all of the ships were packed with people, like this one. One ship carried livestock: cows, sheep, and goats. Another carried horses. Still another ship, its boards bleached nearly white, was carrying medical supplies and personnel. But all Lily could see now were the sails, little more than faint gleams under the dying moon.

They carried Jonathan to the rear of the ship, a place where few people chose to sleep, because the rigging blocked the view of the eastern horizon. At Tear's direction, they balanced the body carefully on the railing. Lily's arms ached, but she gave no sign of it. The burn on her palm had broken open again, oozing pus, but she hid that as well, surreptitiously blotting it on her jeans. She wished she had some clean clothes. She hadn't showered in days. Other people were still wearing the same outfits as the night they'd launched; what would they do for clothing in the new world? There were so many uncertainties, and the only man who could answer them was Tear . . . but now wasn't the time. Beyond the helm, the eastern sky was turning pale, but when Lily peeked over the railing at the stern, she could see nothing but darkness.

"Jonathan hated the water," Dorian remarked hoarsely, and Lily realized that she was crying again. "After what they did to him. He fucking hated it."

"Not this water," Tear replied.

Lily said nothing. They had known Jonathan well, both of them, and she had never even learned his last name. She wanted to think of something to say, something important, but when she closed her eyes all she could see was Greg on his knees, Jonathan holding the pistol to his head. That was the greatest kindness anyone had ever done for Lily, but it wasn't an act she could tell Tear and Dorian about. So she remained silent, though tears had begun to work their way slowly down her cheeks.

"Well, old friend," Tear finally said, "we're off to a good land. Let's hope you're already there."

"Amen, South Carolina," Dorian added, and then, by unspoken consent, they lifted the body over the railing. Lily didn't help this time, only stood back. There was a muted splash, and then Jonathan was gone forever. Dorian waited another moment, then left without a word, walking quickly toward the stairs.

I killed him, Lily thought.

"It was his choice," Tear repeated, making Lily wonder if she'd actually spoken out loud. She looked around, but they were still alone at the stern.

"What happened? Where did we go?"

"Nowhere, Lily. We crossed, that's all. That's how I've always thought of it."

"Is it—" Lily forced herself to bring out the word. "Is it magic?"

"Magic," Tear repeated. "I never thought of it that way; to me it seems the most natural thing in the world. But maybe magic is a good word."

He reached into his pocket and came up with something clenched in his fist. "Have a look."

Lily held out her uninjured hand and felt him drop something cold and hard into her palm. She held it up, squinting, trying to make it out. The sky had lightened now, in the sudden way it did just before dawn, but it still took Lily a few moments to identify the object.

"Aquamarine?"

"Sapphire," Tear replied. "My family tree is documented all the way back to Cromwell, but that jewel has been with us since the Dark Ages. Maybe even further back than that."

Lily held the sapphire to the light, trying to see through

it, but the sun hadn't appeared yet, and it was only a dark rectangle against the pale sky. "How do you know?"

"It told me."

Lily snorted, but Tear hadn't cracked so much as a smile. She couldn't tell whether he was joking, so she handed the sapphire back and leaned over the railing, staring down at the dim lines of white left in the ship's wake.

"Are you healing, Lily?"

That was a difficult question to answer. During the day things were fine, because the sky was wide open and Lily could look from horizon to horizon. But she didn't sleep more than a few hours at a time before jerking awake, certain that she would see the accountant standing in front of her . . . or worse, Greg. They were out of reach of all of that now, the ship's prow cutting smoothly toward the better world, but Lily felt a sudden, terrible foreboding. All of the people around her, sleeping on the deck . . . surely they brought their own stories, their own violence. How could anyone build a better world, a perfect world, if people brought along their own nightmares of the past?

"It won't be perfect," Tear answered, staring moodily over the railing. "I knew that, almost as soon as I knew I would try to do it. The world will be better, but not easy. In fact, in the early going, it's going to be very difficult."

"What do you mean?"

"Look at what we've left behind, Lily. We have no electricity, no technology. While I was asleep, Dori had the computer techs dump all of their equipment overboard, along with the guns. It has to be that way; technology is convenient, but we've long since passed the point where convenience outweighed danger. Tools of surveillance, of control . . . I knew, long ago, that these would have to be the first things to go. But think of the other things we won't have! Fuel. Heat. Textiles. I've brought drugs and antibiotics, on the white ship over there"—he gestured northward—"but they'll go bad long before the decade is out. We'll have none of these things, unless we figure out how to make them ourselves, with whatever we find."

Lily struggled to remain silent. She worshipped this man, she realized now, and it was a difficult thing, to hear him tear himself to pieces. But she suspected that he could not voice these doubts to anyone else, certainly not to all of the loyal people who had followed him for years.

"There will be animals in the new world, for meat, but we're all going to have to learn to kill them without guns or machinery, to cook from scratch over an open fire. We'll have to grow food. We'll have to learn to build our own houses, make our own clothing. I have several people who know the process, from sheep to wool to weaving, but the rest we'll have to learn. There was no way to do this without throwing nearly everything away, and if we want to keep anything, we're going to have to learn to do it all over again."

"You think we can't?"

"We can, certainly. The question is whether we will. It takes effort to build, Lily. It takes effort to put the community's needs before your own. But in the coming period, everyone will have to do that, or we're doomed to fail."

"Socialism has never succeeded anywhere."

"So we keep on trying. These are civic-minded people. They will raise civic-minded children. I chose them as such."

"Me as well?"

Tear smiled. "You as well."

"How do you know I'm civic-minded?" Truthfully, even Lily didn't know if she was; there had been so little opportunity to find out. Her entire life with Greg played out inside her memory, an ugly feedback loop.

"I told you, Lily: I've known you all my life." Tear held up the sapphire, displaying it on his palm. "I saw you here, long before I ever knew who you were."

"Why?"

Tear stared at her for a moment, his gaze contemplative. "Are you healing?"

"Yes. My shoulder barely even hurts, except when I try to sleep. My hand's being a pain, but I can bandage it again once there's enough light."

"You don't fool me, Lily. Your injuries aren't physical. You're not healing yet, but you will."

Lily felt her cheeks flush, wondering if he could look straight inside her and see the nightmares, Greg constantly lurking. It seemed likely that Greg would always be there, dug into some part of Lily that refused to let the past go.

"It might be that way for a long time," Tear told her. "But I promise you, you will heal."

"How do you know?"

Tear closed his fingers around the sapphire for a moment, staring off into some place that Lily couldn't possibly begin to imagine. Then he held it out to her.

"Have a look."

Feeling foolish, Lily lifted the jewel to the sky again, squinting. For a moment she saw nothing, but then the sapphire began to glow from within, a tiny blue flame against the lightening sky.

"What—"

"Shh. Look."

Lily stared at the sapphire, trying not to blink, and after a moment she realized that a figure was forming, far beneath the surface. At first it was shadowy, only a silhouette against the blue background, but then Lily gasped, for she saw herself. This was a different Lily than the one she had seen in the mirror all of her life: careworn and slightly hardened, her arms muscled, her skin dark with sun. The woman turned, and now Lily saw what Tear had meant her to see: her stomach, rounded with late pregnancy, protruding against the blue.

"How are you doing this?" she asked. "Is it an illusion?"

"No illusion, Lily, only the future. I promise you, it will come to pass."

Lily stared at herself, fascinated. The woman in the jewel had not had an easy life, clearly, and yet she radiated contentment. Flowers had been braided into her hair, and on her back was what appeared to be a bow and a quiver filled with arrows. But for the rounded belly, she looked like the picture of Diana in the old *D'Aulaires'* Lily and Maddy had shared in their childhood. Then the image abruptly vanished.

Distressed, Lily shook the sapphire, trying to bring the woman back, but there was nothing more.

"I'm sorry," Tear told her. "Even the little things will tax me for a while."

Lily stared at the sapphire for another long moment, and then handed it back to him. Something seemed to tug at her as the jewel left her fingers, and Lily had the odd sense that a piece of herself had gone with it. Seeing part of the future was almost worse than seeing none of it at all; she turned the vision over, wondering whether it was real, whether the baby was a boy or a girl.

"A boy," Tear murmured beside her. "It'll be a boy."

"How can you know that?"

"Sometimes I just know." He smiled at her, but Lily had

the sense of something hidden behind his eyes, some future that she couldn't yet glimpse. Tear didn't elaborate, only clasped her shoulder. "But that's years away. I have something else for you, something much closer."

"What?"

"Look out there." Tear pointed to the north. "That ship, the third away."

"The white ship?"

"No, the one just past it."

Lily squinted. The sky had lightened to a deep cornflower now, and she could just glimpse the ship he meant, a faint dark stain to the north, barely visible through the fog that clung to the surface of the ocean. "What about it?"

"One of my best people is in charge of that ship. She's been with us for a long time, ever since she was fourteen years old. Two prison sentences under her belt, and she's not afraid of anything. Dorian worships her, so much so that she even tries to dress like her, do her hair the same way."

Something struck inside Lily, a deep vibration like a bell. She stared at him, her eyes wide and pleading. "What's her name?"

"Madeleine Freeman."

Lily turned to stare northward.

"I promise you, Lily, you'll heal."

Tear's footsteps retreated, but Lily barely noticed, too busy staring at the third ship. Maddy's face the last time she had seen her, her hair tied in knots and a black skirt two inches shorter than the dress code . . . a teenage girl trying to look like a woman. But now Maddy *was* a woman. Lily's eyes searched the eastern horizon, looking for the tiniest hint of white against the blue, the first faint sign that there might be land in the distance. She thought of something then, and called softly after Tear. "Maddy's a diabetic! She needs insulin."

"No, she doesn't."

Lily stared after him for a moment, then turned back to the north. She couldn't think of Maddy, she realized, or she would go insane with waiting for the journey to be over, so she boxed her sister up inside her mind, putting her away. Someday she might see Maddy again, if all of this was real. She thought again of that fantastic vision inside Tear's jewel, and for a moment she wondered if she was crazy, but she knew she was not.

"A boy," she whispered. Tear had said so, and she believed him. She placed a hand on her own flat stomach, her eyes full of tears. She could almost feel him there, this child who was still years in her future. Tear was not lying, nor was he crazy. Lily would have a son, she would bear him in the better world, and she would raise him to be free.

She had already named him Jonathan.

Acknowledgments

Three people helped to make this a much better book: Maya Ziv, Dorian Karchmar, and Simone Blaser. As always, I am grateful to everyone at both Harper and William Morris Endeavor for their continued support as I move through the Tearling, but these three women put in effort above and beyond, and the book has benefited enormously. Maya, Dorian, and Simone also listened patiently to an awful lot of unjustified whining over the past year, so there's that. Thanks to Jonathan Burnham, who lets me keep writing, and also to Heather Drucker, Amanda Ainsworth, Katie O'Callaghan, Ashley Fox, Erin Wicks, Miranda Ottewell . . . and a special thanks to Virginia Stanley, my spirit guide in taking no crap.

Thanks and love to my family, particularly my dear husband, Shane, who endured a great deal of artistic temperament over the past year and a half and never flinched once, and Sir and Monkey, who keep me laughing. Thanks also to my good friend Claire Shinkins, who gives just the right amount of love and support, and to the kind and helpful crew at my local Peets Coffee (especially you, Michi!), where I wrote the bulk of this book.

Quite by accident, I found the writing buddy I had needed for a long time. Thank you, Mark Smith, for listening and giving good advice always, as well as being brave enough to take the Tearling on. Not an easy world, this.

To all of the wonderful independent bookstores and libraries—and bookstore employees and librarians—who helped to get my first book out to the world, thank you. There's no praise higher to me than that of people who love books, and your hard work on my behalf means a great deal.

Most of all, as always, thank you, readers. Without you, none of this is possible.

COMING SOON

The breathtaking concluding volume in
Erika Johansen's thrilling, acclaimed and bestselling
'Tearling' trilogy.

In less than a year, Kelsea Glynn has transformed from
an awkward teenager into a powerful monarch.

As she has come into her own as the Queen of the
Tearling, the headstrong, visionary leader has also
transformed her realm. In her quest to end corruption
and restore justice, she has made many enemies –
including the evil Red Queen, her fiercest rival, who
has set her armies against the Tear.

To protect her people from a devastating invasion,
Kelsea did the unthinkable – she surrendered herself
and her magical sapphires to her enemy, and named
the Mace, the trusted head of her personal guards,
Regent in her place. But the Mace will not rest until he
and his men rescue their sovereign from her prison in
Mortmesne.

The endgame has begun and soon the fate of Queen
Kelsea – and the Tearling itself –
will be revealed . . .